A MIRACLE OF SPACESHIPS

MUSKETEER SPACE
BOOK 2

TANSY RAYNER ROBERTS

You loved me once
    Laid your hands on me and broke my skin
    (I let you in)
    You peeled apart my metal doors
    (Thought I was yours)
    Shattered my plexiglass

And when there was nothing left of me to fly
    (watch me try not to cry)
    You built yourself a brand-new miracle
    & sailed away into the sky
    I remember you.
    A spaceship never forgets

"MEDITATIONS ON HEARTBREAK,"
*COLLECTED POEMS OF THE
MUSKETEER ARAMIS,* © SOLAR
IMPERIAL 39835.PARIS

CONTENTS

CHAPTER 1
CHASING SPACESHIPS

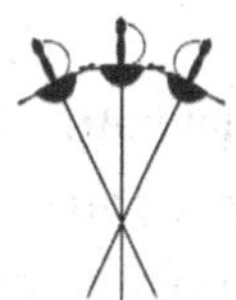

This was not the first time that Athos had lost a spaceship he loved.

It was not even the third time.

He always promised himself he wouldn't get attached. Avoiding intimacy was something he found easy when it came to people (most people), but spaceships had a way of getting under his skin.

It didn't help that he always refused to get a bland factory settings ship. Oh, no. He had to go hunting for one with personality.

Here we go again.

"Where old spaceships go to die," he said aloud.

This was the storage yard that time, space and Musketeers forgot. It was full of salvaged ship debris: a low-ceilinged treasure trove beneath the Musketeer space dock. Engies came here from time to time, rummaging for spare parts. Finding enough scrap to assemble a complete dart was a pipe dream.

He still intended to try.

"I can't believe Treville made you come here for a replacement for the *Parry-Riposte* instead of printing you a new ship," said Porthos from where she sat on the hull of a beautiful dart that had once been called the *Saucy Nancy*, but had been sliced into four separate pieces during a laser battle.

Athos remembered that battle. The Musketeer who piloted her had ended up in three pieces.

"I can," said Aramis, poking at the rubble of a broken tail fin with her boot. "She threatened to, after he lost the *Balestra* last year."

"That was one time, and I found her again!" Athos protested.

"I can't see how that redeems you for literally losing a spaceship."

"At least when he blew her up, it was in service to the Crown," Porthos teased.

"I did not – I hate you all."

D'Artagnan's laugh, loud and enthusiastic, rang above their bickering. It was her first visit to the land of broken spaceships, and she looked like a wide-eyed child at Joyeux. She always looked like a child to Athos.

He had to keep reminding himself that she was twenty, not twelve, and that the three of them didn't actually *have* to feel guilty that their friendship was going to corrupt her irretrievably.

Well. Maybe they should feel a little guilty.

"Why do they hang on to this stuff?" asked D'Artagnan, whose spacer mentality had trouble computing that so much yardage on a space station might be reserved for slabs of steel and spare parts, instead of dissolving it down to its atoms to be re-used as freshly printed ship.

"You can't print personality," said Athos. "Who wants a ship without any scratches on the hull?"

"Me, I do, my ship is perfect," Porthos said, waving a hand as if she was volunteering in class. "You take too much pride in saving broken things."

Athos refused to respond. He didn't want anyone to start assuming metaphors where none existed.

Grimaud emerged from behind a stack of cables and hatchways, her usual headphones slung around her neck instead of clamped over her ears. "Treville offered him a new ship," she said. "He refused to accept until he was sure there wasn't something down here that could be salvaged." With that betrayal, his engie stood there and smirked.

Athos calmed himself by imagining several ways that he could kill her, silently, with no one ever suspecting him.

Aramis and Porthos shot identical looks of delight at Athos.

"You ROMANTIC," Aramis howled.

"I might swoon," Porthos agreed.

D'Artagnan grinned all over her baby face.

Athos growled at them all.

"Speaking of," said Grimaud, and crooked her fingers. "Found something, boss."

He might be furious at her for ganging up on him with the other women, but he still trusted her implicitly when it came to spaceships. Athos followed Grimaud deeper into the yard, with the others trailing behind.

"This one is a possibility," said Grimaud, tapping a silver dart with most of its side attached. "Someone's stripped out the internals, but the hull is sturdy enough to save."

"And?" Athos said patiently. He knew a red herring when he saw one.

"And then there's this fellow." Grimaud stopped, and everyone else bumped into Athos, craning their necks to see.

"Oh," said Aramis in a baffled sort of voice.

"Seriously?" said Porthos. "Is that even a dart?"

D'Artagnan clambered around all of them, half-tripping over her own pet engineer, whose name Athos could never remember. Pigtails? Pigtails spotted what they were all looking at a few seconds before D'Artagnan and responded with a shrill sound and a clap of her hands.

Athos did his best to ignore them all as he took in the sight. It was an old musket-class dart, practically an antique.

"He's even older than the *Buttercup*," breathed D'Artagnan, which meant nothing to Athos.

"He's so *ugly*," said Porthos, sounding giddy.

He was old and bulbous and an odd greenish colour that Athos had never seen on any ship ever. He was so far from a modern dart that Athos wasn't sure that the designation fit. He wasn't streamlined and elegant like the *Parry-Riposte* had been.

Athos was in love already.

"It's a classic, I suppose," D'Artagnan said doubtfully, trying to be polite.

"He's amazing," Pigtails said, punching Dana lightly on the arm. "I'd love to get my hands on him. So jealous, Madame Grimaud."

"Please," said Aramis heavily. "Please tell me you're not taking him home, Athos. He's not a stray cat, he won't benefit from a little food and attention…"

Athos held his hand up to silence them all. "I'm being seduced," he informed them. "Don't spoil our moment."

Grimaud gave him one of her rare, dazzling smiles. "Guess what he's called?"

"I can't even," said Athos, slowly circling the hull. This marvel was even ugly from behind. He had never seen such an awkward-looking ship.

"The *Pistachio*."

"I am not going to be seen in public with you in that ship, war or no war," Porthos threatened.

It was too late. Grimaud smiled, and Athos twitched his mouth back at her. Pigtails was already begging them both to let her help with the restoration.

"Some battles, you have to let yourself lose," D'Artagnan told Porthos, patting her on the shoulder.

"He's *hideous*," Porthos whispered back, as if the ship was physically hurting her with his unfashionably retro appearance.

"On the bright side," Aramis said, blowing Athos a kiss. "Our boy will probably crash or explode him within a few months."

"That is no consolation!" Porthos wailed.

"How much work does he need?" Athos asked Grimaud.

"All the work," she said with a wry smile. "Give me four days, and I'll make you a miracle."

The Great Restoration took over everyone's lives. Dana suspected that Planchet was hiding her return to Paris from Madame Su so that the other engies wouldn't get to have all the fun. The *Pistachio* challenge had swallowed all the engies – not only Grimaud and Planchet, but Bonnie and Bazin too.

This period, between the declaration of war and the shipping out date, was what Musketeers called 'the chase after outfits.' Each of them had to get their helm and harness (AKA their entire equipment for war) in good order. While most were lucky enough to have an intact ship, there were still weapons systems to install or upgrade, repairs to be made, and so on.

Dana had none of this to worry about, which left her far too much time to worry. Not only about her friends who would be seeing direct action in the battles to come, but also about the disaster back on Gascon Station. Messages from her family were few and far between, and she had only managed to speak to her Papa for a couple of minutes, in between his burn treatments.

The news cycle was all Gascon Station all the time, because the images were more constructive and dynamic than the silent, unmoving siege of alien ships around the orbital cities of Truth that occasionally punctuated the media feeds.

Waiting was a quiet agony that was never openly discussed.

Today, Dana found Athos in the storage yard. He lounged in a low-slung deck chair sipping the largest cup of coffee she had ever seen, as he 'supervised' the work of the engineers. He wore over-sized safety goggles and had his feet up on an antique computer bank.

Dana pulled up a jettisoned slab of air ducting and perched beside him. "What's the pink line about?"

It was drawn in chalk, a wide shape around the work-in-progress that was the *Pistachio*. A second chalk line encircled Athos and his deck chair.

"Grimaud and I have come to an agreement," he said, taking a slurp of his coffee.

"Are you not allowed to cross the chalk lines?" Dana realised. "Not at all? I mean, I understand her not wanting you poking your nose into the ship…"

"Thank you very much."

"But why aren't you allowed to leave the yard, either?" Surely Grimaud would prefer Athos to be anywhere but here.

"We needed some new parts – the harness in particular, but other bits and pieces that we couldn't reclaim from the yard."

Dana didn't like the cagy tone in Athos' voice. "And?"

"And the budget that Treville gave me for a replacement ship shrunk somewhat when she found out about the expenses from The Gilded Lily back on Valour." He winced. "There was shouting."

Not undeserved, Dana thought, but did not say aloud. "How did you get the parts?"

"I played for them against a bunch of Mendaki smugglers."

Dana blinked several times. "I thought Porthos was the problem gambler."

"We don't all keep our vices in separate boxes, D'Artagnan," he said sharply. "Sometimes Aramis drinks too much. Sometimes I fuck people I shouldn't…"

"Okay, I get the picture. Did you win the parts?"

"Eventually."

"So —"

"Grimaud found out that I used her as a stake in the betting," he grumbled. "She's taking it personally."

"You are the worst," Dana said, smacking him in the chest.

"She's the most valuable resource I have. Everyone wants her as their engie."

"That's not a good excuse for putting her up as a stake, Athos. That is the complete opposite of a good excuse!"

He lifted his safety goggles so she could see the swelling black eye he was sporting. "Grimaud agrees with you."

"I'm not even slightly sympathetic," Dana told him sternly.

They fell into a long silence together, Athos sipping from his coffee. "I owe you an apology," he said after a moment.

Dana almost fell off her temporary seat. "You what now?"

"The business in the cellar," he said, waving a hand vaguely. "I said more than I should have. My past is not something with which I want to burden others."

"What's said on Valour stays on Valour," Dana said lightly. "There was a lot of wine. I hardly remember what you told me."

Athos gave her a narrow look. "You're lying."

"You can't prove it."

"Hmm." He was unimpressed by her attempt at tact. "Anyway. I'm sure my vast wealth of miserable experience will serve as some form of useful life tutorial for you."

"Don't trust pretty men who talk sweetly about politics?" Dana suggested, thinking of her own recent adventures.

Athos' mouth twitched. "Damn straight."

Bonnie and Planchet went past, carrying lengths of cables and tubing. Planchet gave Dana a wave, delighted to be working on an actual musket-class dart. Athos stood for a moment, his feet brushing the very edge of the chalk circle that Grimaud had drawn around him. "Not the b-clips!" he called after them. "I don't care if it adds to the authenticity of the model, I want silver connections in the harness."

A hand that must be Grimaud's emerged from the hatch of the *Pistachio*, gave him a rude gesture and disappeared again.

"Grimaud says she knows what she's doing," translated Planchet with an apologetic smile.

Athos scowled and dropped back into his chair. "What about you, D'Artagnan? I presume Commandant Essart requires you to outfit yourself for war? Hope that metal monster of yours is in decent condition."

"I'm not with the mecha squad anymore," Dana admitted.

Athos tore his goggles off to stare at her. "What's that supposed to mean?"

"Amiral Treville seconded me," she said, trying not to grin too obviously. "Not as a Musketeer – supplies transport. But I'll be in the middle of it all, not stuck back here on defensive detail, so…"

There was something unfamiliar in his expression. Athos looked at her for a long moment, then shrugged. "If you really want to make sure you see action, there's always the Cardinal's Sabres, I hear they're recruiting…"

"Shut up," Dana said gruffly, poking him in the knee with her boot. "I have *some* self-respect."

Athos clapped his hands. "Speaking of self-respect, dinner tonight at Hotel Coquenard. Prepare to witness awkward mating rituals."

"I – don't even know how to reply to that sentence," said Dana, dizzied by the rapid switch in tone. "Isn't that a fancy hotel over in Gilles Section? How can we afford it?"

"It's who you know," said Athos. He looked smug, which in retrospect Dana should have taken as a big neon warning sign.

Dana was so out of her depth that she was practically floating in space. She had allowed Aramis to raid the suitcase of frocks borrowed from the Duchess of Buckingham, which seemed a reasonable way to get rid of the bloody things, but somehow this turned into them both playing dress-up. An hour later, here was Dana in a formal gown, including long lace gloves and uncomfortable shoes.

This was not the plan. She hadn't realised that there needed to be a plan, but if there had been a plan, it would have been everything that wasn't this.

Aramis wore Buck's clothes as if she were a Duchess. She had re-inked her henna tattoos since their return to Paris, with an extra loop of stars and leaves painted on to the back of her neck, dipping down below the sweep of the gold satin of the dress she poured over her willowy body.

Dana, shorter and more muscular than Aramis, and with a much flatter chest, had never attempted to wear that particular gown, as she was sure it would look indecent on her body. On Aramis, it was the graceful, awesome kind of indecent that she could totally rock.

Aramis had forced Dana into a simple but devastating black cocktail dress that went past her knees. She insisted that Dana wear the Prince Regence's opal on her cheekbone instead of hidden away near her elbow.

The appearance of Porthos swept away any concern that Dana might be overdressed. Porthos was squeezed into a purple corset and layered tulle skirt, with a fierce collection of garnet and pearl jewellery wrapped around her neck, wrists and fingers. Her wig was high, as dark red as the jewels, and her face glowed with professional warpaint.

"I'm missing something, aren't I," Dana said in a low voice to Aramis as they followed their friend into the fiercely expensive lobby of the hotel and made their way to a restaurant that belonged in a Palace. "Where's Athos?"

"Athos was never going to turn up," said Aramis as they were escorted to a table for three. "He hates these scenes."

Dana tried not to freak out about this, but it was difficult. "I also hate scenes," she said in a desperate whisper. "Why did no one warn me there was going to be scenes?"

Porthos gave her a lipsticked smile as the waiter fussed around them. "Because revenge is best served cold, possibly with a nice soup and salad to start," she said, not bothering to keep her own voice down.

"Porthos is here to make a point to one of her gentlemen friends," said Aramis, perusing the menu. "You and I are here for damage control, in case things get out of hand."

Dana decided right in that second that Athos had to die. Slowly, by fork.

CHAPTER 2
THE HOTEL COQUENARD DELUXE BATHROOM EXPERIENCE

Fancy restaurants in super fancy hotels were desperately uncomfortable for Dana. She was going to roast Athos in a *pie* for dropping her into this without warning, and without back up. He knew she would hate it. The bastard probably thought it was funny.

Aramis and Porthos were both enjoying themselves amongst all the wealth and glamour. Dana was also going to roast them in the aforementioned pie.

"Captain Porthos, how lovely," said a voice that was both chilly and welcoming. It was an impressive feat. An older woman in a designer suit bore down upon them with a smile that did not reach her eyes. "Always a pleasure to see the Royal Musketeers here at Hotel Coquenard."

"Madame, it's been too long," Porthos replied graciously. They kissed each other's cheeks as if they were the best of friends.

Creepy.

"You remember Captain Aramis, and this is our friend,

Arms-Sergeant D'Artagnan. My friends, this is Madame Coquenard, our host."

Dana blinked several times before remembering that indeed, her new position came with a new rank. Why was the name Coquenard familiar?

"Delighted," purred the evidently-not-delighted Madame Coquenard. "I shall send Remy out to discuss the menu with you."

"If it's not too much trouble," agreed Porthos with a gleam in her eye.

As the manager moved on to another table, Dana leaned in to her friends. "What the hell have you dragged me into here?"

"No idea what you're talking about," Porthos said, widening her eyes so much that her long lashes got tangled in her ruby-red wig.

"It's all going to be fine, and we get a nice meal out of it," said Aramis, though it was obvious that her attention was elsewhere.

Dana followed her gaze and saw a familiar figure sitting at a table at the far end of the restaurant. Captain Tracy Dubois, with what looked like several elderly relatives, and not a husband in sight. Their eyes met and they shared a long, slow smile across the length of the room.

"Oh you have got to be kidding me," Dana moaned.

She was going to kill Athos so hard. He wasn't even worthy of a pie.

Chef Coquenard was a large, handsome man who approached their table with great trepidation, as if he expected to be greeted by his very own personalised Death By Pie. He greeted them, and managed to explain the more complex and artistic quirks of the menu in between a whispered argument with Porthos about why exactly he had failed to come to her aid back on Chantilly, while she was wounded and stuck for funds.

Other bullet points of the argument included the inappropriate nature of tonight's confrontation, under the eye of Madame Coquenard who preferred to keep up the illusion that they were still married to each other, for business reasons. Yes, of course dinner was on the house, because Porthos was on the verge of causing the most spectacular Scene of Righteous Fury, and Chef Coquenard agreed that he mostly deserved it.

Also, the beetroot foam was not to be missed.

Dana could have lived without being asked to weigh in with opinions about the preferred sauce to be smeared alongside sashimi escargot, and how she felt about vintages from the islands of Truth.

Aramis was so busy flirting with her girlfriend across the restaurant that she did not participate in the debate about *Paris Gateaux* versus *Crème d'Honour*.

"I feel better now," said Porthos as her lover returned to the kitchen to start their appetisers. "Good to resolve relationship issues before they fester."

"I'm so glad for you," said Dana, viciously stabbing her bread roll.

Madame Coquenard returned to pour their wine with a politeness that made it clear she disapproved thoroughly of Porthos but was never going to publicly admit it. Dana made for the ladies room as fast as she could in stupid frock and stupid heels.

As she swung around the grand staircase, she saw a table concealed in a far alcove and almost stopped breathing for a moment as she recognised one of the occupants.

Milord Vaniel de Winter. How was it that he kept crossing her path? Paris Satellite was a big place. Perhaps the universe was trying to tell her something – like she was running out of time if she wanted to rescue Conrad Su before she was sent off to war.

She crept closer, keeping an ornamental shrub in a gilt-lined pot between herself and Milord. Perhaps she might overhear something of use.

As she moved in, Dana realised that she recognised his dinner companion. Milord had finally won the attention of the Marquise de Wardes, that political candidate from Valour who had captivated his attention back on the train.

Well, now she was practically obliged to eavesdrop on their conversation.

The Marquise de Wardes was as effortlessly beautiful in person as in all the newscasts. She was a similar height, colour and build to Dana herself – her deep brown shoulders were surprisingly muscular for a woman who was famous as a fashion plate, not a kickboxer.

Speaking of her fashion choices, the Marquise was all in silver for the fancy restaurant; poured into a sheath dress that looked like it had been welded from sheet metal. Her hair fell in black twists with silver beads that must have taken hours to set in place.

Milord de Winter had gone to some trouble as well. His suit was grey, with a shirt embroidered with silver threads. Had he called ahead to make sure their outfits matched?

That was disturbing. But if he really wanted to match colour schemes with the Marquise, why wasn't he wearing his silver secret agent hair?

Dana shifted closer, but couldn't hear what they were saying to each other. The mood had shifted from politely flirtatious to something tense – Milord spoke too fast, leaning in. The Marquise tilted her whole body back, as if to make extra space between them.

Finally, the Marquise de Wardes rose, speaking loud enough that Dana could hear her from her hiding spot. "Don't think I'm not grateful for your interest, Milord de Winter, but I have so many political advisors already. I'm not sure you are making as strong a case as you think you are."

"Please, give me a little longer to convince you," pressed Milord. "And accept this token of my professional esteem." He pushed a small, pretty object at her. It looked like a retro powder compact, decorated with a gleaming mother-of-pearl surface.

The Marquise sighed, but accepted the gift. "I need a spot of fresh air," she said coldly. She swept off in the direction of the bathroom. De Winter, left behind, looked like the popular boy in school receiving his first ever rejection, and not sure how to handle it.

Dana hesitated for a moment before realising that as a woman, she could follow the Marquise without raising anyone's suspicion.

Aramis and Porthos gave her confused looks as she moved past their table and kept going, doing a lap of the restaurant.

The ladies bathroom of Hotel Coquenard was a gleaming treasure. It was like stepping inside a jewellery cabinet, or a hover-chandelier. Every reflective surface sparkled and gleamed.

There was no hiding in here – Dana found her face staring back at her from a dozen different angles.

At the enormous central mirror, the Marquise de Wardes touched up her makeup, swiping lipgloss across her mouth and turning a dial on her wrist to adjust the colour. "Honestly," she sighed, meeting Dana's eyes as if they were peers. "I think I preferred it when men were after me for my looks rather than my political value."

It occurred to Dana that the practiced charms of her alter ego Lexie Charlemagne might be of use here. "I noticed your gentleman friend," she said lightly, joining the Marquise at the mirror. "If you think he's not interested how you look, you haven't been paying attention. He couldn't take his eyes off you."

The Marquise made an unimpressed huffing sound. "You say that, my dear, but believe me, he's only thinking about my potential career in public office – and what he can get out of an alliance. He turns on the charm when he wants to, but everything beneath the surface is cold as ice."

Dana readjusted her neckline, since she had no more than half a centimetre of hair to primp. "I know what I saw."

The Marquise gave her a thoughtful look, trying to work Dana out. "What a darling gown you're wearing," she said after a moment. "I am sure I saw the Duchess of Buckingham wearing one like it last month."

"She's a trendsetter, all right," Dana said with a smile.

If she was going to keep up this espionage thing, she might have to invest in frocks that weren't Buck's hand-me-downs. What a horrendous thought.

"Well, I hope you're having a better evening than I am," said the Marquise, making for the door.

Dana spotted the compact clamshell, where the Marquise had abandoned it near the sink. "You forgot this."

"Keep it," said the darling of the fashion broadcasts with an airy wave. "And if that handsome, silver-tongued date of mine asks anyone if they've seen me, please don't volunteer that I slipped out through the kitchens to avoid him."

The bathroom door swung closed behind her. Dana reached down and picked up the compact clamshell. It was unlikely that Milord would have put any evidence of Conrad Su's latest kidnapping on this thing before presenting it to the Marquise de Wardes, but she could not afford to discard any possible clue.

It occurred to her that if the Marquise de Wardes could escape this bloody hotel through the kitchens, then Dana could do exactly the same thing. She felt a brief prick of guilt about ditching Aramis and Porthos, but not for long.

Dana put the clamshell in the tiny evening bag that Aramis had pressed on her because the stupid dress she was wearing was apparently too fancy to include pockets, and made a break for it.

The hotel didn't have a back entrance so much as a giant blank wall, but Dana managed to double back and leave the hotel by the main lobby without being spotted by either her friends or Milord de Winter.

That didn't mean that she made it out scot-free. A few steps from the hotel entrance, a strong pair of hands grabbed her around the shoulders and dragged her into the alleyway around the side.

Dana was prepared to fight, but when she saw her assailant, she lowered her fists.

"Hello, Lexie," said the no-longer-friendly voice of Bianca "Bee" de Winter, the Countess of Clarick. "How perfectly lovely to see you again."

"Hello, Bee," said Dana warily.

"Or should I call you D'Artagnan?"

Cover blown, then. Dana wrenched away from Bee's grip, straightening her dress to give herself a moment to collect her thoughts. "It wasn't personal, Bee," she said calmly. "I was working. With a brother like yours, you should understand what that means."

Bee de Winter wore loose clothes, as if she had come here straight from a yoga class – or fencing training, Dana considered. Bee looked lethal here in the alleyway, a sword and gloves hanging on one side of her belt and an arc-ray on the other.

Perhaps Dana wasn't the only one who had been playing a role on that train.

"Nothing personal," repeated Bee. "And next you're going to insist that you're not stalking my brother-in-law."

Dana spluttered at that. "Are you serious right now?"

"Vaniel has a lot of enemies," Bee said. "I was hoping you weren't one of them."

Dana saw red. The old familiar buzz of anger burned through her. "I serve the Crown," she snapped, shoving

Bee further away from her. "If that makes me Vaniel's enemy, that's his choice, not mine. I wasn't even *here* because of him tonight. My friends tricked me into a stupidly fancy dinner I didn't even get to eat, so —"

"What is going on here?" broke in a sharp, beautiful voice. Milord de Winter stood at the mouth of the alley in his silver suit and brown hair, either exasperated or amused. Possibly both.

"Vaniel, darling," said Bee without taking her eyes off Dana. "Did you know that our friend from the train was actually a Musketeer spy called D'Artagnan?"

Milord went very still. "I did not know that," he said calmly. "How enterprising of her."

"What are you going to do about it?" Bee demanded.

"I'm not going to start a scuffle outside a five-star hotel, sweetness. I'll see you back at the ship later. Unless you'd rather walk with me now?"

Bee looked confused. "I'm meeting friends," she said.

"I will bid you good night then, Bee. Good night, Dana."

"Good night, Vaniel," said Dana. Apparently they were on first name terms now.

Then it was just Dana and Bee, staring awkwardly at each other.

"So what?" Dana said impatiently after a moment. "Are we going to fight, or are we going to make out against the wall for a while? Even better, we could go back to reading trashy magazines and painting each other's nails, because that was a super good time."

"My family is everything to me," Bee hissed. "I don't know what you're up to, but I'm going to make sure you stay well away from us."

"Good luck with that," Dana snapped back. "I've been trying to avoid your family all week but here I am getting hauled back in."

Bee's eyes went dark, and then she pulled the padded gloves out of her belt and slapped Dana in the face.

It kind of hurt, but Dana barely noticed because she was recovering from the fact that she had been hit with a pair of gloves, like something out of a vid drama. "Are you challenging me to a duel, or do you just like hitting people?"

"Name the place and time," Bee said in a steady, angry voice.

Dana opened her mouth, but was interrupted by a chorus of aristocratic voices.

"Bee, honey, there you are!"

"Yo, Clarick!"

Two men and a woman, all athletic and wearing the same kind of designer sports gear as Bee, crowded into the mouth of the alley.

"We only have the practice rooms till 2200, what's going on with you, love?"

"I was busy," Bee said between gritted teeth.

Dana would now have to shove her way past three more people in order to get out of this damned alley. She hated it when there wasn't a clear exit. "0600 behind the Luxembourg," she said, keeping her gaze steady on Bee. "If you're so keen to address your issues with me."

"Done," snapped Bee.

"Hang on," said one of her friends. He was a head taller than Dana and his shoulders were crazy wide like he had been built out of lamb shanks and robot parts. His meaty hand slammed down on Dana's shoulder. "A duel, Clarick? And you're leaving us out of it?"

"Take your hand off my shoulder," said Dana calmly.

The idiot ignored her, leaning more heavily as he continued speaking to Bee. "You know it's been on our bucket list since we arrived here. Paris isn't Paris without an illegal duel…"

"Move your hand right now," breathed Dana. "Or I'm going to make you move it."

"Doncaster," Bee said, sounding exhausted and pissed off. "If you can't find your own damned duel, I don't see why I should share mine."

Dana stepped aside from the enormous New Aristocrat who had been using her as furniture, swung around neatly and punched him in the face. Pain shot through her hand all the way up to her elbow, but it was worth it.

"0600 behind the Luxembourg, everyone's welcome," she announced, glaring at the other two New Aristocrats until they stepped quickly aside to let her out of the alley. "I have three friends, you have three friends, *let's have a party*." Dana gave Bee a lazy salute as she made her exit. "For future reference, if you want to fight duels over your brother-in-law's honour, check he has some first."

CHAPTER 3
THE NEW ARISTOCRATS

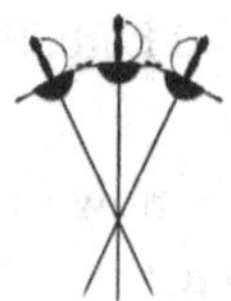

Athos answered the door with a drink in his hand. His eyes went to Dana's knuckles, which were swollen and grazed. Without a word, he stepped back to allow her into the apartment.

She sat at his kitchen bar and poured herself a glass of brandy from the open bottle while Athos raided his medical supplies.

"The service at Hotel Coquenard isn't what it used to be," he ventured, as he cleaned her sore hands with a sonic wand.

Dana winced at his touch. "The fight happened after I left the hotel."

Athos' eyes sparkled with something like humour. "How was dinner?"

"Excruciating. I am never again going to trust any of you to take me anywhere that requires a dress, or prior knowledge of Porthos' love life."

"Seems fair."

Dana's right hand was tingling and sensitive as Athos slapped a medipatch across the back of it. "Ow."

"Fists," he muttered. "You have a pilot's slice and a pearl stunner, but you go straight for the fists."

"I'm good with my fists."

"You're good with a sword."

Dana gave him a wary look. "I am?"

"You are a promising pupil," he admitted.

Dana felt warm all over. "You've never said that before."

Athos rolled his eyes. "If you keep up this kind of mindless thuggery, one of these days that brain of yours will get so bruised you will never pilot another ship. And then what would we do?" He looked embarrassed to have said so much. Dana flung herself at him for a hug, and he bore it manfully for at least five seconds before shrugging her off. "That's enough of that."

Dana grinned. "You'll be pleased to know that I ended the fight by challenging them all to a duel."

His eyebrow twitched. "Goodness, how many were there?"

"Four."

"The perfect number."

"I told them I had friends to even things up..." she added, almost shyly.

Athos leaned back, pleased now. "Make my day," he purred. "Tell me they were Red Hammers. I haven't had a decent skirmish in weeks."

"Oh, better than that," she assured him. "Tourists."

An odd light came into Athos' eyes. "Tourists?"

"New Aristocrats off the boat from Valour."

He hummed with delight. "Is it my *birthday*, D'Artagnan?"

"I thought you'd like that," she smirked back at him. "The Luxembourg, 0600."

"Ah," Athos said, pushing the bottle away from them both. "We'll need an early start. Should we warn Aramis and Porthos now, or surprise them with it in the morning?"

Dana, who was not above a little petty revenge on her friends, pretended to think about it for a moment or so. "I like surprises," she said finally. "Surprises are good."

Neither Porthos nor Aramis were delighted to be dragged out of bed early enough to make it to the Luxembourg for a 0600 duel. Porthos, at least, got into the spirit once she arrived, doing warm-up stretches and lunges.

Aramis was far less amenable. "I only got to bed three hours ago," she scowled, her hands wrapped around her second cup of coffee.

"Poetry again?" Athos said unsympathetically. "It's bad for your health." He turned to Porthos. "How went your siege of Chef Coquenard?"

"Mixed results," said Porthos.

"Ha!" said Aramis. "Like she didn't take him home with her last night."

"He wasn't there when I woke up," Porthos shot at her. "He chose bread-baking and *sous* prep over me. But at least mine doesn't require me to write poetry."

"You have no romance in your soul."

"I'm confused about why you're putting so much effort

into Dubois when *she's* the one who broke it off —
shouldn't she be courting *you*?"

Aramis smiled to herself. "I write better poetry."

"So you're trying to win at relationship."

"It passes the time."

"Will you all shut up about your love lives?"
complained Dana, sick of them both.

Athos gave her an amused look. "That's my line."

"Yes, darling," said Aramis. "We all know D'Artagnan
is your favourite. Will you shut up and let me finish this
stanza before our playmates arrive?"

The New Aristocrats were late, and made a swag-
gering entrance. Porthos and Dana matched their
swagger with their own, while Aramis perched on the
nearby Artifice rocks, scribbling notes in her poetry book.
Athos hung back, looking bored, though Dana knew
better.

She saw his shoulders relax, as he took in each of their
faces. Perhaps he had worried that they might recognise
him from his own New Aristocrat days on Valour?

The tourists wore formal fencing attire, each of them
displaying the flag of Valour somewhere on their person.
Athos rolled his eyes so hard they nearly rattled.

Bee wore grey and white, matching her chilly expression. Even she was embarrassed when her large friend, the
Earl of Doncaster, pronounced the Artifice field appropriate for an 'authentic Parisian duel.'

"Sightseers," Aramis sighed.

"They should put us in the guide book," Porthos said,
undaunted. "Can I have the big one? He looks fun. I bet he
makes a loud noise when he hits the ground."

"Housekeeping before we begin," said Athos, whose

New Aristocrat accent was particularly pronounced today. He held out a tablet. "Your signatures, if you please."

Bee's eyebrows almost hit her perfectly coiffed hairline. "A contract for an illegal duel? That sounds like the definition of a terrible idea."

"As you say, illegal," said Athos. "And extremely dangerous. *Amateurs* —" and he let a beautiful sneer curl around the word "—have been known to get hurt in bouts such as these. By putting our names to the release, we free each other from liability should any of us be wounded."

Dana stepped closer to Porthos. "Why have I never heard of these releases before?"

"We don't bother against Hammers or Sabres," Porthos whispered back. "They're bastards all, but honourable duellists. Dirtsider tourists, you can't trust as far as you can throw. We've lost good Musketeers to the service because some arsehole decided to sue over a scratched finger or a severed artery."

"All the more despicable, because duels between peers aren't even illegal on Valour," Aramis added. She laid her notebook and stylus aside, and stood shoulder to shoulder with Porthos.

Athos collected the thumbprints and assent of Lady Moire of Normandie and the Earl of Doncaster, as well as Bianca, Countess of Clarick. The last of their party took one look at the tablet and scoffed. "These aren't real names. Most of you haven't put down more than one. What does 'Aramis' or 'Porthos' even mean?"

"Sheffield," said Doncaster. "You're ruining the duel for everyone. Stop being a prick and put your thumb on the tablet."

Sheffield — Dana was starting to revisit the idea that

he was friends with the other New Aristocrats, as they all looked thoroughly sick of him — thrust the tablet rudely back at Athos. "I am a gentleman and I have standards," he announced. "If you can't produce an opponent worthy of the name Baron Sheffield, I shall not participate."

"I actually want to kill you right now," said Bee between gritted teeth.

"If he's not playing, I volunteer to sit out," said Aramis quickly. "On account of this poem that I would really prefer to be working on…"

"I can solve this," said Athos.

Dana saw the look that Aramis and Porthos exchanged, and oh crap, she knew that look. It meant Athos was about to do something stupid and take the rest of them down with him. She lunged forward to grab the tablet from him, but it was too late.

Athos stepped into Sheffield's personal space, crowding him with a dangerous smile. "I have another name," he said, making his accent very, very obvious. Posh oozed from his veins. "I believe you will find it worthy of you, second son of a Baron that you are. Not quite in line for the title, not with all those pesky nieces and nephews your older sister keeps popping out, but I see why you feel the need to flash the title around since you're far from home with hardly anyone to call you on your deception."

Sheffield looked at him, confused and angry but not moving away. "I say —"

"Let's play a game," said Athos. "I'll tell you my real name, and you can decide if I'm worthy of crossing swords with you."

"Athos," warned Aramis.

"But if I tell you," Athos continued. "You understand,

it's not something I want known in general circles, since I am believed by most to be dead. So I'm going to do my damnedest to kill you. How does that sound?"

"It sounds bloody stupid," said Bee with a huff.

Dana silently agreed. Why couldn't they get it over with? They could all be having a post-duel breakfast by now.

Sheffield examined Athos from top to toe. It was obvious that he loved the idea of knowing something that should not be known, courting death at the hands of a Musketeer. "Tell me," he breathed.

Athos leaned in, his beard grazing the other man's ear, and whispered for a moment. "Does that suffice?" he said finally, rocking back on his heels.

Sheffield was flushed across the top of his cheeks. He looked as if he had been hit over the head. "Y-yes," he said, stumbling over the words. "Perfectly acceptable."

"I'd like to make it clear that I don't give a fuck who I fight as long as it happens sometime this century!" said Doncaster loudly.

"What he said," Porthos moaned.

"Begin, then," said Athos with a small smile on his face as if he was very much planning to enjoy this duel. "*En garde.*"

Fencing Bee was no chore. This was enough to make Dana wish they had got in a few fencing bouts on that train back on Valour, instead of gossiping about clothes and boys. Bee was a competent, measured duellist, and the anger of their previous night's encounter had bled out of both of them by the time they saluted and began.

Dana won the first bout with a scratch to the side of Bee's neck, and a ribbon reclaimed from her hair. Bee won the second, slicing a button from Dana's sleeve, which was going to be annoying to hunt for in the Artifice grass.

"I could say I'm sorry I lied to you and your brother, and we could call it a draw," Dana offered.

Bee gave her a confused look. "After all this?"

Dana shrugged one shoulder. "Doncaster got his duel, at least. We Parisians like tourists to come away with the full experience."

They sat on the grass together for a while, watching the others fight. Aramis worked quickly, her mind on that poem of hers instead of the fight, and she finished off her second bout with Lady Moire with the same breathtaking efficiency she had used for the first; having won both, Aramis retired from the field and picked up her stylus again, though not before kissing Moire's hand and (Dana could not help but notice) collecting her comm code.

Doncaster and Porthos had fun. He had the reach on her, being taller and wider; she pulled out all her favourite fancy tricks and he matched them with some of his own. The two of them smirked at each other every time they added a different sword flourish or piece of fancy foot-work. They could be at this for hours.

Athos and Sheffield had an entirely different kind of duel. Athos fenced with as much calm and method as if he were teaching a class — indeed, he exhibited far more cool restraint than he ever had when training Dana.

Sheffield was sweating, despite the regulated temperature of the field. It was clear he could see his own death spelled out with every stroke of Athos' sword.

"Is he going to kill him?" Bee asked.

"He said he would," said Dana. She shivered at the blank expression Athos wore. It was nothing like the usual manic energy he displayed when fighting with Sabres and Hammers.

This was work, not play.

"Tell me why you have been following us," said Bee, as they watched Athos school Sheffield on fencing technique. "What is your interest in Vaniel? It might have been a coincidence that you were at the hotel," she added. "But you were definitely watching him — and I saw you follow the Marquise de Wardes in the restaurant. You're up to something."

It was not Bee's skill with a sword that made her dangerous, Dana reminded herself. She was aligned with Milord, and he had Conrad's life in his hands.

Time for Lexie Charlemagne to save the day. For once, Dana was not going to try to punch her way out of a problem. She was going to be smart about it.

"It's embarrassing," Dana said, biting her lip to look younger and less threatening. "But it's not a professional interest. I met you for the first time when I was working under another name, and I'm sorry about that, because it's ruined everything, but —" She gave Bee a helpless look.

Bee looked doubtful. "You're not…"

Dana summoned up all those odd feelings she had glimpsed on the train, when she realised how much she enjoyed Vaniel's company. "I was watching him in the restaurant because I like him," she sighed. "That's it, no mystery. You can laugh at me now."

Bee did laugh, a delightful sound ringing out across the Artifice meadow. "Oh no," she gasped.

"I know nothing will come of it," said Dana, avoiding Bee's gaze for oh so many reasons. It sold the idea rather well. "I can't help myself."

"Does this mean I challenged you to a duel over his love life?" Bee laughed. "Air and fire, he'll never let me hear the end of it."

Dana gave her a stricken look. "You mustn't tell him." The thought of Milord de Winter's sister-in-law telling him that Dana D'Artagnan fancied him was genuinely excruciating. She didn't have to fake her reaction at all.

"You'd rather nurse your crush in secret and let him continue to throw himself uselessly at the Marquise de Wardes?" Bee challenged.

Dana sighed. Athos had managed to slash both sleeves off his opponent. He drove him steadily closer and closer to the church, proving with every step that he was the stronger duellist.

"Vaniel would make a terrible boyfriend," Bee continued. "Really, he talks about politics all the time, and his work is everything to him. I love him dearly, but he was a dreadful husband to my sister."

"You care about him, don't you?" said Dana. It was a mystery to her that Bee — who seemed like a genuine and open person — was so convinced that Milord was worth caring about.

"Family stick together," said Bee staunchly.

"I like hearing him talk about politics," Dana confessed, and managed a small laugh that she hoped came across as girlish and romantic. "It doesn't matter. I know he'd never be interested in me."

"Give me your comm code," said Bee in a thoughtful sort of voice.

"You're going to help me?" Dana said in surprise.

"We'll see."

Only after they had exchanged codes did Dana look up, to see Athos bearing his opponent roughly on to the grass, sword-first. "Oh, fuck, he *has* killed him," she exclaimed, forgetting to be 'Alix Charlemagne slightly embarrassed in love' for a moment. She leapt to her feet and ran full pelt for the other Musketeers.

"Let's get out of here!" Bee shouted to her other friends. They fled the scene, skirting around the Luxembourg and away.

Sheffield lay on the grass with a sword in his chest and a sucking sound coming out of his mouth.

Aramis cast her notebook aside and approached the fallen man with a grim expression and a medikit. "Athos, I hate when you do this."

"I know," said Athos, breathing hard from his duel. "But how could anyone be expected to meet a man like that and *not* put a sword in his chest?"

"One of these days I'd like you to invest in some anger management techniques that don't involve collapsing someone's lung," Aramis said primly. "Porthos, lift!"

Porthos reached over and yanked the sword out of Sheffield's chest. He yelled in pain and flapped his mouth uselessly for air as blood soaked the fine linen of his fencing jacket.

Aramis ripped the jacket open and slapped a medipatch over the wound on Sheffield's chest. He gasped, and then fell unconscious.

"The thing about a collapsed lung," said Athos,

sounding almost cheerful. "It's traumatic enough that the healing process keeps them comatose for hours, and you can almost guarantee twenty to forty minutes of memory loss."

Dana stared at him. "He won't remember the duel."

"Or any words that might have been exchanged shortly before the duel. That's right." Athos bounced lightly on the balls of his feet. "Anyone fancy breakfast?"

"I'm going to punch you now," Dana informed him.

"Give me a minute to finish this off and I'll hold him down for you," said Aramis. "Porthos, kindly drop Athos' victim off at the nearest medibay before you all go for a victory breakfast, and leave me alone to finish my fucking poem."

CHAPTER 4
IS IT LOVE OR JUST PARIS?

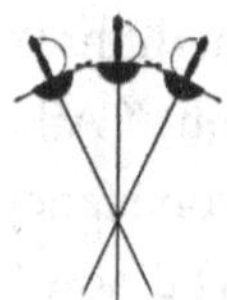

ater that day, once a certain poem had been put to bed, and long after a certain amnesiac Baron's son had been delivered to a medibay, Dana threw herself on the mercy of her friends.

"Let me get this straight," said Porthos, sprawled on Aramis' couch with her feet in Athos' lap. "You got in a fist fight with the Countess of Clarick last night, we fought a duel with her friends before breakfast, and now you have a hot date with her brother?"

"Brother-in-law," Dana corrected, staring at her own image in the mirror. Aramis had taken the 'God, no more dresses' plea to heart, and dressed Dana in a sweeping black tunic with a neckline that could only be described as 'dramatic,' over figure-hugging bronze trousers.

Since she wasn't hiding her identity anymore, Dana wore metal Musketeer dog tags on a chain around her neck instead of society-styled jewellery. Treville had sent them around that morning — flying the Musketeer troop carrier, Dana was entitled to a tag and a blue flight uniform, though not the jacket yet.

So close to being a real Musketeer. She would take it. She would take whatever she could get.

"I'm impressed," said Porthos, handing over the appropriate shade of lipstick. "I was a Musketeer for two years before I started setting my own honey traps."

"I am not a honey trap," Dana said hotly.

"So you're *not* planning to seduce this Milord to find out what he knows about your missing Conrad?"

Dana scowled. "I might be slightly a honey trap."

"I disapprove," Athos volunteered from his position on the couch.

"No one asked you," said Aramis. She encircled Dana's wrists with bronze spiral bracelets. "This looks amazing. He won't be able to resist."

"Not sure you should go in without backup," Porthos said thoughtfully. "A fake date would make you look less obvious, and could help with extraction if it all goes pear-shaped. You should take Athos."

Dana and Athos exchanged appalled looks. "No," they decided in unison.

"I'll be fine," Dana added. The thought of trying to flirt with Milord while any of her Musketeer friends were in earshot was horrible.

Athos pushed Porthos' feet aside and came over to stare meaningfully at Dana. "You're sure this is a good idea, D'Artagnan?"

She lifted her chin defiantly at him. "Not all problems can be solved with wine and swords."

"That shows a distinct lack of imagination on your

part," he replied. "Is he pretty, this minister assassin kidnapper person?"

"A bit," she admitted reluctantly.

"Pretty people are very untrustworthy. Just look at Aramis."

"Hey!" Aramis protested.

"Pretty men who talk politics are the worst of all," he went on.

"You're not actually trying to give me romantic advice, are you, Athos?" Dana asked in a very small voice.

There was that appalled expression again. "God, no. I'm going to stop talking now. Have a good night. Don't do anything Porthos would do."

"*Hey!*" Porthos protested, but then paused in reflection. "No, that's fair."

So this was awkward. The gathering to which Dana had been invited by Bee included not only Milord Vaniel de Winter, who had his nose in a clamshell in a far corner of the room, but also that morning's duellists: Lady Moire, the Earl of Doncaster, and "Baron" Sheffield who remembered nothing about the duel but was unsettled and cranky.

In retrospect, Dana should have brought Porthos, since she and Doncaster had bonded over trying to wound each other in the most grandstanding ways possible, and that could only translate to dinner party gold.

Bee and Vaniel turned out to not be staying in Paris Satellite accommodation, but in a dagger-class scout ship called the *Matagot*. He looked like a plain black raven ship from the outside – for security purposes, Bee claimed, but inside was as beautifully furnished as a royal apartment.

Dana was shown into a parlour (what kind of spaceship had a parlour?) by Miss Columbina ("Call me Kitty!"), Milord's very pretty personal assistant. Kitty Columbina had hair that fell in soft purple curls around her round face, and she wore a dress that consisted mostly of silk butterflies.

"How do you know the family?" she asked Dana.

"Oh, I met Vaniel on a train, and then this morning I fought a duel with Bee and three of her friends," Dana said, hoping to see Kitty's eyes widen in surprise.

Instead, the other woman laughed. "That's the tamest way they've ever befriended a new companion. No bear-wrestling, or pirates? For shame."

"I suppose you see a lot, with the de Winters as your employers," said Dana, wondering if this girl might be a useful resource.

"You're certainly going to have to try harder if you want to shock me," said Kitty, and she gave Dana a look which suggested she rather wanted her to try. "Let me get you a glass of champagne, Captain D'Artagnan…"

"I'm —" Dana started to say, but Kitty had already flitted away towards the bar before Dana could wrap her mouth around the words 'Arms-Sergeant'.

"Dana." Bee greeted her warmly, with a hint of humour in her eyes. She had to be encouraging this whole 'set up Vaniel and Dana' game out of mischief, rather than any genuine interest. Of course, Dana wasn't in it for genuine reasons either.

Flirting at this gathering was not the difficult part; any and all of the de Winters' guests were more than happy to flirt with the mysterious Musketeer who was dressed to kill. But Vaniel de Winter was a harder nut to crack.

So much for being a honey trap.

Half an hour in, and Dana had entirely failed to be alluring and intriguing and all those other things that seemed like good ideas at the time. She had exchanged exactly three sentences with Milord, each polite and not especially interesting.

"You look you want to run out of here," said a soft, amused voice near her ear.

Dana turned and saw Kitty the assistant, standing very close. "I don't do well at these sorts of parties," she admitted.

The other girl smiled at her. She had glitter in her lipgloss, Dana noticed. "Fancy the grand tour?"

This, this could be useful. "Absolutely!" Dana said.

There was no spaceship more alluring or attractive than a musket-class dart. Dana's loyalties were set in that regard. Okay, she had been slightly turned on by the Moth fighter, but she was only human. No one would kick a Moth out of bed.

Matagot was a raven-class scout, and there was nothing remotely sexy about them. Dana had hated the idea of flying one of these when she was considering (not really considering) job options outside the Royal Fleet.

This particular raven-class scout might be the exception to her rule. Never mind the glamorous decor, and the gym that wouldn't have been out of place in a Paris Satellite rec hub. It was the flight deck that interested her, and the engine.

Miss Kitty Columbina had to duck back to the party for a moment or two, to check that the champagne levels were still flowing, or whatever. While she was gone, Dana dropped herself into the flight seat at the helm. The console had been tricked out and customised, by the looks of it. No way the standard design for ravens involved this much chrome.

Something beeped.

Dana lifted her hands in the air, hoping she hadn't set off any security alarms. The beep repeated, over and over.

It was coming from the beaded evening bag that Aramis had pressed on her, because taking a military issue belt-pack to a cocktail party was "inappropriate".

There wasn't much in the tiny bag — only lipstick and Dana's pearl stunner. But then she remembered the compact clamshell she had been carrying around with her since the Marquise de Wardes passed it to her in Hotel Coquenard's bathroom.

Dana opened the clamshell slowly, checking that the camera setting was not on. It wasn't an incoming call, but a text. The words:

> Have you given further thought to my suggestion?

hung on the screen, waiting.

Dana froze for a moment. What did Milord think he was doing? Why ignore her at a party only to — oh. He didn't know that she had the clamshell. He had given it to the Marquise de Wardes.

As she stared at it, a second text came in.

> I can tempt you, if you let me.

Dana summoned up what she remembered of the Marquise, to reply:

I would prefer it if you were after me for my looks. One gets so tired of being a political pin-up.

> Who says I'm not interested in everything you have to offer?

Why, Milord de Winter. That was almost smooth.

> Perhaps you make me nervous in person.

I refuse to believe you've ever been nervous in your life. That would require you to stop thinking about work for ten minutes, at least.

> I'll have you know I spent fifteen minutes yesterday ignoring work altogether. Of course, I was asleep at the time…

He sleeps. Not an android replica, then?

> Sorry to disappoint.

I've always wanted to flirt with an android.

> My sister-in-law is hosting a gathering on our ship tonight. I don't suppose you'd run away from whatever boring occasion you are stuck at, and join us instead?

How do you know I'm stuck anywhere?

> You're finally talking to me.

I can't get away.

But you're tempted?

Go back to your party guests, Milord. Find someone to flirt with in person. I hear that practise makes perfect.

If I do, will you be jealous?

Dana smiled to herself, and then typed in:

Desperately.

So. Dana had successfully carried out a flirtation with Milord de Winter. Sure, it was under the wrong identity, but it still counted as a win, right? She had no idea whether this correspondence would turn out to be remotely useful, but she had to hope it was a crack in Milord's forcefield.

Dana returned to the parlour where the party was going on, and caught sight of Kitty who waved apologetically to her from behind the world's largest tray of *hors d'oeuvres*. Obviously she had been caught slacking and put to work.

"I've been neglecting you, Dana," said a man behind her.

Dana's body betrayed her with a hum of excitement in response to that voice. "Milord de Winter. You're not neglecting me anymore than your other guests." She smirked at him, thinking of his complaints to the imaginary Marquise. "On a scale of 1 to 10, exactly how much do you hate parties?"

Vaniel returned her smile, and rubbed slightly at his

messy brown hair, playing that distracted political obsessive whose company she had enjoyed on the train. "All the numbers," he confessed.

She shouldn't like him — shouldn't enjoy this chance to make a connection with him. He was the enemy. Wasn't he? Dana was almost certain that he was the enemy. It wasn't fair for the enemy to be this adorable.

"I also hate parties," she admitted.

"I'm sure Miss Alix Charlemagne simply *adored* parties."

"Yes, but I didn't convince as her for long, did I?" Dana said dryly.

There was interest in Vaniel's eyes. He kept looking at her like he wanted to see what was inside her brain, and it made her shiver in a not-entirely-good way. *Milord, not Vaniel. This man is not your friend.*

"I'm not sure why I bother talking to you," he said after a moment. "You're too young to have anything intelligent to say, and you don't know anyone worthwhile. You're not useful at all."

Dana blinked very slowly at him, and then smiled. "Must be my natural charm winning you over. Or you have a thing for sarcastic people."

That made him laugh. It was a bitter sound, his laugh. "You're more right than you know. Do you want to come to dinner with me one night soon?"

"Sooner rather than later," Dana replied. "I'm not sure when we're shipping out, but it won't be long."

He raised his eyebrows. "The Siege of Truth?"

"I'm just driving the truck so I'll probably be the last to know." Dana pinched her lips together. "Why invite me to dinner? If it's to insult me further, I already have friends who do that."

Milord gave her a wicked smile that didn't fit his baffled political expert persona at all. "I want to make someone else jealous."

Dana glared at him. "That is so unflattering I can't even tell you." Was he messing with her now? The sudden thought that he might want to make the Marquise jealous *with Dana* burst into her head and then it was all she could do not to crack up laughing. "Yes, fine. I have no shame when it comes to someone else buying dinner."

"Excellent," Milord said, and leaned in to brush his mouth against her cheek. "This is going to be interesting," he promised.

This close, his presence was overwhelming. How embarrassing was it that she was this attracted to someone who had probably kidnapped the man she had been hoping to have an affair with?

The sooner Dana was sent off to war, the better. She shouldn't be allowed out in public on her own.

CHAPTER 5
SEXTING THE ENEMY

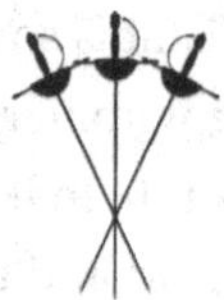

"They look like teardrops," Planchet observed at one point.

"Nothing so innocent," Athos replied.

No matter where you went on Paris Satellite, the vid-feeds were there to remind you about the Siege of Truth Space.

The Sun-kissed ships were grey-silver streaks of metal – 'teardrop' was an accurate enough description for the shape of them, but it did not come close to conveying the lethal force within their shells. The first wave of Cardinal's Sabres and Royal Musketeers had reached Truth Space already, positioning themselves around and between the silent Sun-kissed fleet.

No shots had been fired. No diplomatic exchange had been made. To the extreme frustration of those Sabres and Musketeers left out of the first wave, there was no word yet as to when reinforcements would be called to the front.

"The first war with the Sun-kissed started when we broke ranks and shot first," Porthos said. "I'm not surprised that the Regence is holding back, this time around."

"She can't seriously think we can make peace with those monsters," Athos said with a chill to his voice.

"But wouldn't it be nice if we could?" Aramis sighed.

Dana had heard similar conversations among her friends every day for the last week, and they were still no closer to being sent to war.

What she had been doing, in the week since the party on the *Matagot*, was dating Vaniel de Winter.

One dinner, she had thought, maybe with drinks and dancing afterwards. Getting close to him made a lot of sense, to investigate whether he was the one responsible for the kidnapping of Conrad Su.

Also, it took Dana's mind off the whole going to war thing, not to mention the infrequent, unsatisfying subspace communications she had managed to exchange with her family on the beleaguered Gascon Station.

Somehow, one dinner had turned into another, and another. The location was always based on where the Marquise de Wardes was dining, with friends or political allies or on one occasion a very attractive and muscular young man whose dinner suit had no sleeves.

Dana flirted half-heartedly with Milord at these dinners, but flirted with far greater enthusiasm with him via clamshell, still pretending to be the Marquise.

Milord enjoyed the game so much that he had not tried to speak with the Marquise in person again. Instead, he made conversation with Dana at the restaurant, coldly 'ignored' the Marquise in public (who needed no prompting to likewise ignore him) and then spent hours afterwards typing flirtatious banter at the woman he believed to be her.

Dana was dating Milord twice over. It was exhausting, but exhilarating as well, to be skirting the edge of danger.

He was dangerous. She had to keep reminding herself that he was dangerous, because he was also clever and witty and occasionally so awkward that she wanted to mock him or kiss him, possibly both at the same time.

Thanks to Athos and Grimaud's exciting project of 'let's build a ship from random parts because life isn't difficult enough', Dana and the others spent much of their downtime scavenging the junk field and the shipyards, or hanging out in the maintenance workshop where the *Pistachio* was taking her final shape.

When asked, they referred to it as 'helping.'

Today, Dana was lying full length on a welding bench, flirting via text message. So basically acting like she was fifteen.

She had quite enjoyed replying to:

> What are you wearing?

with:

> A welding mask and steel capped boots.

Though it had required quite a lot of explaining afterwards as to why the Marquise de Wardes might have worn such an outfit. It was amazing how far the phrase 'diplomatic tour of the city' got you.

Dana had teased him with:

A fashion thing, you wouldn't understand

before shifting into a description of lingerie and where exactly she would like him to put his hands someday.

"Sexting your boyfriend again?" Porthos asked. Like Dana, she was 'helping' with Athos' new ship by staying well away from the newly painted hull or any of the essential jobs. Everyone knew that Porthos was prepared to accidentally break things in order to not be asked to perform certain tasks, and so Athos had not even tried.

"I don't have a boyfriend," said Dana, barely looking up from the clamshell where her conversation was about five minutes away from cybersex. "I have a mission."

"Still not clear on how you're planning to rescue one fellow by hooking up with another," said Athos, climbing out of the *Pistachio* specifically to move Porthos further away from the tail fin of his new ship, which was about to have a new tattoo printed on to it by sonic wave. "Is this a 'kids today' situation?"

"Everything involving dating ever is a 'kids today' situation for you, Athos," said Aramis, who had taken charge of the sonic wave, programming in the design for the spray. "No one wants your romantic advice."

"I give excellent romantic advice," said Athos, sounding hurt.

"All you ever tell me is that love is for idiots, pretty people aren't to be trusted, and I should stop flirting with obvious villains," volunteered Dana.

Athos tilted his head slightly at her. "Those are extremely wise words which all sound like things I might have said. What's your point?"

"So this is fun," said Dana, ignoring his question. "But it's late enough in the day that we're probably not going to be summoned to the Siege of Truth, and I have a date tonight."

"Wear something pretty," said Porthos.

"Dance like it's your last night alive," said Aramis.

"Don't sleep with a man just because you think he might have kidnapped your boyfriend," said Athos.

"I'm going to take your recommendations under consideration!" Dana said loudly, and left before they could say anything else.

Tonight's date was not technically with Milord de Winter.

Actually it wasn't at all with Milord de Winter.

Dana had been visiting the *Matagot* a lot this week, meeting with Vaniel before their dinner dates, as well as taking tea with Bee and her appalling New Aristocrat friends. Every visit, every excuse, was for a single purpose: continuing the illusion that Dana D'Artagnan had an innocent but genuine crush on the Valour Minister of the Interior.

And every time she stepped on board the ship, there was Kitty Columbina.

This was the part that Dana felt slightly bad about, but only slightly, because Kitty did work for a criminal mastermind.

Kitty flirted with Dana, quite a lot. And Dana had been flirting back.

So this evening, with Milord and his sister-in-law off at some Palace shindig (which did not, thank goodness, include the Marquise de Wardes as an invited guest, otherwise the jig would be up), Dana visited the *Matagot* specifically to spend time with Kitty.

Kitty was fascinating. She was bubbly and warm and sarcastic, all qualities that Dana admired. Tonight, Kitty wore earrings shaped like strawberries, and a mini dress with flying ponies printed on it.

She also hated her boss.

It wasn't obvious at first, not with all the smiling and the banter and the public politeness. But Dana had discovered by process of elimination that the best way to make Kitty smile was to say something disparaging or sarcastic or downright mean about Milord de Winter.

This was useful, it had to be useful, but Dana didn't really want to think about useful right this second, because that was going to make her feel guilty about the fact that she was kissing her way down Kitty's neck, making her giggle with the teasing trace of her fingertips.

If Dana was a good person, then she wouldn't have decided ahead of time to kiss Kitty. It would have been an accident when their friendly flirtation shifted into the slide of soft mouths together, and the shivery feeling of leaning so far into another person that you could share each other's heat.

Dana D'Artagnan was not a good person. She was a Musketeer at heart, and Musketeer didn't always mean *good*. She had a man to rescue (if it was still possible). She had helped a lot of people, since first setting foot on Paris Satellite. Why couldn't she rescue Conrad Su, one last time?

She was going to be summoned to war any day now. Dana was running out of time, and the fastest way to figure out what Milord was hiding might well be via Kitty's knickers.

An assistant who hated her boss was a traitor waiting to happen. Dana needed to earn her trust fast, and this, she had convinced herself, was the best way to do it.

It didn't hurt that Kitty was really good at kissing. She arched back against her desk, scattering tiny plush animals in all directions. "What was that you were saying before we got distracted?" she laughed.

Dana leaned in, kissing her nose and then her cheek, their eyelashes fluttering together. "I forget. I like your office."

"Milord's is nicer," breathed Kitty, one hand squeezing Dana's upper arm. "Wow, you're strong. All those muscles."

"I work out. Why is his office nicer?"

"Because he's the boss, he has more money than anyone needs, and he has the best couch in the known universe."

Dana grinned wickedly at that. "A couch, you say?"

Kitty squealed as Dana picked her up and carried her into the office, which was conveniently unlocked. She had made her decision. She might fail this mission, but if there was a chance she wouldn't find Conrad, or he was dead already, and it was all Milord's fault…

If that was true, then eating out a hot girl on the bastard's couch was the least she could do.

"KITTY!" called a voice from the outer office sometime later. Dana and Kitty stared at each other in dishevelled shock.

"He's back early!" Kitty gasped.

They weren't entirely naked, but there were several items of clothing that had to be reclaimed or adjusted before Kitty looked even slightly respectable, and even then, there was a wildness about her hair and a sleepy well-fucked expression on her face that wasn't going anywhere anytime soon.

Hopefully Milord wasn't observant about these things. For a professional spy.

"I'll keep him out there," Kitty whispered, straightening her clothes one last time, while Dana hid behind the couch, pulling her boots on as she did so. On impulse, she reached up and gave Kitty a last heated kiss, just to make her blush.

"What the hell are you doing in there?" snapped Milord, sounding irritable as Kitty burst out through the doorway.

"Sorting out those meeting notes for tomorrow, like you asked me to, even though I haven't had a night off in three weeks and some of us don't get invited to gallivant around palaces, eating caviar sandwiches and goosing duchesses or whatever." Kitty managed to sound bored, sarcastic and casual all at once. Dana wanted to applaud her.

"It's not as much fun as it sounds," said Milord.

"Whatever. Next time, bring me back a dish of gold-plated cupcakes." There was a sound as Kitty smacked him in the chest with a tablet. "Here, all the prep work is done. You're welcome. Get an early night or go chase after one of your smart ladyfriends. I'm going to watch the holo-soaps in your office, because you've got the biggest wall screen."

"It's your respectful attitude, Kitty, that's what I appreciate most about you," Milord drawled. Obviously he enjoyed a lack of respect in his employees. It was one of many odd facts that Dana had mentally filed about him.

"Oh, sorry. I'm going to take full advantage of your giant wall screen, if that's okay with you, *sir*." There was a pause, as Milord looked over the work Kitty had handed him. "No hot date tonight?" she asked archly.

"Not for me," said Milord. "I did bump into the Marquise de Wardes at the Palace dinner –"

Dana held her breath, wondering if the two had spoken to each other and figured out about the stray clamshell.

"Oh, your adorable political crush," Kitty laughed. "The way you mix work and pleasure is so screwed up, it's almost artistic."

"I live for your amusement."

"Did she swoon into your arms after all that sexting?"

"She pretended not to know me. It's a very special connection that we share. These notes are adequate, thank you."

"A compliment? You must be in a good mood. If it's not the Marquise de Wardes putting that smile on your face, what is it?"

"Let's just say, the Cardinal and I have come to an understanding."

Kitty gave a squawk at that. "You're not sleeping with *her*, are you?"

"Mind out of the gutter!"

"She's a bit old, and I wouldn't have thought she was your type. Then again, I wouldn't have thought Little Miss D'Artagnan was your type, and you've been wining and dining her all week."

Dana froze at the mention of her name. What was Kitty up to? Was this a trap?

"You're such a gossip," said Milord, sounding almost fond.

"There isn't much to do around here since I have to work the same stupid hours as my boss and that means I don't get a life…"

"You know perfectly well that I'm not romancing D'Artagnan for the fun of it."

"I guessed as much," said Kitty, with half a yawn as if this wasn't massively important information. "Keeping an eye on her for the Cardinal?"

"I'd rather have her within line of sight if she's going to pull another stunt like that business with the diamond studs, yes."

Dana almost stopped breathing. Milord knew? He knew she was the one who had foiled the plot with the diamonds. Did that mean that the Cardinal knew too? How much trouble was she in?

"Her Eminence wants that mess hushed up, doesn't she?" chimed in Kitty now. "*So* embarrassing for her."

"For all of us," Milord said sharply. "Believe me, if it wasn't for the Cardinal insisting we not move against her, I would have had my revenge against that D'Artagnan child already."

"Instead of dating her." Kitty laughed, sounding

utterly relaxed. Dana had never heard anyone lie so comfortably – it was impressive and kind of scary.

"There are many ways to enact vengeance," said Milord. "The Cardinal needed me to take the tailor out of the equation – and if that works as a punishment for D'Artagnan as well, it's a bonus."

Rage burned through Dana. She wanted to burst through the doors and punch Milord in the face. But Kitty had given her this gift, and she did not want to waste it. She waited and listened, anger settling cool and deep in her stomach.

"Go to bed, sir," Kitty said now, all brisk like a medic. "Go on, get out of here. I bet you haven't slept in days, stupid man."

"There's that respect again, Kitty. It shines out of your pores like sunshine and rainbows."

"I want to watch my stories, and I don't want to have to peel you out of bed in the morning. You don't pay me enough for that. Speaking of which —"

"No, Kitty, no pay raise," Milord said, and he did actually sound tired. "It's all going to be worth it, you'll see."

"Yes, yes, nefarious plots, we love it when a plan comes together, whatever. Go away and be unconscious for a while."

There was a shuffling sound, then a door opening and closing. Dana stretched her legs out, leaning against the wall of Milord's office.

Finally Kitty came back in, raising an eyebrow. "That's the sort of thing you were after, I suppose." All business now.

Dana stood up, feeling awkward and grateful. "Kitty, I don't know what to say."

The assistant frowned at her. "People always think I'm stupid. Because of the hair and the bling and the attitude. But it's actually pretty hard to fool me."

"Why?" Dana blurted out. "Why all this tonight, if you knew–"

"That you were only spending time with me to get the dirt on Milord?" Kitty shrugged a shoulder, giving Dana a tiny smile. "You're hot. And I wanted you. I'm *not* stupid. I work for someone who is basically evil, but pays really well. I'm not ditching him or this job. The occasional rebellion is how I sleep at nights."

Dana leaned in and kissed her, meaning it entirely. Kitty kissed her back, but only for a moment before she pulled away. "Get out. I think there might actually be some torture devices along with the treadmills and Pilates machines in that gym of his. You don't want to get caught here."

"Do you –" Dana hesitated. "I hate to ask more of you."

"No, I don't know where he's keeping that boy of yours," Kitty said, her tone cold. "I don't get let in on the super-secret stuff, like where they keep high profile kidnapping victims."

"If you find out, do you think you could get in touch?"

"I don't know, Dana. That's asking a lot."

Dana reached out and took Kitty's hand, grazing the back of her knuckles with a kiss. "Okay. I won't ask." *For now*, she added silently.

CHAPTER 6
CONCERNING THE QUESTIONABLE LIFE CHOICES OF DANA D'ARTAGNAN

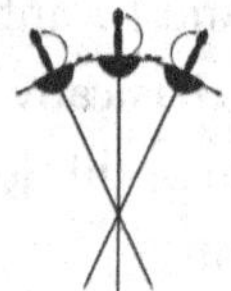

For two days, "the Marquise de Wardes" did not reply to the bantering texts sent to her by Milord de Winter. Dana could not bring herself to put on that flirtatious coat again, not when she knew for certain that Milord considered her an enemy.

It had felt like a game. But now she knew that the only reason he had not attacked her outright was because Cardinal freaking Richelieu wanted Dana to stay in one piece.

The mission with the diamonds no longer felt like a triumph, not with Conrad lost as a result.

The preparations for war continued. Aramis had fixed up the damage done to the *Morningstar*, thanks to financial contributions from several of her former girlfriends who were used to subsidising the military in this way.

A credit stud with a sarcastic message attached had even arrived from Madame (no longer Minister) Chevreuse, who was now working as the press secretary for the Daughters of Peace United Government. Aramis, pleased to learn that Chevreuse was not living on Artemisia anymore and so was a safe distance from the Siege of Truth, showed Dana the message. Dana noticed that it mentioned nothing about the impending happy event that Chevreuse (and presumably, her husband?) were expecting.

There was no tactful way to check if your friend knew her ex-lover was heavily pregnant, and so Dana continued to say nothing on the topic.

"I suppose there are some benefits to staying friends with every woman you've ever slept with," drawled Athos, who never explained how he had acquired his own war chest, despite outlaying more on the refurbishment of the *Pistachio* than it would have cost him to buy a freshly printed ship.

"I only have affairs with patriotic women," Aramis said loftily.

Porthos preened over the brand-new helm and harness that she turned up with one day, for Bonnie to install in the *Hoyden*. "A gift from Chef Coquenard," she said, sounding pleased. "He's still feeling guilty about the whole leaving me stranded on Chantilly thing."

"You're all so shameless," Dana laughed.

Athos gave her a sharp look. "And your flirtation with a certain dangerous politician? You're not using his credit to secretly outfit a ship, are you?"

"No!" said Dana, almost but not quite offended. "I'm after information, not sponsorship."

"Still," said Porthos, giving the others a shifty look. "You might be down to pilot a supplies transport, but having a dart on hand for emergencies, that wouldn't be a bad thing, would it?"

Dana was confused. "What are you talking about?"

"It was going to be a surprise," said Athos, glaring at Porthos.

"Does that mean we can tell her now?" asked Aramis, bouncing on her heels.

There was no stopping them. They called for Planchet and the other engies to join them, and the whole gang dragged Dana across the yard to where a very familiar spaceship was docked and waiting for them.

It was the *Buttercup*.

He had been freshly painted, in exactly the same dreadful shade of yellow. Dana swayed on her feet, staring. She couldn't believe her eyes. This was Papa's old dart, the one he had so lovingly restored before sending her on her way to Paris.

(*Nice ship. What do you call that colour?*)

"We found her in the trading yard on Lunar Palais when we were hunting parts for the *Pistachio*," said Planchet excitedly. "He was going to be broken down for scrap and molecules, but Bonnie thought there might be some useful parts, but then Grimaud said we'd probably be better off restoring him and selling him on, and we all figured out that maybe you could do with a ship..."

"You had one like this, didn't you?" said Aramis, her eyes twinkling. It wasn't like she, Athos and Porthos had not heard the story of *Buttercup* and Agent Ro a dozen or more times. There was something about a third glass of wine that brought Dana's simmering resentment about the matter to the surface, every single time.

Dana had no idea what to say. It was too much. Her hands shook.

"I have to go," she said abruptly.

It was Athos who first realised there was something wrong. The others caught on fast.

"Dana, what is it?" Porthos asked.

Dana shook her head wildly. "It's fine, it's — I love him. You did good. I have to go." Before any of them could stop her, she turned and ran out of the engie dock.

Oh, Papa.

Her main thought was to get away, far away, because she couldn't bear to break down and cry in front of her friends.

There was another reason that Dana couldn't bring herself to play the Marquise de Wardes flirtation game over the last two days. A few hours after she had left Kitty and the *Matagot*, Dana had received a curt, too-brief call from one of her sisters. That was followed by a longer, but still emotionally restrained call from her Maman.

It seemed impossible in this day and age, that anyone could receive injuries that were not immediately reparable by medipatch. But the power outages and regular equipment failures on Gascon Station had taken their toll, in the medibays most of all. The death toll from the Sun-kissed attack rose every day, without a further shot being fired.

Dana's Papa had not been a young man. Half his skin was regrafted a generation ago, before his retirement as a Musketeer engie. This time around, he had not been so lucky.

An aneurism, in the end. He had gone fast, though after weeks of pain management it didn't feel especially merciful that it was quick.

It had now been two days since she learned he was gone, and Dana had not cried. Crying had never worked for her. Hitting things was easier, but finding casual sparring partners was difficult with her friends wrapped up in the preparation of their ships.

She couldn't make herself tell them the truth, not yet. Any kindness would wreck her.

So Dana paced and she chattered and she made herself useful, and until her friends gave her the generous, beautiful gift of her *Buttercup*, she had managed to hide her grief even from herself.

She had to do something now, to keep that grief at bay.

Not crying, not fencing. What was left?

Dana walked, with no clear idea where she was going, except away from anyone who might be nice to her. She walked the streets of Paris Satellite, her head full of war and anger and frustration and explosions and skin grafts and…

She had not been there. She was not sure if she could ever forgive herself for not going home the second she heard that Papa had been injured. She had always meant to leave them, to escape the limited options at home. She had spent her teen years planning and working and learning to fly like a demon, with a single goal in mind: to come to Paris Satellite and become a Musketeer.

Even with the *Buttercup*, she wasn't a Musketeer. She had washed out. That was what she had left her family for. A failed, unreachable dream.

By the time Dana was on her second circuit of the Stellar Concourse, her anger had turned outward again. She was furious with the solar system, with the unfairness of it all. Her Maman had flown hundreds of combat missions. How was it that Dana's sweet, harmless engie Papa was the one to be killed in an act of war?

Dana found herself heading for the Luxembourg, which made no sense at all. The last thing she needed was church – she had never been more likely to punch a member of the clergy as she was today.

What she needed was a duel, and she wasn't likely to get one at the Luxembourg without picking a fight first…

A fight. Never mind swords and duels. Dana needed to get her knuckles bloody. She needed to head-butt someone in the face, and know they had deserved it almost as much as she did.

Which bars were popular with Red Hammers? Athos probably kept a list somewhere on his person. She could call him, but that would involve talking, and he'd probably want to know why she was so upset… oh, wait, what was she thinking? He was *Athos*.

Dana stopped in the middle of a busy thoroughfare and sent Athos a text via her comm stud, her fingers tapping the virtual keyboard on her arm.

> Name three bars where I'm all but
> guaranteed a fist fight with a Red Hammer
> or twelve.

There was barely even a pause before she received the following:

> The Crimson Duck, Santa Antonia's, the Bastille. Want company?

Not yet. I'll let you know

she sent back, and kept walking.

The Bastille was the only one of the three that she knew, because it was the closest bar to the Armoury, and a short distance from Madame Su's. She wouldn't have far to crawl home.

Dana strode in and went to the bar to order a drink. The room was full of red uniforms, and the back of her neck prickled in a promising way.

She hadn't even got to order before she heard the words "Hey, isn't that the wannabe Musketeer who runs around with those three assholes?"

Dana gave a savage grin. *Perfect.*

"Dana?" His voice was far away. "Is that you?"

She opened her eyes, and regretted it. She was – in a corridor, curled against a white, blood-stained wall near a drainage vent. She closed her eyes again, moaning. Her face hurt. All of her head. Her ribs. And…

An arm reached around her waist, steady and reassuring. "Let's get you somewhere safe, sweetness."

Her thoughts were jumbled and she wanted to throw up again, but there was something warm about the voice, something she trusted. "Okay," she whispered, and it came out more like "Urgh."

Steady arms drew her to her feet, and pain stabbed hard into her chest.

"Bleeding," she choked.

"Actually," said the warm and reassuring voice. "I don't think that's your blood."

"Some of it is."

Her saviour's hand jarred against her thigh and the burst of pain sent blackness spiralling through her vision again. She dropped.

Dana dreamed of the Buttercup, of her father's hands as he restored the old spacebucket from the inside out.

"Papa, yellow?" she complained.

"It's a good colour, chicken. You'll never mistake it for anyone else's dart in a line-up. Also, I got the colour cheap and your Maman says I can't use it in the kitchen."

Dana dreamed of Conrad, of making out with him on the couch in the Prince Consort's room, of the odd sort of smile in his eyes when he realised she had arranged for espionage pastries as a distraction technique.

"This isn't a seduction," she told him.

He shoved her. "Good, because you're terrible at it!"

Dana dreamed of Rosnay Cho, who watched her through dark, sympathetic eyes. "If Milord has your boyfriend," she said, wetting her lips. "I'm sorry, buttercup, but you're not getting him back."

Dana awoke, choking on air. She tasted blood in her mouth and then the pain flowed through her one jagged wave at a time. Stocktake: knuckles, ribs, face — jaw, especially. Nose, oh hell. She had lived nearly twenty-one years without getting her nose broken, and here she was, thoroughly smashed up.

"Ugh," she managed.

"That sounds about right," said the voice she had followed, the one that tapped directly into the part of her that responded to trust and reassurance. Her rescuer.

Dana's eyes flew open. Holy hell in a handbasket. She stared into the amused face of Milord Vaniel de Winter.

This was not the *Matagot*. The walls were too flat and straight – even the most decadently decorated rooms in that frivolous spaceship of his had curved walls. A hotel room? Dana was stretched out on a crisp sofa, and Milord had pulled up an elegant chair near her. A clamshell lay discarded on the coffee table within reach – had he been working while he waited for her to wake up?

That was either comforting or really creepy. Dana couldn't figure out which until she was a lot more awake.

"Now you're alert, perhaps we can see about medi-patches?" Milord suggested mildly. "I wasn't sure what the priority was, once I fixed the knife wound in your thigh."

"Face," Dana muttered. "Ugh."

"I didn't like to assume." He looked hesitant, which seemed out of character. "There is a medibay on this block, perhaps I should have taken you there."

"No," she said, so quickly it made her head spin. "I'm fine, just – medipatches?"

"In the bathroom. Do you need help?"

She frowned at her legs. There appeared to be nothing wrong with them, and the one with a medipatch already glowing at her through the rip in her cargo pants felt better than it had in ages. Still, they weren't responding as quickly as she would like. "To my feet. I can take it from there."

Milord's hands were warm as he drew her up, and she resisted the urge to fold herself against his chest. It looked warm and inviting, but that might be the concussion talking.

The bathroom clarified that yes, she was in an extremely expensive hotel: *The Antoine*, according to the dozens of tiny soaps and lotions with matching packaging.

Several medipatches had been laid out for her near the sink, along with gauze and tape. Dana worked on her face first, placing the medipatch along the underside of her jaw and breathing in and out as it had an immediate anaesthetic effect. She placed an urgent patch over her nose and yelled out as it set hard.

There was a knock at the door. "You all right?"

"Nose," she managed, halfway between a grunt and a wail. "I'm fine."

She didn't do anything to the ribs or the hands. They were bruised, not broken, and the dull pain in both of them grounded her. There wasn't a lot of point in throwing yourself into a brawl if you made all the marks go away instantly.

Dana picked up a sonic spray, cleaning blood from her skin, until her face felt closer to human. She removed the medipatch from her nose, leaving the one on her jaw because it was sending all kinds of good endorphins into her bloodstream.

Dizzy, but in a pleasant way, she stepped out of the bathroom. Milord passed her a glass of what turned out to be cognac, and she took a sip, enjoying the heat of it in her mouth. "Thanks for the rescue."

"Not exactly that," he said, his voice thrumming with what had to be false concern. "I found you lying in a corridor, some distance from what I hear was an epic bar fight. You rescued yourself long before I happened along."

"Well," Dana said with a smile that didn't hurt nearly as much as it might have five minutes ago, when her nose was still broken. "Thanks for scraping me off the floor."

Milord leaned in, his glass grazing hers with a clink. "You're not at all what I thought you were, when we met on that train."

She wanted to laugh. Thanks to Kitty, she knew how much he despised her, but he was good — so very good at this. He saw the opportunity for a seduction and here he was, playing that card in the hopes of what, drawing her further into his web?

Here was Dana, feeling self-destructive.

"Vaniel," she said in a low, husky voice, drawing her glass back to swallow more of the cognac.

Her enemy gazed back at her. In this light, his grey eyes were almost silver. "Dana," he said, making her name a caress.

"Let's stop pretending." She reached up, her hand grabbing the back of his collar, pulling him down to her.

His mouth found hers. He still thought he was the seducer in this scenario, so he kissed her slow and sweetly, like a dance. That wasn't what Dana wanted, and she told him that through nips and bites, increasing the pressure.

Milord's hand brushed against a bruise she hadn't even known that she wore on her hip, and she gasped into his mouth, taking him deeper.

They didn't make it to the bedroom, the first time. She backed him against an antique desk, and he lifted her up on it, so as to more easily strip her of shirt and the soft sports bra she wore underneath. He licked his way down her ribs, tracing the darker patches of bruised skin with his tongue, and Dana sank her fingers into his hair, tugging hard.

His clothes came off more smoothly than hers did, and she took the opportunity to shed her boots and blood-stained cargo pants. After only a moment's hesitation, she ditched her knickers as well, because it wasn't like they were being romantic.

"Implant?" he breathed into her mouth when he came back for another kiss.

Dana nodded and showed him the small medical tattoo on her unbruised hip. "You?"

Milord drew her hand forward to wrap around the base of his cock, which felt heavy in her hand. She found the barrier stud nestled there, against his pelvis, and scratched a nail thoughtfully across it. "Well then."

They kissed again, mouths knocking roughly together, and he swiped a couple of fingers against her to feel how wet she was before taking her there, in a couple of fierce thrusts against the delicate woodwork.

This was better than a fist-fight. Dana wanted it hard and fast, and Milord obliged.

The journey they made from the edge of the desk to the bedroom at the far end of the suite, caused the following damage: one broken chair, a stubbed toe (hers), a bruised elbow (his), and a smashed lamp. All worthy sacrifices.

CHAPTER 7
ALL CATS ARE GREY
(IN CYBERSPACE)

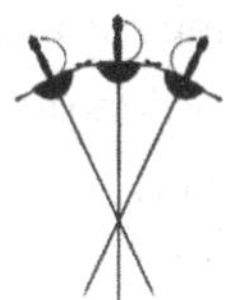

Dana awoke slowly, groaning as yesterday's bruises made themselves known all over again. She was an idiot for refusing to heal them. Then the secondary pain hit, the realisation that her Papa was gone.

She was alone and naked in the decadent, Regence-sized bed of the man who had kidnapped Conrad Su. Dana no longer had an inappropriate crush on Milord Vaniel de Winter; instead she had the intense, visceral memory of his mouth and his hands and the hot, slick feel of his body pressing hers against the desk, the wall, the bed.

Athos had officially lost his 'king of poor decisions' crown.

Dana found a shirt which was not hers, and took a deep breath before committing herself to the embarrassing process of locating every item of clothing she had discarded between the antique desk and the bedroom.

Milord actually sat at that desk in the living area of the

hotel suite, tapping away at his shiny black clamshell. His eyes followed her as she made the rounds of the room, and his mouth creased into a small smile. Dana could not help returning it, rolling her eyes at him.

Would the situation be funnier if he knew that she knew that they were enemies?

"I'm just going to –" she said, waving her armful of clothes in the general direction of the bedroom.

"Take your time," he said.

Keep it light, Dana. Don't get weird. Just because he dragged you home from a bar fight does not mean he trusts you.

Asking about Conrad Su right now would be obvious and dangerous, but when was she going to get another chance? It wasn't like she was going to let this happen again.

Dana left the bedroom door ajar as she dressed herself, tossing Milord's shirt back on to the bed. She could hear his fingers tapping over the clamshell, and wondered if he was attempting to contact the 'Marquise.'

"Hot piece of correspondence that couldn't wait?" she asked as she strolled back into the room, attitude firmly back in place. She was the brash young wannabe Musketeer with a crush on him. Nothing more or less.

"A correspondent who won't respond," said Milord, frowning at the screen.

"Sucks to be you," Dana said unsympathetically.

He rolled his eyes at her. "So kind."

"I'll be —" she started to say, because her extraction from this hotel room was her highest priority right now. The door chimed.

"Enter," said Milord before Dana could protest, and in strolled Miss Kitty Columbina.

Kitty wore lavender today, a tulle skirt beneath a tiny crop top that stretched the image of a space unicorn around her impressive cleavage. She didn't bat an eyelid at Dana's presence, but held her empty hand out to her boss, making grabby motions. "Since apparently a Raven isn't good enough for your highness?"

"This gift requires the personal touch," Milord said calmly, and placed a small box wrapped in gold tissue into Kitty's hand.

"Just reminding you that I have this afternoon off," she said and trotted back out the door, her heels clicking against the polished floor. "It's non-negotiable, because pedicures are involved. Don't call me!"

The second she was gone, Dana gave Milord a sheepish grin. "I should go too."

"I highly recommend it," he said. "My sister and her awful friends will be coming back to the suite shortly."

"How's Sheffield doing?" she asked, not entirely caring except that she didn't want Athos carted off for murder. Not everything could be fixed by medipatch.

"He has been cured of his interest in authentic Parisian duels," said Milord with a smirk.

Oh no, not this. Dana couldn't let herself like him, not even a little. She gave him a small wave, *oh let's be so casual about this*, and let herself out of the hotel suite.

Well, that was less awkward than it could have been.

"Arms-Sergeant D'Artagnan!" called out a voice, not three paces from the hotel entrance. *Spoke too soon.* Dana spun around and realised that she should have kept on walking.

Kitty Columbina stood leaning against a decorative pillar, unimpressed.

Dana could see her point.

"Playing with fire, aren't you?" was all Kitty said.

Dana winced. "It's complicated."

"I'll bet." Kitty marched forward and handed the parcel to Dana.

Startled, her fingers curled around it. "What's – I don't understand."

"Milord de Winter sent me to present this to the Marquise de Wardes, as a token of his ongoing affection and interest," said Kitty, reciting it as if it was a poem. "But I'm not an idiot, so."

"So," Dana repeated, because apparently she was an idiot. "Hang on, what?"

"I know," the assistant said slowly. "You ended up with that clamshell, didn't you? The *Matagot* screens all electronic devices taken on and off the ship. You've been carrying on some kind of — weird fake romance with Milord via text message as the Marquise and to top it off you decided to jump his bones as *you*." She batted her glittery eyelashes at Dana. "Don't freak out, I'm not going to snitch. But I am judging you very hard."

Dana shifted on her feet. "Why would you keep my secret?"

"I told you. Little rebellions, that's how I sleep at night." Kitty crossed her arms under her unicorn boobs and scowled. "Also, you're not a completely terrible lay."

"Thanks, I think."

Kitty leaned in. "If he catches you out, don't you dare take me down with you."

"Understood," said Dana, swallowing.

"Fine," said the assistant, turning around with a sniff. "My work here is done. Enjoy your present and don't feel super guilty that you basically stole a priceless gem under false pretences."

Once Kitty was out of sight, Dana tore the tissue off the little box and stared at the gleaming blue stud inside. Milord had decided to express his affection for the Marquise de Wardes via an antique sapphire.

Dana's fictional love life had become embarrassingly profitable.

Dana headed for the Musketeer dock, rather than going home. It was early, and she didn't see anyone she knew on her way. Even Treville was not yet ensconced in her plexiglass office.

The dock was deserted. Dana kept walking until she reached the four familiar ships, lined up in berths next to each other. *Morningstar. Hoyden. Pistachio*, freshly restored and ready for war. *Buttercup.*

She walked all the way up to the ship that her friends had found for her, and leaned her chin against the hull, like she used to when she was a little girl, begging Maman and Papa to tell her stories of the old days, of the Royal Musketeer fleet.

A discreet cough alerted her to the fact that she was not alone. Athos stood at the open hatch of the *Pistachio*, holding a freshly brewed pot of coffee. "Breakfast?"

For the first time in three days, Dana thought she might be capable of letting herself cry without the solar system coming to an end. Not in front of Athos. That much emotion might damage his circuits. But soon.

She gave him a smile instead. "When you say breakfast…"

"I basically mean coffee."

"Works for me."

Dana sat on the narrow bunk in Athos' aft cabin, holding a cup as he poured the coffee for her. "I am obliged to tell you," he said formally. "Porthos and Aramis and Engineer Pigtails are all concerned that they upset you yesterday. I present this information without comment."

"Noted," said Dana, sipping the hot, black coffee gratefully. "You know her name's not Pigtails, don't you?"

"I'm using it as a placeholder until I care who she is. Do you need medical attention?"

"No, I'm good," said Dana, flexing her bruised hands. "Not good. I'm – medically attentioned."

"Fine."

She leaned her head against the curving outer wall. "You are *terrible* at this."

Athos nodded gravely. "It is a crime and a tragedy that I found you first, but we shall have to make do. There will be no hugging."

"Understood. That's what Aramis is for."

"Exactly."

"Papa died," Dana blurted out, all at once, not making eye contact with him. "I didn't – but the ship – that's why – it's all still sort of recent. But I'm fine, or I will be, I just." She stopped talking.

Silence came from Athos. After a moment, Dana risked a look in his general direction. His face gave her no clues.

"I was wrong," he said eventually. "I am the right person for this one."

"Really?" she said in astonishment.

Athos joined her on the bunk, setting down the pot of coffee between them in case she changed her mind about the hugging thing. "Dying was the worst thing my father ever did to me, too."

"Oh," Dana said softly. She had not expected that.

Silence unfolded between them, like a coffee-scented blanket.

"I don't think the others would understand," Athos added. "Aramis' family were terrible to her; her life really began when she cut off all contact. Porthos never had a family to speak of. But believe it or not, I once had a father that I loved very much."

Dana nodded. This was useful information. "When did he die?" she asked.

"I was twelve. Away at school. Suddenly he was gone, and I was expected to *be* him."

"The Comte?" she supplied, remembering what he had said about the Comte de la Fere in the basement of the Gilded Lily.

"I won't talk about that side of it," Athos said sternly. "But yes. I hated him for a while. He would hate the person I have become. Yours wasn't like that, I expect. But I can share the general father-mourning experience, if empathy is at all useful."

"Papa was proud of me, even though I didn't make it as a Musketeer," Dana admitted. "He'd – be happy to know you got the *Buttercup* back for me. I'll reimburse you," she added. "I have the opal, and a sapphire now too, I suppose. I *know* the three of you didn't let Planchet bankroll the purchase."

"It's a good thing you're keeping the ship," said Athos. "Pigtails is attached already, and I'd hate to see her cry."

Dana stared at her hands, tracing the bruises with one finger. "Athos, I've done the stupidest thing."

"What are you, twenty?" he scoffed. "You're barely getting started."

"No, I mean specifically today. Last night. I made a mistake which I can't even count as a mistake because I knew what I was doing the whole time and I still did it."

"And yet you're richer by a sapphire? I should make such mistakes."

"It was a present." Frowning, she showed him the new stud on her wrist. "You remember how you told me not to sleep with the bad guy?"

There was something awful about Athos' face when he saw the square-cut sapphire set into her wrist. He reached out, his hands closing around her forearm as if he wanted to snap it in two.

"Athos," Dana whispered. "Athos, breathe."

He squeezed her arm painfully tight. "D'Artagnan, where did you get that thing?"

"From last night's mistake," she said, still not understanding what had got into him. "I spent the night with Milord."

"Oh," he said, and there was an odd twist to his mouth, not a smile, but something cruel and self-mocking. "Your pretty Milord de Winter. Yes, that makes sense. I had one like it, once. Don't mind me." For a moment, he leaned into her, his forehead resting against hers. "You have to stop this. Throwing yourself at dangerous men is a distraction you can't afford. We have a war to fight."

"So what?" Dana said, her voice shaking. She would not cry in front of him, she had promised herself that. "I should forget Conrad?"

Athos tugged her sleeve back down, so he didn't have to look at the sapphire stud. "If Conrad Su is still alive, let him damn well rescue himself."

Sometime later, over-caffeinated and swamped with emotions that she needed to jettison directly into outer space, Dana returned to the *Buttercup*.

It wasn't exactly the same – there had been some restoration work here and there. She wondered how many hands the musket-class dart had passed through, between Meung Station and Paris Satellite.

The sonic shower worked, which meant Dana could clean her clothes and remove the last sticky traces of her night with Milord. She refused to let herself dwell on it, though it was nearly impossible to think of anything else.

She lay on the familiar old bunk and composed the chilliest, least-affectionate break up text that she could summon. Not for herself – he would not expect to hear anything from Dana D'Artagnan, but from the woman he was actually fascinated with: the Marquise de Wardes.

Athos was right. Time to let this game go. Kitty knew too much. It wasn't like Dana had managed to acquire any useful information, except that Milord was more dangerous to her than she had ever imagined.

She had to get her head into the war, or she wouldn't survive it. Conrad and Milord were distracting her from what she had come to Paris to do, so many months ago. To serve Crown and Solar System.

> Milord de Winter.
>
> I thank you for your gift, though I hardly think our acquaintance so intimate as to make jewels appropriate. I think perhaps you have misconstrued our recent correspondence.
>
> I shall consider the sapphire an appropriate parting token.
>
> Yours,
>
> Marquise Illehandra Conchita Mullholland de Wardes

It was the meanest thing Dana had ever written. She kept reworking it, trying to soften the words, before remembering that Milord was basically (probably) evil, and it wasn't a real relationship she was ending.

When Milord did reply, a full 24 hours later, it wasn't a reply to the Marquise at all.

It was a stark request for Dana D'Artagnan to attend him on the *Matagot* at her earliest convenience. Dana stared at the blinking message for a long time. It didn't make sense for 'Dana' to ignore him, and it might be suspicious if she ditched him so soon after the Marquise did the same.

She would have to keep up the pretence that she was crushing on Milord for a while longer, maybe until the call to war. One more visit, to throw him off the scent, that couldn't hurt.

No sex, though. Their night together had been intense and memorable and exactly what she needed in that moment, but Dana could only give herself one pass on sleeping with the enemy. More than that would make a very embarrassing pattern. One visit, no sex. Easy.

Dana hid the sapphire stud and the mother of pearl clamshell in a storage compartment on the *Buttercup*. With her valuables concealed, she set out to play Dana the Admirer one last time. She dressed in a fresh tunic and cargo pants, with her fleur-de-lis dog tags, the pearl stunner in her pocket and the pilot's slice swinging in a business-like fashion from her belt.

She would have worn the blue Arms-Sergeant uniform if she thought she could get away with it, but it was hanging freshly-printed in her rooms. Dana didn't want to risk not being ready when the call to Truth Space finally came.

"He's not in the best mood," warned Kitty. She wore three star-shaped piercings in her lower lip today, and worried at them with her teeth as she showed Dana into Milord's private parlour on the *Matagot*. He must have evacuated the hotel suite again to avoid his sister and her New Aristocrat entourage.

"He asked to see me," said Dana, deliberately not saying 'he clicked his fingers like I was a German Shepherd and look at me, I came running.'

Responding to his summons was a terrible idea. Why hadn't she thought of claiming she was sick?

Milord was a streak of fury in a beautiful suit. He paced up and down in front of an exquisite false fireplace (a vintage fireplace, on a spaceship, who even does that?) and waved his hand impatiently when Kitty announced Dana as if he could not even bother speaking to his assistant.

His eyes gleamed with anger. For one awful moment, Dana thought he knew everything. Kitty disappeared around the door in a swish of glitter and hairspray, closing it behind her.

"You like duels," Milord grated out between his teeth, barely even looking at Dana. "Would you take one on for me? I have someone I want publicly humiliated."

Dana approached him cautiously. She could feel the danger rolling off him as if he was a snake about to bite. It made her want to stroke his head and make him feel better. What was wrong with her?

"I'd do anything for you," she said, and didn't have time to think about whether she meant it or not (*in too deep, Dana, get out while you can!*). He grabbed her around the waist, and kissed her with a savagery that made her dizzy. Dana could not help but push back, giving as good as she got.

All her good intentions fell away as Milord pushed her into a tapestry chair, and began to bite her out of her clothes, one piece at a time. Damn it all, but he was good with his mouth.

It wasn't until she sprawled naked in the chair, with Milord's tongue opening her up, his fingertips digging into her inner thighs, that Dana realised this was her last chance to find out what she needed to know.

She was never going to let herself set foot on the *Matagot* again. She would stage her own intervention if she had to, call in Athos and Aramis and Porthos to ensure she kept her word, that she stayed away because obviously she couldn't – couldn't be trusted – ohh – and there –

She dragged him into the chair and rode him hard, gaze locked with his. It was the first time they had made more than perfunctory eye contact during sex.

"Does she look like me?" Dana breathed in short gasps against his mouth. "The woman you're feeling so vengeful about. The one you want me to – challenge."

Milord flexed his fingers hard against Dana's scalp, as if he wished she had enough hair for him to pull. "What makes you think it's a woman?"

She tipped her head back, moaning quite genuinely as he pulsed inside her. "You want me to challenge someone in a duel, to humiliate them, shouldn't I know more about who they are?"

"I don't see why," he said, grazing the dark curve of her shoulder with his teeth. "You don't need to know someone to pierce their heart with a sword."

He genuinely thought she would act as his assassin? Damn, she had been convincing.

"Who – is – it?" Dana asked as they quickened their pace together.

"The Marquise de Wardes," he said, with venom.

Dana laughed as she came, the vibrations hitting them both. Milord was only a minute behind her, groaning into her breasts so that she could not see his face.

Interesting. Dana caught a handful of his brown hair and tipped his head up, catching a flash of an unexpected colour in his pupils before they settled back to their usual grey. "What will you give me, if I kill her for you?"

She still held him in place with her thighs, though she knew he could push out of the hold if he wanted to. She had more muscle tone, though she had learned from their previous dalliance that he was strong for a man who spent most of his life at a desk.

"Anything," said Milord, and kissed her almost politely on the mouth.

Dana was so damn tired of pretending to be someone that she was not. "The only thing that I want, you can't give me," she said in a hard voice.

He tilted his head back, curious. "What is it you want, Dana D'Artagnan?"

She shoved herself off him, backing away on bare feet. "I want Conrad Su, alive and well. And *you know it.*"

Milord's eyes blazed silver. He looked her up and down with an expression of contempt that he had never allowed her to see before. "How much do *you* know?"

"Everything," Dana snarled, and punched him because what the hell else was she going to do at this point? She was naked and her weapons were – much like her clothes – scattered half across the room.

It was a good hit – she had been aiming for the jaw, but over-compensated for the height difference and got him in the nose. He jerked back in pain, hands shielding his face.

Again, a flash of brightness, not only in his eyes. Lights reflected in tiny motes from his skin – no, the lights were part of his skin. Milord lit up like a constellation of stars against a scarlet sky. A terrible, overwhelming realisation rushed at Dana like a sonic engine to the face.

Milord lunged for her, and she was ready for him, her punches jabbing at his throat and solar plexus even as he slammed her to the ground. She clawed at his face, going for the sensitive parts of his mouth and eyes, and there, where her short nails dug into his lip, she saw it again.

"I know what you are," she choked out as red and silver burst across his skin like she had thrown boiling water on him, like there was an explosion inside him trying to get out, like he wasn't human.

He wasn't human.

Sun-kissed, sun-kissed, sun-kissed.

It made too much sense. Milord was one of them, an alien spy. Dana had known she was sleeping with the enemy but this – this was worse than she had ever imagined.

"Do you think I won't kill you to protect my secret?" Milord hissed down at her, his body pinning hers to the floor.

Dana stared at his bright red skin from hairline to fingertip. His eyes burned with hatred, and his skin glowed like fireworks.

"Well," she said. "You can *try*."

CHAPTER 8
MILORD, AND HIS SECRETS

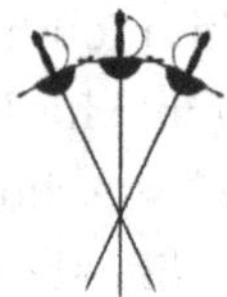

They grappled together, Milord's body heavy over Dana's, his hands pinning her shoulders to the floor of his fancy spaceship parlour.

Who even has a parlour in a spaceship? she thought, not for the first time. She should have known he was an enemy alien, from that.

Dana lay still, waiting for him to make the first move. Athos had taught her that. If she had learned anything from her fencing lessons, it was that patience paid off.

Do you think I won't kill you to protect my secret?

Dana breathed, regaining her centre, and Milord took control of himself again. His skin paled to its usual pinkish white, and the bright constellation of stars faded away. His hair framed his face, metallic silver.

Secret agent hair. With Vaniel de Winter there had always been a promise of danger well-hidden under his witty, judgy, grumpy surface. But he was pure Milord now, sharp as a knife.

Dana breathed, and waited for him to shift his weight.

"It would be in your interest," he said in a low, threatening voice. "To come quietly, sweetness."

He had never used pet names in bed, but was willing to pull them out when trying to kill her? Oh, that wasn't creepy at all.

"And what?" Dana asked, borrowing the bored, 'you can't touch me' tone that all three of her Musketeer friends employed before leaping into bar fights. "Surrender like a good prisoner? You don't know me at all."

"I'm starting to," said Milord. He pushed up from her, his hands hard on her shoulders, as if his strength was enough to keep her down.

Yes, he was strong. But Dana was pissed off, and that counted for something. She dropped one hip, knocking his balance off by a fraction, and head-butted him in the face.

Milord fell back enough that Dana was able to slam an elbow into his neck and slide out from under him.

Clothes, she had to grab her clothes and her weapons and get the hell out of here, because running naked out of a spaceship dock was completely not on her list of things to do today. As she put space between them, she saw his feet, *his bare feet*, and a dizzying memory swept over her. Oh, fuck. How had she not put it together before now?

Milord lunged for her and Dana picked up the pace, rocketing across the room away from him.

A weight slammed into her bare back; he grappled her around the ribs. She dug a punch into his side and swung her shoulder into his entire arm, hard enough to break a bone though she did not hear a reassuring crack.

Did the Sun-kissed even have bones?

Milord could not get purchase on her hair, his nails sharp against her scalp, but Dana went down beneath his body, the air bursting from her lungs as she hit the floor. His arm wrapped around her throat, hard enough that stars sparked behind her eyes.

They were on top of her clothes, and that meant her weapons were *right there*. Dana slid her hand beneath her own stomach, hoping that the hard lump she could feel under her hip was the pilot's slice and not a random candlestick or whatever rich people accessories Milord kept in his fancy parlour.

No, she realised as painful black circles spun in her vision, and her whole body battled to breathe. *Not the pilot's slice* at all. Her fingers had closed around the handle of the pearl stunner.

Good enough.

She brought it up wildly, hoping not to catch the rebound as she sent a burst of bright white energy directly into her attacker's face.

Milord collapsed on top of her, a dead weight on her shoulders and spine. Dana angled herself to shove him off her, not caring that his head hit the floor with a hollow sound.

It wasn't like he was human.

She tugged on her underwear, not daring to take her eyes off the unconscious alien. He did not revert to his Sun-kissed form in unconsciousness — that would have been a giveaway every time he fell asleep. He had only lost control of his disguise when he was hurt.

His silver hair fell in soft tangles around the back of his neck. Dana knew that neck, but not from any of her own interactions with Milord. She examined his feet, to confirm the fleeting impression from the fight.

Milord's hair, his bare feet, *the back of his neck* – she had seen him in a dream, long before the train on Valour.

Dana could not deny it anymore. Milord Vaniel de Winter was not only a Sun-kissed spy *like* Athos' pretty husband. He was the actual ghost who drove her friend to drink and misery, the sleeping lover he kept locked inside his guilty conscience. The traitor who had married the Comte de la Fere.

Dana was still sticky from having sex with him.

"Shit," she said aloud.

She had to get off this ship. She had to get less naked, and she had to get off the *Matagot*, and she had to get well clear of the ship so this traitorous Sun-kissed spy didn't murder her to protect his secret.

There were lots of steps to go through before Dana had to start panicking about how to break it to Athos that she had fucked his dead husband.

Milord lay crumpled over Dana's clothes. She shifted him with her foot, reaching down to grab the pilot's slice. It felt better, to have her baton in one hand and the pearl stunner in the other, even if she was still only wearing a pair of black knickers.

She reached for her cargo pants next, but as she leaned over his body, Milord's eyes snapped open.

Alien biology, Dana realised. The pearl stunner must not work on him for long. By the time that thought had sunk in, she was already running, crashing out of his bedroom and along the corridor.

This damned ship was so big, and she didn't dare take the most direct route to the hatchway, not if he was coming after her. Once she was two twists of the corridor away from his room, she leapt up the walls and levered open an air duct panel, slipping up and into the narrow space in the ceiling. She pulled the panel closed behind her, as Athos had taught her to do, then slithered quietly along the crawl space.

She heard shouting, and at one point lay still and terrified as Milord thundered along the corridor, calling for the Red Hammers stationed outside the ship. She heard words like 'treason' and 'assault' and was glad she hadn't tried to brazen it out at the main hatch.

No, she would be better off dropping out via one of the storage hatches underneath the ship, once the fuss had died down and they thought she was gone. But she would be even better off if she was wearing clothes.

After a couple of false starts, Dana got her bearings enough to slither into the air duct directly above Kitty's office. There was no sign that Milord was nearby – and given how furious he was, she was sure she would hear about it.

Kitty, wearing a purple lace coverall with spiky silver earrings, sat at her desk, absorbed in some kind of social media site rating celebrity hairstyles. The Marquise de Wardes was top of the poll.

Dana whistled between her teeth, and when Kitty did not look up, rapped lightly on the inside of the grate.

Kitty frowned, and tipped her head up.

Dana loosened the panel and smiled hopefully down at Milord's assistant. "Hey, babe."

"I seriously don't want to know," Kitty said in a scandalised whisper. "I am *so* not helping you escape, he's spitting spark plugs. *I did not see you.*"

"Um," said Dana. "I've figured out an escape route, but I need —"

"WHAT?" Kitty demanded. "What can you possibly need from me?"

"Clothes."

There was a long pause, during which Milord's assistant rolled her eyes hard enough to make Dana wince with embarrassment. "Really?"

"I'll take anything," Dana begged.

Kitty smirked, and stood up, then walked to the cupboard on the other side of the office. "You're lucky. I keep a spare outfit for nightclubbing emergencies."

"Um," said Dana, wondering if she wouldn't after all be better off escaping through Paris in a pair of knickers and nothing else.

"Don't worry," said Kitty, opening the door to reveal a sparkly mini-dress covered in a print of happy baby dragons in astronaut costumes. "I have the matching shoes."

The *Buttercup* was docked a few levels from the *Matagot*. Dana went there first, reclaimed her jewelled studs, and hid out in the old dart for an hour or two until her pulse had calmed down. She couldn't get the printer to produce more than basic supplies – no replacement for the space dragon dress, no shoes, not even decent coffee. She would have to get Planchet to check it out before bringing the dart with her to war.

It was surreal to be thinking about war while wearing a sparkly space dragon frock.

The best option would be to call Planchet to bring a flight suit and a pair of boots from her place, but Dana didn't think of that until she was halfway across Paris Satellite. To be safe, she used the most populated route, which meant a whole bunch of people got a good look at her in the sparkly dress, walking barefoot through the piazzas and boulevards of the city.

Talk about a walk of shame.

Aramis' apartment was closer to the docks than any of the other Musketeer digs in the city, including Dana's own lodgings. She told herself firmly that she was making this decision out of pure practicality – it had nothing to do with the fact that she was not ready to look Athos in the eye, or that she would literally rather die than have Madame Su catch sight of her in this get-up.

Aramis opened the door, and the expression on her face as she took in the sight of the sparkly space dragons was about what Dana had dreaded.

"So," said Aramis. "There's a story behind this?"

"I need to borrow your sonic shower and a change of clothes and please don't ask," Dana moaned as she pushed her way into the safe privacy of Aramis' living room… which featured Porthos on the couch, and Athos printing coffee at the kitchen bar. Yep, Dana was completely and utterly not ready to look him in the eye. She made an embarrassed squeaking sound and scrambled for Aramis' bedroom.

"Borrow whatever you like," a bewildered Aramis called after her.

Dana found a spare black flight suit and threw it on the bed to change into after her shower, then stepped into the tiny cubicle and turned on the sonic spray. She couldn't have her meltdown just yet, couldn't even think about all the ramifications of what she had learned when Milord turned on her.

She wanted to throw up and die, possibly not in that order.

When she stepped out of the shower, wrapped in one of Aramis' fluffy towels, she found Athos on the bed, leaning against the headboard. Waiting for her.

Dana swallowed.

Athos turned politely away, so she could get dressed without being observed. "I have been nominated," he said. "Believe me, I'm no happier about this than you are."

Dana dressed quickly in the soft, protective black folds of the flight suit. She felt like herself again, even if she had to roll up the sleeves and ankle cuffs because Aramis was so much taller. "I can't talk to you about this, Athos."

"Fine with me. I'll get Porthos —"

"No," Dana blurted out in horror. "I don't want to talk to *anyone*. I'm not ready to think about it in my own brain, let alone inflict it on the rest of you."

Athos glanced over his shoulder at her, and settled back against the headboard once he saw she was respectably dressed. "We're worried about you, D'Artagnan. All this running around, playing at spy — you're out of your depth."

Dana burst into hysterical laughter, her hands pressed to her mouth. She could feel the sobs surging up inside her.

Athos stared at her in horror. "I'm getting Porthos."

"No," Dana said, hands still pressed to her mouth as she calmed herself down. "Give me a minute. It has to be you." When she could breathe without breaking down, she climbed on to the bed, sitting beside him. She had to do this, or it would eat away at her until there was nothing left of their friendship.

She held her wrist out to Athos. When he did not react, she peeled the antique sapphire stud off her wrist and placed it on his, beside the vein. "It's yours," she insisted.

"I know," he said, unflappable. "I recognised it. But that was in another life – it's probably passed through a dozen pawn shops since then."

"No, I need to you to take it. It's *yours*."

"I don't understand what you're saying." He grazed the jewel with the soft pad of his thumb.

Dana tried to make the words come, but they got stuck in her throat. What if she was wrong? "Have you ever seen a picture of Milord de Winter?" she tried.

"I don't think so. I don't pay much attention to politics these days, especially Valour politics. I left that planet behind for a reason."

Dana grabbed a tablet from Aramis' side table and ran an image search. Milord had covered his tracks — there were hardly any pictures of him on Gossipnode, no official portraits attached to the Valour government website, or anything like that. But his 'Vaniel de Winter' identity brought up a few candid shots from social occasions at the Palace, and the de Winter estate. There was a portrait of his wedding, deeply archived. He was younger, his soft brown hair worn long down one side of his neck in an aristocratic braid.

No images of him with his silver secret agent hair, but this would do. Dana pushed the tablet at Athos. "He's a shape-changer," she said flatly. "A Sun-kissed. And I think

– I recognised him from the visions we shared back on the *Parry-Riposte*. I really want to be wrong."

There was a long silence as Athos scrolled through the images.

"You're not wrong, D'Artagnan," he said finally. "There are – subtle differences about the face. But he looks a great deal like the man I married."

Not *husband*, Dana noticed. *The man I married.*

"Maybe they all look like that," she said in a small voice. "I mean, they're shape-changers. They could use the same human design." Was that worse? She should shut up.

"But this one had the sapphire," said Athos, tilting his wrist to look at the stud.

"Yes," admitted Dana.

"He's alive." He had something like wonder in his voice, as if this was not entirely terrible news.

"Alive and dangerous," Dana reminded him.

"Yes, of course. Alive and dangerous."

Dana turned away, not wanting to see Athos looking at pictures of his dead husband like it was a miracle. "He tried to kill me. He can't afford to let me tell anyone who and what he is."

Athos set the tablet aside on the bed. He pressed his hand firmly against the back of Dana's neck for a moment, a reassuring touch. "D'Artagnan, I will not let that happen."

There was a knock on the door, and Aramis opened it. "We've had our orders," she sang out cheerfully. "Day after tomorrow, we ship out to motherfucking La Rochelle!"

Dana looked down at her wrist, where a message light was blinking on her comm stud. She passed her thumb over it, and read the contents. "All of us, it seems."

Athos nodded, checking his own messages. "That's good news. You only have two days to avoid the alien secret agent who is trying to kill you, and then we get to go into battle against his people."

Aramis blinked. "We are totally getting drunk later so I can get that story out of you two."

"Later," Athos promised, sounding oddly bright. "First, I have to pawn a sapphire. I think this particular jewel will bring in enough to cover the restoration bills for both of our darts, D'Artagnan. Nice to start a war without too much debt."

"It's yours," Dana said, a little shocked. "I mean, if you need the money — that's fine, pawn it, sell it, whatever, but you said it belonged to your *family*. Don't you want to keep it?"

"Believe me," said Athos, tapping idly at his wrist. "I'm not sentimental."

"I won't take your money," she said stubbornly. She was feeling guilty enough about this Milord business without profiting from it.

Athos arched an eyebrow at her. "I could throw the dratted stud in one of the ornamental fishponds on Lunar Palais, see if we can bag ourselves a trout instead of two fine darts to serve the solar system."

Dana glared at him and he returned her gaze, eyes dancing at her.

Forgiveness, then.

"Fine," she muttered, looking away first.

Athos clapped her around the shoulders. "Good choice."

"Dana," called Porthos from the other room. "You have a visitor, pet."

Dana and Athos both tensed. She had not yet put on her belt or her pilot's slice, but was gratified that Athos' hand went straight to his. He was taking the threat of Milord seriously.

"Who is it?" Athos asked, guarded. He stepped through the door ahead of Dana. On any other day, that protective instinct would have annoyed the hell out of her.

Porthos was alone. "Not here," she said. "Planchet called me, because you haven't been answering your comm? Some girl turned up at Madame Su's, asking for you."

Aramis raised her eyebrows. "Business or pleasure, Dana?"

"How should I know?" Dana said defensively.

"Apparently she's sparkly," Porthos added.

Dana sighed heavily. "Kitty." What on earth did Milord's assistant want with her?

"Could be a trap," Athos mused.

"Excellent," said Porthos. "We haven't walked into a trap for ages. It's important to keep in practice."

CHAPTER 9
TEA, AND THE CARDINAL

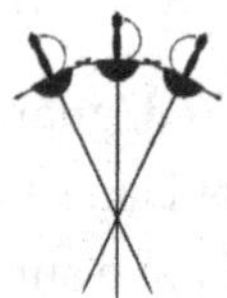

The last thing Dana wanted was for all three of her Musketeer friends to follow her home and witness whatever Kitty had to tell her, but she didn't have a choice in the matter.

When they arrived at Madame Su's Bed and Board, Dana was alarmed to see that Planchet was nowhere in sight. Madame Su herself had cornered a dishevelled and cranky-looking Kitty in the workshop.

"So this is your landlady, Dana!" Aramis announced, pouncing on Madame Su with a delight that might or might not be feigned. "You didn't tell me she was so fashionably turned out. Hello, Madame, I'm Captain Aramis of the Royal Fleet, so glad to meet you at last!"

Porthos jumped into the charm offensive with both boots, giving Madame Su a hearty smack between her narrow shoulder blades. "I hear you've been taking good care of our Dana," she said heartily. "So nice when neighbours take care of each other. That's what I always say about Paris Satellite – we might be a giant space station orbiting the moon of an over-heated desert planet no one in their right minds would ever visit, but we're also a *community*."

"You do always say that, Porthos, it's true," said Aramis, nodding. "Madame Su, you must tell me where you got that darling silk suit – I've been looking for something like it for ages. Not that my figure is quite as dainty as yours…"

Madame Su was helplessly pinned between the two friendly Musketeers, which gave Dana an opportunity to draw Kitty out of earshot, further into the workshop. Athos followed her, one hand hanging casually close to his pilot's slice and a harmless expression on his face that was in direct contrast to the set of his shoulders.

Kitty darted a look at Athos, and got the picture quickly. She wasn't going to get to speak to Dana alone.

"I have your dress," Dana said, handing the folded frock to the other girl.

"That's a good start," Kitty snipped back. Her eyes were red-rimmed beneath the glitter-pink eyelashes. She had been crying. "How about finding me a new job while you're at it?"

"I thought you were sticking with Milord," said Dana, genuinely startled.

Kitty stabbed a finger into the middle of Dana's chest. "That was before you sent him absolutely ape shit. He accused me of helping you – which I did, by the way, you're welcome – and when I tried to leave the spaceship he *attacked* me and locked me in my own office!"

"How did you get out?" Athos asked in a measured voice.

"Same way Sergeant Grateful here did, through the

ducts," Kitty snapped. "He scares me, and I am *not* going back. So you had better find me somewhere to go, Dana D'Artagnan. You broke my boss."

Dana sighed. "You know he was always evil, right?"

"Not with me, he wasn't!" Kitty hugged herself, looking more distressed than a girl wearing sequinned high-top sneakers ever should. "I have to get off Paris Satellite, somewhere safe, and *you are going to help me.*"

"Fine," Dana said, folding her arms. "We'll get you out of here." She had no idea how to accomplish that, and looked to Athos for help.

He sighed. "Aramis knows someone who works for the Daughters of Peace united government. Is that far enough?"

"You mean Madame Chevreuse?" Dana asked.

Athos nodded. "I'm sure she can help this young lady find work in the press secretary's office – though we'd need good reason to give a reference." He gave Kitty a stern look.

"I'm a fucking aces personal assistant," Kitty said, stabbing Dana's chest with a polished teal fingernail.

"I believe you," Athos said mildly. "But that's not what I meant."

Dana caught on. "Kitty, you need to tell me everything you know about the kidnapping of Conrad Su, and where Milord is keeping him."

Kitty rolled her eyes at her. "You've got *another* boyfriend on the go? How do you find the time?"

"Conrad's not mine," Dana assured her. "It's Athos here who's in love with him. I'm just being a good friend," she added, giving Athos a pat on the shoulder to show what good friends they were.

Athos said nothing. This was for the best. His sarcasm levels were currently broadcasting a frequency only robots could hear.

Kitty was unconvinced. "What's this got to do with the old broad over there?" she asked, nodding at Madame Su, who was ushering Aramis and Porthos into her office to discuss pattern books and fabric imports over tea.

"She's Conrad's wife," Dana admitted. "That's why we have to be so discreet about his affair with Athos."

"Yes, D'Artagnan, 'discreet' is the first word that comes to mind," Athos grated out.

"But she's been working with Milord," said Kitty. "She's one of the Cardinal's spies."

"I knew that," said Dana after a horrified pause. "Slipped my mind for a moment."

"Quickly," said Athos, taking his chance. "Before Madame Su comes back and gets a good look at you, Ms Columbina. Tell us everything you know about the whereabouts of Conrad Su."

"Aliens," said Aramis, as the four of them sat around a table on the Promenade. Athos and Dana had decided to catch Aramis and Porthos up with recent events, in case it was the last time they were all together for a while. It wasn't a story they wanted to share over comms.

"You've both had sex with aliens," said Porthos.

"The same alien," Dana corrected.

"Yes, that is the most important detail," Athos growled. He was on his second espresso, and deeply angry at the coffee for not being alcoholic.

"I'm not trying to be insensitive," Porthos added. "It makes more sense now, that's all."

"What makes sense?"

Porthos gave Athos a friendly shove. "*You*, you miserable, self-destructive sod. None of this was your fault, you know."

"Apart from my failure to properly execute an enemy of the solar system," Athos said, staring at the table.

Aramis drummed against the table with her long, tapering fingers. "Dana, I have put a certain Kitty Columbina on the solarcrawler to the Daughters of Peace, with a suitcase full of plastic unicorns, a reference stud for Chevreuse, and an assumed name. It doesn't sound like she had much to offer in exchange."

"Kitty confirmed that Madame Su is working as a spy for the Cardinal, and has had dealings with Milord," said Dana. "She knows that there is an outpost called 'the Tower' where Milord keeps his enemies, but she couldn't tell us where it was."

"It doesn't matter," said Athos flatly. "It's too late, D'Artagnan. We ship out tomorrow, and we don't have time to stage a rescue even if we knew where he was. The best we can do is pass this information on to Prince Alek and hope he has the resources to be useful."

"I know," Dana said, squeezing her hands into fists. "At least Milord won't be able to go after me in Truth Space."

"Uh," said Aramis. The others looked up: first Porthos, then Athos, and finally Dana.

Special Agent Rosnay Cho – Ro, to her friends and colleagues – stood in the middle of the Promenade, in a peach flight suit. Her long black hair swept down her back, and her scarred face was quite calm. She beckoned Dana over to her.

"So, that's a trap," Porthos said conversationally.

"It's convenient when they're obvious," said Aramis.

Athos laid a hand on Dana's arm. "Don't," he said firmly.

Dana patted his fingers, and stood up. "I'll be okay."

"If you go anywhere with her, I will stun you, I'm not even kidding," warned Porthos.

Dana walked over to the special agent. So much had happened since they saw each other at the Fountain of Tranquility. They had felt like allies, that night. Still, Dana knew better than to trust her.

"You've been busy," said Ro.

Dana's immediate thought was *how much does she know, oh hell*. She could feel her eyes widening like saucers.

"Wow," said Ro with a laugh. "That bad?"

"Did you want something?" Dana meant to sound businesslike, but a plaintive edge slipped in. She felt twelve years old in the presence of this capable, terrifying older woman.

Ro drew a paper envelope from one of the many pockets of her pretty flight suit. "I have an invitation for you. Thought I'd deliver it specially."

"I was going to say that's nice of you, but I'm pretty sure it's your actual job to screw with my head, so – thanks, I think?" Dana was proud that her thoughts came out that coherently.

Ro gave her a salute – an actual salute. "I hear you're shipping out tomorrow, Arms-Sergeant D'Artagnan. Thank you for your service. Try not to get your baby-faced head blown off."

"I –" said Dana. She didn't have the faintest idea what to say in response to that, not at all. Her lack of a snappy comeback was fine because Ro was already striding away.

Three pairs of Musketeer eyes locked on to her as she headed back to the cafe table.

"What is it?" Athos asked at once.

"Never mind what is it, what was *that*? Dana how many of your suspiciously hot sworn enemies have you been flirting with lately?" Aramis demanded. "This one's my favourite, she is sizzling."

Dana opened the envelope, and took out a gold-edged card inviting her to take tea with her Eminence, Cardinal Richelieu, in two hours. She stared at it.

"So," said Porthos, sounding far too cheerful, "*that* is a trap."

The Cardinal's office at the Palace was a stylish salon, not the ominously dark room Dana had pictured on the way over here. There were no historical portraits, no dusty religious statues and there was certainly no angry antique power desk.

Dana had been so sure the Cardinal was the type to have an angry antique power desk.

The ceiling was painted in a traditional sacred starscape, depicting the view of Honour from orbit, as seen through the viewscreen by the cosmonaut crew of the Third Venturer. The mural was the only part of the room that was remotely religious.

A grey-haired woman in military dress reds sat by a window that spilled a flood of artificial light into the salon.

She looked like a scholar, or a teacher, with a volume of poetry open on her lap. At Dana's approach, the woman looked up and smiled, and Dana gave up all hope that this was the Cardinal's kind-hearted secretary.

"Arms-Sergeant D'Artagnan," said Cardinal Richelieu. "We meet at last."

"You honour me by the invitation, your Eminence," said Dana, which was not untrue even if this was a trap. It was bizarre for the leader of the Church of All and closest advisor to the Regence to take an interest in a low-ranked pilot.

"I thought we had better meet here," said the Cardinal dryly. "Your friends are likely to panic less about the Palace than my private residence."

Dana agreed silently. Athos, Aramis and Porthos were all standing guard along the gallery across this floor, with an eye to the possible exits. She had no doubt that they would have locked her in a cupboard rather than let her attend upon the Cardinal in her own home.

Bad enough that she had walked past several Red Hammers and at least three Sabres on the way to Richelieu's salon.

"You are from Gascon Station, are you not, Arms-Sergeant D'Artagnan?" asked the Cardinal. She gave Dana a searching look, as if she could see every thought that passed through her head. "Your mother was a Musketeer, and your grandmother before you."

"That's right, your Eminence," said Dana.

The Cardinal waved her to sit. "They will bring us tea shortly, while we extend our acquaintance. I believe you stopped at Meung Station on your journey to Paris."

That detail surprised Dana, though it should not have

done. Of course, the Cardinal would know all about her first encounter with Rosnay Cho, and probably every time their paths had crossed since. "Yes, your Eminence."

"Such a shame that your paperwork was lost, and that you were not able to present yourself properly to Amiral Treville," said the Cardinal, with a sympathetic smile. "Still, our fearsome Amiral would have been hard-pressed to find employment for you among her troops. The Musketeers have so few resources these days."

"So I believe, your Eminence," said Dana, wondering where this was going.

"And oh – so many adventures since then. Your friendships with the infamous Inseparables, your romance with a certain tailor, even your journeys – two journeys, no less – to the picturesque planet of Valour. You see, I know all about you, young D'Artagnan. Our Prince Consort has particular reason to value your adventurous spirit, and your loyalty. You are to be commended."

Dana shifted uncomfortably in her seat. "Your Eminence is too kind."

The Cardinal was amused by what she found in Dana's face. "Oh, my dear. Did you think I called you here to reprimand you? What authority is it that you think I have over the Regence's own Musketeers?" She laughed, her eyes dancing.

Dana was more confused than ever. "Why *did* you want to see me, your Eminence?"

The tea arrived, brought in by servants who tidied the Cardinal's book away and set a table between the two women, resplendent with a silver teapot, vintage china cups, and a towering display of pastries.

The Cardinal poured for them both, adding milk to the

dark, fragrant tea in the cups. "You are brave, D'Artagnan," she said. "Youth, bravery and talent make such a compelling combination. The best pilots – and the best soldiers – are strong of head and of heart. Don't you agree?"

"Yes," said Dana helplessly. She could do nothing but surf alongside this conversation and hope that she came out alive at the other end.

Cardinal Richelieu smiled warmly, as if Dana's agreement meant something else altogether. "I believe that you need guidance, my dear. So far from home. Grieving your recent tragic loss. I would like to take you under my wing."

Dana had judged it safe to bring the cup to her lips and take a sip of tea; it now took all of her personal reserves to hold back from a spit-take. "Your Eminence?" she said, pouring enough confusion into her words to make it clear that she was asking a question, though she didn't know what the question was.

Cardinal Richelieu sipped her own tea with infinite grace. "D'Artagnan, I hereby invite you to take up a commission as a Sabre in the Red Fleet. What do you say?"

CHAPTER 10
DRIVING THE ARQUEBUS

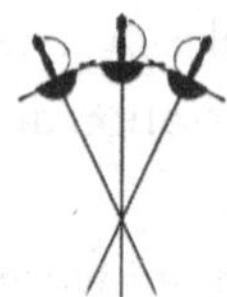

Dana opened her mouth, and nothing came out. She was so used to thinking of the Cardinal as her enemy. Could this offer be genuine?

"You would be flying a sabre-class dart into Truth Space within the week," said the Cardinal, gripping her cup of tea with the same elegance she did everything else. "I know Treville brushed you off with some grunt work – supplies transport? Far beneath your capabilities, I would have thought. My dear Jeanne so often displays a remarkable lack of imagination when it comes to personnel."

Dana's teacup rattled against its saucer, and she put it down in a hurry. The last thing she wanted was to break some antique crockery in this beautiful room.

"I see potential in you, D'Artagnan," said the Cardinal, as if Dana wasn't staring at her like a gaping goldfish cartoon. "I only recruit the most talented, the most energetic, the most courageous young pilots. You will accept, of course."

It wasn't a question. If Dana didn't say something, she

would be signing a contract in pastry crumbs and icing sugar right here at the table.

"I – no," she said faintly. "I'm sorry. But I'm happy where I am."

And there was the Cardinal Richelieu that everyone was so afraid of. The woman's face didn't change; there wasn't a twitch of difference to her expression or her body language. But the light had died in her eyes, leaving her flinty; carved out of stone.

"I cannot think why you would refuse," she said. "Don't you know that an offer like this is what great careers are built upon?"

"I serve the Crown, however Commandant Essart and Amiral Treville choose to employ me," said Dana, sounding remarkably normal considering that she was almost certainly going to be stabbed with a cake fork.

"You realise, of course," said the Cardinal, "That the Red Fleet serves the Crown. If you fly for Paris, you fly for our beloved Regence."

"I know that," Dana said desperately, "But –"

But I don't trust you. I don't know how deep your loyalty to the Crown goes. All I know is that you and Milord have worked together, and that means you could be allied with the Sun-kissed.

"I made this offer for your sake, D'Artagnan. I have had reports of your extracurricular activities, and it seems you have spent many days and nights doing the precise opposite of serving our beloved Regence Royal."

The chill of those last few words was intense, like staring into an ice comet.

"You see now," said the Cardinal, after a silence that was far too long to be considered polite, "why I offer my protection."

For one shameful moment, Dana considered how she might look in the smart red-and-gold livery of a Sabre pilot.

"If I may speak honestly," she said, playing for time.

"From what I hear, Arms-Sergeant, you do not usually hold back your opinions."

Dana took a deep breath, trying to construct her thoughts in the formal, political language that was popular in the Palace. "Nearly every friend or ally I have made since coming to Paris has been associated with the Musketeers, or Commandant Essart's Mecha Corps. I have not tried to make enemies, but I now have several, and *all* of them have at one time or another been in your employ."

The Cardinal raised a sarcastic eyebrow. "Do go on. This is fascinating."

"If I accept your offer, I will have enemies on all sides."

The Cardinal smiled with all her teeth. "I forgot how young you are. Who but a child would deny herself a career because of what her friends might think?"

My friends would think taking your offer was in my best interest, Dana thought fiercely. *That is why they do not get a vote.*

"That is my answer," she said simply.

The Cardinal stood. Their interview was at an end. "When you fall into misfortune, young D'Artagnan – and you will – I hope you will recall that I extended the offer of friendship to you, and that you rejected my help."

"I am grateful for your generosity," said Dana, the words feeling like mining grit in her mouth.

When she left the salon, Dana found Agent Rosnay Cho leaning casually against the wall of the gallery.

"Should have taken the offer," Ro said in a low, considering voice.

Dana met her gaze steadily. "I'm not so easily bought."

Ro rolled her eyes. "She was right. You're a child."

That night, in the Abbey of St Germain, over many cups of wine with her closest friends, Dana shared the story of what she and the Cardinal had said to each other.

Aramis and Porthos, distracted by the farewells they had to make to their various lovers, both gave Dana supportive hugs and insisted she had made the right choice.

Only Athos, who had no one to farewell except an excellent vintage bottle of brandy, gave Dana's refusal more serious thought. "You did what you had to do," he said. "I would have done the same. And yet – that doesn't mean it was the right decision."

Drunk enough to be daring, Dana leaned in and gave him a smacking kiss on his forehead. "Athos, you always know exactly what to say."

"It's a gift," he agreed.

"Welcome to Supplies Team Delta!" said a cheerful young man with a shaven head and whorled tattoos that covered him from scalp to shoulder. "I'm Bass and this is Chantal." He indicated a remarkably short and cheerful white woman with pierced fingernails and two dainty silver horn implants protruding from her forehead. "We're your team leaders. I'm the Maintenance Specialist, Chantal is Printing and Inventory."

"And you're the pilot," Chantal added helpfully. "Welcome to the *Frenzy Kenzie*, Arms-Sergeant D'Artagnan!"

Dana had never met two less military people in her life. "I guess you can call me Dana?" she offered.

Bass gave her a friendly hug. "We're going to get along great! Sorry your orientation is so last minute – we ship out in three hours – but the boat was still being rebuilt until early this morning."

"Acidsplosion," Chantal said gravely.

The 'boat' was a massive, dark blue tube of arquebus-class venturer. Dana had piloted something similar when she was a trainee back on Gascon Station, because Freedom still used arquebus-class venturers for supplies and trading. This one was newer than the ship Dana had practiced in, though the front half was a lot older than the back half, which had been all but printed from scratch in the rebuild.

It was traditional for a new pilot to walk entirely around her ship before coming aboard. With the size of the *Frenzy Kenzie*, that wasn't practical, but Bass and Chantal dragged Dana into a storage buggy so they could drive her around the perimeter.

For the first time, this felt real. They were going into a war zone. A war zone where no shot had (yet) been fired, but still.

It was so bloody huge. The ship, not the situation. Yes, also the situation.

When she saw the tail fin of the venturer, Dana let out a bark of a laugh. "Who designed the tattoo?"

"It's mine," said Chantal, looking pink with embarrassment. "I mean, my kids drew it. You can put your own on if you'd prefer."

"No, I like it," Dana said quickly. It was a children's drawing of three people waving madly under a squiggly rainbow. "Is it really only three of us crewing her?"

"There's also Wheels, our meditech, she's kitting out the medibay right now," said Bass. "But she hates healthy people, so don't talk to her unless you're bleeding. Chantal hired two assistants to help with the fetching and carrying, and I have a couple of baby engie interns to train up, they're coming too."

"I don't suppose I get an assistant to pilot the ship while I'm sleeping?" Dana asked dryly.

"Ha!" said Bass appreciatively, then realised that she hadn't been joking. "Oh. Ah. This is awkward."

"Nope, it's just you and the autopilot," said Chantal with a smile. "But you can borrow our assistants some-times. If you ask nicely."

"I did pick baby engies who claimed to be able to pilot boats this big," Bass said, as if it had been an afterthought rather than a major requirement.

"Oh," said Dana, even more overwhelmed. "That's… good."

The helm and harness of the *Frenzy Kenzie* were heavier and more old-fashioned than the set-up Dana was used to from darts, or even the transporter she had been piloting to and from Luna Palais for so many months. She hesi-tated, not sure where she should even start with all the cables and attachments.

"Let me help you, boss," said a familiar voice. Planchet popped into her field of vision. The girl wore her red hair in its usual pigtails, but she had found a Musketeer-blue coverall from somewhere, with the ship's name embroidered on the chest.

"Planchet!" said Dana, half alarmed. "Are you a stowaway? I think that's treason."

Planchet laughed. "Don't worry, boss. Stowing away is a misdemeanour at worst, and it doesn't even count as a crime until we leave dock."

"Planchet."

"I'm kidding," the teen engie said, wide-eyed. "I signed on with Arms-Sergeant Bass as an intern. It will look good on my resume when you finally become a Musketeer and need a proper engie to look after the *Buttercup*. Can you believe they're keeping an antique like this running? I can't wait to get my hands on her insides."

Dana wasn't going to complain. Having Planchet here helped with the overwhelming sense of isolation she had felt ever since she parted ways with Athos, Aramis and Porthos.

"Quick, help me get into this helm and harness before the rest of the team figures out I have no idea what I'm doing," Dana begged.

Fifty gleaming red sabre-class darts in perfect spiral formation exploded out of the Church Dock of Paris Satellite. They hung in the sky for a dramatic instant before boosting in a co-ordinated jump across the solar system.

Next came thirty blue musket-class darts – the Muske-teers of the Royal Fleet, pouring forth from Lunar Palais.

"Must be true, then," said Bass, who had joined Dana and Planchet in the cockpit of the *Frenzy Kenzie* with a larger-than-regulation tub of popcorn. "The Regence herself is flying out with this wave."

"Into battle?" Dana said in surprise. "No one expects that of her, surely."

"Rumour has it that her siblings have been sniffing around, campaigning to be allowed back from exile," said Chantal, who was flipping through a gossip app on a large clamshell. "The tall one who won all those medals, in particular. I guess the Regence wants to prove to the adoring public that she has military cred."

"The Cardinal's definitely with this wave," said Bass. "Saw footage of her Eminence waving at the crowds on the way to her Sabre after breakfast. The two of them must have left the dragon prince at home to watch over Paris."

Dana frowned at the slang term for Prince Alek. "Less chatter," she said sternly. "We're about to –"

Her dash lit up with the command to detach from their berth and take to the sky.

"No worries," said Chantal. "War involves heaps of waiting around in between the exciting parts. There will be *so* much time for gossip."

CHAPTER 11
SPACE JUMP

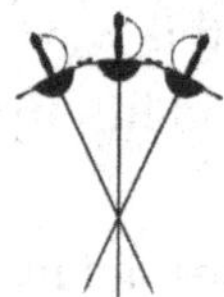

The jump system was only legal for military operations within Crown Space, on the basis that they were the only ones with robust enough comm frequencies to be trusted with the technology. No one wanted to be part of an interstellar pileup after civilian spaceships had literally materialised inside each other.

The *Frenzy Kenzie* and other arquebus-class venturers (like the Church Fleet's own *St Konstantina*, chugging alongside them) were too large and antiquated to be fitted for jump engines. Their steady pace of star travel was roughly equivalent to the recharging time that dart engines required between jumps.

As systems went, it worked fine, except for the high boredom factor of pilots in general, and Musketeers in particular.

Dana was on constant rotation, flying the support transport, while her friends were stuck in their own darts with literally nothing to do between jumps but use

Fleetnet to message her, and each other, about the most trivial things.

It would take six jumps and eight days for the Second Wave of the Combined Royal Fleet to reach Truth Space. By the third time Dana had caught up with the Inseparables, she was amazed that they had not yet started challenging the Sabres to dogfights out of sheer boredom.

FRENZYKENZIE3: Porthos, I don't want to hear about your stomach.

HOYDEN: Jump always makes me feel so sick.

FRENZYKENZIE3: Considering you and Athos just woke up from a twelve-hour sleep rotation while I was the only person fielding Aramis' insecurities about her girlfriend for did I mention twelve hours, I'm going to go with no. No pity. None left.

MORNINGSTAR: No one is insecure, who said I was insecure? Have you been talking to Tracy about me?

FRENZYKENZIE3: Porthos, is this a group chat??? Warn a person first.

HOYDEN: It's not my fault you started talking about our friends behind their backs.

FRENZYKENZIE3: Nothing I haven't said to their faces.

PISTACHIOGRUMPYFACE: I ALREADY REQUESTED TO BE TAKEN OFF ANY AND ALL DISCUSSIONS ABOUT ANYTHING SHORT OF WAR-RELATED EMERGENCIES.

When a message from 'unknown user' clicked through her comm, containing only a set of spacial co-ordinates, Dana assumed it was Aramis or Porthos pissing about, stripping their ID from the message for a joke.

But it wasn't obvious or funny enough, especially when Dana checked the pre-programmed flight path to discover that they were already due to cross the co-ordinates in question – and none of the musket-class pilots were cleared to know the exact flight path of the *Frenzy Kenzie*.

Should she divert to avoid those co-ordinates? A diversion would show up on her daily report, and she wasn't sure if this message constituted a threat, or a promise.

In the end, she did an extra scan on the area while allowing the arquebus to continue on the route as planned.

Five minutes before Dana reached that point in space, the main screen above her dashboard filled with static, picking up a signal from a local transmitter. There were no satellites in their path, so if there was a transmitter it was tiny, and had been left here like a message in a bottle.

After a minute of static, the screen dissolved into footage from an old fleur-de-lis game. Dana knew it was old, because it showed the original Emerald Knights team: Prince Alek, Conrad Su and Minister Marie Chevreuse opposite a team called the Burly Lions.

For a moment, she allowed herself to become caught up in the game – the fluid movements of the athletes powering through the zero-gravity tank. The glee on their faces as they racked up points between the three of them.

And oh – *Conrad*. His blue hair was longer in this footage, spiking low into his eyes. He and Prince Alek and Chevreuse moved together as a single unit, like their brains matched as well as their bright green uniforms.

At one point, Conrad fell face-first into the camfeed, and threw a flirtatious grin directly at the viewer – at Dana – before spinning backwards in a series of somersaults that took his opponent by surprise and allowed Chevreuse to bodyslam that player halfway across the tank.

Why would someone send her this footage?

Dana checked her instruments — the *Frenzy Kenzie* would move out of range of the transmission shortly. She flexed her fingers and her thoughts into the ship's engines, powering down to slow drift. She sent a message to Bass with an excuse:

> Getting odd readings from power spheres,
> can you check the couplings? We can still
> make the rendezvous on time if we drift
> for 15 mins.

The part about the time buffer was true. She didn't want to miss any important information from this transmission, but she wasn't willing to risk making the entire Second Wave of the Combined Royal Fleet late for a battle.

Bass' response was a series of exclamation marks, and an emoji that looked like either a thumb's up or a dick joke. She was going to assume it was a thumb.

The game footage ran to static. Dana's first thought was that she had slowed the *Frenzy Kenzie* too late, but then the screen cleared again, and she saw what looked very much like a dark, stone-walled cell.

"Do you have nothing to say to your wife?" a voice said from behind the cam. A familiar voice, Dana realised with a chill down her spine. Those smooth tones belonged to Milord.

A dark shape shifted and turned towards the screen. Dana bit her lip as she recognised the tired, pissed-off face of Conrad Su. It was a livestream, according to the date and time numbers running along the bottom of the screen. He was alive.

Conrad stood slowly, stretching his legs, showing no sign of injury. He walked towards the cam. There was no gorgeous grin now. He stared into the screen, head tilted slightly, eyes blazing into it. "Whoever you're doing this for, *Slate*, I know one thing. It's not my wife."

"Oh, but that's interesting," purred Milord. "Which of my many enemies is it that you think you're talking to?"

Dana clenched her fists, because otherwise she would be reaching out for the screen like an idiot, as if she could actually drag Conrad through it to safety.

"I'm friends with the Prince Consort," Conrad said fiercely. "It's not difficult to work out why you might think you can use me to hurt the royal family."

"I was hoping you had more than muscle between those ears of yours," said Milord, sounding bored.

Conrad turned the full force of his glare into the screen. "Luckily Alek knows better than to take stupid risks just because he doesn't want to run tryouts for a new pole attack."

Dana rolled her eyes at his bravado, and her own fool-ishness. She forgot sometimes that Conrad had been wrapped up in court intrigue long before she breezed into Paris.

He probably didn't even remember her name.

"You'd be surprised how many enemies I have who think you're worth rescuing," said that hateful voice behind the cam. "Say hello to Arms-Sergeant D'Artagnan."

Conrad's head flicked up and away, his face registering something – surprise? Irritation? Dana barely got a chance to see before static overwhelmed the screen all over again. This time, the footage did not return.

"All clear, Sarge!" Bass said cheerfully through her comm. "The ship's security picked up a magnetic transmitter-bot in the area, probably some new spyware thing trying to register our location. Zapped it good, so it won't be able to trace us."

"Good," said Dana, more calmly than she felt. "That's good work, Bass."

Spyware. Damn it all. She should have steered clear of this location, avoiding the co-ordinates. She couldn't risk the Fleet for one man, especially when Conrad himself was so determined to sacrifice himself for Prince Alek. If Milord wanted her to see that transmission, nothing good would come from it.

"Get a grip, D'Artagnan," she muttered to herself. "War before boys."

But she couldn't erase that image of the stone cell from her mind.

Conrad Su was still alive, for now. But he was in Milord's custody, and Milord wanted revenge on Dana.

The second last rendezvous before the final jump to Truth Space was an otherwise empty stretch of space, halfway between Peace and Truth. As the *Frenzy Kenzie* chugged towards the co-ordinates, Dana noticed that the usual heat signature grouping of 80 darts was not registering on her dash.

That was when she realised three hours had passed without any trivial Fleetnet message pinging her screen from Aramis, Athos or Porthos.

> FRENZYKENZIE3: Is there an issue with the rendezvous?

> STKONSTANTINA1: Have received no alerts.

> FRENZYKENZIE3: The Fleet's not where it's supposed to be. How far out are you?

> STKONSTANTINA1: Twenty minutes ahead of you. Looks like they jumped early – update pending.

Dana waited and tried not to fret. Chantal joined her on the bridge to wait for news, which she appreciated because the silence of the comm was unnerving.

"This happened to me on a long-haul mission once before," said the Printing and Inventory Specialist, in a voice that was probably supposed to be motherly and comforting, but mostly set Dana's teeth on edge. "Usual protocol is that they leave one pilot behind in stealth mode, to deliver new co-ordinates in person."

"But our next rendezvous is Truth," Dana argued. "I mean, it's a planet. It's not like it can have moved."

Chantal gave her an almost-pitying look. "If our orders

have changed, maybe we're not heading to Truth anymore."

When the stealth ship connected to the *Frenzy Kenzie*, it was with a clang that reverberated across the whole ship.

"Official protocol, you say," Dana said, swallowing hard.

"Either that, or we've just been boarded by the enemy," said Chantal.

"That's not as comforting as you think it is."

"It wasn't supposed to be comforting!"

Bass spoke to them both over the comm. "It's a silver moth-fighter. One of ours."

"You can tell that from the noise it made?" said Dana, impressed.

Bass covered a laugh with a snort. "Oh, honey, no. The main airlock has a plexi-glass window. I can see it from here. Hang on, welcoming our visitor on board."

The next ten minutes felt like an hour, punctuated only by a short message from Bass confirming that their messenger's ID checked out; she represented Cardinal Richelieu and the Church Fleet.

That was even less comforting.

Dana managed to unhook herself from helm and harness, to greet the Church pilot as she entered the cockpit. There were a quarter of a million Moth fighters in the solar system, and yet Dana was completely unsurprised when her stealth visitor removed her helmet, and a long fall of black hair swung out.

"Hey, you," said Agent Rosnay Cho.

"Are you even in the Fleet?" Dana blurted. She was used to seeing the special agent in candy pastel colours, far too cutesy for her vivid looks and sharp tongue. She looked good in red, with the Church Fleet jacket of scarlet and gold over a matching flight suit.

"I am now," Ro said with a smirk. She held up a small clamshell. "Eyes only, Captain D'Artagnan. Especially for you."

"Arms-Sergeant," Dana corrected, but gave Chantal and Bass a nod to clear out.

Ro shook her head with a devastating smile. "You know the code, Dana. When you're steering the ship, you're the Captain, regardless of rank."

Dana was tired. Tired of hiding and secrets and not knowing whom to trust. Tired of worrying about Conrad and her friends and the whole fucking solar system. "Where the hell is the Fleet, Ro?" she asked, and didn't even care that the nickname slipped out.

Ro's smile softened for a second –Dana later thought she must have imagined it – and then she was all business. "Three hours ago, the teardrop armada made their move." She clicked open the clamshell to show a series of images: the now iconic picture of the grey teardrop ships of the Sun-kissed hanging in orbit around Truth, then the shocking development of the ships replicating in twos and threes, until there was nothing but a cloud of grey wrapping around the entire planet.

"That's —" said Dana, and swallowed hard.

"You can swear for a while if you like," Ro said helpfully. "The Captain of the *St Konstantina* is still thinking up new synonyms for 'fuck' — I left her to it after the first ten minutes."

"Have they still not fired any shots?"

"It depends what you mean by *shots* and *fired*," Ro said grimly. "This particular manoeuvre coincided with a power wave that knocked about forty Fleet ships out of their orbital position, and sent all electronics screwy for a three-click radius. They managed to get a subsonic message to the incoming reinforcements, warning that all systems had been compromised. That's why the Cardinal and the Regence moved the rendezvous. And that's why you're about to make a course correction."

Ro passed over a new set of co-ordinates and Dana returned to her helm and harness, programming in the new flight path. Her radar picked up the *St Konstantina*, already tracking ahead of the *Frenzy Kenzie*.

When Dana finally looked up, Ro was sitting in the co-pilot's seat beside her, making herself comfortable. "Moth spheres need recharging," she said. "You don't mind if I hang around for a few hours?"

"Do I have a choice?" asked Dana.

Ro grinned. "Nope."

Dana gave herself over to the navigation of the ship, ignoring the intruder. When she darted a look under her eyelashes at Ro, the other woman appeared to be napping.

"Cardinal Richelieu is in league with the Sun-kissed, you know," Dana said in a low, conversational tone.

Ro's eyes flew open. It was the first time Dana had ever seen her ruffled. "Damn it, D'Artagnan, you can't say things like that."

"It's true."

"I know you Musketeers are basically children who think it's all about taking sides in the playground," Ro said after a strangled pause. "But that's *stupid*. Her Eminence has always done what she thinks is best for the Crown and the whole fucking solar system, that's the remit of the

Church – to protect humanity. The Sun-kissed have no part in that."

"She's compromised, and so are you," said Dana, keeping her hands steady on the controls despite the anger that flooded her whole body. "How many of the Cardinal's plots involved Milord de Winter?"

Ro narrowed her eyes. "I warned you he was dangerous," she reminded Dana.

"You didn't tell me he was Sun-kissed."

There, she had surprised her. The special agent sat there in silence for a few minutes, while Dana steered the smooth metal tube that was the *Frenzy Kenzie* on course to their new rendezvous.

"How exactly did he compromise you, Dana?" Rosnay Cho asked after a long moment. "How deeply did you have to dig to find that particular secret?"

"I don't want to talk about it."

Ro huffed to herself. "Yeah, that's what I thought."

"Did you know?" Dana asked.

Ro looked at her from beneath her sweeping fringe. "Of course I didn't bloody know. Just because the Cardinal doesn't gambol around covering up evidence of royal adultery like *some people* doesn't mean she would betray the human race." She scowled darkly. "And neither would I."

"You know now," said Dana. It was odd, having the upper hand. She did not have the faintest idea how to use it to her advantage. It felt refreshing, to speak honestly. "What are you going to do about it?"

Ro shook her head. "Give me more than two minutes to assimilate this upsetting piece of intelligence. I'll let you know."

Dana felt oddly relieved, just as she had when she had confessed to Athos, Aramis and Porthos about Milord. She was no longer alone with this terrible news, and she would not have to work out what to do with that knowledge, without help.

What did it mean, that she was feeling this way about Agent Rosnay Cho?

CHAPTER 12
FLEET UNITED

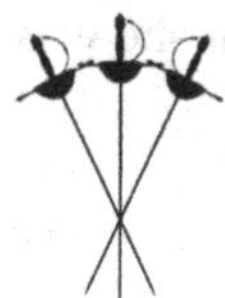

The Second Wave of the combined Royal Fleet that set out from Paris six days ago was now in orbit around Chaillot Station, a deep space recharging satellite twice the size and three times as grimy as Meung.

Walking into the briefing room on the Regence's flagship with Agent Rosnay Cho at her back made the memories of that particular stopover even sharper in Dana's mind.

"Don't suppose you fancy a duel, for old time's sake?" suggested Ro in a mocking voice. Dana glared at her, and Ro held up her hands in innocence before crossing to the other side of the room, where the Regence stood with Cardinal Richelieu and Amiral Treville.

Someone seized Dana's sleeve, and she found herself dragged into a hug by Porthos, who led her over to the corner where Aramis and Athos were waiting.

"Making new friends?" Athos said dryly.

"Befriending old enemies, I think," said Dana. She did

not know what to think of Rosnay Cho, but war did that sort of thing, didn't it? It brought unlikely allies together in a common cause.

"Because that worked out so well last time."

Dana gave Athos a startled, wounded glance. He took a sip from a flask that was decidedly non-regulation. "Too soon?"

She punched him in the arm. "It's never *not* going to be too soon, Athos."

Aramis put placating hands on both of them to make them quiet down. "Treville's about to speak."

But the Amiral did little but wave at the crowd of pilots to command silence, before introducing the Regence.

Lalla-Louise Renard Royal was bright-eyed and animated in her plain flight suit, with none of the usual cosmetic enhancements or hair baubles she favoured for public appearances. Her hair was pinned up in a severe top-knot like the one Aramis always wore on duty. As if the Regence was a real pilot.

In a grave, majestic voice, the Regence outlined the situation: the enemy had engulfed the planet of Truth in a storm of ships, creating what looked like a wall wrapping entirely around the planet.

Satellite images suggested that part of the 'wall' effect was an illusion created by some kind of gas, but the fact remained: they no longer had individual targets to aim at, only a single enormous target that held a planet as hostage.

"Is it possible –" Dana began to ask without thinking, then clamped her mouth shut as she remembered where she was.

The Regence's eyes flicked in her direction, and the traitorous Athos gave Dana a shove out of the corner, so she could more easily be seen.

"You have a question?" the Regence suggested in a mild voice.

"Arms-Sergeant D'Artagnan," the Cardinal supplied before Treville could speak up.

"Arms-Sergeant D'Artagnan," added the Regence.

Dana swallowed. Everyone was looking at her now. She had no choice but to follow through. "Pretty much the only thing we know about the Sun-kissed is that they are shape-changers," she said. "Is it possible that their technology – that their ships, can also change shape?"

All three commanders – the Regence, the Cardinal and Amiral Treville, went very still. Dana didn't know if it was because this was a new, terrible concept to them, or if they had already been working from such a theory but had not intended to make it public.

"That is entirely possible," the Regence said finally.

Dana heard the Musketeers and the Sabres muttering quietly around her, the muffled noise rising and falling in urgent waves. She didn't blame them.

It was bad enough to have to fight against ships they couldn't see, without those ships potentially changing size or shape at any moment.

"That's the best theory we have for how their fleet expanded so quickly," the Regence admitted after the muttering died down.

"But of course," said the Cardinal, moving nearer to the Regence. "We have God on our side."

The Regence Royal smiled as if this act of togetherness was spontaneous, instead of painstakingly rehearsed.

"With Church and Crown working together, nothing can stop the Combined Fleet," she said, her voice filling the room powerfully. "United, we have so much to fight for – including the very future of the solar system."

She paused and placed a hand very deliberately on her abdomen, and it was clear from the quick look she received from the Cardinal that this part came as a surprise to her as much as anyone else.

For a moment, distaste crossed the Cardinal's face – the very idea of producing children by natural rather than scientific means was not against the teachings of the Church of All, but was certainly not preferred when it came to royal heirs and expectant mothers flying into battle. It smacked of pandering to the Elemental populace, including Prince Alek himself.

But the expression passed so fleetingly that Dana could not be sure afterwards that she had really seen it. With her usual polite benevolence, the Cardinal led the assembled Musketeers, Sabres and other military personnel in a prayer for the safety of all members of the royal family, present and future.

After the briefing, Dana considered heading back to the *Frenzy Kenzie*, though they weren't due to make the final approach to the Siege of Truth for another twelve hours and she was pretty sure she needed as much of a break as she could get from Bass and Chantal. The two of them would be vibrating with excitement over the possibility of a royal pregnancy.

Dana wanted to be alone with her thoughts about the

transmission she had received, and what it might mean for Conrad Su.

In the end, she didn't get a choice in the matter. Porthos slung an arm around her waist, preventing Dana from disappearing into the crowd. "Come and drink with us," she insisted. "We've clearance to head down to Chaillot as long as we're back in our bunks by 0:00 hours."

Reluctantly, Dana agreed. "Drink with us" turned out to mean sharing a booth in the corner of a rather loud nightclub called Dovecote Red with Athos and Porthos, surrounded by most of the Combined Fleet.

"She's gone to subspace transport," said Athos, when Dana asked about Aramis. "A message from a friend that had to be collected in person rather than sent over the comm, so she'll spend half the night in a queue." His weary expression, lit up by the blazing pyrotechnics that poured from the domed ceiling of the club, suggested that he was entirely bored by Aramis and her social life.

"Speaking of friends," said Porthos, her eyes gleaming. "What the hell is going on with you and Agent Scarypants, Dana? You were cozy when you arrived at the briefing. Isn't she supposed to be your nemesis or something?"

"Or something," said Dana.

There was drinking and dancing and the night was surprisingly fun considering that they were literally on the brink of war. The club's light show was heavy on scarlet and crimson filters, making all the sweaty dancing look grisly after a few drinks.

With only 45 minutes before the curfew came down,

Dana headed to the bar for a final refill when someone smacked into her from behind. She turned and found herself with an armful of warm, drunken Aramis, who pressed her face into Dana's collarbone as if wanting to inhale her entirely into her lungs.

"Um," said Dana. She caught sight of Athos over Aramis' shoulder. He rolled his eyes as if this was no more than he had expected of the two of them. Porthos grinned and made an encouraging gesture that was entirely unhelpful.

If she let go now, Aramis would surely slide on to the floor, presuming she was as drunk as she seemed. Just as Dana had this thought, Aramis slithered a little higher to nip her on the earlobe and whisper. "Go with it, we need an excuse to be alone."

Dana opened her mouth to complain that the pretence was unnecessary given that the entire Fleet knew they were friends, and it would hardly be out of character for the two of them to slope off to some quiet corner together without the need for gratuitous making out.

Her mistake was in opening her mouth, because now she had Aramis' tongue to deal with, and there was no thinking about anything remotely practical when she was having the very breath kissed out of her.

"Well, that was discreet," Dana managed to complain, eight lingering kisses later when they finally tumbled through the door of a private room above the club.

"Possibly there was a side bet with Porthos about how

enthusiastically you'd respond to espionage kisses," Aramis said, throwing herself on the bed.

"Like kissing hasn't got me into enough trouble already," Dana sighed, perching on the edge of what was either a very uncomfortable bed or a very soft massage table. "What on earth is all this about?"

Aramis produced an antique pearl ear-drop. When she laid it on Dana's dark brown wrist, it burrowed into her skin like any other data stud. "I was asked to collect a message from a mutual friend of ours – big surprise, since it was news to me you'd even met."

Dana gave her a bleary look. "I've been flying a giant space boat for nearly a week with minimal rest cycles, do you think you could explain without all the flourish?"

Aramis pouted, and wriggled back on the bed until her head hit the pillow. "Flourish is my best thing."

"Aramis, come on!"

"You know how your Conrad was teammates with Prince Alek and my ex, Chevreuse?"

Dana hesitated. "Yes." That seemed safe enough.

"Well, while you were running around Paris trying to seduce the relevant information out of that backstabbing alien bastard who broke Athos' heart –"

"Without flourish, Aramis!"

"Turns out that Prince Alek launched his own rescue mission, the second that the Regence left Lunar Palais for the front. Without involving a single Musketeer, which I'm trying to not take personally." Aramis tapped the new pearl stud on Dana's wrist and smiled. "Want to watch a handsome prince save your boyfriend?"

✤ ✤ ✤ ✤

Dana sat through the holographic recording, trying not to hyperventilate. This was the same transmission she had viewed back on the *Frenzy Kenzie*, before Bass' security measures severed the connection. The clip from the game, then the footage of the cell with Milord standing out of the range of the cam, taunting Conrad and, by extension, Dana.

Milord had intended her to see that footage. She knew he had. It was overwhelming to think that this version was coming to her from friends instead of enemies.

"You'd be surprised how many enemies I have who think you're worth rescuing," she heard Milord say again. "Say hello to Arms-Sergeant D'Artagnan."

Conrad's eyes flicked towards the cam in surprise, then away. "You almost got me," he said dryly. "But D'Artagnan's not the one who's going to get me out of here."

"Such little faith," mocked Milord.

"He's a piece of work, this de Winter fellow," Aramis muttered. "Could he be any more villainous?"

"He's skilled at hiding that side of him," Dana sighed. "Under all the charm and the pretty."

"Whatever you say, baby doll." Aramis smirked. "He's not *my* type."

Conrad's eyes darted past the cam, seeing something beyond the lens. Even in the dingy light, his face lit up in a genuine moment of joy. "On the contrary," he said. "I have *so much* faith right now, Slate."

There was a noise: a meaty thump that suggested a fight of some kind, flesh on flesh. Conrad disappeared from sight.

After more grunts and smacking sounds, the cam spun around to show the collapsed, unconscious figure of

Milord de Winter on the stone floor, his fancy suit gathering dust.

Conrad leaned into the camera with the practised ease of a famous athlete who had to put up with paparazzi interviews all the time. "If you're watching this, Dana," he said. "Don't worry about coming to rescue me. My team has it covered."

"Su, stop pissing about," said an impatient, aristocratic male voice. Another figure swept past the feed. This man was masked, wearing the uniform of a Red Hammer, but Dana knew would have bet her life it was Alek of Auster, Prince Consort.

Conrad blew a kiss into the cam, and ran after his rescuer.

Dana stared at the fallen figure of Milord, before the cam feed finally bled once more into static.

"They should have finished him," she said in a low, vengeful voice. "I should have finished him. When I had a chance."

Aramis lay her smooth hand on Dana's shoulder, stroking the side of her neck. "It's a specialised skill, killing people in cold blood. We don't all have the knack for it."

The static jumped to a new piece of footage, dated only a few hours ago. It was Madame Chevreuse herself, her hair pearl-white and cut into a tidy bob instead of the elaborate locks she had been sporting when Dana saw her last.

"Hey Aramis," she said with a warm smile. Dana could practically feel her friend glow in response. "Just to let you – and your Gascon friend – know that the tailoring package has been delivered safely to me. I plan to keep it well away from Paris for now."

Chevreuse's hand came into view long enough for her to blow a kiss. "Be valiant in battle, win the war, and get home safe, both of you. I'll see you again."

There had been a tension inside Dana for so long: guilt and fear about Conrad. He looked good, despite all that time in Milord's custody. She was going to see him again someday, when the war was over.

"She looked puffy," said Aramis with a twist of her mouth. "Do you think she looked puffy? I mean, the extra weight suits her, Chev was all cheekbones and sharp edges when we were together, but she looks *exhausted*, what are they doing to her on the Daughters of Peace? I can't imagine that a life without the Cardinal breathing down her neck is somehow less stressful than –"

"She's pregnant," Dana blurted out.

Aramis blinked and looked at her. "Excuse me, now?"

Dana felt hot. She hadn't meant to say it, possibly it wasn't a thing even, but. "At least, she was pregnant when I saw her on Luna Palais a couple of months ago, so she must be almost completely done with being pregnant now, but there was definitely a – uh."

"Huh," said Aramis thoughtfully. "I guess that explains why she wasn't along for the rescue, punching Milord in the head and all that. I wonder why she never mentioned it. I never thought her husband was the type to insist on that particular clause. But they were re-negotiating their contract, when she left Paris." She shrugged and smiled. "Fancy visiting Peace once we're done with this whole alien armada thing? We'll have some rec leave banked up. I can buy outrageous outfits for Chevreuse's baby, and you can visit your boy."

"Sounds like a plan," said Dana.

Aramis gave her a big, squeezing hug. "Better now? Conrad will be safe with Chev until your squishy romantic reunion. Hey, he's a tailor, right? He can *make* tiny outfits. Every baby needs a flight suit with sequins."

Dana nodded, and hugged Aramis back. Safe. Conrad was safe.

WHATEVER HAPPENED TO THE DUCHESS OF BUCKINGHAM?

In recent weeks, Georgiana Villiers or "Buck" to her friends has become a shell of her former self. From being one of Valour's most-tracked celebrities, she's fallen into a social media black hole.

Heartbreak? Drug addiction? Mental breakdown? Or something more sinister?

Our reporter, Coral Wishlist, was able to capture Buck for some one-on-one time earlier today. As you can see from the footage, the Duchess of Danger Sports lacks her usual energy, and has gone for a dramatic image change.

CORAL: You look amazing, Buck. What are you wearing?

BUCK: The silk dressing gown is from Shania's latest collection. If you're going to wear pyjamas during the day, they should at least be as expensive as a new car, right?

CORAL: That quote's going straight up on our website!
[They laugh]
Seriously, the world has been worried about you since you dropped out of sight! Tell us the truth: was it rehab?

BUCK: I wish it was that easy. I've been working through a few emotional issues, and my life coach thought it best that I stay out of the spotlight to gain some perspective. I spent a week on an ornamental llama farm, and a fortnight at a meditation retreat in the foothills, specialising in mindful silence and therapeutic yarncraft. I'm feeling much stronger now.

CORAL: I'm glad to hear you're taking care of yourself. But I hope you'll be tweeting again soon – the digital space isn't the same without you!

BUCK: Believe me, I'm planning my social media comeback.

CORAL: Did all that mindful silence allow you any time for romance?

BUCK: Watch this space!

After the reporter and her cams had gone, Buck staggered back up to her private suite and splashed water on her face. She looked in the mirror for a long time, her finger-tips brushing over the short curls that were all that remained of her once wild, tangled bronze locks.

She had been sober for two weeks, and Winter had not made an appearance in her head. That was good, right? Perhaps he was done with her. The implant, or whatever it was, might simply have dissolved after a certain amount of time.

Or perhaps he had got better at erasing her memories without leaving a trace. No, she couldn't think like that, she couldn't.

She really would go insane.

A trill caught her attention as a subspace call came through. Since she was already sitting at her bathroom mirror, she patched the call through.

"Hey Buck!"

To Buck's astonishment, it was Chevreuse – a smiling, tired-looking Chevreuse, holding a bundle in her lap.

"Babe, is that your baby?" Buck blurted out.

"It's a baby, I made a baby!" Chevreuse held up the tiny bundle long enough for Buck to see a pink, scrunched up face. "They're so much better on the outside, believe me, but noisier and messier. I'm so not doing the organic method again – capsule hatching all the way for future heirs to Montbazon's fortune." Her voice dropped to a more business-like tone. "Are you alone?"

No, never alone, never safe, never clear, don't trust me. "Of course. What's up?"

"Our Conrad's got himself into a bit of trouble. Alek and I just rescued him from this godawful tower on a freaking asteroid where he'd been held prisoner for more than a month. I'd keep him here, but people will start asking too many questions, and it's not safe to send him back to Paris yet."

Buck forced her face into a smile. "You want me to take him? I don't think that's a good idea …"

"Your place is huge, and there are always guests in and out. It'll be fine, as long as you can keep his face off social media. Maybe find him a cozy monastery somewhere? Valour has monasteries, right? I know you're all about the historical reenactment bullshit. I'm putting him on a shuttle to you today."

"Chev –" but Buck's mouth wouldn't work, wouldn't let her voice craft an excuse.

"You have to keep him clear from any government officials, especially Milord de Winter. He's the Secretary of the Interior on Valour, I think? In fact, keep Conrad clear of all government officials until after the Fleet have dealt with the Siege of Truth. After that, some Musketeers will be coming by to pick him up – or I will, if they can't make it. Got it?"

No, no, no.

"No problem," Buck found herself saying, the words coming out with an easy smile. "I'm sure we can keep ourselves occupied. I'm having a zero-gravity tank installed in the summer house."

Chevreuse laughed and blew kisses. "Awesome. Alek sends – well, you know. Completely platonic but genuine and politically-neutral expressions of friendship. You'll have Conrad in two to three days. He'll message you when he docks. Keep our boy safe."

The call cut out, leaving Buck to sit at her bathroom mirror in a haze of shock. She could hear laughter inside her head. No, not inside at all. She wrenched back the shower door to find the silver-haired man who called himself Winter lying in the empty cubicle with his bare feet up against the edge of the tub, laughing hysterically.

"So glad I stuck around in your brain," her personal hallucination managed to sputter out, half-choking on his amusement. "This is going to be *marvellous*."

CHAPTER 13
THE BOYS FROM AUSTER

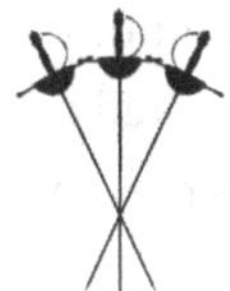

"Well," said Conrad Su, his arms folded comfortably behind his head as he settled into the co-pilot's seat. "Can't say I'm not disappointed."

"I am sorry it's not up to Sir's usual standards," replied his rescuer with light sarcasm. "Sonic shower not hot enough?"

"It was tolerable," Conrad said with a smirk. "You'd think a fancy crate like this would run to a proper clawfoot tub. And maybe a spa."

Prince Alek rolled his eyes, and punched his friend lightly in the shoulder. "I'll have one put in for Sir's next voyage."

There were many things they were not going to talk about. Like the weeks and weeks of imprisonment that Conrad had endured in the abandoned asteroid base that felt every inch the medieval tower.

Like the interrogation at the hands of his kidnapper, the grey-eyed man who called himself Slate.

Like the fact that Conrad's wife Jingfei – with whom he had entered a marriage contract that he assumed was based on mutual trust and pragmatism – had been selling secrets to the Cardinal.

Like…

He closed his eyes for a minute.

"You all right?" Alek asked hesitantly.

"Fancy decor's giving me a headache," Conrad muttered.

He had never seen this particular ship before. Prince Alek's *Jacaranda* was a moth fighter, sleek and ordinary on the outside, but decorated inside with detail worthy of a Palace boudoir.

The colour signature was matte purple, with highlights of glossy purple, shot through with contrast details in violet, iris, lavender, and at least another dozen shades that Conrad would call something other than 'purple' if he was talking about bolts of cloth. The walls were lined with actual satin, and punctured with the occasional cluster of genuine pearls.

The *Jacaranda* was the perfect frivolous gift one might give a prince if one knew absolutely nothing about him.

When Conrad had gone to clean himself up in the cabin, he discovered that the back part of the ship was far less objectionable – someone with taste had stripped the soft furnishings off the walls and replaced them with wood-panel lining, along with holographic windows that displayed familiar scenery from home.

The country of Auster, in the southern hemisphere of Honour, with its scalded red hills and dry, grey-green foliage and the occasional, *yes*, flutter of purple flowers among the dryness and the heat. A place where having a pattern of scales down your amber-brown neck didn't mark you out as an exotic freak.

Conrad had been wrong. The rear half of the spaceship was worse. It made him homesick in a way he hadn't been for years.

He didn't want to think about Auster. Not now, when they were travelling to entirely the wrong planet. Valour, of all places. Chevreuse had laughed at the expression on his face, when he realised he wasn't being sent back to Paris.

"We can't afford to have the Prince Consort of the Solar System regularly disappear on rescue missions, you know," she chided. "He's supposed to be keeping the home fires burning on Lunar Palais while the Regence gets all the military glory."

"You don't know I'd get kidnapped again," Conrad sulked in reply.

Chevreuse had laughed again, and wrapped her arms around both of her boys until their shoulders relaxed into the friendly embrace. It was so long since they had been together, the three of them.

Conrad missed the old days – back when he and Chev and Alek were a team. Practicing TeamJoust was the only time that he and Alek could be equals instead of master and servant.

He should be used to it by now. Conrad's family had served Alek's since they were both children. But it was hard-going when your oldest and closest friend had the power of life and death over yourself and your family.

"Valour will be good for you," Alek said now, breaking the silence between them. "You haven't had a holiday in years."

No, because I couldn't afford to leave you unsuper-vised, Conrad thought but did not say aloud.

"I don't like the idea of you back in Paris without friends close by," was what he did say. Between the machinations of the Regence and those of the Cardinal, Alek had become isolated from his allies at court. The companions and servants who had originally accompanied him from Honour had been stripped out one by one, and then the new supporters like Chevreuse went the same way.

Conrad was the last of them, and he couldn't help Alek while hiding out on some country estate with the Duchess of frigging Buckingham.

"I wish I was staying with you," Alek said with a twisted smile.

"Yeah, no way that could go terribly wrong," Conrad said dryly. After all the trouble he and Chev and the Musketeers had gone to — after all the risks they had taken to enable Alek and Buck to be together, however briefly. No, letting the two of them near each other again was the ultimate bad idea.

"That's not the reason," Alek said, sounding remarkably serious. "I mean – yes, obviously, that's the reason. I promised I would keep my distance from Buck for the remainder of my marriage contract, and I mean to keep my word. But that's not the reason I need to return so hastily to Paris."

"Go on, then," said Conrad, his eyes fixed on his friend. "Surprise me."

Alek relaxed his hands from the ship controls, and unfastened his embroidered jacket, letting it fall open. Underneath, he wore what looked at first to be a tactical armour vest, though it had no military identification marks on it.

Conrad leaned in, curious about the unfamiliar garment, and then jerked back when he realised what the flat silver pouches in the front of the vest must be. "Are those—"

"The future Regences of the Solar System?" Alek said with a wry smile. "God willing, they are."

Conrad pressed his hands to his mouth. "But I thought — didn't she agree to try body pregnancies rather than capsules? It was a clause in your marriage contract."

There had been nights where Conrad had scoured that marriage contract, checking over the precise meanings of words and phrases, because he was terrified his friend was going to start a civil war by breaching it. He knew every line by heart.

"It was never going to happen that way," said Alek in a flat sort of voice, which made it clear he did not want to discuss the details. "Anyway, the Cardinal would not support the Regence uniting the Fleet and going personally into battle without some insurance left behind, for the future of the Crown. Lalla-Louise agreed to fake a body pregnancy to placate my family and the Elemental factions on Honour who already think I betrayed them with this marriage. It's not a bad idea for security reasons, anyway."

Conrad was tempted to reach out and touch the silver pouches, but kept his hands to himself. The enormity of Alek's sacrifice crashed in on him. Conrad was not a particularly devout Elemental, but it had always been important to Alek to follow his family's faith as closely as he could, even when his marriage to the Regence meant that he had to publicly join the Church of All.

Damn it, the future sovereign was sitting on Alek's chest, along with a bunch of their backup siblings, and Alek had *still* thrown himself into a physical fight to rescue his friend.

"Why on earth would you risk them to come after me?" Conrad blurted, horrified.

"Well, I wasn't going to leave them behind," said Alek, which didn't answer the question at all. He reached out, and cuffed Conrad lightly on the back of the head. "It's fine. The capsules are like armour, built to withstand laser fire and sword thrusts. It's supposed to be good for them to experience different sounds and vibrations while they're gestating. Develops the brain better, or something."

"Sounds and vibrations like you punching that bastard kidnapper of mine in the head?"

"Exactly."

The *Jacaranda* was supplied with discreet New Aristocrat protocols that allowed the ship to bypass most of Valour's security requirements. They landed in a green field, instead of an official air dock.

"Behold the beauty and glamour of the prettiest planet in the solar system," said Alek with a wave of his hand.

"I'd prefer desert and eucalyptus any day of the week," Conrad muttered as the hatch slid open. Valour smelled wrong. It was all grass and buttercups. Elemental, yes. The planetary gravity was heavy and welcoming. But this whole rolling green pastures business was going to take a lot of getting used to.

"You're so fucking spoiled," Alek laughed. "Go braid some daisies."

"Such a productive use of my skills," Conrad sighed. He didn't want to go. Alek might have pod babies to protect, but he was terrible at looking after himself. "We should go on to Paris together."

"Nope," said Alek, leaping up from the pilot's chair and physically manhandling Conrad out the hatch. "Embrace the dirtside lifestyle. I hear they grow their own vegetables down here."

Conrad butted his head lightly against that of his prince. "Vegetables are overrated. You're going to end up assassinated, and badly dressed. You need me."

"Yeah," Alek said, his voice dropping its usual archness. "I need you, mate. So keep yourself alive until that cute Musketeer of yours comes to rescue you."

"She's not a Musketeer," Conrad muttered. "And she's not cute, either. She's — kind of amazing." Dana D'Artagnan. He could wait a long time for a woman like her. "Fine, I'll lock myself in another fucking tower, start growing my hair like the damsel I obviously am."

Alek's eyes danced with amusement. "Or find some decent fleur-de-lis players to practice against while you're here. They've closed the league for the war, but next year — next year is *ours*, baby."

Conrad grinned at that. "I'll work on staying alive, you grow some fetuses, and arrange to get Chevreuse transferred back to Paris. We'll have the old team back together by next year."

They exchanged manly punches, and then Prince Alek stepped back into the *Jacaranda* and flew away.

Conrad stood on his own in a green field, surrounded

by dandelions and bluebells. In the far distance, he could see a large estate that had to be Buck's formal residence.

"Right," he sighed to himself, beginning to walk. "A package holiday on the wrong planet, in the middle of nowhere, with the Duchess of Buckingham. Could be worse."

Buck swam. She hadn't used this pool in years, except as a site for decadent parties, and even then she preferred to swan around in amazing outfits instead of actually getting wet.

Over the last few days she had come here regularly, to swim methodical laps. The ritual of it was comforting, and made her think that maybe she could get through this.

On the rare occasions she held her breath too long, allowed herself to flirt with the possibility of drowning herself, the first thing she saw when she burst clear of the surface would be Winter.

Winter. She had watched footage of the real Milord de Winter, Minister for the Interior, and while he was similar to her parasite in so many ways, she knew that he was a different creature.

Weapon. Creature. Weapon.

If Buck swam hard and fast enough, until her limbs shook with exhaustion when she finally clambered out of the pool, then sleep without dreams became a possibility.

Not today. Today, there was a pretty young man with amber-brown skin and dark eyes, grinning at her from across the pool. His hair had been electric blue last time she saw Conrad Su, but now it had grown out to its natural shiny black with blue at the tips. A pattern of gleaming gold scales ran down the side of his neck and under his shirt.

"Hey," said Buck, spitting out a mouthful of water, because she was cool like that.

"Thanks for letting me crash here," said Conrad, shielding his face against the bright sunlight. "You sure it's okay?"

As Buck stared at him, she saw Winter approach Conrad on his silent bare feet. His hair blazed silver in the same sunlight. Winter leaned in and licked the side of Conrad's neck.

Conrad did not react because he could not feel the touch of the other man — Winter did not exist except inside Buck's head.

That didn't mean he was not a danger to them both.

Buck shivered, the sun-warm water around her body dropping in temperature. "It's fine," she said. "Glad to have you. We're going to have some fun together."

CHAPTER 14
ANJOU WINE

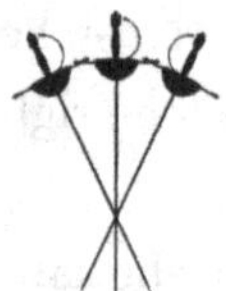

The support vessels *Frenzy Kenzie* and *La Konstantina* remained in position at the edge of Truth Space, close enough that ships and personnel would be able to reach them for medical assistance and supplies, but not so close that they were at risk of being taken out by long range shots from the Sun-kissed fleet.

Dana had known when she chose this assignment that she would not be going into battle herself, but she had not realised quite how far she would be stationed from the front line.

Communications were patchy at best. Assuming that the Sun-kissed would not be able to tap into their most secure military frequencies was a mistake made during the last war. Never again. Fleetnet and personal comms were now blocked for everything but official notifications from the command posts. The flippant chatter of Dana's Musketeer friends had driven her up the wall on the journey, but this silence was worse.

She would do anything for a snarky tweet about Porthos' love life right now.

Dana's war began when three sabre-class darts arrived unannounced, their hulls scarred with laser burn, to be taken on board the *St Konstantina* for medical attention and repairs.

What followed was eight days of hell.

Ships – mostly darts of sabre and musket-class – might appear at any time of the 24-hour clock, often in packs of at least three, sometimes with multiple crews crammed into them, depending on how badly other ships had been damaged.

Bass and his engie interns, and Chantal with her supply assistants, were run off their feet, printing and fixing Musketeer hardware to allow ships to be sent back into the field.

Dana, left with little to do but monitor the *Frenzy Kenzie's* drift, found herself conscripted into the medibay to help Wheels manage and monitor the wounded alongside her squadron of medical androids.

The technology did most of the work, but an extra pair of human hands (and lungs, and brain cells) was always useful. Dana's main responsibility quickly became supervising the movement of damaged pilots from the airlock to medibay so they didn't keel over in a corridor *en route*.

The *Frenzy Kenzie* and the *St Konstantina* weren't the only support vessels. There were at least two others based on the far side of Truth Space, so even if Dana's favourite Musketeers were injured or dented, they wouldn't necessarily end up here.

As much as a base for supplies and repairs, the *Frenzy Kenzie* became an unofficial gossip hub, with every tale of

Sun-kissed action passed on to the next wave of patch-jobs. One wall of the main airlock was given over to scrawled messages from the pilots and engies to their loved ones and comrades because it was assumed that everyone would come through here sooner or later.

Dana saw all manner of familiar faces on her ship, including Amiral Treville at one point: escorting the Regence herself after a nasty sortie. Lalla-Louise Renard Royal had flashburns down one side of her face, and was discreetly lodged in a private room behind the medibay while she healed up.

"Are we winning?" Dana could not help but ask Treville in a low voice, as she handed over fresh supplies for the flagship, including a crate of meal bars and fresh-printed uniforms.

Treville was exhausted. She downed a whole tube of chilled water without pausing for breath. "We're not losing," she grunted, which wasn't the same thing.

On Day 6, Dana found herself climbing into a familiar dart to slice Captain Tracy Dubois out of her helm and harness, after the metal had been fused to the dashboard by an unknown Sun-kissed weapon that scared the hell out of everyone.

"I saw Aramis two days ago," Dubois reported. Dana would have hugged her, if she wasn't busy trying not to cut her skin off along with the melted cables. "She was doing well — the *Morningstar*'s barely been grazed. I saw the *Hoyden* at a distance this morning, Porthos was in the thick of it. Took out three Teardrops in under a minute.

Athos' wretched green thing has been all over the place. He's impossible to miss."

Small fragments of information like that were better than nothing, Dana told herself. But 'alive two days ago' didn't mean safe and sound today.

She worked, and she worried. One day melted into another, as the Siege of Truth wore on.

On Day 8, a Musketeer that Dana barely knew handed her a package. "I had it from Juillet, who had it from Valentin, who had it from Borlois who had it from Treville," he said, barely glancing at Dana as he stepped into the bright white medibay. "Hey, Wheels, here I am again."

"Didn't I just patch you up, Mikhail?" complained the stern, grey-haired medic, spinning around in her hover chair.

Dana didn't open the package until much later, as she lay down in her bunk at the beginning of a regulation six-hour shift, hoping something like sleep might happen.

The box contained two vacuum flasks of well-packed wine from Anjou, one of the finer vineyard countries in Honour, north of the equator.

Dana wasn't sure who had sent it. Her first guess was Chevreuse, given her recent habit of mysterious communications. Maybe even Conrad, who was supposed to be staying with Chev? But deep in the package, underneath the flasks, she found a holo-card that made her grin ridiculously.

It was a pic of Porthos, Aramis and Athos, squeezed

into the same bed in an unknown medibay — aboard the *Sherwood*, perhaps, or the *Belizze* — with medipatches wrapped around every visible limb.

They were alive and recuperating. The message on the back read:

DRINK IT FOR US, WE'RE BANNED.

Dana considered it. God knew she was unlikely to sleep without some kind of chemical assistance. But she packed the flasks under her bunk to keep them safe for later, and allowed the feeling of relief to wash over her like a blanket.

All three of them were alive and safe, for at least a couple more days by the look of those medipatches. She could breathe.

It would all be over soon. Waiting to drink the wine with her friends would be no hardship.

Over the next 24 hours, Dana thought about that Anjou wine a lot. She was dragged out of her bunk when a dozen or more darts appeared at once, and it was all hands on deck to separate the damaged ships from the damaged pilots.

An hour later, another six ships turned up. Then another wave, the hour after that.

Dana was practically hallucinating about the Anjou wine at that point. She promised herself that as soon as there was a lull, she would drag Planchet or Chantal or anyone she could find back to her room and make them drink with her until their skulls were ready to float into space.

The next wave of ships included the *Pistachio*.

Dana didn't realise at first. Bass was on a sleep shift, and so his assistants and Dana were run off their feet fitting out several darts to be spaceworthy again, so they could free up space in the cavernous docking level.

Dana and Planchet waved the last of these into Airlock One and watched them punch out in military formation, only to turn and watch three more ships power slowly into Airlock Two, ready to be rolled inside.

One of the ships was green.

Planchet moved first, calling for support droids to crack open the other ships, and for the second engie assistant – Dana couldn't even remember her name, something beginning with Z? – to check their crews for medical triage.

Planchet herself went straight for the *Pistachio*, beating one fist on the chassis before hunting for the external lock release. The hatch folded open, and an exhausted-looking Grimaud hovered at the top of the steps.

"Superficial damage to the ship," she reported. "Minimal repairs needed to get him back in the field." Then she turned her head and shouted: "UNLIKE THE PILOT, WHO IS A COLOSSAL ARSEHOLE!"

"I'm glad you're okay," said Dana, running up to her. "What's wrong with Athos?"

"What *isn't* wrong with Athos?" Grimaud muttered, and started discussing technical specs with Planchet. She clearly had no interest in talking to pilots today.

Dana let herself into the *Pistachio* and found Athos in the cabin, stretched out on his bunk, too pale to be healthy.

His eyes were open, but he didn't seem aware of her presence. "Are you drunk?" Dana demanded, leaning in. His pupils were blown wide. "Are you *high*?"

Nexus. Of course he was still taking pilot drugs. But this reaction was too intense for that. She went back to the hatch and called Grimaud. "How many different stims are he on right now?"

The engie stared back at her, silent.

Dana was prepared to wait all day if necessary. "Medical treatment is confidential, you know that. Tell me."

"You use automated medical systems on this base," Grimaud reminded her calmly. "During military operations, all medibay computers and androids automatically report inappropriate drug usage found in patients."

Dana winced. "Shit. Is a Sobriety patch going to make a difference if I give it to him before we log him in?"

"He's had two already. They reacted badly to the caffeine implant. And that's not taking into account the three different strains of pilot drugs he has been bouncing between over the last two days."

Anger stabbed through Dana's chest. "Is there a chance that me smacking him upside the head will make the situation worse right now?"

"That's the only reason he doesn't have a black eye from me."

"Grimaud, I don't know how you do it," Dana sighed.

"Most pilots are idiots," the engie said flatly. "The trick is finding one you're willing to take stupid risks for."

"Athos is worth it?" Dana thought so, but she'd always wondered about Grimaud's fierce loyalty.

"He doesn't make small talk. That goes a long way as

far as I'm concerned." Grimaud frowned. "It's possible I have Stockholm Syndrome."

"I'm taking him somewhere quiet for a proper med assessment," Dana decided. "I'll keep the androids away from him if I can, but honestly — if he's being this dangerous about stim usage, we should *let* them report him."

Grimaud gave a short nod to concede the point.

The walls of Medici College were butter-yellow, as if they were doused in sunshine even on cloudy days. Olivier Armand d'Autevielle sprawled in a window alcove with a text reader spread across his knees. He was paying little attention to the revision he had to do.

"You could come home with me," he suggested.

Auden: a beautiful, too-thin boy with silver hair and cut-glass cheekbones, leaned against the glass of the window at the other end of the alcove, soaking up the sunlight. "You want to turn up for the holidays hand in hand with a no-name scholarship kid and announce that we'll be sharing your fancy four poster bed or whatever it is that rich families sleep on — gold-plated sheets and caviar throw cushions? That will go down marvellously, sweetness."

Olivier hated that. He hated that Auden could be so cutting and funny while putting himself down, as if he was accustomed to thinking of himself as worthless but entertaining. "I don't know if you've heard, but I'm the Comte de la Fere now. I don't care what my family thinks."

"You've been the Comte for years, and you've always cared." Basking in melancholy was high in Auden's skillset, up there with sarcasm and dead languages. These were all things that Olivier loved about him.

Love. So, there was that.

"Now I'm of age," said Olivier, speaking lightly so that Auden would not catch on that he had been struck by a life-changing, lightning strike of a personal revelation. "They can't stop me doing whatever the hell I want."

When Auden smiled, it was like the sunlight of the ivy-draped courtyard outside was here in the room with them, warming the walls, lighting up the ancient bookshelves and wall portraits. "And you want *me*?"

Olivier grinned in return, pulling his boyfriend into his lap and to hell with the text reader, which fell to the floor. "I always want you," he said honestly.

It was a dream. Of course it was a dream. Athos hadn't let himself remember the good times in years, while he was awake, but his subconscious mind was a traitor and a love-struck fool.

Other dreams weren't nearly so pleasant.

Athos dreamed of his ship crumbling around him, of the gravity of Valour ripping through the *Parry-Riposte* on their way down to the surface. He dreamed of getting D'Artagnan killed in that stupid crash, while the pursuit ships fired upon them. He dreamed of Grimaud, wounded and limp in his arms.

He dreamed of the planet he had always thought would swallow him whole, and the mountain that he had once believed would be his eternal resting place.

Valour.

Athos.

The ship exploded around him, metal scattering in vicious shards. Athos saw Grimaud dead, and D'Artagnan dying. He could not save either of them.

He stared at his feet, where the soft green grass of Valour curled gently around his ankles. Bare feet. When he looked up, he saw the face of his husband, beautiful and sad, with bright silver hair tousled around his slender neck.

"You're not going to do this," said Auden in a low voice, the voice that had always made Athos – *Olivier* – shiver with want. "You're not going to give up what we have. I love you. I trust you. I always have."

Olivier Armand d'Autevielle, the Comte de la Fere, spoke without a hint of emotion. "There's only one way to kill a devil."

"Is that honestly what you think I am?" Auden's voice was a howl, a screech, several octaves too high. An alien, unfamiliar sound.

Alien, oh yes. There was that.

"It doesn't matter what I think," Olivier ground out between his teeth. "I lost the right to happiness when I lay down with the enemy."

The sword was real, a family heirloom. It felt heavy and metallic in his grasp, warm to the touch. Not the cool, perfectly-distributed weight of a pilot's slice.

Humans knew little about the Sun-kissed, even after surviving a war against them, and yet one fact stood out: to kill them, you take the head.

Auden tilted his head to one side, basking in his own beauty. Of course he was beautiful. His face was manufactured: everything from the pale grey eyes to the sculpted face. He was created to be admired; to make humans weak at the knees for desire of him. "Kill me then, sweetness," he breathed. "Let's see how much better it makes you feel."

Olivier swung the sword, severing his husband's head from his neck. His duty, he reminded himself as the ugly thud vibrated through his arms, and his heart. Duty above everything. It had to be him who struck the blow. How could he trust it to anyone else?

His hand closed around a glass of whiskey, relishing the way that it felt against his palm before he poured the contents down his throat.

That didn't help, either.

Athos' eyes snapped open. He hadn't dreamed of that in years – oh, there had been dreams, terrible torturing dreams that regularly ripped his heart out of his chest, but not that, not the moment when he performed the execution.

The failed execution.

Cutting off their heads doesn't work after all. I should warn someone about that.

"Where am I?" he muttered. "Grimaud?" It came out as a slur of unrelated consonants, and he realised too late that this wasn't his bunk on the *Pistachio*. Damn it, had he totalled another ship?

He found a flat white medipack fastened to his bare chest, and sat up in a hurry, groaning as his head churned and the bright lights of the medibay hurt his eyes.

"You're alive, then." It was a chirpy voice. Athos glared at it until the blur resolved into a familiar person.

"Pigtails," he said flatly.

"You know that's not my name," the redhead said, not offended. She passed him a cup of ice chips. "Dana would have hung around but she said she was likely to smother you in your sleep if she did, so she's gone back to work."

"Grimaud?"

"Much the same only she said, 'break his limbs' instead of 'smother him' and she's overseeing the repairs of the *Pistachio*."

Athos nodded slowly. He didn't hurt as much as he might have expected, but he still felt shaky. "Am I grounded?"

"Inappropriate stims usage in the field, three days out of combat," said a different voice, breaking into their conversation. "You're to report back to Treville at Chaillot Station as soon as you're fit to travel so she can shout at you in person." A fifty-something medic in a hover chair whirred over towards them, peering at Athos through her thick glasses with professional interest. "You're getting off lightly, kid."

Athos had a long history with Wheels, the Musketeers' longest-serving medic, and he was well aware that things could have gone much worse.

"Always a pleasure, sweetness," he drawled at her.

Wheels gave him a dirty look. "Don't even think about

trying to flirt with me, Mr Posh Accent. I haven't slept for forty-eight hours, and I have no sympathy for self-destructive pilots. Were you trying to kill yourself? Suicide by Front Line?"

Athos was taken aback. "No," he said, and meant it. There were times he had come close to that, but no — Aramis and Porthos would never forgive themselves, if he let it get that bad. They had enough of a hold on his heart that he curbed his more self-destructive impulses.

Perhaps he was due for recalibration about what exactly counted as self-destructive.

"Good to know." Wheels made a check mark on the clamshell that rested on the arm of her hover chair. "You will remain here for three more hours under my observation, and then you can get the hell out. Planchet says Cap will let you bunk with her while you're on enforced downtime."

Athos blinked, not used to the idea that their baby-faced D'Artagnan was a Captain now. "Am I allowed to know what happened to my pants?"

Dana was dog tired, worn to the bone, and while she wanted to check in on Athos in the medibay, she didn't have any energy left for the angry rant she had building inside her head. Sleep first, shouting later.

She let herself into her small quarters and toppled headfirst on to the bunk. She lay there still and silent for at least ten minutes, trying to work up the energy to take her boots off.

If she sat up, she could get at that wine. She would

need to hide it when Athos was well enough to bunk with her. But she was going to drink some of it first, and to hell with hypocrisy.

In order to drink, she had to get up.

Her door chimed once, twice, three times, and even before she could react to it, she heard an urgent thumping against the door. Damn it all to hell and back. Dana rose slowly, staggering with exhaustion, and thumbed open the door.

Athos stood on the other side, wearing medibay-printed pyjamas and an agonised expression.

"What?" Dana snapped.

"Pigtails told me about the Anjou wine," Athos blurted out.

Heat surged through her body. Her anger and fear about what the fuck he had been doing to himself resolved into a single, furious punch.

Athos went down like he'd been felled by a cinquefoil pole, and Dana didn't even feel guilty about it. She stood over him, yelling about how much his friends loved him, and how he was a stupid, selfish addict who was going to break all their hearts when he got himself killed out of sheer drug-induced idiocy.

When Dana paused to take in a shaky breath, Athos tried to speak. She cut him off with another round of ranting, then sat on his chest, and hit him a couple more times.

Finally, she ran out of words and fury.

"D'Artagnan," Athos started to say. Dana raised her hand to smack him again. He caught her hand and flipped her on to the ground, leaning over her with her wrists pinned hard above her head. "Dana, this is all very touching," he snarled into her face. "But if you would stop emoting at me for half a minute, I didn't come here because I was *thirsty.*"

Dana glared up at him, breathing hard. "Then what?"

Athos sighed, still not relinquishing her wrists. "Aramis and Porthos and I have not been inside the same medibay since this damned war began. We've barely seen each other since Chaillot Station. *We never sent you any fucking wine.*"

CHAPTER 15
DOVECOTE RED

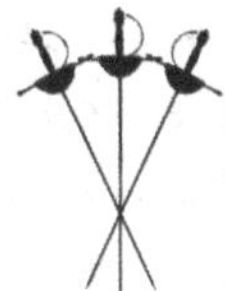

Nothing about the flasks offered a clue – they held the stamp of the Cotillard Vineyard in Anjou, and a postal seal to show they were authorised for interstellar export. There was no sign that they had been tampered with since leaving the vineyard.

Athos took over Chantal's testing chamber with a surprising demonstration of charm and tact, long enough to learn that the contents of the Anjou wine contained enough poison to wipe out a whole platoon of Musketeers, let alone a single Arms-Sergeant Captain.

Back in Dana's cabin, Athos sat on the bunk poring over the holo-card that had accompanied the poisonous gift. "I remember this picture; it's from a year ago. Chevreuse took it in the medibay after the three of us were involved in a training accident, when I lost the *Merci Beaucoup*. She posted it on Fleetnet with the caption 'Inseparable in Idiocy.' Treville had a copy on her dartboard for at least a month. Anyone could have got hold of this."

"How many ships have you lost, Athos?"

"I'm hoping my luck changes with the *Pistachio*. No ship that ugly is ever going to be blasted out of the sky." He blinked, and looked up at Dana. "He is all right, isn't he?"

Dana was touched. Athos pretended he wasn't soft about his spaceships, but she knew true love when she saw it. "The *Pistachio* is fine. Nothing we can't patch up. Grimaud is also fine, by the way, though I doubt she'll be speaking to you by the time you ship out again."

"That's just how I like it," said Athos, his attention drawn back to the holo-card. "You couldn't tell this was old? It's from before I grew out my beard."

"Since you started shaving it close again it looks exactly the same."

Dana fiddled with one of the flasks, and Athos moved quickly, his hand covering her own. "Keep your fingers to yourself. We don't know what other surprises your murderous friend has in store for you."

Dana's hand stuttered on the flask. "Point made."

"I'll take them with me when I ship out," he said. "This is a matter for Amiral Treville."

"There's more," said Dana, and quickly told him about Conrad, and the transmission Aramis had shared with her, via Chevreuse. Athos went very still when she confessed that it was Prince Alek who had staged Conrad's rescue.

"This is bad," he said in a low voice, once she was finished. He tapped his comm stud. "Grimaud, when will he be ready to return to base?"

"I hate you, I hate your face, I hate your ship," his engie said calmly. "Six hours, if it's an emergency, but only if you can prove you've had actual sleep, and I take the helm."

"See you in six hours." Athos cut her off without further conversation. "See? Grimaud's fine."

"Don't tell her you're bringing poison on board, it would be far too much of a temptation," said Dana. "Are you really going to take this to Treville?"

"Oh, yes. All this –" Athos waved a hand at the flasks with a troubled look upon his face. "This is personal, not political. Cardinal Richelieu has lived too long and survived too much political bullshit to indulge in personal revenge, and if she ordered your assassination it wouldn't be so amateurish. Who else wants you dead? Should we consider that pilot with the scar and the fierce hair?"

"You don't get to mock anyone's hair, given yours when we met," said Dana, reaching over to rub her palm over the blond stubble of his scalp. "And no, I don't think – Ro and I have an understanding. If she wanted to kill me, I honestly think she'd prefer to be there for it."

"How romantic," Athos said sarcastically. "Well, then. I can think of one suspect."

"So can I."

They didn't say it – any of the names by which they knew Milord. They could not speak of the alien spy without feeling him there in the room with them.

"I can believe it," Dana said finally. "He was furious before Conrad escaped. After – everything in Paris, I can well believe that he is taking it personally, about me."

Athos nodded, and sat in silence for a moment. "I have to have a very detailed and very uncomfortable conversation with Amiral Treville. It's long past time that we put this Sun-kissed creature in the ground."

Dana felt a painful tug at her stomach. "Do you have to go straight away?"

Athos smiled, and tapped her lightly on the nose. "The war won't last forever, D'Artagnan. We'll all be back, drinking and brawling in Paris before you know it."

Dana said nothing. It felt a terribly long way away.

"Six hours," Athos reminded her. "I can crash here, yes? Let's see if this sleep thing is as worthwhile as everyone claims."

"Fine," Dana groaned, looking at the narrow bunk and wondering how on earth they would both fit. "But take your damn boots off."

Forty-eight hours after Athos and Grimaud left to make their appointment with Treville, the *Hoyden* rolled into the main dock of the *Frenzy Kenzie*.

Dana stared at it for a full minute, gathering her courage to check on whether Porthos was alive and well inside her dart – though, in fact, the *Hoyden* didn't look like it had taken any damage at all.

Bonnie was the first one out, and she waved off the intern that Bass sent over for a damage report. When she caught sight of Dana, she crooked her finger.

Huh.

Dana headed to the *Hoyden,* wondering what in space was going on, only to stumble over her feet when a tall and elegant figure in a violet flight suit stepped out, instead of Porthos.

Rosnay Cho gave her an enigmatic smile, and held out her wrist. "Captain," she said lightly.

Dana leaned in, her wrist brushing against Ro's. Her comm hummed as the new orders rattled in.

"What happened to your Moth?" she asked, because there was something about Ro that made her blurt out the first thing that came into her mind, every single time.

"Crashed and burned in the last sortie against the Sun-kissed," said Ro, and laughed out loud at the horror that crossed Dana's face. "Honey, I didn't know you cared."

"That was a beautiful ship," Dana muttered.

"I'm sure the Cardinal will present me with a new one for services rendered."

Dana glared at her. "So what are these orders?"

"Oh, I'm relieving you of duty for 48 hours," said Ro in an offhand sort of way. "You don't have to show me the way to the captain's chair – I'm sure I remember it."

Dana blinked. "You're what? I'm — what?"

Rosnay Cho was already walking away, a knapsack tossed casually over one shoulder. "Read your orders, D'Artagnan," she called out behind her. "You'll find them enlightening."

Porthos explained everything on their way to Chaillot Station. She made Bonnie pilot the *Buttercup*, so that Dana — still without an engie of her own given Planchet's continuing duties on the *Frenzy Kenzie* — could share the *Hoyden*'s flight deck, and they could talk without the use of comms.

'Explain' wasn't entirely accurate, given that Porthos had no idea what was going on, and why Rosnay Cho of all people had been rotated on to cover for Dana on the *Frenzy Kenzie*.

"Athos is cooking something up with Treville, and they want us part of it," was all she had to share. "Spy stuff."

Dana nodded miserably. It had been categorically proven that she was terrible at spy stuff, but if Athos thought she could be useful, she wasn't going to let him down. "How's he doing?"

Porthos gave Dana a cagey look, as if trying to work out how much she already knew. "Grimaud has threatened to quit if he doesn't cool it with the pilot drugs and the stims," she said.

"Grimaud threatens to quit every week," Dana sighed.

"She means it this time. She showed him a job offer she received from Claudine Jussac of the Red Fleet, and he promised not to call her bluff."

Dana was skeptical. Grimaud had been enabling Athos for a long time, like the rest of them. It was hard to imagine he would let her force him into a corner. "*Is* he actually going to cool it with the pilot drugs and the stims?"

"He's hopped up on caffeine. I haven't seen him drunk since he got back from his near miss," Porthos said. "But he's spent most of his time behind closed doors with Treville, so maybe he hasn't had time." She hesitated to continue, her fingertips tapping idly against the cables of her harness. "He's taking this Milord business personally."

"Wouldn't you?" Dana demanded.

Porthos gave her a long, hard look. "He's acting like it's his fault the bastard tried to poison you."

"Oh," Dana groaned, because of course Athos would blame himself. "Typical."

"There's also a problem with the Prince Consort," Porthos went on. "Prince Alek is supposed to be back safely on Lunar Palais — leading the home guard, or tattooing the nursery walls or whatever else an expectant father does while his pregnant wife is out winning a war against aliens. Instead, he's been bombing around the solar system, punching spies in the head and rescuing his tailor from sinister asteroid prisons."

"Does Athos blame himself for that too?" Dana asked tiredly.

"Nope," said Porthos, hiding a grin. "I'm pretty sure Treville is going to blame you."

Dana expected to be taken to the Regence Royal's flagship, or the armoured command base: the *Saint-Gervais*. Failing that, she thought Treville might have an office somewhere on Chaillot Station. Instead, Porthos led her directly back to the nightclub they had spent the evening in before the proper battle began – Dovecote Red.

"This is official business, right?" Dana asked as they made their way through the grinding bodies, pulsing music and spotlights that turned everything blood-red. "You haven't kidnapped me to show me a good time?"

"Such trust," Porthos laughed, catching her by the hand and pulling her onwards through the club. At the far end of the bar, she gave a discreet password, and was led through to a mostly sound-proofed back room.

There, surrounded by barrels and bottles, two Musketeers sat at a game of cards, with a bottle of wine between them. Aramis and Athos.

"About time you showed up," said Athos as he laid down his hand.

"It's been forever," said Aramis, giving Dana a friendly hug and hooking her arm around Porthos' neck.

"No Treville?" Porthos said with a frown, pushing Aramis off and pouring herself a drink. "I expected her here by now."

"Is this or isn't this official business?" Dana asked, unsure whether to make herself comfortable. There was an odd tension in the air.

Athos looked up, his eyes locking on to hers. "Not all councils of war can be held in the open," he said.

There was a knock at the door.

Dana's friends froze, their hands going to their belts. Athos' fingers hovered at his pilot's slice, while Aramis and Porthos reached for stunners.

"So we're not supposed to be here?" Dana hissed. She had been right to be suspicious.

"That isn't Treville's knock," Aramis said in a whisper.

The door spun open. The bright red-gold lights of the club poured across the threshold, along with the thumping beat of the music. Six Red Hammers filed into the room, lining up against one wall. A woman in full battle dress and steel-grey hair stepped in after them. The door whirled shut behind her, keeping out the music and the blazing lights, though the thudding backbeat continued to vibrate through the floor.

"Musketeers," said Cardinal Richelieu. "How fascinating."

There was a strangled pause. Athos moved first, one hand curling around the neck of the nearest wine bottle. "Your Eminence. May I offer you a drink?"

Dana thought for a horrified moment that she might burst into laughter, but she managed to swallow it down.

"Too kind," said the Cardinal. "I am here for a meeting, but I seem to have been shown to the wrong room. A glass of wine would be most hospitable." She came forward to take the empty seat at the table, the one that Dana had not taken for herself.

Aramis scrabbled the cards and coins out of the Cardinal's way. Athos poured a glass of wine and handed it to their visitor with the aristocratic manners that he dusted off for special occasions.

The Cardinal sipped,. "It's the Comte de la Fere, is it not?" she said, eyes on Athos and his bright blue jacket.

"I prefer Athos," he said flatly. "That other fellow died a long time ago."

"Of course, Athos. A simple name for a simple man."

"I like to think so, your Eminence."

Her eyes flicked around the room. "And young D'Artagnan, I see you there. Are you enjoying your work on the supply line?"

"It keeps me busy, your Eminence," Dana said, keeping her tone even and polite.

"I suppose you all know each other," said the Cardinal, waving a hand at her stony-faced Red Hammers. Two of them wore the uniforms of Sabre pilots, while the others were grunts.

"Paris may be the greatest city in the solar system, but those of us in the same line of work do tend to find each other," said Athos, with a charming smile that Dana had never seen him use before. "Your man Boisne there had a friendly altercation with Aramis only a fortnight ago. Not with blades, of course, because duelling is illegal. Arm-wrestling is a time-honoured way of settling grievances while keeping things friendly."

"How thrilling," said the Cardinal. "Who won?"

"It was a draw, your Eminence," said Aramis with a smile that matched the one Athos still wore. "I took a cut in the arm, which was easily fixed, and I believe that Boisne regained the full use of his legs within 24 hours."

"Thank goodness for today's medical marvels," said the Cardinal. "Really, Boisne, you know I disapprove of fighting between the ranks. We're a Fleet United now. Even *arm wrestling* has its dangers."

The Red Hammer in question was well aware that this conversation was a trap, but managed to say "Yes, your Eminence," without shifting his steady gaze from the Musketeers.

"All in the name of friendly rivalry," Athos went on. "You wouldn't want your guards to be lacking in fighting spirit, would you, your Eminence?"

The Cardinal's eyes darkened. "I've never heard it put so succinctly before," she said. "Of course, we also value restraint."

"Your pilots are paragons of restraint," Athos agreed. "Why, last time Captain Hardoin and I had an informal sparring session, we didn't even try to draw our swords, did we, Yvonne?"

One of the Sabres, a muscular woman with the shape of two crossed knifes shaved into the side of her scalp, gave Athos a grin that was all teeth. "Nope," she said. "You threw me out a window instead, baby."

"I paid for the damages," he shot back. "And dinner."

"And dinner," Yvonne agreed.

Oh, God, were they flirting? Dana could have done without this insight into Athos' love life. There was no way this conversation could end without extreme violence, and multiple arrests. It was all so civilised, and yet the tension was unbearable.

"And you, Captain-lieutenant Porthos?" said the Cardinal. "Surely you have never come to blows with any of my guards?"

Porthos ran her eye along the line of them, considering. She lingered on the smallest Red Hammer, a man who had to be younger than Dana. He blushed under her gaze. "There may have been an incident involving a tavern bench, but the guidelines on fighting with furniture are more of a grey area."

The Cardinal laughed, a bright and happy sound. "You are all such entertaining company. I can see why D'Artagnan is so attached to you."

Athos' grip tightened on his wine glass.

Another knock sounded on the door. Everyone flinched except Athos and the Cardinal.

One of the bar staff opened the door, looking mortified. "Your Eminence, I am sorry, I believe your appointment is – waiting for you upstairs."

"I thought it must be something like that." The Cardinal drained the last of her wine glass and set it on the table. "I apologise for intruding on your evening, my dears."

"It was a pleasure and an honour," said Athos, rising with her. The Cardinal held her hand out to him. He bent over her ring, kissing it.

"Good evening all," said the most powerful religious leader in the solar system, and made her graceful exit.

The Hammers and Sabres filed out behind her. The door closed.

Dana let out a shaking breath. Aramis and Porthos did the same.

"What was that?" Aramis said incredulously, and then swung around to point an accusing finger at Athos. "Who *are you*? With the manners and the charm and the…"

"The smiling," said Porthos with a shudder.

Dana said nothing. Like the others, she was staring at Athos. She had seen that manic gleam in him before, usually when he was about to throw the first chair, or stab the first attacker in a bar brawl. He glowed all over.

"Ladies," said Athos, purring his words. "This war just got *interesting*."

CHAPTER 16
ATHOS IN THE WALLS

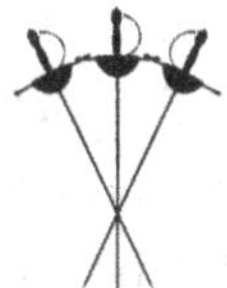

Dovecote Red was Athos' idea of hell. He had never been one for nightclubs: all that noise and movement. Even in his university days, he had not been the one who dragged them out to 'paint the town,' it had been…

No, he would not think of Auden here and now. He was on a mission.

Athos liked having a mission. The best thing about being on duty as a Musketeer was having a straightforward task to achieve, even if it was as simple as 'fly in a straight line from Station A to Satellite B' or 'keep the royal family alive during a public appearance.'

Athos liked being given orders, and he lived in a constant state of background dread that Treville would make one allowance too many for his extracurricular shenanigans, and put him in a position where he was the one giving those orders.

He preferred to be as far as possible from his former self – that young Comte who bore too much responsibility on his shoulders, and screwed up his life so thoroughly that there was nothing but ash and rubble left behind.

The best thing about a war was that you were technically on duty all the time. You had constant purpose.

Tonight, Athos could see his mission parameters as clearly as if Treville had written them out for him in calligraphed longhand on the back of his arm.

His mission was to find out whom Cardinal Richelieu was meeting in an upstairs room of this dive of a nightclub. His duty was to keep his friends safe.

"Wait here for Treville," he said abruptly. "I won't be long." Before Aramis or Porthos or D'Artagnan could protest, he was out the door and striding through the club.

A dark-eyed boy with silver eyeliner – too damn young for Athos, that was for sure – lurched out of the noise and the lights, covered in glitter. "I like your jacket," he said, eyeing Athos up and down.

All his instincts told him to brush this kid off before he got too close – Athos' usual method of getting laid involved arguments or swordplay, and he saved it for opponents who didn't expect him to be kind. He drew the line at flirting with anyone D'Artagnan's age (possibly younger, God, it was hard to tell under all that glitter).

But this was a mission, and he'd look less suspicious going upstairs if he had company. Athos offered the easy, charming smile he had so recently been practicing on the Cardinal. The d'Autevielle smile: a family heirloom.

"Do you want it?" he asked the young man, crowding into his space and sliding off the jacket to wrap it around his shoulders. "It's yours."

Huh. Flirting was easier than picking fights. That was a thought to be examined at a later date.

Ten minutes later, Athos was upstairs with a keycard, arm slung around the glittery boy. It hadn't taken much to convince the club manager – who had served with Treville in the previous war – to hire him a room near (but not suspiciously close) to the Cardinal's rendezvous.

It had been embarrassingly easy to convince the beautiful young man who now owned Athos' Musketeer jacket to come upstairs with him. Charm was a dangerous tool.

The Cardinal's honour guard were positioned along the way, two of them at the top of the stairs, two more in the corridor and the last pair playing cards outside the hired room. None of them paid much attention to the glitter-smeared couple that went past, though Athos was pretty sure at least one of the Sabres gave him a wink.

Inside their room, Athos peeled the young man off him and made for the wall vents. He'd spent a few nights in this club years ago, on a protection detail for the Regence's hen party, and had pulled at least three would-be assassins out of the walls.

Dovecote Red had terrible lighting, awful music and a drinks menu that priced itself far too highly, but its ventilation system was spacious and comfortable.

The glitter-strewn boy threw himself on the bed, watching Athos with a calculating gaze. "This is a spy thing rather than a hookup thing, yeah?"

Couldn't argue that, already busy removing the grate. "Sorry," said Athos. "There's a war on," he added.

"Don't bother me, mate, makes for a better story tomorrow." The boy smirked. "I get to keep the jacket, right?"

Athos rolled his eyes, and hauled himself up into the vent. It was more difficult than it had been three years ago.

Maybe it was time to cut down on the wine. "Yes," he drawled. "You can keep the jacket."

Athos made good time crawling down to the room where the Cardinal and her guest were meeting. All he could hope was that *her* appointment was a spy thing and not a hookup thing, or he had wasted everyone's night.

"… seems to me that your time on Paris Satellite has been entirely wasted." The Cardinal's voice came clearly through the vent. Athos stopped moving. She was angry. "The Marquise de Wardes continued her loyalist sympathies regardless of your involvement – and the Valour government has all but washed their hands of us. What was the point in making it possible for my own agent to take an influential position as Secretary for the Interior if you wield so little of that influence in my favour?"

Athos stilled when he heard 'Secretary for the Interior,' because that answered his question as to the Cardinal's companion in the worst possible way.

Milord. He must think of him as Milord, because if he even began to think of that man as Auden d'Autevielle, he would not get through this.

A warm mouth on his neck, a sly smile in the sunlight, bare feet padding across the ancient floors of the house of his ancestors… Blood, so much blood spilling out across the grass.

"Your Eminence," said a voice that chilled Athos to the bone, "There is a fine line between influence and the ability to steer an entire planetary policy in the opposite direction."

Athos leaned his head against the cool wall and

listened to the voice, to the inflection of every word. He had known about this ever since Dana spilled her secrets but there was a difference between believing it, and hearing it with his own ears.

How are you still alive?

"Your so-called influence has been entirely toxic," the Cardinal replied. "First Minister Beautru was previously neutral on the matter of Valour independence, and never once failed to commit troops and ships to the Crown when requested."

Milord scoffed. "First Minister Beautru is four months away from retirement after three terms of inactivity. His Fleet is controlled by the New Aristocrats who fund each individual regiment. They all see Beautru as a relic of the past, and take their cues from the electoral candidates. While the Marquise de Wardes has indeed managed to spark some of the younger New Aristocrats to her royalist sympathies, the most powerful tastemaker is still the Duchess of Buckingham with her Independence Faction."

Ugh, politics. Valour politics. Athos had gone to a lot of trouble to ensure he never had to care about New Aristocrat posturing bullshit. Now he had to listen to it in his dead husband's voice?

"Buckingham and the rest are obliged to put ships into the air and join this war," the Cardinal said, all but vibrating with fury. "They are not independent yet."

"True enough," said Milord, sounding arch and amused. Did nothing faze the man? "The defence of our solar system is a trending topic, and I might well have been able to convince the charming Buck to join the party as a final gift to the Crown before she rips Valour out of the alliance. Unfortunately, she recently suffered a personal setback culminating in weeks of rehab. Hardly a development that I could have prevented. In Buck's absence from the Gossipnode, it has been assumed that she doesn't give a damn about the war against the Sun-kissed, and therefore the rest of the New Aristocrats of Valour don't have to either."

Cardinal Richelieu was unimpressed. "I am hearing excuses, Milord, when I want solutions. I need fifty new ships at the battle zone by the end of the week, and I want Valour to be the one who provides them."

"We have two obvious options," Milord said, sounding delighted by the challenge. "Either the Duchess of Buckingham must be convinced to lead an armada to war – or the other New Aristocrats must be inspired to do so, by some dramatic event. Nothing like a tragedy to bring people together, don't you think?"

Athos sucked a breath in. He had known for years that his husband was a murderer and a criminal – not to mention an alien spy. Was he really about to hear him plot an assassination?

"Now you're thinking creatively," said the Cardinal. "The Duchess of Buckingham has proved herself a diplomatic liability."

"Are you asking me to kill her, your Eminence?" God, it sounded like Milord was flirting with the woman — a cat offering a dead mouse to his mistress.

"I ask you to use your own judgement," the Cardinal replied.

She couldn't know. Cardinal Richelieu was working with the military needs of the Crown and Solar System as her main priority. She could not possibly know that the agent she had hired was one of the Sun-kissed himself.

If she knew she would never give him this opportunity to control the reinforcements for the Fleet. Would she?

"I will not use my own judgement, your Eminence," said Milord – Auden – Milord, a sharpness in his voice. "Given the high profile of the target, I shall require personal protection to ensure I don't find myself reclassified as 'a diplomatic liability' in the future."

The Cardinal spoke as if words were being physically dragged from her: "Tell me what you have in mind, so that we do not speak at cross purposes."

"I am, as you know, a devout follower of the Church of All, your Eminence," said Milord. "I'd like you to sign a contract."

During the pause that followed, Athos heard his own breathing loudly in his ears.

"Milord de Winter," said the Cardinal, on the verge of laughter. "Do you think it would be appropriate for me to sign a contract ordering the assassination of a popular politician from a planet on the verge of declaring independence?"

"Nothing so specific," said Milord. Clearly he was going to get exactly what he wanted. "But I do require your protection, should I be caught. A sealed stud declaring that the bearer has done whatever they have done in your name and for the good of the solar system – that should be enough."

"Only that?" the Cardinal said. She did laugh this time. "Why, you could commit any murder you liked and be assured of a pardon."

"Yes," purred the man that Athos had once loved more than life itself. "I could, couldn't I? I think I'll start with Dana D'Artagnan."

When Athos returned to the hired room, the boy was gone, leaving only a rumpled bedcover and a pillow covered in a fine film of glitter. That saved him from one awkward conversation.

Athos replaced the vent, washed dust from his hands and face, and checked his messages. There were a series of emoticons on his comm stud from Porthos and Aramis, conveying surprise, impatience, concern, and their mutual belief that he was a dickhead.

From Dana D'Artagnan, he only had a single message:

??

Athos typed:

a little longer

to all three of them, and stepped out into the corridor in time to see the backs of the Cardinal and her guards as they swept out of the premises. There was no sign of Milord.

One moment Athos was standing in the corridor, considering what to do next, and then he was standing before the other door, one hand raised and the sound of his knock still in his ears.

So, they were doing this.

His husband opened the door.

Athos could no longer pretend that he was facing political mastermind and murderous secret agent Milord de Winter, not when the tired and sullen man with the silver hair standing before him was quite obviously the snarky troublemaker he had fallen in love with at university.

He had one moment, one breath in and out to feel glad about it, in a terrible sort of way. Then the anger took over, burning a hole through his chest and propelling him forward, into the room before Auden could shut him out.

"You're here," his husband said, falling back with his eyes wide and troubled. "Olivier…"

"That's not my name," Athos said in a harsh snap. "Believe me, I know the names you're going by these days, *Milord*. Slate. De Winter." Athos had not put it together before, but he remembered a compelling, quiet man in service to the Duchess of Buckingham when she first visited Paris as Ambassador as far back as Joyeux. "Mr Gray." That man had taken the fall for sabotage of the station, gone to prison… but a shape-changer could escape anything. How long had Milord been playing the villain under a variety of faces?

This face was so close to that of his own Auden that it devastated Athos. Why would a shape-changer hold on to the face of a dead man?

Milord's surprise bled away, leaving behind a more professional demeanour. "How lovely to catch up with old friends," he said, closing the door behind Athos. "Shall I print coffee, so we can gossip about the good old days?"

Auden had always been good at turning on that slick, artificial charm. He had used it on professors, on girls trying to flirt with him, on authority figures and members of the close-minded aristocracy who disapproved of their union. He had never before worn his false face at Athos when they were alone together.

Wasn't that a colossal joke? Athos kept forgetting it had

been a false face all along, *every second*, because the memories jumped between what he knew now, and what little he had known then.

Husband, criminal, traitor, assassin.

"Are you a devil after all? You're supposed to be *dead*." Athos meant it as a threat, but it came out half-sad, half-frustrated. "Why are you still here?"

"That's rich, coming from you," snarled Milord. "There's a grave marker on Valour with the Comte de la Fere's name on it."

"Yes," said Athos. "But the difference is, I actually thought I killed you."

Milord smiled, with that familiar twist of his pretty mouth. "Surprise!" he said, deadpan.

"My condolences," Athos drawled, after gathering his dignity around him like a coat. He had to regain control of this conversation, despite his old insecurities. "On the death of your most recent spouse. Delia de Winter, wasn't it? Was your wife aware that you were still contracted to me when you put the ring on her finger?"

Milord gave him a new smile: one Athos had never seen before. "Death ended that contract, sweetness."

"You didn't die," Athos ground between his teeth.

"You have no idea what I did," his husband retaliated. "What I have done."

That made Athos laugh. "I know more than enough. You have crept back and forth from Paris for months, running errands for the Cardinal. Stealing diamonds, drugging the Duchess of Buckingham, kidnapping Conrad Su, and oh yes, attempting to poison Dana D'Artagnan. Not to mention, five minutes ago, you accepted a commission to assassinate a member of the New Aristocracy peerage, in exchange for the Cardinal turning a blind eye to a murder of your own. Did you think I wasn't *paying attention?*"

Milord's eyes widened, as the list – barely a footnote, surely – of his crimes spilled out from Athos' mouth. "You called me a devil," he said finally, with a tilt of his head. "I rather think you are one."

Athos needed to pace, to punch something, to hold a sword in one hand and a drink in another. He held himself still because if he moved, they would be fighting, and he would get none of the answers he needed. "Is your ego so fragile that you would kill a child out of revenge for a spoiled plot or two?"

Milord laughed at that. It didn't sound like Auden's laugh – it was bright and cold and bitter. Athos' husband had been all of those things at one time or another, but he had not laughed like this. "Do you mean Dana? She was a full-grown woman when I took her to my bed. Would you like details?"

"She's barely twenty," Athos ground out. "I don't give a damn about your seductions, but if you hurt her, there will not be enough pieces of you left to stage a second miraculous return from the grave."

Milord leaned back in his chair, humming beneath his breath. "It's killing you, that you don't know how I escaped your murder."

"It was an execution," Athos replied coldly.

"Tell yourself that, sweetness, if it helps you sleep at night." Milord's grey eyes glittered fiercely. "You severed my head from my neck, and you still couldn't put me down. It's eating you up inside."

The only known method for killing one of the Sun-kissed is to sever his head from his body, and burn them both. I did that, it nearly killed me to do it, but I did. What did I do wrong?

Athos threw his arms up in the air, losing the temper he had been holding back for this entire conversation. "Why are you here? Why are you pissing about with the Cardinal's plan to expand the Fleet, of all things? Shouldn't you be with your friends on the other side of the war, ready and aiming to shoot us out of the skies? Or are you still nothing more than a common or garden spy?"

"I have no friends," said Milord, unblinking. "I am not who you think I am. I never was."

Athos stepped towards him. They were an arm's length apart. Then a hand's span. He stopped with barely an inch between their knees, looking down at the seated figure. Milord tipped his head up to maintain eye contact, silver hair falling back from his face. "The teardrops. The alien ships. Your people are at war with ours."

"You are assuming a lot," Milord whispered. "To think that I am working for them."

It was a lie. Of course it was a lie. Athos slid the arc-ray from his belt and pointed it at his husband's face at close range. "If you have no loyalty to your people," he said, allowing a sense of dangerous calm to flood through his body. "Then all you have to bargain for is your safety. Shall we find out how many methods of execution you really are immune from?"

Milord's eyes flickered, but only a little. "I don't fear you, sweetness."

Another lie.

"Give me the stud," said Athos. This was an order he could make.

"What?" Milord was surprised at that, his eyes still fixed on the weapon.

"The sealed stud that the Cardinal gave to you," Athos elaborated. "The contract. I want it."

Milord hesitated. Athos pressed the barrel of the arc-ray directly between his eyes. The alien spy made a frustrated sound and held out his wrist.

There was a dozen or more studs along the pale skin near the vein (did Sun-kissed even have blood in their veins? There had been so much blood when Athos severed his head from his body, but perhaps that was a trick). The one from the Cardinal was obvious – a flat bead of platinum with a red fleur-de-lis stamped into it. Athos peeled it from Milord's wrist, and let it burrow into his own, before activating it with a finger swipe.

Words glowed in the air above his arm:

> *It is by my orders and for the good of Crown and*
> *Solar System that the bearer of this stud has*
> *done what they have done.*
> **Cardinal Richelieu, timestamp 987398Red,**
> **identity sealed.**

Athos nodded, and stepped away from Milord. "Bite us all you like, snake. You will face judgement for your crimes, like everyone else in this damned war."

Having the last word was enough for now. He had realised five minutes ago that he was not capable of killing his husband for a second time, and it was important he not make that weakness too obvious.

Athos, formerly Olivier d'Auteville, the Comte de la

Fere, left the seedy hotel room and walked away from Milord de Winter without looking back.

CHAPTER 17
PICNIC UNDER FIRE

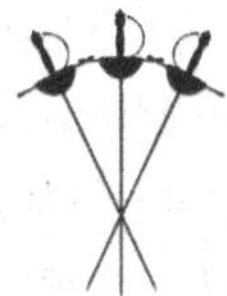

Porthos was worried about Athos.

Porthos always worried about Athos. It was a familiar background noise ever since she and Aramis found the miserable drunkard clinging to the side of a mountain, half-dead and drenched in the mud of Valour so many years ago. Not worrying about Athos was like not sonic-cleaning her teeth – uncomfortable and itchy and *wrong*.

Having said that, there were times in her life when she had particular reason to worry about Athos. His recent brush with a stims overdose in the middle of battle was a fine example, not to mention the many ships he had managed to crash and burn since becoming a Musketeer.

He was made of steel, but fragile. Porthos had seen Athos at his lowest ebb last Joyeux, when he fell victim to a terrorist drug that gave him hallucinations of his dead husband and drove him near suicide.

Now that the husband in question was still alive, *and*

an enemy alien – it should have broken Athos harder than ever.

Porthos was still waiting for evidence that it had not.

When Athos returned to their back-room rendezvous in Dovecote Red, his eyes alight with energy and a goddamn smile on his face, the last thing she expected him to say was: "I know where Milord is going next. And I know how to stop him. Where's the boss?"

"Hang on," said Porthos, wanting to get this straight. "You saw him?"

"Yes, we had a lovely chat. Seriously, where's Treville?"

"She couldn't make it," Aramis said. "Sent a brief coded message by Fleetnet – she's stuck on the Bastion for the foreseeable future. They're under extreme fire from the Sun-kissed, and no shuttles can safely go back and forth."

"Fine," said Athos, grinning like a lunatic. "We'll go to her. Pack a picnic. It'll be fun."

Aramis blinked. "They're under extreme fire from the Sun-kissed right now. *No shuttles can safely go back and forth*," she repeated with greater force.

"Darts are faster and more manoeuvrable than shuttles," said Athos as if that was a reasonable response.

"Athos," said Dana. "You spoke to Milord? Why didn't you arrest him?"

"He's so far in the Cardinal's pocket, she'd spring him before we had the handcuffs closed," said Athos cheerfully. "But he's already failed her once, with the diamond bullshit. If we make sure he fails his next mission, I think she'll finally wash her hands of him. That's when we can move in and nab him for good."

"And what is his next mission?" Porthos asked, seriously wondering if they needed to call in a medic to give

Athos a shot of something. When had he last slept? When had any of them?

"To assassinate the Duchess of Buckingham," said Athos. "Come on, to the Bastion. I wasn't kidding about the picnic. Treville's always more amenable to crazy stunts if she's not hungry. Is there anywhere around here that sells pastry?"

At least he was admitting that the stunt was crazy. "Athos, we can't get to the Bastion," said Aramis. Treville's command ship, the *Saint-Gervais*, was referred to as 'the Bastion' because it had almost impregnable space armour. "We'll get shot out of the sky by the Sun-kissed if we try to board her."

"I know," said Athos. "But if we disappear in the middle of this war without warning Treville, it will be our own people who shoot us out of the sky. I say it's worth the risk. Also, pastry." He nodded, as if he was making complete and total sense.

"You're going to get us killed," groaned Dana. "Mercilessly. If not by the Sun-kissed, then by Amiral Treville."

Porthos sighed. "I can source the pastry," she admitted.

There was nothing in the known universe Porthos had achieved in her life more fortunate than hiring an engie who was a stress baker. Bonnie was easy-going most of the time – with her huge, sprawling family who genuinely seemed to like each other, and her no-nonsense philosophy on life, she was the most well-adjusted person that Porthos knew.

When they were setting the *Hoyden* up together, back

when Porthos first joined the Musketeers, Bonnie's one demand had been a bread oven along with the more standard food printer. When Porthos protested, (she hadn't known any better) Bonnie devoted the next twelve hours to teaching her the difference between printed and freshly-baked bread.

Porthos had never argued with Bonnie (about anything kitchen related) ever again.

That was before she realised that when under pressure, or stressed, or bored (or any combination of the three), her engie would bake her way into infinity and beyond.

War, with its long waits between short bursts of terror and danger, was highly stressful, and allowed for a great deal of uninterrupted baking time.

Porthos had no idea if Athos knew that her ship was basically full of baked goods at this point, or if he had subconsciously picked up the scent of chocolate ganache croissant where it had infused into her uniform, but his request was, for once, easy to fulfil.

At least, the pastry part was.

Two hours after Athos burst into the back room with wild eyes and a determination to crush Milord and the Cardinal in a bizarre pastry-related scheme, Porthos stood on the bridge of the *Saint-Gervais* musket-class base, holding a covered basket and feeling like an idiot.

Amiral Treville, her massive, muscled shoulders expanding as she faced them down, vibrated with fury. "WHAT THE HELL KIND OF STUNT WAS THAT?"

Athos gave Treville his wickedest grin, the one he

saved for special occasions, like having to explain how he nearly got himself and his friends shot out of the sky while technically off duty.

Not that special, once you started adding all those occasions up.

"Boss, we had urgent intelligence and it really couldn't wait…" he began, but Treville cut him off.

"The four of you sailed directly through a barrage of enemy fire, during an active operation, to board a command vehicle without prior notification over the comms? Oh, and you did it in a bright green dart which is not yet cleared for battle. Nor is its stupid, foolhardy, reckless addict of a pilot."

Athos's grin widened. "You forgot to mention the part where we brought you pastry. Pastry!"

Treville's eyes bulged. Porthos had never seen her angrier.

"I'd like to interject at this point and let you know that I personally checked Athos' blood readings before letting him fly us here, and he's sober," Aramis said helpfully.

Treville took this new intelligence on board. "Is there some reason that should be a surprise to me, Captain Aramis?"

Aramis thought about what she had just said. "No," she said finally. "But it might also be of casual relevance to the conversation that he's also not currently on any narcotics. Except coffee."

Porthos was trying to look like an innocent accomplice but she thought it more likely that her own face currently said: 'looking for an airlock to jump out of.'

"So this…" Treville said, waving vaguely at Athos'

chipper demeanour, and the way he was bouncing enthusiastically on his heels.

"Natural high, boss," Aramis informed her.

"No," Treville decided. "There's nothing natural about that smile on his face."

Athos blew her a kiss.

"Ready room, all of you," Treville barked, marching towards her private quarters. "Lacroix, you have the helm. Try not to get us blown up while I'm shouting at Musketeers."

"To be fair, boss, that is the way you'd want to go out," and oh, Porthos had said that out loud. What the hell had got into her?

Treville gave her a filthy look. "Bring the damned picnic, Captain Porthos," she ordered.

The basket contained a warm orange honey cake that Bonnie's grandmother had taught her to make, something sticky involving chocolate and cherries, and a pastry affair with cinnamon custard that Porthos wanted to hug to her chest and defend from the harsh perils of the solar system.

For Treville, whose tastes always leaned more towards the savoury, there were a selection of croissants, sausage rolls, and crumbly quiches that smelled of three kinds of cheese, rosemary and happiness.

Since Athos had supervised the packing of the basket, there were also two flasks of champagne, and three of hot coffee. Under Treville's judgy eye, while Porthos served out pastries and wedges of cake with napkins and tiny forks, Aramis poured the coffee and discreetly nudged the champagne back under the cloth for later.

"So," said Treville, once she had downed one and a half cups of powerful espresso, and fully appreciated several bite-sized quiches. "Athos. What the fuck."

"Sentiment echoed over here," said Aramis, waving her own fork. "Assassinations. Milord. Conspiracies. Buckingham. Discuss."

"Right," said Athos, who had not touched the pastry in front of him, but held on to his cup of coffee as if he planned to live there forever. "This might be a long story."

"I will actually kill you," Porthos remarked.

Athos got to his feet and began to circle the room. This was bad. Athos always had trouble organising his thoughts when seated, and preferred to be active. If they weren't careful, he might end up doing sword lunges in the middle of their impromptu picnic.

Porthos stood up, went to him, unfastened the pilot's slice from his belt, and returned to the table. "Continue," she suggested, and saw everyone around the table give a small sigh of relief that he was no longer armed.

Athos gave her a wounded look. "Fine. The Cardinal has hired Milord de Winter to assassinate the Duchess of Buckingham." He glanced at Treville. "We're going to need your official order to head to Valour at all speed and arrest the assassin, before he gets to her."

Treville considered this. Chewed and swallowed a mouthful of buttery croissant. "With all due respect to the Duchess of Buckingham, she has her own security. Explain why I am going to allow four essential members of personnel – because it's too much to fucking hope that you don't all expect to go on this mercy dash together – to leave the battle zone and play bodyguard to a pampered aristocrat from a planet about to secede from the solar system any minute, that has barely contributed any resources to the war effort?"

'Why I am going to,' Porthos noted, not *'Why should I?'* Honestly, none of them deserved the trust that Treville placed in them. Athos least of all, when he had pissed away so many second chances.

"Because," said Athos, circling the table full of Musketeers and pastry as he arranged his thoughts, one foot in front of the other. He struggled to get further than that. "Because…"

"If you could manage to explain without further maligning the reputation of her Eminence the Cardinal, that would help," Treville added.

"Yes, I can see that," Athos mused. "It's a challenge, but I'll try. The Cardinal's plan is well-intentioned. She blames Buckingham's influence – and her recent well publicised breakdown and retreat from public affairs – for the lack of enthusiasm towards this war. Among the New Aristocrats on Valour, anyway. She believes that if carefully managed, Buckingham's death would work as a call to arms."

"Interesting," said Treville. "Tell me again why I am against the scheme if it means more ships on our side?"

"Because," said Athos. "What the Cardinal does not know is that her agent poses a terrible danger to the Crown and the Solar System. He cannot be trusted to follow her agenda, or to do anything that is in the interests of humankind."

Treville finished her croissant, and started on the sausage roll. Porthos had eaten one already — they were pleasantly spicy and just the right temperature. "You think de Winter is a spy for the enemy?"

"He is a Sun-kissed," Dana blurted, and then drew her eyes back down to her cake. "We know that much."

"We know more than that," said Athos, throwing a sympathetic glance at Dana, though the kid didn't look up in time to see it. "Milord has infiltrated the Valour government, rising to a high position. He has acted directly against Crown and Solar System, and I believe he is responsible for acts of terrorism in Paris last year."

Porthos almost swallowed her cake fork. "The Joyeux attacks? Athos, are you serious?"

"I knew it when I looked into his eyes tonight," Athos said calmly, as if he was not talking about a man he had once loved and married. "We know he goes by pseudonyms like Slate and Winter in the course of his work – and the suspect we arrested for those crimes called himself Gray. I thought at the time there was something familiar about him, but could never quite place it… and, you might remember, he escaped prison custody after faking his own death. A favourite trick."

There was the bitterness Porthos had been waiting to hear, some hint that yes, this was personal for Athos. She had worried that he was compartmentalising the situation a little too effectively. Now she had whole new things to worry about.

"You want us to thwart Milord in this scheme, hoping that the Cardinal will drop her protection of him, and we can bring him into custody permanently," Dana said softly, lifting her face to Athos as if the two of them were the only ones in the room. "Save the Duchess of Buckingham, catch the spy."

"And convince Buckingham to lead the New Aristocrats of Valour into this war," Athos added. "That's the carrot for you, boss. We'll follow the Cardinal's wishes and bring you ships of Valour to help with the siege – and we'll do it without assassinating anyone."

"An alien spy and a flotilla of imaginary ships," said Treville. "Is it my birthday, Athos?"

"We did bring pastry," he said hopefully.

The Amiral nodded. "And does anyone wish to tell me why this de Winter – who, regardless of the Cardinal's protection, is a high-ranking New Aristocrat official of the Valour government and thus has considerable resources of his own – is of any interest to my Musketeers? How can you be so sure that he is a Sun-kissed spy, and why does it matter so damned much to you that he be stopped?"

Athos stopped pacing near Dana, and stared at Treville as if she had shot a puppy in front of him.

"Milord personally requested to be freed from the legal consequences of murdering D'Artagnan as a reward for his work," he said quietly. "He holds a grudge."

Treville gave him a thin smile. "That sounds like the end of a story, Captain Athos, not the beginning."

Dana took a deep breath, ready to take over her part of the conversation. "I should probably explain about Conrad Su…"

"No," Athos said, his hand briefly brushing her shoulder. "No, shut up, D'Artagnan, it's okay. It's time she knew all of it." He glanced at Porthos with a silent entreaty.

"Come on, you two," Porthos said brightly. "Let's go take a turn about the deck and see how many aliens are shooting at the Bastion right now. It will be fun." She hooked one arm around Aramis's elbow and collected

Dana on the way out, leaving Athos and Treville facing each other down across a crumb-strewn meeting table.

"So," said Athos, as the door spiralled open to let his friends out of what Porthos was already mentally dubbing The Embarrassment Zone. "Fun story, boss. I used to be married…"

After twenty minutes or so loitering outside Treville's door, Dana D'Artagnan was making herself sick with worry. Or possibly she had eaten too much cake. "She won't actually kill him and ditch the body out an airlock, will she?"

"If she was ever going to do that to Athos, it would have been when he grew the beard," Porthos assured her.

"He's her favourite," Aramis added gravely.

Porthos had literally bet on Athos in the 'Musketeer most likely to be murdered by our boss' sweepstake, but she wasn't going to argue with either of them.

When Athos finally emerged, he looked wrecked, as if Treville had beaten him around the head with her office furniture. He had lost all of the manic picnic energy that he had used to fuel their flight here.

"So?" asked Aramis. "Are we riding into the sunset to rescue you-know-who and arrest that other fellow?"

"Subtle," Porthos complimented her.

"I thought so," Aramis preened.

"No," said Athos in a rough voice. "No, we're not." He looked directly at Dana, as if this was only the start of the terrible news he had to break to her. "Treville's not letting us go, and I can't change her mind."

CHAPTER 18
I JUST CALLED TO SAY I'M GROUNDED

The four of them hustled off the bridge and along a series of grey corridors on the Bastion, which mostly went around in circles. Dana suspected they weren't heading anywhere in particular, but that Athos was moving for the sake of not punching walls.

"She wouldn't let us go after Buckingham?" Porthos asked.

Athos growled under his breath. "Need somewhere we won't be overheard. In here." He lurched them into a storage space that turned out to be more of a cupboard than a room, full of humming printers.

"Is it me?" Dana asked. "She wants me to go back to my duties on the *Frenzy Kenzie*?"

"No, you're definitely off that detail," said Athos with a vague wave of his hand. "Porthos and Aramis are to return to their own ships in the armoured shuttle after the next ceasefire. But you and me, Dana, we're assigned to the Bastion for the foreseeable future."

Aramis and Porthos stared at Athos with wide, startled

eyes. "Athos, what did you *say* to her?" Aramis asked in alarm.

"The truth," he said impatiently.

Dana swallowed hard. "How much of the truth?"

"Pretty much all of it. I was trying for honesty points." Athos looked weary.

"And how did that work out for you?" asked Porthos.

Athos winced visibly. "I made a major miscalculation. Two miscalculations, but at least one of them was based on information I didn't even have at the time."

Aramis leaned into Athos, one hand stroking his hair. "Breathe, darling, and try to talk at human speed for the sake of us mortals. What's the problem?"

Athos calmed down at Aramis' touch. "Our problem is that Treville doesn't give a fuck about whether the Duchess of Buckingham lives or dies. She thinks the Cardinal's plan to squeeze more ships out of Valour is stupid and won't work, but she's not willing to let all four of us scupper it."

"But she knows now about Milord," Dana burst out. "Surely she must understand how important it is to discredit him in the eyes of the Cardinal…"

"… And get him out of play," Porthos added grimly.

"Yes," said Athos. He looked miserable. That couldn't be good. "She does understand that. But Treville has her own priorities. It turns out that the Sun-kissed have made diplomatic overtures. In twelve hours, the Regence will be communicating directly with whoever is in charge of all those shape-shifting red blobs in their shape-shifting grey teardrop ships, and we get to find out if there's anyone still alive down on Truth."

Aramis' hand stopped stroking Athos' hair. "Oh," she

said in a whisper. "I can see how that is more important than an assassination attempt on Valour."

"But that has nothing to do with us," repeated Dana. "Not directly, at least. Right?" She was still trying to get her head around the part where she had been released from her duties on the supplies transport. Why?

Athos gave Dana an apologetic look. "The problem is – the other problem, on a very long list of problems – is that I just revealed to Treville that you and I have both had recent personal experience with a Sun-kissed spy. So she wants to keep us here on the Bastion, in order to answer all the intrusive and embarrassing questions that may or may not come up during the negotiations with the Sun-kissed."

Dana let her head fall back against the nearest printer with a thunk.

"You know," Porthos said after a moment of long and awkward silence. "I always thought if one of us ended up entangled in a highly political alien sex scandal, it would be Aramis."

Dana kicked her in the ankle.

"What now?" Aramis asked, her fingers continuing to scratch lightly at Athos' scalp. "How long before Porthos and I have to be back on regular duty?"

"Two hours until the next shuttle back to Chaillot Station," said Athos. "Which gives us a short window in which to save the Duchess of Buckingham's life and screw over Milord de Winter without leaving the war zone. Any suggestions?"

"Chevreuse, obviously," said Aramis.

"Yes," said Athos. "She can warn Buck, at least. Maybe send support, though we're going to need someone on the ground. Who do we know on Valour?"

"The Countess of Clarick," said Dana thoughtfully.

That took Athos aback. "You mean the one with all the New Aristocrat wanker friends we had the duel against?"

"She's Milord's sister-in-law. She's crazy loyal about her family, but – I don't know if she'd still be on his side if she knew the truth about what he is and where he comes from."

"Devious," Athos said admiringly. "I like it. There's also the embarrassing possibility that I'm still married to the bastard, which means I get to have a delightful conversation with her about breach of contract and bigamy. Porthos. Got any convenient boyfriends in positions of power, influence or really sharp swords anywhere on Valour who could get to Buck before Milord does?"

"My boyfriends tend to be conveniently located around Paris," said Porthos. "Not that it's not still faster to get to Valour from Paris than from here. But…" She looked at Aramis, who rolled her eyes and groaned with genuine pain.

"No."

"It's not a bad idea."

"It's a *terrible* idea."

"Well, if you will go having affairs with married women who storm off to become important people on other planets…"

"But she *hates* me."

"We're not talking about Chevreuse again, are we?" asked Athos, frowning.

"Felton," sighed Aramis. "We're talking about Jan Felton. Who quit the Red Hammers to take up a position as a Planetary Marshal on Castillion, two years ago."

Athos blinked again. "But Jan Felton *hates* you."

"She hates me so much," Aramis agreed.

"We'll bring her in. Can't afford to be choosy. Comms centre, let's get messaging." Athos made a shooing motion, and pushed Aramis and Porthos out of the printer cupboard. He glanced back briefly over his shoulder at Dana as he went. "Oh, and we have to call D'Artagnan's mother. Add that to the list."

Dana was startled. "Maman? Why?"

Athos waved his hand airily. "Treville finally promoted you to Captain-lieutenant, as a Musketeer. Mothers like to know that sort of thing."

Aramis and Porthos crowed with delight. Athos grabbed each of them by the neck and propelled them along the corridor, leaving Dana gaping on her own in a cupboard full of printers.

"What," was all she could think of to say. "No, really. *What?*"

The *Saint-Gervais*, AKA the Bastion, had many facilities and resources not enjoyed by standard Fleet ships – not only the impregnable shielding and a complete inability to use offensive weaponry, but also a state-of-the-art comms centre.

Athos had been right to bring them here. The Bastion was designed to be the final hold-out for high-ranking personnel, and not only boasted a good range of highly secured military frequencies (the lines of communications that made jump engines feasible) but the luxury of privacy booths and access to those same securities for personal calls.

Aramis and Porthos stayed long enough for Aramis to make discreet calls to Chevreuse, and to Marshal Felton. They had to leave after that, queuing for the shuttle back to Chaillot Station so they could return to their ships and the Fleet.

Dana knew that it was less dangerous for Aramis and Porthos to fly back on the official shuttle than it had been with Athos in the *Pistachio*, dodging and weaving the laser blasts from the Sun-kissed on their way here, but it felt worse somehow, whenever the four of them were separated.

Not Dana and her three Musketeers. They were the four Musketeers now. It would take her a while to get used to that idea.

Athos was enclosed in one of the privacy booths, continuing a long and possibly painful conversation with Bianca de Winter, the Countess of Clarick. Dana had squeezed in there with him long enough to make the introductions – should Bee fail to recognise the man who had so effortlessly kebabbed one of her friends with a rapier-length pilot's slice back on Paris Satellite – but she withdrew once Athos began telling his story.

Dana was proud of him. He had concealed his true identity for so long, keeping Athos the Musketeer as far as possible from the troubled and officially deceased Comte de la Fere. Now it was all spilling out, for the sake of Crown and Solar System and the life of the Duchess of Buckingham.

What would Athos do without that layer of secrecy?

They had attempted to get a call directly through to Villiers House, where the Duchess of Buckingham lived. According to the app Planchet had made for Dana a million years ago, which gathered all of Buck's appearances on the Gossipnode, the athletic duchess had become a digital hermit in recent weeks. There was no hint that she had stepped outside her home in days. So why wouldn't she accept the call? They kept trying.

Perhaps Chevreuse would have better luck.

Dana leaned back against the smooth, white curve of the privacy booth wall, wondering if Athos was done with his call yet, and whether Bee would prove to be an ally. They had decided to tell her the truth. It wasn't like Athos had not already tipped Milord off that they knew his plans.

At least – and it was a small thing to be grateful for – Milord no longer had that sealed stud from the Cardinal, promising amnesty for any crime he cared to commit. Dana had been trying very hard not to think about the fact that Milord wanted her death as a personal reward.

Worst fling ever.

She hit the call key again and watched a still image of Villiers House, in the duchy of Buckingham, on the continent of Castillion, on the planet Valour, fill the screen as she waited for the signal to tell her that the call had not been accepted.

This time, the screen flickered and gave way to a friendly amber-brown face with gold scales running down the edge of his cheek and neck, and blue-tipped spiky black hair.

Goddamn, she had forgotten how beautiful Conrad Su was. He wore loose practice gear, caught in the middle of laughing at someone else's joke. "Villiers House," he said, and did a double take at the screen. "Holy shit."

"Hey," said Dana, laughing at him. "Miss me?"

"Always," Conrad said, recovering a little of his usual swagger. "How did you even know I was hiding out here?"

"I didn't. I called for Buck."

"Now I am disappointed." Conrad pulled an expression that made her want to reach through the screen and smack him, or possibly kiss his face off.

Yeah, who was she even kidding with those options.

"I'm being serious," she told him sternly. "Has anything unusual happened lately?"

"Buck keeps to herself. I've hardly managed to get her to joust with me at all, though she has a kickass zero-G practice tank in her back garden. Luckily she hires security guards who like their sport, so I can usually find someone off duty to play with me. Keeps me from going completely stir crazy."

Dana grazed her lower lip with her teeth. "No security issues?"

"We've had word from the local Marshal to be on alert, and we've stepped up house and perimeter patrols," said Conrad, his face losing some of its customary humour. "You had something to do with that?"

Felton was on it, after being alerted by Aramis to the situation. That was good to know.

"There's been an assassination threat," said Dana. She hesitated to say it out loud, but these comm lines were the best they were likely to ever have access to, and it wasn't as if they wanted it to be a state secret. Still, part of her felt that if she said the name out loud, then Conrad would figure out everything – her stupid behaviour around Milord, for a start – and she hadn't realised until now that she really, really did not want him to know what an idiot she had been.

Huh. Something to emotionally unpack at some point. But not right now.

"A threat to Buck?" Conrad asked, switching quickly from flirtatious to businesslike.

"Given your history with the assassin in question, you're both at risk."

"Ah," Conrad sighed, tilting his head tiredly to one side. "Our silver-haired friend?"

"He doesn't always look the same," said Dana. "He could look like *anyone*, Conrad."

The tailor whistled beneath his breath. "I've heard of tech like that."

"So have I," Dana said pointedly. "But he doesn't have to use it."

His expression froze over as her meaning got across. There was only one known alien race that could change their faces as easily as their clothes, and the solar system was currently at war with them.

"Fuck," said Conrad.

"I know."

"I mean, *fuck*. We took on new security today, Dana."

"He's not there yet," Dana assured him. "He can't be. He was on Chaillot Station less than six hours ago. Even if he uses jump, even if he switches ships at Peace so there's no waiting, it will be at least another day before he gets to Valour."

"But when he gets here," Conrad said sombrely. "He could look like anyone, and he'll be gunning for Buck."

Dana could see his brain working behind his eyes. He was already figuring out the best way to keep the Duchess safe. Conrad had spent his whole life doing this for Alek, and now he had another selfish, privileged New Aristocrat to babysit.

"Get out of there," Dana urged him. "Hop a transport for Paris, you're not his target yet."

If Milord turned up at Villiers House and found Conrad Su there, so soon after Prince Alek had freed him from captivity… it was impossible to believe that he wouldn't take a moment to enact a personal revenge.

"Yeah, that's not going to happen," said Conrad with a biting smile. "Anything else I should know?"

Dana hesitated. There was something else, something that had been churning around in her head since her own first trip to Valour. She hadn't articulated it to Athos and the others. She wasn't sure if it was too crazy for even them to accept.

"When I met Buck," she said slowly. "You know, when I went to collect – that mission you sent me on." Secured line or no secured line, she was not going to say the words 'Prince Consort's diamond studs' aloud.

"I remember," said Conrad, his mouth curving into a smile that made Dana feel warm all over.

"She was having a breakdown. She seemed to think – she called him Winter. She said that a version of him, the scary silver-haired assassin version, was actually inside her head. Watching her. She kept herself drugged or drunk or both, to keep him at bay. It could just be paranoia…"

"But she could be compromised," Conrad said slowly. "I get you."

"I mean, a person can't just climb inside another person's brain…"

"Can't they?" said Conrad, his dark eyes fastening on

hers. "I get it, Dana. You're saying that I can't trust that Buck's decisions will be in her own best interest."

"Yes," said Dana, blowing out a sigh of relief. "That's what I'm saying."

"Good to know." He gave her a smirk. "When can I expect you to ride in to save the day?"

"You can't." Guilt rose up in her. "We have orders to stay here. Hopefully – he won't even get near the house. But keep your guard up."

"Always do." Conrad winked at her. "Don't suppose you have a personal comm code I can use? To keep you in the loop."

Dana hadn't even thought of that – this was how unsettled she was, just from seeing him. She leaned in and pressed her wrist to the transmission screen, giving Conrad the code of the Prince Consort's opal that she still wore. She and Athos had pawned the La Fere sapphire to fund the restoration of the *Pistachio* and the *Buttercup*, so she was free to hang on to the opal for the time being.

It felt appropriate for Conrad. It made sense to keep him off her general comm, from which she received Fleetnet communications.

Conrad grinned as he received the code. "I like the jacket, by the way," he observed. "The Musketeer look is so hot this season."

Dana felt her cheeks grow warm. "It belongs to Aramis. I haven't had a chance to print one of my own yet, and she didn't want me to wait."

"I assume that means congratulations are in order," Conrad said slyly. "Captain D'Artagnan. I knew you were going places the first time I laid eyes on you."

"Oh?" Dana teased. "Was that before or after I tackled you to the ground?"

"Definitely during." He kissed his palm and pressed it to the screen. "Take care of yourself, Dana. With that whole interstellar war thing you've got going on over there. Come home in one piece, yeah?"

"You too," she said, her throat feeling dry. There was something so intimate about him asking her to 'come home'. Slowly, she leaned in and brushed her lips to the screen. "Keep in touch, Conrad."

"You too, babe. Bring me back something pretty from the war."

End call.

CHAPTER 19
SUNRISE AT THE
SIEGE OF TRUTH

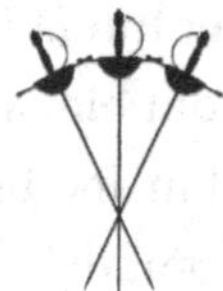

Athos was wrecked after his private call to his former (current?) dead husband's sister-in-law. Dana was equally wrecked after the conversation with Conrad, followed by the emotional tennis match that was her call to Maman.

Every silence between their words was heavy with the loss of her Papa, and how Dana hadn't been there, not only for the disaster on Gascon Station and the medical fallout that came after, but also the hard work that was going on right now, to restore the station and save the community.

They were all so far away. Truth was technically closer to Freedom. But there were whole hours, entire days, when Dana's chaotic life had distracted her so sufficiently that she almost forgot that her Papa was dead and her childhood home in ruins.

Because of the Sun-kissed. It always came back to them.

Even with the good news to share about her promotion

(*your Papa would be so proud, your Papa always believed you would make it*) to the rank and status of 'proper Musketeer,' Dana felt a stab of guilt as if her Maman knew that Dana did not spend nearly enough time thinking about home.

When they emerged from their respective privacy booths, Athos and Dana looked at each other, and both said: "You look like shit," in unison. They calculated the time, and decided that since they were officially off duty until this meeting with the Sun-kissed, they could afford two hours to get filthy, stinking drunk and another six hours to sleep (if sleep was even possible) in the basic bunks Treville had assigned them on the Bastion, before slapping on all the Sobriety patches in the solar system and pretending to be respectable members of the Royal Fleet.

It was not the most responsible decision Dana had ever made, and she was well aware of her hypocrisy at enabling Athos in his self-destructive behaviour, when she had been so very angry at him back on the *Frenzy Kenzie*.

But damn, she needed it.

They woke up tangled together in a single bunk, fully clothed and feeling like death warmed up.

"Why didn't we use the Sobriety patches before we went to sleep?" Dana groaned with her head pressed underneath a fresh-printed pillow so stiff it might give her a paper cut.

"Wouldn't have slept if sober," Athos grumbled.

After a brief tussle in which they discovered that old age and treachery was indeed superior to youth when it came to fighting over who got to use the sonic shower first (who knew that Athos had quite so many elbows?) they dressed themselves in flight suits and jackets. Dana still had the one from Aramis, while Athos had to suffer a newly printed garment after some sort of mishap at Dovecote Red that he would not discuss. They buzzed each other's hair short, and stepped back to examine the results in the mirror.

"The pride of the Royal Fleet," Athos said with grim satisfaction.

Dana trod on his foot. "Don't be bitter. We scrub up okay."

The first day of intergalactic diplomacy was dull. Athos and Dana were relegated to a side gallery where they could observe and be called upon if necessary.

It was not necessary.

The Regence, the Cardinal and Amiral Treville sat together at a central table. Surrounding them were what turned out to be a team of expert linguists, xenobiologists and code-breakers, all there to aid communication between the Sun-kissed and the representatives of the human Solar System.

Three Mendaki were present among the 'alien experts' presumably because they were aliens themselves, though Dana was not sure how that meant they had any perspective on the psychology of the Sun-kissed. Still, they had brought a hefty array of translation units with them.

Five minutes before communications formally opened, a messenger arrived, and had private words with Cardinal Richelieu, before climbing the short stairs to join Athos and Dana in the side gallery.

Dana was not even surprised that it turned out to be

Agent Rosnay Cho, with her usual sweep of hair tucked under a black Raven cap, and a black flight suit to match. Dana was used to the idea now that Ro might turn up anywhere, at any time.

"What are you doing here?" Dana asked, nevertheless. "Who's in command of the *Frenzy Kenzie*?"

"Classified," said Ro, placing a finger to her lips. "And also, I don't remember. A Sabre, I think. Jussac?"

"That's worse than you," said Dana in horror.

"I'll take that as a compliment," preened Ro.

"The *Frenzy Kenzie* is a Musketeer supplies transport, why would they put a Sabre in command?"

Ro lifted one shoulder in a lazy shrug. "Perhaps the Regence has finally accepted that the solar system would be more efficient if the Church ran everything?"

"Let me guess," Athos drawled. "You're in here because you're another member of the 'I have intimate knowledge of Milord de Winter' club."

Ro smirked as she took a seat a little way from them both. "Well," she said. "Not as intimate as you, as it turns out."

Athos glared at her. Ro stared back, her mouth curved up, and the two of them faced off against each other in a long, silent challenge.

The only thing that stopped Dana beating her head against the wall was that she was starting to worry about brain damage.

It didn't get better once the Sun-kissed delegation appeared on the bright digital screens of the meeting room, largely because they refused to communicate in any known language.

There were sounds, and bursts of light, and some kind

of static chatter. The experts all scrambled to identify the language, but it was harder than they had imagined.

"Now we know something new about the Sun-kissed," Athos said quietly as he observed the chaos in the main gallery.

"Yes, they're arseholes," Ro replied, deadpan.

Athos gave her a look that was half surprise and half appreciation.

Dana stifled a laugh. "How do you figure that?"

"They speak our language," said Athos. "We know they do. Aud – Milord isn't the only one. The last war saw at least forty or fifty spies dropped among the Fleet itself, and seeded in the various planetary communities – and that's the ones we know about. They looked like us and they damn well spoke like us. They can do it any time they like."

"The Amiral and the Cardinal were both active during the last war," Ro observed. "They're well aware of this."

"Must be why her Eminence is twitching so much," said Athos.

"She's big on the value of time," said Ro. "Wasting time is up there with Elementalism on her Eminence's list of personal hates."

"It's not a waste, though, is it?" Dana mused. "Surely it's better for us to learn how to communicate with them properly if we're going to have any kind of long-term diplomacy with their people."

Athos and Ro exchanged a weary look.

"She's so young," Athos said conversationally.

"Tell me about it," agreed Ro.

Dana was indignant. "I don't need you two ganging up on me! You're only cranky because you know I'm right."

Six days later, Dana was prepared to admit that she was wrong. She still believed that it was important that humans learned to communicate with the Sun-kissed in their own language. On the other hand… was there *seriously* no way to hurry the process up?

Some progress had been made. The last two days had featured more muttered, excitable conversations among the translation team, and less of the glazed eyes and desperate panic that had characterised the early sessions.

For Dana, Athos and Ro, it had been an interminably dull week in which lights flashing on screens and experts getting excited about sound frequencies were not the focus of their attention.

No, *their* focus was on the tournament of noughts and crosses between the three of them, and the elaborate system of rewards, forfeits and handicaps they had devised to make the game more of a challenge.

Dana might or might not have lost too many matches because of the deeply unfair 'lose a mark off the board if you smile at a cute text from your non-boyfriend in exile' rule. She was dangerously close to earning a dread 'truth or dare' forfeit when Treville interrupted them.

"Fruit break already, boss?" Athos asked languidly, not even looking up from where he was sprawled on the bench. "You spoil us."

Treville looked at the three of them with a mixture of impatience and resignation. "I don't suppose you were paying attention to today's work?"

"We did try," said Ro, who had a startled school child expression on her face, obviously less accustomed to

Amiral Treville taking notice of her, let alone disapproving of her behaviour. "But the effects of paying attention are so similar to the effects of a migraine, that…"

"Yes, I get the picture. What about you, D'Artagnan?"

"I wasn't napping?" Dana ventured. "What was it you particularly wanted our feedback on, boss?"

It was the first time she had called Treville 'boss' since becoming a Musketeer, and it sent a little thrill through her.

Treville crossed her arms. "We've been making progress. The latest breakthrough in communications has revealed something of our adversary's motives."

Athos looked at least slightly alert. "What about Truth?"

"They've promised us that they will open a channel to the planet to prove that the majority of the population are still alive down there."

"That's good," said Dana. "Isn't it?"

"That depends," drawled Ro. "On what it cost."

Treville flicked her gaze in Ro's direction, and nodded. "They want something from us as a gesture of good faith."

"Is it something within our power?" Athos asked, all seriousness.

Treville blew out a breath. "They believe we are harbouring a criminal who has been condemned to death in absentia by their government, and they are prepared to destroy us, planet by planet, to get him back into their custody."

Athos frowned. "So why can't we just…" and then he paused.

Dana was way ahead of him. Her own awkward pause joined his to become an epic silence of embarrassment.

It couldn't be, could it?

"Holy shit," said Ro, and started laughing maniacally. "I guess you two are here for a good reason after all."

"We don't know for certain," said Treville. "There are – roadblocks to identifying this criminal."

Athos squared his shoulders. "Show us what you have, and D'Artagnan and I will see if it's who we all think it is – shut the hell up, Agent Cho, it's not funny."

"It really is kind of funny," Ro gasped. "Because, come on. Who else is it going to be?"

Milord Vaniel de Winter stepped off the *Matagot* and into a cluster of assistants and bureaucrats ready to inform him about all the work he needed to catch up on between the space dock and Prime House, the centre of government on Valour.

He did love politics but oh, there were times when the paperwork seriously got in the way of being a covert assassin.

Vaniel was like a comfortable, finely tailored suit – Milord had something of a soft spot for this identity, who was kinder and wittier than most of the personalities he had developed over the years. More ambitious than Linton Gray, the soft-spoken diplomatic aide (and covert religious terrorist); more clever and careful than Slate the Raven (and occasional kidnapper); certainly saner than the wildly destructive Winter, who existed mostly as a hallucinogenic virus inside the heads of his enemies.

The mission prickled under his skin, a constant distraction as he signed forms, made decisions, and agreed to meetings he probably would never attend.

"First Minister Beautru wishes to receive you at your earliest convenience," said Nonja, a flat-faced and humourless young woman who was excellent at scheduling but hell to share an office with.

Milord missed the snarky, glitter-strewn irreverence of Kitty and her space ponies. There were many reasons for which he wished to murder Dana D'Artagnan with his own bare hands, but depriving him of his favourite assistant was high on that list.

"Back at the office," he said firmly. "We'll sort out a timetable for essential appointments."

There was a government-issue skimmer waiting for him, to transport him across town to Prime House. Milord hesitated. If he got in, several of these hangers on would pile in with him so as to keep him signing and agreeing to appointments. He hadn't intended to go to Prime House today, not with a Duchess to kill.

As he thought rapidly of how to express his wish to travel alone and unaccompanied, a familiar voice broke into the buzz.

"Vaniel will be riding with me. Affairs of state are all very well but family comes first."

The Countess of Clarick strode towards her brother-in-law as if she expected anyone and everyone to leap out of her path. She wasn't wrong.

"Bee," Milord said faintly.

"Vaniel, darling," she said, kissing him on each cheek and then tucking her arm into his. "Come along. I have my own skimmer waiting and it will give us a chance to talk."

He allowed her to steer him away. It solved the problem of government distractions.

What it didn't solve was the problem of a sister-in-law. One did not take a sister-in-law along on assassinations.

Once they were both comfortably seated in the padded interior of the de Winter skimmer, Bee flicked a few autopilot options. The skimmer arced up into the air, and Bee leaned back to place her booted feet on the dashboard. "Time we talked, brother dear. I've had some fascinating chats with a Musketeer since we last spoke."

"What are you talking about?" Milord asked, in his usual careless drawl. "Musketeers are like drones, sweetness, that's like trying to have a conversation with a random piece of Palace furniture."

"This one had scads of interesting things to say," said Bee, her mouth hard. "Vaniel. I think it's time you and I talked about family loyalty."

Well, this was unlikely to be pleasant.

CHAPTER 20
THE COMTE DE LA FERE IS A GHOST STORY

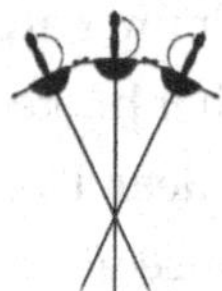

The de Winter family skimmer was a masterwork of comfort and elegance in design. Milord had always been rather fond of it.

Bee sat with her boots up on the dash, waiting him out.

"Where are we going?" he asked, choosing not to address the implied knowledge and accusation in her voice.

There were at least sixteen methods he could use to kill her, right this minute. It would be a shame – Bianca de Winter had been a worthy ally. Her loyalty to family had provided him with a certain layer of protection in the cutthroat world of Valour politics.

Milord had always known that it would be temporary. *Olivier, you taught me that. The second I disappointed you, my life was forfeit.*

They were a ruthless race, these New Aristocrats of Valour. Only four generations ago, their ancestors had set foot on a barren rock and turned their machines against it until it transformed into a land of storybook beauty, worthy of their distant myths and legends.

If Milord had learned anything from the university courses he took to snare his first valuable spouse, it was that humans were stupid in the face of beauty. Having conquered this planet and made it perfect, the New Aristocrats thought themselves above it all.

Oh they had religion, but was it a surprise that so many of them preferred Elementalism to the more forward-looking and inclusive Church of All? By worshipping the earth and the trees and the very air, they worshipped themselves all over again. Who was it that made the earth rich and fertile on this planet? Who was it that shaped the rivers and the mountains and altered the air so it tasted sweet in human lungs?

The fucking New Aristocrats, that was who. Their religion, like everything else, was all about them.

The de Winter family were as bloated and self-congratulatory as the d'Autevilles had been. But Milord had learned from the Comte de La Fere. By the time he presented himself on a platter to Delia de Winter and her arrogant, brash older sister, he had shaped a history that allowed him to play Someone of Note rather than an outsider, craving acceptance.

He loved his title. How could he not? As the husband of the Comte de la Fere he had been merely the Honourable Auden d'Auteville, which made it clear he was of lesser status to everyone else in the backwater noble family he had chosen to infiltrate.

When he came to marry Milady Delia de Winter, younger sister of the Countess of Clarick, he had expected much of the same. But Bee was generous, and pleased with the money and political influence that 'Vaniel Greywater' brought to the marriage. She allowed him to share Delia's title, and somehow…

Somehow, as Milord, he had become someone new. Perhaps these New Aristocrats knew what they were doing after all. The title was meaningless, and yet.

He was a different man when he wore it. There was a confidence to him that only arrived when he became Milord, distancing himself from the ragged remnants of the previous identity that had nearly destroyed him.

Bee waited now for him to speak, her boots twitching impatiently. Did she realise that he was considering the potential risks of killing her right here, in the skimmer? Had she password-locked the autopilot? It would not do to arrive, bloodstained and breathless, at the de Winter estate in the county of Clarick with the recently-murdered corpse of his sister-in-law.

"Aren't you going to ask me what I know about you?" Bee made herself pretend her usual careless amusement.

"I have already asked you a question and received no answer," Milord replied, matching her light tone. "Goodness, darling, what have those surly Musketeers been telling you?"

Bee leaned in. Milord's gaze swept over the pulse at her throat, the one that he could pinch out so easily. She had no idea how strong he was, how much more than a human she had trapped here in the metal skin of this skimmer.

Unless, of course, she did know.

"One Musketeer," said Bee, tipping her head back against the soft leather of the pilot seat. "His name is Athos. You're acquainted, I believe?"

Milord was careful not to allow anger to show in his body language. "We met for the first time some days ago."

Bee's expression went hard. "Really, Vaniel? Is that the truth? I got the impression you had known each other long ago. Or is it a lie that you were once married to the Comte de La Fere, under another name?"

Milord huffed out a laugh. "The Comte de La Fere? Someone has been telling you fairy tales. The Comte de La Fere is a ghost story."

"Indeed." Bee looked unimpressed. How had Olivier got under her skin so quickly, turned her trust into suspicion? "I'd never heard of the estate, but I've had time to research it while waiting for you to show up. It's found in the peak district of far north Castellion – a long way from civilised society. Far enough north that they use the old language – comtes and comtesses, ducs and duchesses. As it turns out, there was a Comte of those lands until five years ago, and he had a husband."

Milord had not wasted a thought on what happened to the estate after he left. He knew – had read somewhere – that Olivier d'Auteville disappeared after the execution of his husband, and was eventually declared dead. Perhaps one of the hangers-on that orbited the family had taken the lands for themselves. Perhaps they stood empty still.

He had been happy there, for a time. When he thought of it now he remembered the chilly grey winters and not the fresh green warmth of the summers.

"Have you been listening to gossip from a dead man?" he asked Bee.

Her mouth broke into a broad, cold smile. "Such fascinating gossip."

Milord's gaze was drawn to the viewscreen that was full of blue, bright blue. "We're skimming over water."

"Yes," said Bee. "I'm sorry to disappoint you, brother dear. But we're not going to Clarick."

His attention snapped back to her, calculating. "Then I'm the one who's sorry. I don't think we have anything left to talk about."

Milord moved, and Bee twisted away from him. He had a blade in his hand by the time her boots smacked down on to the floor, but she did too. His was a killing knife, the kind that concealed so easily in a sleeve, though the SmartMetal allowed it to bend and warp to whatever length or width was most useful.

Bee had a sword. She had kept it hidden beside her seat, but the hilt was in her hand now, the tip directly pointing at Milord's throat.

Her weapon had the reach on him, but she was a sportswoman and not a killer. He took a step, intending to let her impale him. A thin blade sucking through the middle of his throat would nicely take the sword out of play and do little to slow him down as he slit her throat and let her bleed out on the floor of the luxury skimmer.

A hard snap locked around his ankles, forcing him still. Cuffs. The chair had cuffed him in place – some sort of automatic system? He growled, flexing against the hard metal that restrained him.

Bee de Winter, the Countess of Clarick, lowered her sword. "I was never as stupid as you believed," she told him.

Milord snarled at her, no longer having to pretend. "Isn't that *inconvenient*?"

Finisterra. This was Finisterra. Milord knew it from the moment Bee led him – cuffed at the ankle and the wrist – from the skimmer and on to the hard grey rock of the island.

Delia had brought him here once. She hated the place as much as any member of her family did. Finisterra was where New Aristocrats went to remember how good things were on the rest of the planet. It was one of the few patches of Valour which had never been successfully terraformed – oh, the air was breathable enough, and the bitter blue ocean as teeming with life as any other body of saltwater on this over-designed planet.

But nothing grew on Finisterra. The de Winter family had sold stone blocks hewn from this grim island for generations, to build castles all across Castellion, though the New Aristocracy preferred butter yellow sandstone from the eastern quarries to the pale blue-grey rock of the islands. Eventually the quarry was closed down.

There was a tower here, built high and sure above the island, with a clear view across the ocean to mountains that must, it occurred to Milord, overlook the land he had first infiltrated when he arrived on Valour.

This was a northern island, so he was closer to La Fere than he had been since his execution. Ironic, that he might meet a second execution here. Full circle, one might say.

Good luck with that, Bee, Milord thought as he trudged the path from the skimmer to the grim tower that awaited him. His ankles were weighed down by magnetic cuffs. His sister-in-law held an arc-ray on him as she followed his steps. *I wonder if you have any idea how difficult I will be to kill.*

Milord made his way inside the tower as a prisoner. The de Winters hated Finisterra but they loved their grey stone. Bee and Delia's grandfather had built a similar tower on an unnamed asteroid after winning the ownership title of the space rock in a gambling debt. The asteroid was one of many random properties assigned to Milord's care after the death of his wife, and he had made use of it recently to house Conrad Su.

The Finisterra tower was colder and less welcoming than the asteroid tower had been.

"I haven't been here since I was a child," Bee remarked as they entered the arched gate to be greeted by a flat-faced unit of guards, all wearing the de Winter crest. "I do hope there are dungeons."

"You are making a mistake," Milord said, keeping his voice soft and unthreatening.

Bee leaned in to him, making sure to keep at an arm's length. Even with his wrists heavy in cuffs that matched the weights on his ankles, she did not trust him. And so she should not. "Was that someone else's hand wielding a knife in my face a few hours ago?"

"I feared for my life."

"From me?"

"You have been bewitched by the words of a madman."

Bee smiled at that. "Mad is he, your handsome Musketeer? I thought he was a ghost story."

"Bee, for the sake of our family…"

She actually hissed in her throat. "Family. You dare say that to me? I have trusted you as a brother and a friend, and this – what you have done to my family is *indescribable.*"

"It's the dishonour that burns, is it?" he shot at her. "How embarrassing, to have Musketeers spreading lies about your kin."

Bee looked as if she had been slapped. "You think I brought you here because you are an embarrassment? Darling boy. I brought you here because I want answers."

Milord wriggled his fingers, flexing his wrists against the cuffs. He could get out of them now, if he changed shape, but he did not yet know the lie of the land. If he could be sure those six men and women in livery were the only guards on the island, he would be prepared to risk it. But he had not got this far without patience, and caution.

"I am an open book," he said, projecting an aura of harmlessness. "What do you need to know, sweetness?"

"For a start," said Bee. "Did you murder my sister Delia?"

Oh, that.

Well.

That was a long story, and the truth would not endear him to Bee tonight.

Better to say nothing.

Milord was taken, not to a dungeon, but to a room high in the tower. Suitably melodramatic. He was impressed by Bee's commitment to the role of ruthless jailer.

There were twelve guards in all, presided over by a resentful woman in the emerald-and-gold sash of a Planetary Marshal.

"Aren't you overqualified for guard duty?" Milord asked the Marshal, calculating the size and shape of the room, the electronic seals on every window, and the active security system that would monitor him every second of every minute of every hour of every day.

"Marshal Felton is here at the First Minister's request," said Bee, as she checked the accommodations. "I've done my research on you, since that informative call from Athos. Her Eminence the Cardinal was especially forthcoming about your past activities."

Milord raised an eyebrow. "I bet she was."

"The government of Valour took it as a personal favour for me to discreetly remove you from the public, to minimise the scandal," Bee went on. "I might get a knighthood for it."

"Betrayal is such a lucrative business these days."

Her face frosted over. "Don't you dare, Vaniel. You wormed your way into my family, married my sister – who died so *conveniently* a year after the wedding, after a brief illness. I never doubted you for a second. All this time."

"Bee," he said, still hoping he could convince her to take his word over that of his former husband. "Be reasonable."

"Reasonable?" Bee hissed. "This isn't a minor skeleton in the closet to be tidied away. My sister is *dead*, and my only heir turns out to have been fathered by a scum-sucking alien. I'm not in the mood to be reasonable, Vaniel. I'm done with you. If you have any confessions, give them to Marshal Felton, and we'll see if anything you say is worth trading for a swift and private execution, instead of the publicly humiliating spectacle that the Valour government is preparing *as we speak.*"

She stormed out of the room, leaving only Marshal Felton behind.

Milord took a deep breath, and gave her a charming smile. "I'm sorry you had to see that. Family tiffs can be so awkward. Any chance of a hot cup of tea?"

Olivier, you will die for this, he decided, then and there. *I will make you watch me dismember the girl D'Artagnan before I finally let you fall into your own oblivion.*

CHAPTER 21
FIVE DAYS OF CAPTIVITY

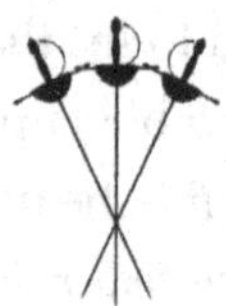

Marshal Felton was a problem.

Milord had been imprisoned many times, under many circumstances, but he was currently short on allies, and every guard on the island was aware that he had the ability to change his shape and his face.

His room, at the top of the tower, was locked. The windows had turned out to be sealed. Plexi-glass, of course. Most New Aristocrats on Valour were willing to sacrifice history and traditional grandeur for security and convenience.

No, the only way Milord was getting out of here was with the help of an ally, and the only one with the clearance to make it happen was the flat-eyed, suspicious and thoroughly sulky Marshal who was in charge of security around here.

How to crack Felton? She was as dry and resistant as the grey rock that had been hewn into this isolated tower, on an island so far north that you could taste ice in the air.

But every soldier had a breaking point. She would crack, sooner or later.

On the first day of captivity, Milord sat quietly and responded obediently to every order. He did not try to scare Marshal Felton, or show her any face other than the one he had so carefully constructed for his identity as Vaniel de Winter, after losing his life as the younger and more cynical Auden d'Auteville.

Milord had won many hearts and opened many doors with this face. There was something about humanity and their susceptibility to a fine pair of cheekbones that he should report back to his own people, sooner or later.

If cheekbones could be weaponised, conquering humans would be easy.

Milord composed himself outwardly while his inner heart burned with rage. Rage against D'Artagnan, against Olivier – no, Athos, it was Athos the musketeer who had brought him so low this time around. Olivier was as dead as the husband he had ruthlessly executed.

He waited.

Finally, the security web on the door hummed in response to a code, and the door swirled open to reveal the implacable figure of Marshal Felton, holding a food tray. Milord examined her through his sweeping eyelashes, considering the possibilities. "I don't think I can eat," he whispered.

"No?" Felton banged the tray on the plain table in the corner. "What's wrong with you?"

"I couldn't begin to say."

As Felton turned her back on him, Milord made his move. He slumped forward, and fell to the floor in a dead faint.

Milord awoke to hear an argument happening over his head.

"What kind of amateur are you?" demanded the dulcet tones of Vaniel's sister-in-law. "Pretending to faint is the oldest trick in the book. I thought you were smarter than to fall for a literal slapstick routine."

"He wasn't pretending," Felton said hotly. "The medic confirmed he was unconscious."

"I told you no one was to enter this room except you and I, and it took him less than a day to compromise your instructions. What's next? Am I going to find you braiding him an escape rope with your own hair? No more medics. No unauthorised personnel. I shudder to think what he could have done with access to medical equipment."

"There are rules on how to treat prisoners," Felton replied. "I will not break those rules simply because…"

"He is not human," Bee spat. "He has betrayed everything about our race and our planet. You cannot treat him like some common or garden prisoner."

"Spy, traitor, alien, whatever he is, we should treat him honourably," said Felton.

"Honourable is not the same as stupid," said Bee. "Stop pretending, Vaniel, I know you're awake."

Milord opened his eyes and stretched lazily. He lay on the floor, with what felt like a bruise across the top of his face. He had induced his entire body into a legitimate faint, knowing that bruising was a possibility. It all sold the story of his misery. "What did I miss?"

"There will be no more swooning," Bee said flatly. "We have been charged to keep you imprisoned until representatives from the Fleet collect you. It is the only way that the de Winter family can escape retribution for harbouring an alien spy in the first place."

Milord rubbed his face. "When you say family, you don't mean those cousins you pretend to be polite to at parties, do you? You mean Morgan."

"Do not speak her name," Bee snapped, and stormed out of the cell. "Felton, if you disappoint me again, do not expect further employment on Valour, or anywhere else in the solar system."

For the rest of the day, Felton brought every meal on a tray, and Milord said nothing.

On the second day of captivity, when Marshal Felton brought in the breakfast tray, Milord saw the star.

It was a tiny thing, tattooed on the inside of the wrist and all but concealed by the sweeping sleeve of the uniform. But it was enough.

The tray contained basic rations, a glass of juice (only the supper tray included wine) and two Elemental bowls, one filled with earth and one with water.

"The Countess of Clarick insisted you have these," Felton said quietly. "The prisoner's charter requires you be provided with the basic tools of worship. I'm afraid she would not trust you with a flame."

Milord shoved the tray away, so that the Elemental bowls knocked together, and nearly spilled. "She mocks me," he snapped. "She knows I do not share her religion."

There, a flicker of interest from the Marshal. A hairline

crack in her armour. "Indeed? What religion do they follow, on your world?"

"You mock me, too," Milord said angrily. "She calls me alien though she has no evidence but the lies of a man who wants to destroy me. I am as human as you are, Marshall Felton, and I follow the stars."

Felton tilted her head to one side. "You belong to the Church of All?" There was sympathy in her eyes.

"One more thing that woman has taken from me. My wife is dead, and Bianca controls my daughter. I am never to mention my own religion, lest I contaminate her!"

Felton's face was unreadable, but Milord knew he had got to her.

"Did you know I have a daughter?" he said in the gentlest possible tone. "I will never see her again. That is why I am here. Nothing to do with war, or politics, or aliens. The Countess of Clarick has found a way to rid herself of her heir's last surviving parent. I will never leave this tower alive."

"You will be guarded and protected in accordance with the law," said Felton stubbornly.

Milord gave her a wistful, melancholy smile, and ate his breakfast. "I am sure you believe that, and I respect you for it."

When Felton brought Milord lunch, and again when she brought supper, she interrupted the prisoner standing at the plexi-glass windows, singing quietly of the cosmonauts who went to the stars, and of the Church who kept them safe once they got there.

On the third day of captivity, Milord was quiet over breakfast, eyes lowered to the ground. It was a magnificent performance of humble melancholy.

He thought perhaps Felton was going to speak to him, but instead she pressed her mouth tightly closed and took the tray without a word.

It was Bee, and not Felton who brought the lunch tray.

"I heard you've switched religions," Bee said cheerfully. "Was it your first spouse who put you on to the Church of All or is there some other husband or wife I don't know about?"

It was tempting to snap back with sarcasm or violence, but Milord could not discount the possibility that Felton and the other guards were watching the interchange.

"You are subtle in your interrogation methods," he said calmly. "Why are you still here? Isn't there a war to fight? I would have thought charging off to blast lasers at an imagined enemy is exactly your kind of sport."

Bee gave him a frosty smile. "I have responsibilities here."

"You know that I was sent on a mission of vital importance to the war effort," Milord tried. "Her Eminence the Cardinal wished me to encourage the Duchess of Buckingham and New Aristocrats like her – New Aristocrats like you – to bring reinforcements to Truth Space. It's brave of you to risk the wrath of the most powerful religious leader this solar system has ever seen."

Bee laughed at him. "You never stop, do you? I know who you are, Vaniel. As for the Cardinal, she has no more desire to be implicated in your crimes than I. No one is coming to rescue you. You are completely alone."

"Ha," said Milord, and gave her a wan smile. "You

never said a truer thing, Bee. There's no one coming for me, and I have no allies."

I am alone. That's what makes me dangerous.

Felton brought the supper tray. Once again she found the prisoner at the window, comforting himself with songs of the stars, and the early spacefarers.

"I can –" she said, and hesitated. "I have permission to bring you tools of worship. A book, perhaps?"

Milord turned his beautiful face up to her. "A knife," he said bleakly. "If you would really help me, there is a small knife hidden in the hem of the jacket I wore when I was brought here. It has a sacred star pattern on the hilt. The Cardinal herself gave it to me as a gift. Bring me that."

Felton approached the prisoner as carefully as if she were a wild animal. "What would you do with that knife, if I gave it to you?"

Milord allowed a tiny puff of a sigh to escape his lips. "I promise, I will hurt no one but myself."

Felton shivered at the very thought of it. "You can't think I'm going to let you commit suicide."

"Why not? It's what she wants."

"The Countess of Clarick wants to hand you over to the authorities of the Royal Fleet. Alive. She made that very clear."

"Ah yes, the Royal Fleet. Not the Combined Fleet, and certainly not the Cardinal's own. Telling, that."

Felton's mouth twitched. "I have no love of Musketeers but you must know that they serve the Crown's justice. They will be fair with you."

"Oh yes," Milord said hollowly. "Fair. They shall be fair judges, fair juries and fair executioners all rolled together into one – or, rather, three. You know the three I mean?"

"Ha," said Felton, rolling her eyes. "Yes, I have some idea. I took a call from the Musketeer Aramis before I received my official orders to hunt you down. They are not my favourite people, and in private life they barely have the morals of an alley cat between the three of them – but I don't think they would be a threat to an innocent man."

"It depends on what you mean by innocent," said Milord, and paused precisely so that Felton would encourage him to speak further. "Do you love the Cardinal, Marshal Felton? I believe you served her once."

"I did," said Felton. "I love her still. I left Paris Satellite for personal reasons."

"You know that the Musketeers have an unreasonable hatred for the Cardinal and everything she stands for. That is why I have ended up in this awful situation. The Duchess of Buckingham – you know of her?"

"I might have heard her name once or twice," Felton said dryly.

"She's a monster. She seduced the Regence's husband, months ago. And now – I can't even speak of what she is doing now." Milord stood, and stretched his legs. "I should eat, to keep up my strength. They will be here for me, soon enough."

Felton waited impatiently while Milord chewed through the dull, rote-printed rations. Finally, she burst out: "Of what do you accuse the Duchess?"

"I accuse nothing. It is not my place." Milord gave her a wry look over one shoulder, letting his silver hair fall rakishly over one eye. "I can't give away all of my secrets."

"But if the Cardinal is in danger…"

Marvellous how Felton had put the story together all on her own, with only a few steering hints from Milord himself. "Grave danger. The Duchess of Buckingham has the Musketeers wrapped around her little finger. They don't realise the extent of her evil, because their hatred of the Cardinal makes them blind. Buckingham used that against them."

Felton stepped forward to take the tray. "I can't – you know I can't let you out. No matter what you say. You must wait and submit yourself to justice. If what you say is true…"

"There will be no trial," said Milord, patting his mouth with a napkin. "I will be dead the moment that the Musketeers or their representatives arrive to take me. And by then, it will be far too late to save her Eminence."

As Felton turned to leave, Milord caught her troubled gaze with his own. "You will never forgive yourself," he said gently. "If I am right, and Buckingham's conspiracy succeeds. But God will forgive you."

On the fourth day of captivity, Felton brought Milord his knife.

"I can't give it to you," she said stumbling over her words. "I can't – the Church of All does not condone suicide, and neither do I. But I thought – it has the sacred constellations engraved upon it, and I thought it might bring you some comfort to see it."

Milord sat by the window, the model prisoner, hands folded submissively in his lap. "Perhaps I might hold it for a moment?" he asked. "You are a strong woman, I know you would stop me if I sought to do violence to myself. But – you are right. It has always brought me comfort."

Felton hesitated for a moment, and handed over the folded knife.

Milord squeezed it tightly to his chest, and traced the star engravings with his fingertip. "You are kinder than I deserve. I would not fear justice at all if you were the judge."

"Would you like to pray?" Felton asked.

Milord gave her a sweet, melting smile. "I would."

They held hands, and they prayed together for some time. When it was over, Milord handed the knife back to his jailer, and went to eat his breakfast.

Felton had not seen the tiny hidden compartment in the knife, nor the silver grain-like beads that Milord poured secretly into his palm.

Now, at least, he had a plan.

He would not die here, on this rock.

"Shall I come again, to pray with you?" Felton asked.

Milord smiled warmly at her. "They're watching us," he said. "I worry about you. I think, once I am dead, they will think that I had too much opportunity to influence you. Why let a single official have so much exposure to me, if not to have a scapegoat when I am dead?"

Felton's face crumpled. "They're not going to kill you," she said. "We don't execute prisoners, not on any planet in the solar system."

Milord gave him a crooked smile. "Buckingham wants them all to think I am an alien spy. Everyone knows that the only way to kill a Sun-kissed is to cut their head from their body." He turned away, as if the expression on

Felton's face was painful to him. "Don't pray with me again. I don't want you to suffer for sympathising with me."

"I'll come when they're not watching," Felton whispered.

"Don't," breathed Milord. "I'm not worth it."

On the fifth day of captivity, the Countess of Clarick delivered the meals to her brother-in-law.

"You have been made a fool, Bee," he said, as she left after supper. "Buckingham is using us both – and the Musketeers too – for a plot that has nothing to do with this planet, or our family. When it is done, I will be dead and you will be left with blood on your hands and nothing to show for it."

"I knew you were poison when she married you," Bee grated out.

"No," said Milord, and the smile he gave her was very different to the one had had been using on Marshal Felton. "You liked me. That's why you're so angry now. Don't let them do this to our family."

Bee banged his tray out of the room with her, leaving the wine glass behind.

It was later, nearly midnight, when Felton came.

Milord was ready for her.

CHAPTER 22
THE MANY DEATHS
OF MILORD

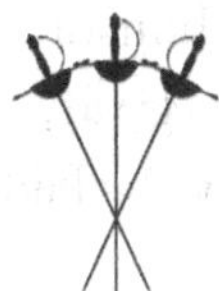

The first time that he died, he was not Milord De Winter, nor was he Auden d'Auteville. His name was a burst of light and shade in his own language: a vision that meant familiarity and home and *me*.

He was one of the Bright Ones, a legion of youngsters charged with scattering themselves across the alien solar system. Their mission: to integrate themselves into the society that called itself humanity.

There were four of them in each pod, hurtling through the galaxy, away from the true suns, away from the light and heat and anything they had ever known.

He (was he even a he at this point?) had no words for this loss, for the fear that swept over them all as they were shot like bullets into a solar system that felt cold and grey compared to their own world.

Why not call it death?

He would never be bright and warm again.

The planet was cold and pale; too far from the sun, which was itself a weak ball of yellow light, hardly worth bothering about.

Two pod-siblings were dead, shaken badly on impact. A third crawled ahead of him, out of the pod and into the wan sunshine. She stood, already forming her flexible scarlet limbs into the body she had learned to make in Basic Training.

He watched as she gave herself two arms, two legs. She grew hair from her scalp, and nails from her fingertips. She stretched her waist thin and her hips wide; made globular breasts too round to be realistic.

"Clothes," she said hoarsely. "Don't have enough… energy to stay warm, without clothes."

Something had gone wrong with her heat source; she was already turning blueish and pale, simply from the contact between her misshapen feet and the fierce white ice-crust of the ground.

Winter, he realised. They had landed on the winter side of the planet. That was not in their mission parameters. It would count as a failing mark.

He could feel his own heat within his core. It kept his muscles relaxed and protected even as he shaped his own body into the design he had worked on for so long.

Male, now. A sleek, practical silhouette with the appropriate musculature. Toes. He had worked hard on his toes, ensuring a deliberate inconsistency between them. To be too perfect was to stand out, and their mission was to integrate, to collect data.

To survive.

His pod-sibling moaned as her skin chilled quickly. Her energy flickered. He stepped forward, pressing his chest to her back, so that she would think she could warm herself on his heat.

As he drained her of the remainder of her light energy, she screamed. There was no one on this ice-crusted land to hear her. He burned with triumph, with the heat that meant survival.

The pod disintegrated, as was always intended, leaving a small beacon behind, dug deep into the ice.

As he walked across the ground, towards the flecks of heat and light in the distance that meant some kind of civilisation, his feet steamed where they touched the snow.

The second time he died, he was the Honourable Auden d'Autevielle, husband to the young Comte de La Fere. He had spent two years befriending Olivier with his wit and sarcasm and beauty, before pouring everything he knew about humanity into a dazzling seduction.

From lovers to husbands: it took only a few months for Olivier to fall so completely that he stood up to his remaining family members and asserted his privilege to marry whoever he damn well wanted.

They were happy in their marriage, or as near to happiness as Auden had ever imagined. Each year he made a discreet pilgrimage back to the snowy wastes of far north Castellion, to pour all that he had learned about these people into the blinking, impersonal beacon.

The war between his own people and the human solar system was over, but the work of spies continued. There would be another war, and he was one of the weapons they were saving for the future.

Every year it became harder, to slide out of the warm bed and the man who loved him, to make that solitary trek and to betray the planet that had become his home.

He was never warm on Valour, and yet he no longer saw it in bleak shades of grey and white. There was colour, if you looked hard enough.

The beacon – his people – knew too much, now. They knew about Olivier and La Fere. The only way Auden could escape would be to destroy that life entirely: all the connections he had made and shared. To destroy his husband, and start again as a different person.

Auden gazed thoughtfully at the beacon, uploaded his report, and returned home to the estate, to love, to Olivier, to warmth.

The following year, he stayed home. He left it a day, and then another, telling himself that he would go tomor-row, that he had not truly made up his mind to turn rogue. The beacon made up his mind for him. At the beginning of the third day that the Honourable Auden d'Auteville failed to make his annual report, his skin began to burn.

The heat was pleasant at first, familiar warmth that filled him with light and urgent energy. But the heat did not disperse. It poured over him in waves, sending him shivering one moment and sweating with heat the next.

It appeared as an illness, to the humans. He fell into a rambling fever; his whole body swamped with pain and heat and punishment.

By the time he had recovered anything like his usual sensibilities, it was too late. He found himself weighed down with heavy chains and cuffs, under sentence of execution by his own husband who had finally – terribly – discovered his secret.

Here is what he could have done:

1. Twisted his hands and feet thinner to easily escape the cuffs.
2. Murdered the guards watching over him.
3. Made a new body and started again, on the far side of the continent, or elsewhere on the planet.

Instead, Auden placed his trust in the love that he had built with Olivier. He believed, right up until the last minute, that his husband was incapable of striking the killing blow.

Humans knew so little about the Sun-kissed, even after fighting a war against them. One thing they all believed was that the only way to kill a Sun-kissed was to sever his head from his body.

It was an extremely useful myth.

There were millions of ways for his kind to die on their own world, but Auden had seen for himself that the only way that the Sun-kissed could die on Valour was if they took damage while their bodies were cold.

Olivier Armand d'Autevielle, the Comte de La Fere, executed his husband on a beautiful sunny afternoon on the village green of Foilles, on his family estate. In attendance were: a planetary marshal, a Servant of the Elements, and several members of local government as well as local villagers.

Auden's body was ritually burned in the Elemental fashion, in two separate locations.

Ten minutes later, his body reassembled itself in a bright beam of burning light, beside the beacon in the snow. He gave his report methodically, taking in all relevant data gathered in the last year, and providing particular account of the human response to his unveiling as an alien spy.

He brimmed with power and unspilled energy, glowing in his own skin after the – what should he call it? Restoration? Extraction?

Rebirth.

As soon as the report had been uploaded into the sky, Auden (not Auden anymore) summoned every mote of energy he had, and blasted the beacon into dust.

Now he was truly alone.

The body he shaped for himself next should have been completely different. It was a dangerous luxury, to keep any feature that resembled Auden d'Autevielle. But that face, those limbs, those feet – he had designed them personally. They felt more like himself than his original bright red body of flexible, mutable limbs.

He liked his cheekbones. He could rule the world with cheekbones like these.

In the end, he shaped his body into a man who could well have been Auden's more stable older brother. He let his hair grow brown rather than silver, widened his nose, added wear and tear to the face, and width to the shoulders and ribcage.

He travelled south, far south, because there was no need to linger near that damned beacon any longer. He went from city to city, acquiring clothes and funds and political gossip: building a platform from which to launch Vaniel Stonewater.

He was an excellent spy, above all things. He built up different faces and bodies, variations on a theme: he became the Raven Slate and the bureaucrat Linton Gray as well as Vaniel. They all had different faces, but the same excellent cheekbones.

Auden and Olivier had adored political theory – but their world had been small, confined to their university and then to Olivier's rural estate. Here in the south, cities ate and drank New Aristocrat politics. Vaniel Stonewater found a game that he could win all the time without growing bored; the rules were always changing.

One night, in a salon filled with beautiful people looking for sex and attachment as much as intellectual stimulation, Vaniel Stonewater met a quiet young woman with laughter in her eyes, whose elder sister was desperate to marry her off so she could start making babies for the family line.

"Milady Delia de Winter," she told him when he asked for an introduction.

"Winter," Vaniel said with an inscrutable smile. "What an evocative name."

"You don't think it makes me sound chilly?" she ventured, flirting a little.

"Quite the opposite, sweetness. Quite the opposite."

Marrying Olivier had been his greatest mistake; marrying Delia was precisely the opposite. As Milord de Winter, he finally became his truest self. Such a shame that Delia had to die, for him to truly profit from the marriage…

Now, in the tower on the island at the end of the world, it was Vaniel de Winter's turn to die. Bee had ruthlessly guarded his safety when he was a part of her family. Now that she saw him as her enemy, she would not hesitate to end him.

It was only a surprise she had not done it already. But she had orders, or a request, at least, from someone with the authority to stay her hand.

It was too much to hope that her Eminence the Cardinal might ride to his rescue. Theirs had been a partnership of convenience, and Milord was well aware that he had ceased to be convenient.

Still, the death of the Duchess of Buckingham would go some way towards repairing their professional relationship. He had a reputation to uphold.

Committing a murder remotely while locked in a tower, far from the victim… oh yes, that would remind people of what Milord de Winter was capable.

Even if he would not be de Winter after tonight.

Marshal Felton came to him at midnight, when everyone else in this wretched tower was asleep. Milord sat with his feet up on the window seat as the chime of the security system indicated that someone was punching in a code.

He had already taken a dose of vision, a clever psychic drug once used by air commanders to see into the minds of their pilots during battle. Combined with the Winter implant, it made for a whole different kind of weapon.

When he closed his eyes, Milord saw through the eyes of Winter: a barefoot, silver-haired creature. Winter was a flirt, a dangerous weapon, and a spy. All of Milord's selves were spies, of course, but Winter was the wickedest of them.

He had built Winter himself, based on a set of programmable micro-studs he bought on the black market from Mendaki traders: he was pretty sure they used them as some kind of long-distance interstellar sex toy.

The micro-studs looked like grains of pepper and could be added to any food or drink. Once lodged inside the victim's skin, they implanted the program directly into their brain.

Milord had no control of Winter once the program was activated. It played out its own games of mockery and subversion.

The Winter he had dosed the Duchess of Buckingham with months ago was a law unto itself. It had certainly performed the necessary tasks – pushing her towards the adultery she already desperately wanted to commit, nudging her to keep the coat that the Prince Consort had been foolish enough to wrap around her shoulders.

The true value of Winter was in the information it provided. Milord could check in with the implant – with everything it had seen and done in the presence of the Duchess of Buckingham – through his use of vision.

Tonight, he learned that Buck had a house-guest: a young man who had thwarted Milord more than once, and had an intimate connection to Dana D'Artagnan. Killing Buck was a matter of duty. Killing Conrad Su would be a delicious treat: something to look forward to, when duty was done.

Milord relaxed, wriggling his bare feet against the cool stone of the tower wall.

Felton stepped into the tower. "Milord," she said in a low whisper.

He had her now. He had manipulated her to make her move against the Countess of Clarick. That was an excellent start. If Milord was to use Felton, really use her, then she must *want* to be used.

"Did you come here to pray?" he asked now, stretching out along the ledge.

"I don't know what I'm doing here," said Felton, her voice trembling.

"It's all right," said Milord. "It's not your fault. You have been caught up in a conspiracy not of your making. You are on the wrong side. But you don't have to be."

"I don't believe you. I don't trust you," said Felton.

Milord exulted. He had cracked her open using only words and ideas. It was the best kind of seduction.

"Here," he said, crossing the tower floor, his warm soles stinging with the cold of the flagstones. "Share my wine, and we'll talk. I will answer any question you have about the crimes my sister-in-law has committed against Valour justice – all in the name of friendship with those Musketeers."

He could not resist a sneer at 'Musketeers' and he saw that Felton subconsciously mimicked him. Of course she had an ingrained dislike and distrust of the Regence's own. She had been one of the Red Hammers on Paris Satellite not so long ago.

Felton wet her mouth with the wine, and licked her lips, though it was more of a nervous habit than any particular thirst. Not enough. She must drink deeper.

Milord continued. "It is Buckingham behind it, of course. Buckingham and her ambitions for this planet."

"This planet," said Felton, taking another swallow of wine. There was something about the twist of her mouth as she repeated the words…

The best tool for a seduction was knowledge. "What is it you most want, Marshal Felton? What is it that you need?"

"Want, need," said Felton, waving the wine glass as if it offended her. "My whole life collapsed because of want and need. I lost Paris because of want and need. I won't make that mistake again."

"Oh," breathed Milord. He took the glass from her and pretended to sip, then passed it back to watch her take a longer swallow. "It is Paris you want. To return there."

That was enough to break the dam. "I hate this planet, with its New Aristocrats and its politics and its *rain*, and Elementals everywhere," confessed Felton. "I was happy as a Red Hammer, happy on Paris Satellite."

"What happened? Who took it away from you?"

"I fell in love with a Musketeer," she said sourly. "With a woman who did not care enough for me. I broke the fidelity clause of my marriage contract for three nights in the arms of the Musketeer Aramis. When we were caught out, *she* moved on to another affair, while I was ruined. Everyone on Paris is an oathbreaker, one way or another, but no one can afford to be caught, especially those who work in service to the Church."

I see," said Milord, watching the long, milky throat of Felton work around the wine that remained in the glass. He could not be sure yet if the implant had taken hold. "What do you want most? Revenge, or Paris?"

"Both, I want both. Even if the Cardinal forgave me my sins, I cannot return to Paris while *she* is there…"

There it was. Swimming with the heightened senses provided by vision, Milord gasped as a wave of heat roiled around the tower room, and the illusion of his younger, charming silver-haired self flickered into existence between them.

Felton staggered back, seeing double. She swayed as the implant took hold, and her eyes focused on a single figure – on the image of Winter.

Milord captured the glass and set it aside. Felton barely even glanced in his direction.

Winter moved towards her, his hips swaying and his smile blazing with heat. "We're going to do such marvellous work together, Jan," he promised her. "We're going to kill a traitor. And when the Duchess of Buckingham is in the ground… I promise you, the Church will welcome you back with open arms. Aramis will never return to Paris Satellite alive."

Milord, meanwhile, would reshape himself anew, into someone that none of the damned Musketeers would ever suspect. All he had to do to beat them was to die one more time…

CHAPTER 23
MISSION TO VALOUR

This was embarrassing.

For Dana it had been an entire week of embarrassment, thanks to the reports she and Athos had been required to lodge, detailing their intimate knowledge of the Sun-kissed agent known variously as Slate, Winter, Milord, Milord Vaniel de Winter, Linton Gray, Vaniel Stonewater, Auden Snow and the Honourable Auden d'Autevielle.

Then there had been the discovery, after a week or more of intense diplomacy and attempts at translating an alien language formed mostly from light and colour, that Milord was wanted by his own people for crimes so grave that they would be willing to pull their troops out of Truth Space in exchange for his living body.

The question as to whether this invasion had been intended for the specific purpose of reclaiming Milord or whatever he was called in his own language – Sparkle Flash Shimmering Sunbeam or something equally untranslatable – had literally been keeping Athos up at nights.

The Regence, Amiral Treville and the Cardinal all agreed that reclaiming Milord from Valour was now of the utmost importance to the war effort. Special Agent Rosnay Cho had been put in charge of a mixed unit made up of Sabres and Musketeers. Porthos and Aramis were both included in the mission. Athos and Dana were not.

Another stinging humiliation, piled on top of so many others that Dana barely felt it.

Athos refused to accept that when it came to Milord de Winter, he and Dana were hopelessly compromised. He argued that they were both needed on the mission, precisely because of their experience with the diabolically ruthless agent. He was not prepared to leave Treville's office until she agreed with him. Treville dug her heels in so hard that there were skid marks on the carpet.

Their fight had been going for two hours and counting. Dana had missed lunch.

Finally, Treville threw up her arms and bellowed. "He's in custody of the Countess of Clarick's personal guards, and a Planetary Marshal! All this team have to do is collect him from detention and bring him back here — a simple operation. What the hell insight do the two of you think you can provide?"

"For a start," said Athos flatly. "There is no risk of either of us looking at this mission as a simple operation. There is no such thing, with this man."

He and Treville stared each other down, silently.

Dana became aware of a frantic buzz of conversation outside the office. "Amiral Treville," she said hesitantly.

Treville held up a hand to silence her, then strode out of the office.

Athos gave Dana a dirty look. She rolled her eyes at him, and followed Treville.

"Have they started shooting again?" Treville barked at her comms officer.

"No, boss," said Comms. "It's just – there's something come through on the interplanetary wire. From Gossipnode and a bunch of other sources…"

"I wasn't aware that Gossipnode was one of the sources we prioritise."

"Not usually, boss," said Comms, blushing. "But they're saying on Valour that the Duchess of Buckingham has been assassinated."

Dana felt cold spread through her body, starting from her neck. *Buck*, she thought helplessly. And then, with a burst of inner selfishness: *what about Conrad?*

Conrad Su's last message to her had been flippant and ordinary:

> This house is too small for me AND Buck's terrible shoe collection. Was looking for the games room, fell into her shoe cupboard & was lost for hours. Send a ball of yarn!

That was yesterday.

"You should have sent us days ago," accused Athos, in a voice low enough that no one but Treville and Dana could hear him.

Treville gave Athos a sour look. "Head down to Chaillot Station and inform Agent Cho to make room for two more. If you come back to Paris in a body bag, I'll blow up that green eyesore of a ship myself."

"They burn bodies on Valour," was all Athos said before he walked away.

Dana offered Treville an apologetic smile. "We'll end this war," she said with all the fervour of a newly minted Musketeer.

"Yes," Treville sighed. "But with Athos involved, you'll have started three more by the time I see you again."

Rosnay Cho had a new Moth fighter. Not the same model as before, but one even newer. This one had a name – the *Ryan Mac* – and it was beautiful, gleaming silver like a beetle. A beetle made out of stars.

Life, Dana D'Artagnan decided, was entirely unfair.

Ro looked singularly unsurprised to find Athos and Dana joining her for the final briefing at the dock on Chaillot Station while their ships were detailed by a group of dedicated and highly caffeinated engies.

Planchet's transfer from the *Frenzy Kenzie* had come through three days after Dana's promotion. She waved cheerfully at Dana from the fin of the *Buttercup* before sliding all the way under to check the couplings on the power spheres.

"Is it true?" was the first thing Athos asked Rosnay Cho. The two of them had bonded during the hellish week of translation.

"We think so," said Ro. "All we're getting is from the media at this point – we haven't been able to make contact with Villiers House or with local law enforcement for formal confirmation."

"Was it him?" Dana asked. She could be as streamlined and efficient as the rest of them.

Ro gave her a steady look. "Our sources assure us that the agent known as Milord is still under guard, on private land on the far north of the continent. It looks like he wasn't involved."

Porthos blew out an unbelieving breath, and even the two Sabres who made up the party muttered 'ha' to each other.

"Our mission is the same," said Ro. "We collect the target from his detention, and we bring him here to the Bastion. It's not our job to investigate the assassination of Buckingham, however tempted we might be."

Dana raised her eyebrows, silently calling bullshit on that one. "But?" she invited.

"But," said Ro, giving her a smirk. "Turns out we have more personnel than we originally planned on, so I'll make that call when we hit Valour orbit. Saddle up, buttercup. A lot of space miles between here and there."

Her first mission as a Musketeer. Dana was playing it as cool as she could. Still, she was excited as they all went to their individual ships, despite Aramis mouthing the words 'saddle up, buttercup' in silent delight.

"Ready to go, Cap," said Planchet as Dana stepped into the cockpit. The pigtailed engie came forward to help her with the helm and harness.

Wish me luck, Papa, Dana thought as they flew in formation out into space.

The *Buttercup* was delighted to be flying again. *Space space! Here we go!* he sang.

The look on Planchet's face – joy that they were finally doing this together – mirrored Dana's own. If it helped to distract Dana from the fact that Conrad Su had not replied to her recent messages, then all the better.

After several days of jumping and recharging their way across the solar system, they were only a few hours out from Valour when a message chimed into the *Morningstar*.

Aramis blinked at the user info.

PRIORITY ONE CALL FROM LUNAR PALAIS

followed by a series of ominous looking security codes.

"Captain-lieutenant Aramis," said Bazin from where he stood plugged into the wall of the cockpit. "There is a priority one…"

"Yes, Bazin, thanks, I can see it." Aramis hesitated only a moment before stabbing at a button to bring up the call. "*Morningstar*."

It was not a surprise to see a business-like Chevreuse filling her screen. The surprise was the origin of the call.

"Why are you in Paris?" Aramis demanded. "What's wrong?"

The other woman rolled her eyes. "I'm here to sit on a royal friend of ours so he doesn't go raging across the galaxy on an unsanctioned killing frenzy."

Oh. That made sense. Chev would have had time to fly to Lunar Palais from the Daughters of Peace once she heard the news about Buck – royal exile or no royal exile, of course she would not leave Prince Alek to deal with the news on his own.

Chevreuse was a good friend to have in bad times.

"This line is secure," she said now in that brisk, no-nonsense way of hers. "At least, if it's not then no line ever can be. Are you on your way to Valour?"

Aramis didn't ask how Chevreuse knew that. Her ex-girlfriend had spent her whole career as a wickedly efficient information hub. "Special team," Aramis replied. "Collecting a package."

"That could be trickier than you think," Chevreuse frowned. "Can you do me a favour?"

"Always," Aramis said automatically, then hesitated. "As long as it's not treasonous."

Chevreuse gave her an exhausted look. "As if I'd ask you commit treason before breakfast, darling."

"Shoot."

"Do your people know how Buck died?"

Aramis stared at Chevreuse through the screen. She was all bright white bobbed hair and business suit – very professional. "No. Information's been sketchy, and it's not supposed to be relevant to our mission." *Collect Milord, take him back to the Bastion.* That was it. That was all they were supposed to do.

Chevreuse leaned in, her bright blue eyes troubled. "Aramis, honey, I can't emphasise enough *how* relevant this is to your mission."

"Tell me."

"Marshal Felton paid a call on Buck, forty minutes before the staff at Villiers House reported the murder."

Aramis blinked at her. "Marshal Felton. *Jan* Felton?" She had never met a stuffier, more rule-abiding person in her life. "That can't be right."

"There were witnesses who corroborated the security records, but all evidence concerning Felton's presence in the house was deleted within six hours of the time of death." Chevreuse choked a little over the word 'death' and Aramis wanted to reach through the view screen to hug her.

"What can I do? We're not going to have much leeway on the planet if you want us to expand the investigation…"

"No need," Chevreuse said, getting more of a hold on herself. "That's not the favour I require. There's one witness who can't be bought, can't be silenced, and I know exactly where he's hiding now because I sent him there. You and your crew must find him, keep him safe. I need you to promise me this one, Aramis, because without that promise I can't stop the Prince Consort from trying to do it himself."

Aramis nodded briskly. "Send me the coordinates, Chev. If your witness is who I think he is, I know a Musketeer who is going to be very pleased to hear it."

Conrad Su must have escaped Villiers House after Buck was killed. No wonder Chev and the Prince were so desperate to secure him. They had already lost one friend this week.

"Good," said Chevreuse with a grin. "I have a soft spot for your D'Artagnan, since she sent me the best bloody personal assistant I've ever had. Kitty is a marvel."

"How's the baby?" Aramis asked, to keep Chevreuse on the line a little longer. It was a million years since they had last talked.

Chev actually looked startled – it was rare that Aramis was able to ruffle her. "How did you know about that?"

"Is it a secret? I thought Montbazon would be shouting it to the sky – he's always wanted an heir, hasn't he?"

Aramis didn't know Chevreuse's husband all that well – one New Aristocrat high-up government official was much the same as another. Chev had kept them as separate as possible, when she and Aramis were dating. Whatever she and Montbazon shared, it had always sounded like a pragmatic, contractual relationship rather than anything romantic.

"He was happy to acknowledge our daughter," Chevreuse said, surprisingly flustered. That was rare. "He's not the biological father, though."

Aramis smirked, leaning her chin on her hands. "Rrreally? Tell me more."

Chevreuse narrowed her eyes. "Oh look," she said. "Signal's breaking up."

The perfectly clear subspace signal that had transmitted her footage all the way from Lunar Palais dissolved into a burst of grey static.

"That was fun," Aramis said to Bazin, who gave her one of his patented judgy android expressions. "Can we set up a secure line between us and the *Buttercup*? I want to chat to Captain D'Artagnan about boys."

CHAPTER 24
SNOW AND STAR NUNS, BUT MOSTLY SNOW

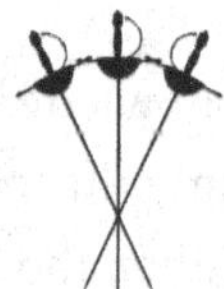

THEN:

Conrad gave Buck her space, as much as possible. Villiers House was her home, and he was conscious of the fact that he was an uninvited guest.

Also, they weren't friends.

They had got along fine last Joyeux, when she was the Ambassador of Valour, palling around with Prince Alek and taking Chev's place to help the Emerald Knights complete their final season. They had played fleur-de-lis together with Chev and Alek, and Conrad would always consider Buck to be a valued teammate. But that wasn't the same as friends.

Buck had been acting strange since Conrad arrived. It was as if she were at least three people.

1) She was a tired, stressed New Aristocrat who made political plans and looked over paperwork constantly, taking calls from supporters and colleagues who had

Opinions about Valour continuing to stay neutral in the war against the Sun-kissed.

2) She was a manic jock who would grab Conrad at the oddest times and haul him into her pool or her Zero-G tank to compete, whether they were racing through the water or sparring with poles.

3) She was a ghost, a pale shade of herself who muttered into her hair, darted away at any sign of company, and did not eat or drink nearly enough.

Buck was cracking up, and while there were plenty of staff and sycophantic 'friends' hanging around Villiers House to address her every need, Conrad seemed to be the only person who noticed what a state she was in.

Chev should be here. Chev could deal with anything. Conrad was used to looking after one impulsive but mostly compliant Prince Consort, not this messy mish-mash of What The Hell Is Going On Inside Buck's Skull?

It was the extra security, he told himself. That was enough to make anyone jumpy.

It was almost a relief when the Planetary Marshal arrived, offering a discreet code at the door to prove her identity. "The First Minister wishes me to revise the Duchess's security arrangements," she said in a clipped voice.

Conrad wondered if Marshal Felton even knew who he was. Dana had mentioned her as a potential ally in one of her recent texts, but did anyone official know why he was here in this house?

"I'll fetch her," Conrad said, making sure that Gus and Loni – two of Buck's oldest and longest-serving personal guards – escorted the Marshal into the Room of Eggs.

It probably had some schmancy posh person name like

a Receiving Salon or a Guesting Suite or whatever, but it was a blue room off the main lobby full of tiny, jewelled eggs on stands that freaked Conrad the fuck out. It was also where Buck liked to meet official guests.

Conrad hated that he even knew that. He wanted to go home. Paris was a yawning ache in his heart, and there was too much pollen on this planet. Pollen and oxygen and grass. Why did they need so much grass?

He found Buck upstairs in one of her listless moods. She was wrapped in a dressing gown that was heavy on the starchy gold brocade. "Marshal Felton is here," Conrad reported.

Buck threw off the dressing gown, unconcerned that she was naked underneath, and walked to her enormous wardrobe, selecting a blue doublet embroidered with pearls. "Felton's been involved in Milord's detention," she said, which Conrad already knew. "I suppose she has news for me?"

"Something about security checks," said Conrad, keeping his eyes aside while Buck dressed. He was used to being treated as furniture by people like her. Alek was the only New Aristocrat who had ever treated him like a person and even then – Alek had his moments of forgetting that Conrad wasn't a personified extension of his own needs. "Do you want me to join you?"

"No," sighed Buck, now dressed. She hadn't put a brush or a sonic wand to her tangled red-bronze hair in days, and it looked it. "Meet me at the pool afterwards. We can swim laps to clear my head."

"Works for me."

Conrad was not a fan of this planet and its oddly disconcerting gravity, but he could get behind swimming in water every day of the week. It was almost as good as being in the tank — which he also got to do every day.

Yeah, here were worse prisons than the Duchess of Buckingham's personal estate. That asteroid tower, for instance. He shouldn't complain.

Though if he never met that bastard Slate or Milord or whatever he called himself again, it would be too soon.

Outside, Conrad peeled off his clothes and stood in a pair of bright emerald trunks, poised to dive into the deep end of Buck's glorious pool.

In the seconds before he hit the water, he heard the low 'boom' of an arc-ray discharging from inside the house.

NOW:

Yeah, there were worse prisons than the Church of All Convent of Carmelline, in the peaks of the Drift Mountains, but it was hard to imagine one colder.

Conrad awoke with a gasp as the sound of the arc-ray shocked him out of the dream, like it always did. He wasn't even sure if what he had heard was the shot that killed Buck. Perhaps it was a chair hitting a wall, or one of the shots that Gus and Loni got off in those last few moments.

All he remembered now was plunging into the water. When he surfaced for air, the world had been different.

He breathed hard now, separating himself from the dream – the memory. The air hit his lungs, cold and unrelenting.

This prison was also more comfortable than Slate's asteroid tower, but that wasn't saying much. Every time Conrad awoke in this place, he was wrenched by desperate homesickness all over again – for the cozy artificial atmosphere of Luna Palais and Paris Satellite. Even for the home he had barely shared with his wife, behind her workshop.

Conrad would give anything to be back among his own people, instead of here.

Hiding from an alien maniac in a freezing stone building in a snowy mountain range. A stone building with glass windows. Not temperature-controlled plexiglass: this was the breakable, old school kind of glass. It let in draughts.

Also, there were star nuns.

To be fair, the star nuns were pretty great.

Conrad dressed quickly, layering tunics and extra wool sleeves before putting on the heavy hooded scarf that the nuns insisted all men wear within their walls, for modesty.

Breakfast was served in the Sharing Hall, on the far side of the frosted courtyard. Conrad took a deep breath and pulled his hood over his face as he walked over the slippery flagstones, towards the smell of food.

A discreet cough alerted him to the presence of the extremely tiny and elderly Sister Ursa, about to make her own trek across the courtyard. Conrad doubled back and offered her his arm.

"Good boy," she said, patting his cheek. She allowed him to help her across to the hall. After the icy air, it almost felt warm inside, though the high glass ceiling (to allow better access to the constellations at night) let in far more cold than Conrad himself would have liked.

Oh, for a space station. Conrad had never felt cold in Paris. Cold never entered the equation there.

As they approached the tables of food, Sister Ursa

released her hold on him and darted towards a prime spot of bench space, within grasping reach of a porridge ladle.

Conrad didn't have anything like her speed, and ended up jammed between Sisters Volantis and Columba, both of whom were far more interested in breaking down this year's fleur-de-lis matches than they were in allowing him to eat his breakfast.

Oh, and that was the other thing. The season. League Fleur-de-lis had been well underway for months before the war called for a suspension of games, mostly without the reigning champions the Emerald Knights in the roster.

With Laurel Slaughter replacing Chevreuse after her exile last Joyeux, the Knights had played barely a handful of games this season.

Conrad knew that everything at the other end of the solar system was more important than a game with poles in a Zero-G tank, but... he mourned his old life, that other life where he was able to prevent Alek from doing stupid things, and Chevreuse was on the ground in Paris to mitigate the Cardinal's more destructive schemes, and the most adrenalin Conrad felt in any given week was in the tank, where he belonged...

After the asteroid, as he recuperated at Chevreuse's new digs, they had barely talked about the sport, except for that one night they got drunk together and bitched about every single member of the 0-League who wasn't them. At Buck's, Conrad managed to keep the vidscreens from displaying any of this season's most recent games, which still screened on a high repeat rotation.

Here at the convent in the fucking mountains, you couldn't escape it, because little known fact about this particular chapter of nuns? They were really into Team-

Joust. They had their own tank, and their own cinquefoil teams (divided by age group – the 60+ Silver Tyre-Irons were especially brutal). They had watched every 0-League game, past and present. They talked about fleur-de-lis, constantly.

If sport was a religion, these nuns had their cake and ate it too.

It no longer surprised Conrad that they had taken him in with only an anonymous character recommendation from Chevreuse's office, had given him shelter despite the danger his presence might bring down on their peaceful community.

The nuns of the Convent of Carmelline thought that having a real-life pro fleur-de-lis player in their midst was the best thing that had happened to them in years.

"So, what was it like playing against the Dido Demons?" asked Sister Gemini from across the table. She at least leaned over and offered him a ladle of the hot herb porridge, while Sister Columba took pity on him and finally pushed the flagon of coffee in his direction.

Conrad smiled weakly and filled his plate, pushing his hooded scarf back a little (not too far) to make eating more practical. "Oh, man, that game almost killed me…"

Yeah, as long as he never ran out of sporting anecdotes, he and the nuns got on fine.

After breakfast, Sister Ursa led them all in a rousing series of songs about star fields and the future of humanity. Sister Magellan was called up to lead a prayer for the United Royal Fleet, and the casualties of war.

Conrad shivered, and not from the chill of the stone-and-glass hall. Dana was out there. His friends among the guards and the Musketeers were out there, most of them.

And then there was Alek. The Prince Consort was supposed to be safe on Lunar Palais playing secret baby daddy, but what were the actual odds that he was going to be safe in a time of war?

As Sister Magellan's prayer came to a rousing finale, there was a knock on the big double doors at the far end of the Hall of Sharing. The doors that led directly to the mountain path. Conrad tensed, remembering all over again that an alien assassin might have a good reason to hunt him down here.

But when the nuns levered the heavy doors open, it was a woman who collapsed through them, in the torn remains of a flight suit. For one confused moment, Conrad thought it was Dana – the same warm brown tones to her skin, the shaven head, the clenched fists – but this woman was taller, and shaped differently. Her face, messy with blood and plasma burn, was broader than that of Dana.

The sisters came forward to help the woman. Some of them gasped as the sleeve of her flight suit came completely away, revealing tangled tattoos all the way up her arm. A fleur-de-lis pattern blended into a star field, familiar because it reflected the tattoos that every Sister of Carmelline wore on her limbs.

Their religious robes were designed to slide back and reveal the sacred patterns to each other, though Conrad had only seen the nuns do it once or twice, for formal cere-monies. It was too damned cold in the mountains to flash wrists and ankles if you didn't have to.

Also it was too cold to make your way up a snowy staircase on a mountainside in a ripped flight suit and ungloved hands. The poor woman was a wreck.

"She's one of us," Sister Magellan said. "Conrad, help us get her to the medibay."

Well, he *was* the muscle around here. Him and Sister Volantis, who could bench-press three of him. Volantis was already moving ahead, shoving open doors and clearing the way.

Conrad scooped the burned, half-frozen woman into his arms, and she nestled into him as if seeking comfort. Her fleur-de-lis tattoos ran all the way up her throat, he noticed.

In his head, he composed a text to Dana even as he carried the woman to the medibay to have her wounds seen to.

> Hey, babe, today I played at being an Actual Knight, with chivalry and everything.

A text he would never send, because after the single message he had got through to Chevreuse when he was on the run, and the location she sent back to him, he had destroyed his comms. Flirting with Dana was going to have to wait until this Milord business was over with, and she came to rescue him.

Dana was worth the wait.

"What is your name, dearie?" Sister Ursa asked as Conrad laid the woman on a bed. "Don't worry, we'll get you fixed up in no time."

The woman's eyes opened wide, as if startled, and Conrad saw that her eyes were grey, an odd combination with her deep brown skin. "I seek refuge," she gasped.

"That's what we're here for, ducks," said the elderly nun, patting the woman's hand.

Conrad stepped back, wanting to get out of their way, but he could not take his eyes off the stranger on the bed.

There was something about her that was so familiar, though he could have sworn he had never seen her before in his life.

"Sister Snow," breathed the patient, as the first medi-patch buzzed across her burned face. "My name is Sister Snow. I need you to help me."

She wasn't looking at any of the star nuns, as she said those words. She was looking directly at Conrad.

CHAPTER 25

TWO KINDS OF WINTER

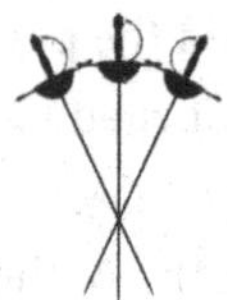

"Fascinating," said Athos, looking around at the bleak grey landscape that was the wind-lashed island of Finisterra. "I did not realise there was actually a more depressing corner of this planet than the province of La Fere. But here we are. And look, there's snow."

Dana knew it wasn't the snow that had him looking so wary and tense, but she wasn't going to say so out loud. Athos had been quiet and remarkably sober for most of their journey, which was not as comforting as it should have been.

"This is a mopping up job," said Porthos. "What are you so afraid of?"

Athos gave her a chilly expression. "Everything," he said.

Dana was caught up with thoughts of Conrad. Aramis had given Dana the coordinates that came directly from Chevreuse. It was up to them to rescue Conrad and take him home. They knew exactly where he was.

But first, there was official business to be dealt with, here at the tower on Finisterra.

Special Agent Rosnay Cho, still in charge of this mission, took point with two Sabres (Ducasse and L'Etoile) and the four Musketeers at her back. They entered the grey slab of a tower with all the gravity of a royal delegation.

Bianca de Winter, the Countess of Clarick, was waiting there for them, her expression as grim as the weather outside. "You know what I'm going to say," she announced without ceremony.

"I expect you're going to tell us that the slippery bastard escaped," said Ro. "There's no need to mince words, your Grace. I worked with Milord for years. I doubt you can surprise me."

Bee looked frosty. "I have done my duty to the letter, Special Agent Cho. My brother-in-law is still upstairs in the tower."

Ro raised her eyebrows. "He never left?"

"He never left."

"Felton carried out the assassination alone, then," Athos muttered to Ro.

"So it seems," she replied. "Milord waiting around for us to take him into custody seems awfully polite, doesn't it?"

"Well," said Athos in the driest of voices. "He *is* a gentleman."

Dana hung back with Porthos and Aramis, watching Rosnay Cho and Bee de Winter, who stared each other down like each was waiting for the other to flip a table and start the bar brawl.

Ro smiled, finally, pretending there was no possibility of animosity between them. "I'd like to question Milord de

Winter, before we make plans to escort him off planet. Captains-lieutenant Athos and D'Artagnan will accompany me, while the rest of my people question your security team, and survey the perimeter."

The Sabres nodded, while Porthos and Aramis managed salutes that weren't entirely sarcastic.

"Of course," said Bee, with a polite motion of her hand. "This way, Agent. Captains."

Dana fell into step behind Athos.

Bee led them up a spiralling staircase to the highest room in the tower. She swiped a card and entered several codes before the door slid open.

And there he was. Milord. His presence hit Dana like a punch to the solar plexus. He stood in a pool of rare winter sunlight, like a cat sunning himself. His hair had reverted to its bright silver hue, long around his shoulders. His shoes had disappeared somewhere. He wriggled his bare toes against the slate floor, apparently feeling no cold.

Dana risked a look at Athos, who displayed no reaction to the presence of his former husband.

"Hello, sweetness," said Milord, his eyes on Ro. She stared him down with a steady, implacable expression. "Miss me?"

"Milord," said Ro.

"So stiff and formal," he teased. "I know that the Cardinal has washed her hands of me, but you too? What does a man have to do around here to inspire a little loyalty?"

Bee and Athos made almost identical scoffing sounds at that, and then glanced, slightly embarrassed, at each other.

Dana noticed a nearby table, and an untouched tray of food. "Has he been eating?"

"Not for a few days," said Bee. "Says he doesn't need to. Alien biology and all that."

"Or I'm too traumatised," Milord suggested. "I feel a little traumatised."

There was something wrong in this room. Dana felt a light buzzing in her ears, as if danger approached. Something important had been missed.

"That's not him," she blurted out.

"What?" Ro and Athos said at the same time.

"It looks like him, but it's not Milord de Winter."

"Are you high?" Bee demanded.

Milord gazed at Dana with a twisted smile on his pretty face. "Give the girl a gold star," he purred. "Or some sort of cake related treat. I know how you Musketeers like your sweets."

"Explain yourself, D'Artagnan," said Rosnay Cho in a harsh voice. "If you're going to claim mistaken identity…"

"No," said Dana. "I'm sure he's responsible for every crime of which he is accused, and more." She did not take her eyes off Milord. "He's not blinking. He hasn't eaten his rations. We've been in here for nearly ten minutes and he hasn't tried to murder any of us."

"It is a terrible temptation," Milord agreed. "And yet I restrain myself."

"He's not human," Athos grated out. "D'Artagnan, you can't assume he will behave in a way that makes sense to us."

Dana picked up a plastic-wrapped fork from the rations tray, and threw it at the prisoner. The utensil went right through his chest and hit the window on the other side.

"Oh, shit," said the Countess of Clarick.

"It's a holo-projection," Athos snapped. "But from where?"

Dana went down on her knees to examine the floor at Milord's feet. "There's something here," she said. "A pocket knife, with a data stud embedded in it. I think that's where the projection is coming from."

Ro's comm chimed. "Boss?" said Porthos over the line, managing to say it with only a hint of irony. "We've got a problem."

"I bet it's not worse than the one we've got here," Ro snarled.

"We've lost eyes on Aramis," said Porthos, sounding worried. "Comms have gone dark."

Aramis was not the most considerate girlfriend, but she was aware of her own shortcomings. She tried to ensure that her partners had fun, that no one's heart got broken (except perhaps her own, but she was robust and could take it), and that she left no one's marriage in a worse state than when she began her seduction.

Even with the best of intentions, sometimes one slipped through the cracks.

Her affair with Jan Felton was the worst mess she had ever been involved with. It ended ugly, and Aramis had not covered herself in glory during the fallout. While Felton was publicly disgraced, divorced and left Paris Satellite under a cloud of scandal, Aramis ignored the drama, acting instead on the long-running flirtation she and Chevreuse had toyed with for years.

The guilt set in later, much later, after Felton's friends made sure to let Aramis know how badly she had fucked up.

Still, she hadn't realised it was quite this bad. Not trapped in a freezing cellar with an arc-ray pointed at her head bad.

Then again, if half of the babble coming out of Felton's mouth matched her state of mind, Aramis wasn't the only one who had screwed with her head. A certain 'Winter' had a lot to do with it.

"Jan," she said now through lips that felt cracked and sore in the chill air. "Did you kill the Duchess of Buckingham?"

Felton snapped out of her reverie, her hand tightening with greater confidence on the arc-ray. "I'm a Planetary Marshal," she spat. "The law is everything to me. He would never ask me to —"

"Because," Aramis went on steadily, "either Milord – or Winter, whatever he's calling himself – either he made you kill her, or he stole your identity to do it. You are wanted for murder right now. He did that to you. Not me."

Felton's face twisted into a snarl. "I'm only on this godforsaken rock because of you," she snapped, digging the point of the arc-ray into Aramis' temple. "I lost every-thing because of you. My wife. My career."

"Not your sense of justice," Aramis whispered. "Not the rule of law. I didn't take those things from you, Jan, I couldn't. He's inside your head, making you act against everything that's important to you. He has hung you out to *dry*."

Felton's eyes gleamed. "Every contract is on the side of law," she said, the words coming out stiff and robotic. "Adultery within the bounds of a marriage contract is against the law. You're the one who made me a criminal. Milord will set me free."

Aramis closed her eyes as the arc-ray twitched in Felton's hand. "You don't want to kill me, Jan," she whispered.

"You'd be surprised," Felton said hollowly.

They both heard the footsteps. Felton hissed, her hand coming around Aramis' throat even as the arc-ray jittered against her scalp. "Who's there?"

"Hello, Jan," said another voice.

Aramis breathed out, her pulse steadying as she recognised Athos. He might be a pure hot mess, but he was the best backup you could ever ask for. Second only to Porthos, who was there too, a step behind Athos. They projected calm, as if they had interrupted a tea party instead of a hostage situation.

"Get out of here," Felton snarled. "I know what you're like, the three of you. *Inseparables*. You laugh and joke and pick fights like the world is your goddamned playground."

"Sounds about right," said Athos. He was at the foot of the staircase now. The shallow pool of light from the cellar's solar lantern cast shadows across his face. "There are some things we take seriously. Loyalty." He looked at Aramis, taking in her position, then his focus snapped right back to Felton.

"I don't think you know a damned thing about loyalty," said Felton.

"I know a lot about the man who climbed inside your

head," said Athos, resting one hand on the banister, still a safe distance from Aramis and her captor. "I've been haunted by him for more than five years, Jan, since I cut off his head and had the body cremated. This is a ghost story, not a love saga. You need to let the ghost go."

"You're crazier than usual, Athos," Jan said fiercely.

Athos smiled with all his teeth. "That's when I'm at my best."

A tiny noise behind them alerted Aramis. She shoved at Felton, pushing the arc-ray aside. A body leaped out of the shadows, knocking Felton to the ground. Aramis secured the weapon before she realised it was Dana. There were four of them, now. Extra backup.

"Where did you come from, baby doll?"

"Fuel chute at the back of the cellar," Dana said, climbing off Felton and helping her up. "I was the only one small enough to fit."

"Excuse me," said Porthos, moving Athos aside. She came forward and punched Jan Felton solidly in the jaw. The other woman went down like a collapsed sack of grain. "Aramis, is now a good time to admit that I've never liked *any* of your girlfriends?"

Aramis spluttered out a laugh, pocketing Felton's arc-ray. "I love you too, Pol."

Athos pressed a Sobriety patch to Jan Felton's neck. "If this doesn't have an effect, we'll have to assume there's some kind of implant."

"Do you think he did the Winter thing to her?" Dana asked.

"No idea," said Athos. "Lucky us, we get to interrogate the prisoner."

Oh, thought Aramis. *That's not ominous at all.*

Whatever generations of de Winters and their staff had poured into that fuel chute over the years, Dana could smell it all over her skin. No time for sonic showers, not now. She took the stairs two at a time, racing up to the tower room.

To Dana's surprise as she entered the room, Milord and Ro were in polite conversation with each other.

"Am I interrupting something?" she demanded.

Ro was as unflappable as ever. "I'm not learning anything that the tech gals won't be able to drag out of the chip directly." She tapped a control on the knife that was the source of the projection, and the smirking figure of Milord vanished in a haze of pixels.

"Shame we can't do that with the real one," Dana said without thinking.

"Don't think you're the first to have that thought," Ro shot back. "Did you find Aramis?"

"Athos and Porthos are questioning Felton now. She never made it off the island."

Ro frowned. "It was Milord, then, who assassinated Buck. He used Felton's face."

"Looks like it," Dana agreed.

Ro picked up the small device from the floor, tossing it from hand to hand. "The bad news doesn't stop there, buttercup. While you were playing in the cellar, I got a ping from the investigators at Villiers House. They've picked up a trace of a comm message between Marie Chevreuse and Conrad Su from the day of the murder. A copy was bounced back to the house server thanks to the upgraded security net."

Dana went very still. "What does that mean?"

"The kind of privacy settings that Minister Chevreuse uses on her messages means we never should have found that message. Turns out the Villiers House server was hacked, hours after the assassin disappeared." Ro raised her eyebrows. "Does the Church of All Convent of Carmelline, in the peaks of the Drift Mountains, mean anything to you?"

Dana felt something break inside her. "That's the safe house Chevreuse provided for Conrad Su." The only people who should have that information were Chevreuse, Prince Alek, Conrad, Aramis and Dana. And the nuns.

Ro nodded grimly. "Makes sense. So, with what we know about Milord, assuming he saw the message from Chevreuse, where do you think he's heading next?"

Conrad, damn it all. I thought you were safe. "The convent," Dana said. "I think that's exactly where we'll find him."

CHAPTER 26
A DROP OF WATER

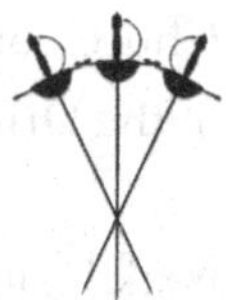

odies were strange. Human bodies stranger than most; though it was so long since Milord had allowed himself to be truly Sun-kissed, to burn bright in his natural state.

To be a female was a new journey. Taking Felton's shape meant more than copying her face, the shape of her rib-cage, her brisk and military manner. It meant shaping breasts and cunt to be hidden beneath layers of uniform; it meant a different way of walking, a different tilt of the hips and length of spine.

Being Felton and being female-shaped were equally strange states after spending nearly a decade as some version of a beautiful young man.

Once it was done, once Georgiana Villiers the Duchess of Buckingham lay dead on her own floor, once 'Marshal Felton' had bugged the communication lines, taken out several members of the security team and found a safe house at a good distance from the scene of the crime in order to monitor and consider her next move…

Once all that was done, Milord had to choose a new face and body. A person that no one would recognise.

He had failed to kill Conrad Su at the house, but the message he intercepted less than an hour after the assassination of Buck provided the location where he was heading. The Convent of Carmelline. The next body he made for himself would also have to be female-shaped.

Only when he had finished the shaping and smoothing of the new identity did Milord realise how much he had borrowed from Dana D'Artagnan – he had become a tall, softer version of her with similar skin tone and facial features. Not close enough to raise suspicion, but perhaps Su would feel a connection to the mysterious stranger.

Milord prodded at the new body, noting where he needed muscle tone or soft tissue, refining the design. When it was done, he illustrated the arms with a tangled pattern similar to those he had seen scrawled across the tail fins of sabre-class darts.

These humans. A few crosses and star fields carved into an object – or a person – and they deemed it sacred.

Tattooed and perfect, wrapped in the robes of a space nun, Milord set out to locate the secret stash of credit studs he had set aside for emergencies when he had been Vaniel de Winter. No need to steal a skimmer when he could purchase one without suspicion.

Revenge was a weakness. He knew that. And yet, he wanted this particular revenge so badly, he could taste it in his new mouth. The job was not complete until Conrad Su was as dead as the Duchess of Buckingham. What else did he have to live for, but to thwart his enemies?

Conrad Su would never see Sister Snow coming.

"This is going to take forever," Dana D'Artagnan raged. "We have to get there *now*. Can't we take one of the darts?"

"Spaceships are not exactly the thing for mountaineering," drawled Bee de Winter. "If you're willing to risk causing an avalanche in the region, be my guest, but I suggest you listen to local advice."

"Skimmer's the only way to cover the area safely," said Athos, rugged up and ready to go. He had found another three layers of woollen clothing somewhere in the tower. "I've called ahead to Brabazon, the nearest city to the Drift Mountains, and ordered two skimmers to be picked up there. We can dock the darts at Portside."

"Hang on," said Aramis, frowning. "There's a good distance between Portside and Brabazon. Is there a bullet train between them?"

Bee laughed suddenly, and then sobered. "Oh, you're serious. The bullet train doesn't go that far north. No one does, by choice."

Athos exchanged a glance with Ro.

If ever Dana had been wary of those two teaming up, now she had all senses on high alert. "What aren't you telling us?" she demanded.

"It's a dirtsider thing," said Ro with a smirk. "Don't worry, it won't kill you."

Conrad stood out on the stone wall, watching the horizon and letting his breath turn to steam. Sister Snow spent a lot of time up here, he had noticed. She was polite to the nuns, but her preference was for silence and stillness away from their friendly buzz.

He was out here because if he had to listen to a nun analyse his fleur-de-lis team history one more time, he might punch one of them.

"Everyone has been so kind," said Sister Snow. She was dressed in robes lent to her by the nuns of the Convent of Carmelline – thick white wool, trimmed in bands of striking red that reflected the dark tattoos still visible at her wrists and throat. Her wounds had mostly been healed via medipatch with only a few spidery scars remaining that would disappear after another treatment or two.

"They do their best," said Conrad. "This is a good place to gather yourself, before the next thing comes along."

Sister Snow turned a smile on him that was surprisingly cheerful, white teeth gleaming. "What's the next thing for you, Conrad Su? Where are you going, when you have gathered yourself?"

"I haven't decided," he said, which was all kinds of lie. He wasn't going to tell a nun that he was running straight back to Paris as soon as it was safe, into the arms of a brave and funny Musketeer instead of his wife.

He wanted Dana D'Artagnan. He wanted his job back. His life. He wanted to return to Alek's side, designing new outfits to conceal the growing pod babies that the wretched Prince had slung inside his shirt.

Conrad wanted to stop feeling bad about Buck, who had been good to him, but whose death made protecting Alek a hell of a lot easier. Wow, yeah, there was the guilt stab, right in the stomach and completely on schedule.

He wanted Lunar Palais and fleur-de-lis and Dana and a chance to breathe air that wasn't made by goddamn trees.

So many things he wanted, but he would settle for one right now.

"I'm ready to go home," he told Sister Snow. What did she care about the details, anyway? "It's not safe yet. My girl will let me know when the coast is clear."

"Oh," said Sister Snow, with an odd sort of smile. It felt as if he had met her before, though Conrad could not place her, for the life of him. "You have a girl?"

"That is a trick question," he said, pointing a finger at her, half-accusing. "You want me to spill my story."

She gave him a merry expression. "What else is there to do around here?"

"My story is long and complex and I'm pretty sure I can't tell it sober."

Sister Snow arched an eyebrow at him. "Luckily for you, the sisters left a flask of wine in my room."

"I do love nuns," Conrad said fondly. "There should be a nun appreciation day."

"On behalf of nuns everywhere," said Sister Snow. "I salute you."

"Horses," moaned Porthos. "It had to be horses."

"It's horses or mecha," insisted Athos. You had to know him very well to spot the amusement behind his flat expression. "Only way to cover the distance to Brabazon."

"Horses," Aramis said quickly. "Seriously. I know we made fun of you, Dana, when you were training for

Essart's squad, but Porthos would destroy the world if she ever tapped into a mecha suit."

"Mecha for me," said Dana. "Oh God, mecha. Please." The thought of it – of riding a live creature that rolled and breathed under her – made her feel physically sick.

"I'll go with D'Artagnan," said Rosnay Cho. "We'll make better time than the three of you on horseback, and take one skimmer from Brabazon. The rest of you can collect the other."

The Sabres had stayed behind with the rest of the ships and the Countess of Clarick. It was clear that Ro wanted to be rid of them as much as the Musketeers did, though Dana hadn't thought too closely about what that might mean.

Athos frowned. "I don't like it. We shouldn't split up."

Dana gave him an impatient look. "We can't delay further. Milord will not hesitate to kill Conrad if he gets near him. Ro and I will go ahead."

"Meanwhile, we get to watch Athos demonstrate his superiority with land-based mammals," Porthos groaned. "Wonderful."

"It's not my fault you were born on an ocean world," Athos said smugly.

"Just you wait until the safety of the solar system hinges on my dolphin-training skills!"

The mecha that Ro and Dana hired from Portside were different to the suits that Dana had grown familiar with on Lunar Palais. They were designed for harsh winter conditions, converting from the usual humanoid form to some kind of snow bike setting with large wheels, a heavy tread, and hover mode.

There was a setting labelled 'blizzard' which Dana hoped she never had to use.

With the map programmed in, she and Ro made good time across the icy plains until the statuesque city of Brabazon came into sight. It was like something off an old-fashioned Joyeux card, with intricate gabled roofs that might have been constructed from gingerbread.

Dana barely even glanced at the city's adorableness as they shifted their bikes back to humanoid setting and headed up the street towards the skimmer dealership: two large metal giants stomping across the snow. "Do you think we made good time?" she asked Ro over the comms.

"Hard to tell," Ro buzzed back. "We don't know how much of a lead Milord has on us."

Enough, Dana thought darkly.

The wine wasn't anything special – not like the vintages that Conrad had been spoiled with during his time as the Prince Consort's companion. It did the job to loosen his tongue as he told Sister Snow a censored but amusing version of his love affair with Dana D'Artagnan, his various kidnaps, and his most recent flight across the snowy northern wastes of Castellion to reach the most inappropriate safe house Chevreuse (or as he renamed her for the story, 'Sheba') had ever provided for him.

"I'm not convinced it's not a practical joke," he admitted. "Was always a bit of a prankster, my mate Sheb. Star nuns with a sports fetish – can't be a coincidence."

"At least you're safe," said Sister Snow. She had been watching him carefully since he first started drinking the wine – barely blinking, in fact.

Conrad remembered the last time someone had watched him like that, and it wasn't a good memory.

"Huh," he said, and set the glass down. "Are you waiting for something?"

Sister Snow's eyes widened and she started blinking again, like a normal human being. "I don't know what you mean, dear."

"It's just – it's kind of obvious now," he said. "That you spiked my drink. I'm assuming not poison, since we drank the same wine. Or you could have taken the antidote already, hadn't thought of that."

Sister Snow tensed. Only slightly, but the shift of body language was enough.

"Yeah," said Conrad with a small nod. "Thought so. Could look like anyone, they told me. Might have been less obvious if you hadn't borrowed half my girlfriend's features."

Now that he was looking for it, he could see how much of Sister Snow's face and body type had been inspired by Dana – not the height, that was Buck if anything, but the shape of the shoulders, the ears, the *eyes*, damn it. No wonder she had seemed so familiar, no wonder he had felt like he could talk to her.

There was a confidence in her – his – her face, a calmness. Conrad had hit the nail on the head. Sister Milord Snow was waiting for something to kick off. Something that was in the drink.

"Thing is," Conrad went on. "I know you only kidnapped me the once, and you weren't after any information at the time, but you worked with the Cardinal's people for years. Do none of you talk to each other? Special Agent Cho figured out in the first five minutes that psych drugs don't work on me. Genetic incompatibility. Luck of the draw. Doesn't matter what kind of braindrain shit you made me ingest – it won't take."

Sister Snow's gaze flicked to the half glass of wine that remained, and then back to Conrad's face. She smiled, and it wasn't the wry smile of a fellow traveller anymore. It wasn't human.

Not for nothing was Conrad a member of the only fleur-de-lis team of all time to have an unbeatable season. He leaped to his feet and hurled himself backwards as Sister Snow – Milord – made his move. Even in stupid planetary gravity, Conrad was more than capable of a quick handspring to the window ledge, where he kicked out the glass – real glass – and watched it shatter across the snow-packed staircase that wound around the outside of the convent.

Milord lunged for Conrad, who launched himself out into mid-air and came down hard with a skid on the landing below. He rushed down the steps even as the freezing northern wind tore through his clothes.

Where to go? This was the safe house, so where to go next? He wasn't even sure where the star nuns had docked his skimmer. Sister Snow herself had arrived via skimmer, but hers had crashed, hadn't it? Or did she fake that?

Conrad saw a shape in the hazy distance of the mountains, cutting through the grey white of the endless winter sky. It looked like a ship. A rescue party, or more of Milord's traitorous aliens?

Something – *someone* – slammed into him from behind.

Conrad turned as he fell, soaring into the air for a breathless moment before he hit the steps, his head cracking with a fierce pain against a corner.

As his vision swam, he saw the white and red blur of a nun and wondered if he was doomed, or saved. "Don't hurt the rest of them," he slurred. "They didn't do anything… soup and porridge. Good nuns."

The nun leaned over him and yanked the scarf back from his head. It was doom after all. Sister Snow nudged him with her foot, looking satisfied. "For what it's worth, I didn't put psych drugs in the wine. I was waiting for the wine to run out, so you would reach for the flask of water."

Wetness fell out of nowhere, a steady flow from a flask on to Conrad's face. He screwed up his eyes and mouth, trying not to breathe, but it stung his skin and he spluttered it through his nose before his traitorous mouth coughed open to take a splash of water inside.

"Just a drop," said Milord de Winter. "That's all I need."

"This is depressing," said Ro, surveying the grey buildings settled into the mountainside, layered in white snow. "There should be more safe houses on beaches and tropical islands."

"I'll make a note of that in the report," Dana sighed, tapping her foot impatiently as they waited on the top step of the convent.

The deep, resounding tone of the bell still vibrated against the walls, but it was a while before they heard footsteps and a tiny, elderly nun pushed open the massive doors to let them in.

"More guests," she said, looking pleased. "I'm Sister Ursa. Welcome to the Sharing Hall. I don't suppose you are famous fleur-de-lis players too? We're hoping to get a team together for an exhibition game."

"I'm the Musketeer D'Artagnan," said Dana as the door closed behind them. Ro started stripping off her heated gloves and snow-damp outer layers, but Dana didn't want to waste time. "This is Special Agent Cho. We need to see Conrad." No point in wasting her time asking for his pseudonym if the nuns were Emerald Knights fans.

Before Sister Ursa could answer, a great clanging alarm shook the walls.

"Sisters!" yelled another nun from the courtyard beyond the Sharing Hall. "We are under attack!"

Dana ran.

She found herself skidding and sliding across a frosted courtyard and up a stone staircase towards a nun with cinquefoil-standard biceps beneath her robes. The nun had the unconscious figure of Conrad Su draped in her mighty arms.

"Sister Volantis, what is going on?" cried Sister Ursa as more and more nuns gathered in the courtyard.

Dana's own feet stopped moving as she stared at the figure of Conrad, unsure if he was even breathing.

"Sister Snow did this," said Sister Volantis grimly. "Who are these strangers?"

"We're his friends," Dana said helplessly. "Is he –"

"Hurt," Volantis snapped, and pushed past everyone to sweep Conrad into the Sharing Hall, laying him flat on the enormous table. "Send for Sister Gemini! We need medic intervention now – head wound."

Yes, there was blood smeared on the table, Dana realised, and in Conrad's blue-tipped hair. As the nuns scattered to arrange medical attention, she stepped closer and laid her fingers over his hand. It was cold, but from the snowy air, she was certain, not a lack of pulse.

"Conrad," she whispered.

His eyes fluttered open and fixed upon her. "Here's trouble."

"Hey," Dana said with a soft smile. "Heard you got taken down by a nun."

"Don't laugh. The nuns around here are mighty and glorious." His eyes glazed over, losing focus. "He's a star nun now. Looks a bit like you."

"Milord," Dana breathed. "It's okay, we've got you now."

"How long ago?" Rosnay Cho broke in. "How far could he have gone?"

Conrad looked confused.

"Head injury, dear," Sister Ursa reminded them gently.

"Water," said Conrad.

Dana looked around. "Can we get him some water?"

Several nuns with medipacks and other equipment, led by a uniformed medic that the others called Sister Gemini, crashed into the Sharing Hall from an inner door.

"No," said Conrad, his hand squeezing Dana's finger with surprising strength. "It was in the water. Sorry about – our timing's *terrible*."

"What was –" and the words caught in her throat as she saw him shudder on the table, his hand falling from hers. "No. Help him!"

The nuns with medical training closed in and around Conrad. Dana stared wildly, wishing that Aramis were here, that any of her Musketeers were here. Last they had checked in with each other, the three of them were in the second skimmer, two hours behind Dana and Ro.

"Poison," said one of the nuns, checking the readings on a medipatch. "It's damaging his blood vessels faster than the tech can repair him."

"But it's not," said Dana. "He can't –"

Conrad's body shuddered again, and the medipatches beeped furiously.

"Heart's stopped," said Sister Gemini, sounding grim. "I can't – what kind of poison is this?"

Rosnay Cho breathed out. It could have been any other breath, but Dana was on high alert for anything, any sign. "What is it? What do you know?"

"This sounds like the illness that Milady Delia de Winter suffered from before she died," said Ro heavily. She moved a hand as if she was going to touch Dana in some comforting way, but stopped before she made contact. "As a point of reference."

"I see," said Dana.

The nuns continued to work on Conrad, attempting to get his heart started again. Dana turned around and walked back out of the warm convent, into the snow.

CHAPTER 27
COLD HANDS, RED CLOAK

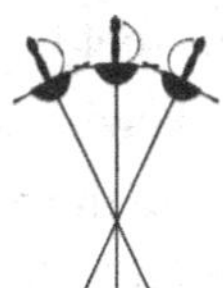

Dana stayed on the snowy landing until warm hands came to take her away. An arm wrapped around her and led her into the echoing meeting hall.

It wasn't until she was inside, breathing air that didn't hurt her lungs, that she realised it was Aramis who had hold of her.

"When did you get here?" she whispered.

"Just arrived," said Aramis, squeezing her close. "Damn it, Dana, you'd been out there for hours. Didn't the nuns try to move you?"

"They may have said some things. Didn't sink in."

She remembered the old one, Sister Ursa, informing her that Conrad was dead, and things got rather hazy after that.

Something clicked inside Dana as she saw Porthos and Athos, still wearing their thick winter gear, talking to several concerned looking nuns. Someone was missing.

"Where's Ro?" she asked aloud.

"Your guess is as good as ours," Aramis said. "She was long gone when we arrived."

Dana huffed at that. Her lungs felt raw and painful as she warmed up. "She went after him," she guessed.

"Entirely possible."

Across the room, Athos met Dana's gaze and then looked away. It was Porthos who came over and held Dana's hand while she broke the news to her. "There's surveillance footage," she said. "Turns out these nuns are as committed to security as they are to fleur-de-lis."

"Lot of good it did Conrad," Dana said bitterly. "They let Milord waltz right in here because he looked like one of them."

Porthos looked sick. "Athos is checking the footage now," she said. "But it looks very much like Special Agent Cho met up with Milord between your arrival and ours. They left together."

Oh. So that was a thing that had happened.

Dana didn't cry. Not even when Athos showed her the footage that proved that ten minutes after Conrad Su officially died, Rosnay Cho was halfway down the fucking mountain, in conversation with a figure that the other nuns identified as Sister Snow, a recent addition to their community.

A murderer.

The two of them left together after what looked like an extremely amiable seven-minute conversation which did not involve anyone arresting anyone else.

Dana did not cry, but she did get angry. So angry that

her friends had to hold her down, pin her to the wall so she didn't rampage through the convent that had failed so badly to be a safe house.

At one point, she came back to herself and realised that she was standing in that damned snowy courtyard again. Athos had been patiently letting her hit him in the chest for… a while.

"Sorry," she muttered and wiped her mouth. Her knuckles ached with bruises and cold.

Athos gave her a thin smile. "Could be worse. You could be grieving on a mountain top, so fucked up that you think joining the Musketeers is a good idea. Oh, wait."

Dana blinked at that, and looked around her. "Is this the same mountain?"

"No," he said calmly. "This isn't the mountain, Dana. That mountain is a long way from here."

"What's it called? I want to see it."

"It's called Athos," he said, and watched her dissolve into a fit of shocked laughter. "Shut up."

"You named yourself after a mountain!"

"It was a significant mountain."

The laughter had been a bad idea, because Dana couldn't stop now and oh, maybe she was crying after all.

A look of panic crossed Athos's face, and he summoned the others. "I only signed up for anger and denial," he said, and propelled Dana into the arms of Porthos and Aramis.

They bundled her away from the courtyard, into a small and comforting room that was almost warm. Dana buried her face in the chilled coat of Porthos and sobbed loudly, messily, while Aramis stroked her close-shorn scalp.

Milord was gone. He had done exactly what he came here for, made the most predictable move, and they hadn't been able to stop him. He had got away with it. Ro, damn her, was helping him, of course she was. The Cardinal must still have some use for Milord de Winter.

That betrayal hurt more than it should have.

A horrible noise was coming out of her now. It was embarrassing, but she couldn't stop it. Tight arms pinned her down, kept her safe, her friends taking turns to hug her as she cried.

Dana felt the sharp stubble of a close-cut beard against her cheek and realised it was Athos who held her now. She could hear Aramis and Porthos talking in low voices, across the other side of the room.

"I don't know what to do," Dana gasped.

"Love is what kills us," said Athos, his voice rough. "Nothing else can destroy the human race half so fast. I suspect he was sent here to hurt us in the worst possible ways. It's the only explanation."

Dana head-butted him lightly. She had no more words.

"Okay," said Porthos in a businesslike voice, coming back to them. "Dana, you ready to get back in the game?"

"Is it revenge time yet?" Dana asked in a small voice. She was tired of all these feelings.

"Here's the thing," said Aramis, bright-eyed and excited. "They left in the hire skimmer, the same one you and Cho arrived here in, Dana."

Dana frowned at her. "So?"

"So, Planchet can track it." Aramis waved a clamshell at her. "We know which way they're going."

"That's good," said Athos. "Let's go."

Porthos and Aramis both gave him a look. Dana knew

that look. It was an expression they usually used behind his back.

"What aren't you telling us?" she said in a low voice.

"From their current route," said Aramis awkwardly. "Planchet suspects they are heading for the province of La Fere."

Athos nodded as if this was no more or less than he had expected. "If anyone attempts to talk to me about *my* feelings," he said stiffly. "I'm going to throw them out of the skimmer. Why aren't we in the skimmer already?"

Porthos gave him a hearty clap on the shoulder. "That's the spirit."

"I will end you," he growled.

They made their hasty farewells to the shellshocked star nuns and headed back out to where the Musketeers had docked the second skimmer some way back down the snowy steps. Athos stayed protectively close to Dana all the way. She wasn't sure whether to hit him or hug him, but she settled for saying nothing at all.

Athos made some calls from the skimmer. He spoke quietly in his New Aristocrat voice: he gave co-ordinates and sent texts, and his face was so thunderous that no one – not Dana, Aramis nor Porthos – dared to ask him exactly what he was doing.

"We're going to have some company in La Fere," was all he told them.

"I've had a thought," said Porthos.

The others looked at her, except Aramis who was piloting the skimmer.

"Well?" Dana said expectantly.

"There's no way Agent Cho didn't know we could track the skimmer. Maybe she's not on his side after all."

Dana stared at her boots, and thought about throwing up.

La Fere was a thousand square kilometres of grey rock, picturesque lavender hills and pale green grazing land. Hardly anyone lived here; there was one medium-sized town near the Bethune border, a handful of rural villages and a scattering of farms.

As far as Athos was aware, the whole place got along swimmingly without any occupants playing lord of the manor from the d'Auteville estate.

Then again, Olivier Armand d'Auteville was believed to be dead. For all Athos knew, the estate could be crawling with distant cousins who had turned the place into a strip club casino.

The thought of a giant disco ball rotating from the ceiling of his Maman's picture-perfect salonniere, or the family silver being sold off to pay for a bulk batch of roulette wheels, would be enough to make him smile, on any other day.

Here he was, chief phantom in his very own ghost story, about to face the worst demon of his past. Sober.

"I don't understand why Milord would return home like this," said Porthos – and Athos had to work very hard to conceal a twitch at the word 'home' in this context – "Surely he knows that the La Fere estate is the most obvious place for us to look for him."

"Sometimes the guilty seek penance," said Aramis, wearing her 'religious contemplation' hat. "The worst criminals often want to get caught."

"He's doing it to make me follow him," ground out Athos. Wasn't it obvious to the rest of them? "To force me to go home. All he has left now is revenge."

"That's why he killed Conrad," said D'Artagnan in a small voice that reminded Athos all over again how damned young she was. "Revenge against me."

"Of course," Athos said, only to be faced with blazing expressions of both Aramis and Porthos, in matching performances of Shut Up, Athos, You Just Said Something Tactless. "I mean – who can truly know the mind of a madman?"

"Good save," D'Artagnan said dryly.

The tracker led them directly to Foilles, the village nearest the d'Auteville manor. *Home.* Aramis brought them down practically on top of the hire skimmer that was identical to their own, on the outskirts of town.

"That's my ship!" said Dana, her head coming up as she recognised the bright yellow eyesore that was the *Buttercup,* already docked on the grass alongside the skimmers and Athos' own *Pistachio.*

"I got in touch with the engies," Athos admitted.

"Good idea," said Porthos.

Athos shrugged uncomfortably, aware that he had been taking the lead on this, something he generally preferred not to do. Responsibility was a terrible addiction that destroyed lives. On the other hand, his husband had just murdered D'Artagnan's boyfriend, therefore Athos was going to accept a certain amount of responsibility until the bastard was dead. He could quit leadership any time he liked. "If there's a chance we can get this sewn up this afternoon, I don't want to waste any time getting us off the fucking planet," he grumbled.

Aramis leaned over and prodded him in the stomach, to let him know that she saw through him, as always.

Like Athos needed a bruised abdomen to know that.

The four Musketeers spilled out of the cramped skimmer and onto the grass. Pigtails and Bonnie emerged from the *Hoyden* and ran towards them with a reluctant Bazin trailing behind.

"No sign of Milord," said Pigtails, the words bursting out of her with juvenile excitement. "But we found Agent Cho easily enough."

"Is it too much to hope she's in the pub?" Athos said wistfully. The home-brewed beer of the Foilles watering hole was one of only three things he missed about his home.

Pigtails blinked at him. "How did you know?"

Grimaud waited for them outside the Fleur and Anchor, swaddled in a thicker star scarf than she usually wore, and scowling at the world. A tension that Athos had not even realised he was carrying unwound at the sight of her. He always felt better when he knew she was near, and safe.

"In there?" he asked without greeting.

Grimaud nodded, peered at him for a moment, checking for injuries, and went back to pretending he didn't exist.

"Musketeers inside, engies out here in case there's trouble," Athos commanded.

The engies grumbled about this distribution of labour.

"For when there is inevitably trouble," Athos clarified. "If you spot our target, or anyone suspicious, do not engage them on your own."

The engies all took on oddly similar expressions at this piece of advice, even Bazin. How did that level of sarcasm even work on an android face?

"It's sweet that you think you're in charge," Bonnie informed him.

Aramis staved off any possibility of an Athos-and-engies smackdown by steering him inside the pub. Porthos and D'Artagnan followed close behind.

Nostalgia swept over Athos like a heavy curtain full of knives. The smell of this place was exactly the same: beer and coffee and browning pastry, soaked into the deep grey stone of the walls and the slate of the floor.

He knew the barman, though he didn't remember his name – an old man with a flat expression who (of course) knew who Athos was the second he stepped in the door.

This was a mistake. No going back now.

After a brief sweep of the room with no sign of Agent Cho, Athos stepped up to the bar. "Black hair, scar?" he said.

The barman made a grunting noise and pointed. "Courtyard."

"Cheers." The lack of further questions made Athos feel oddly lightheaded. It had always been like that in here, he remembered. Everyone knew who he was: the young Comte from the big house who lost his parents too young and married an outsider straight out of university, then later executed his husband on the village green for being an alien spy. No one had ever said an unnecessary word about any of it, when he was in here and needed a drink.

"Does everyone talk like that around here?" he heard Porthos hiss to Aramis. "A whole town full of Athoses!"

They crowded into the doorway that opened on to the walled courtyard: Athos with D'Artagnan beside him, the other two squishing into them from behind.

"Oh no," D'Artagnan breathed.

Special Agent Rosnay Cho paced back and forth in fury, arguing with empty air. She flung her arms, hissed between her teeth, and got up in the face of her invisible opponent. An arc-ray twirled between her fingers.

There wasn't room to draw a sword, so Athos went for his stunner, knowing Porthos and Aramis were blocked from making the shot. He didn't bank on D'Artagnan, who slipped out from his side and marched right up to the raving agent.

"You idiot," D'Artagnan said, shoving her. "You *drank* something he gave you?"

"Of course I didn't," Cho said, whirling on D'Artagnan. Not pointing the arc-ray at her, as such, but not holding it safe by her side, either. "What the hell do you think I am?"

"How about a traitor?"

Cho scoffed, then turned to address empty air again. "Shut up you. Keep out of it."

"You've got Winter in your head," D'Artagnan accused. "Don't you?"

"He slapped a patch on my wrist while I was flying the skimmer," Cho admitted sullenly. "What do you mean, traitor? I'm leading this fucking mission."

"We were supposed to be working together!" Dana howled. "Until you ran off hand in hand with the target."

"I would have brought you along for the ride, buttercup, but you were too busy being catatonic over the death of your boyfriend and somehow I don't think your presence would have made Milord less suspicious of my motives!"

"Shut up, both of you!" Aramis ordered, stepping between D'Artagnan and Cho. "This is all very sweet, getting your feelings out in the open, and usually I'd be all for it, but I'd like to ask a question. Can he –" And she indicated the empty space where Rosnay Cho had directed her non-D'Artagnan-related anger, "Hear what we're saying?"

"How am I supposed to know how this works?" Cho demanded.

"I think he can listen in," D'Artagnan said sourly. "If it's like the others. Why do it otherwise?"

"Then I suggest we get on with arresting our target without a digital spy in our midst," said Aramis.

Agent Cho looked murderous. "You can't leave me out of this. This is *my* mission."

"I think we're past that, aren't we?" Aramis countered.

Athos lost what little patience he had left. He lifted his arm and shot Agent Cho through the head with the pearl-white beacon of his stunner. She crumpled and D'Artagnan caught her awkwardly, lowering her to the ground.

"That's one way to win a conversation," muttered Porthos.

"She didn't tell us which way he went!" D'Artagnan

protested, looking down at the unconscious Cho like she could will her back awake.

"I know which way he went," said Athos. "Come on. We've got one more stop to make first."

He headed back through the pub, with three Musketeers following him. He heard Aramis hang back to instruct the engies about returning Cho to the ships, but did not slow his pace to give her a chance to catch up. That was why she had those long legs, after all.

Finally, Athos stopped at the edge of the village, and knocked sharply at the bright red door of a whitewashed building. A familiar figure emerged: cloaked all in red, her face masked and her hands covered.

"Mother," said Athos, and kissed the gloved hand that extended to him. It felt like ice beneath the light silk. "Time to go."

The red cloaked figure nodded and set out before him, leading the way out of the village and up the well-trod path to the higher pastures and the over-sized house that had been built to overlook the entire province.

"Come on," he said to his friends.

They glanced awkwardly at each other before hurrying after him. "Athos, is that actually your mother?" Porthos asked.

"No," he said honestly, surprised she had thought so. "My mother's dead."

"Then…"

"That is my priest," he explained, following the red mother up the path towards his worst nightmare.

His three best friends in the world followed him without further comment.

CHAPTER 28
THE HOUSE OF ATHOS

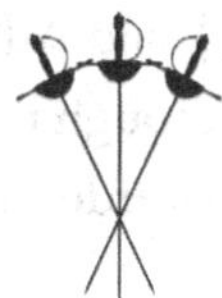

The silence on the walk up the slope was comforting, though Athos knew his friends were burning with questions. It was remarkably restrained of them to hold back.

The red mother did not speak either, and that was a different kind of comfort. He remembered her as an acolyte, holding the cup and knife for the old red mother when he was a child. The acolyte was the one who had taught him the Elemental rituals that were expected of the eldest son of a great family, long before he became cynical about everything else that was expected of him.

The old red mother had passed into retirement or death since Athos had left Foilles. He did not ask the questions that might be expected from a local man, recently returned home. He did not care what had changed in the meantime.

They reached the tall gates, marked with the sacred symbols of fire and water, earth and air. The red mother halted, her dark-painted mouth barely visible beneath her deep red hood.

Athos breathed on the lock and placed his palm there. He did not need to state his name. House recognised him, and let him through the security field.

"Welcome home, your grace," House said in a clear voice that rang out from the empty air.

"These are my guests," said Athos, not wanting to address the title for now, though it made his skin crawl. "The red mother is to be awarded the same security privileges as her predecessor."

"Understood, your grace," said House smoothly. "Welcome to Auteville Manor, mother."

The priest bowed her head in silent acknowledgement.

"House," Athos went on. "Please recognise Porthos, Aramis and D'Artagnan. They are personal guests, to have security privileges for the ground floor zone only."

"Welcome, Porthos, Aramis, D'Artagnan," said House. There was a different note in his voice there, as if he was proud that Athos had returned with friends.

No, that was stupid. House felt nothing. Athos had always let his imagination run wild. He needed to resist such childhood habits.

The red mother and the Musketeers stepped through the security field. Athos led the way up the path again, not looking around to see their reaction as the manor came into view. After years calling a space station home, it was embarrassing to realise quite how much space the d'Auteville family thought was reasonable for them to take up.

"House," he said to fill the silence. "Have we had any visitors since I left?"

House recited a litany of failed attempts by Athos' distant relatives, lawyers and other officials to breach the security field over the last several years. If anyone ever questioned whether it was possible for an AI to demonstrate smugness, here was the evidence.

Athos had been so very angry, in the immediate days after Auden's execution. He was drunk, of course, and furious at the world. He had a vague memory that when he abandoned the manor, he had left the door wide open, and vocalised no orders to preserve the house for his return.

He had never planned to come back here.

Perhaps he had given House some security instructions after all, as part of a drunken rant. Perhaps House had simply and quietly tidied up after him, making an assumption on behalf of the Comte de la Fere when the man himself was unable to make the right call.

Either way, there was one person, he was certain, whose access had never been revoked, because he was dead. Even Athos had not been that paranoid. Not then.

"House," he *interrupted*, as he reached the door. "Have we had any visitors recently?"

"No visitors in the last 48 hours," said House precisely. "A stranger tested our security twelve hours ago but failed the visual scan and fingerprint test, and went away."

Athos swallowed, because the door was so damned big and heavy and he didn't want to open it, not at all. "Is there anyone in residence besides myself and my guests, House?"

"Mr Auden is in the iris library," said House. "He arrived ten hours and fourteen minutes ago."

"That's good," Athos said with a very dry mouth. "Good house. You've done well."

"He's actually here?" D'Artagnan said quietly.

"Too much to hope that the iris library is in the ground floor zone?" Aramis asked pointedly. She never missed much.

"Open," said Athos, and stepped forward into a blinding pattern of black and white tiles that swept across the floor of the foyer. A huge staircase sprawled up one wall, leading to the upper floors. Even the goddamned pot plants were green and leafy as ever.

He had expected to return to a ruin, to something dust-caked, looted and neglected that represented the conflicted feelings he had about his former home.

House, of course, had other ideas. Athos should have known.

His father would approve that House had held up so well. He would not approve of Athos' failure to meet his responsibilities over the last five years.

Time to make up for that by addressing the one responsibility he had failed most thoroughly to accomplish. It was time to rid the estate of a monster.

"The iris library," Porthos growled. "Where is it?"

"Third floor," said Athos, and didn't even smile.

"You're not going up there alone."

"You're *not*," D'Artagnan added. "I want him, Athos. You can't keep me down here and out of the way. I don't need to be protected."

"Of course you do," said Athos calmly. He glanced at Aramis, the only one not currently furious with him. Her calm lack of surprise was somewhat soothing. "I can handle this, D'Artagnan. Trust me."

"You're not trusting us," she complained. "We're a team now. You don't have to run around playing lord and master and lone hero and all those stupid things from the holo-channels. You need back up."

"I brought back up," said Athos, and nodded briefly to the red mother. "I brought all of you. If he gets past me and House, you're here to stop him getting away."

"That's not comforting if he kills you, Athos!" D'Artagnan protested, her fists curled into tight balls.

He felt bad for a moment, but not as bad as if she was bleeding on the ground, because of course Auden – *Milord* would go for her first. D'Artagnan was the youngest and the least experienced, and Milord hated her.

"I'll see you soon," Athos said, and turned to make his way up the enormous staircase. As soon as he reached the lowest step, his friends were unable to stop him.

Hot anger pricked at Dana's eyes and that was so similar to crying that she wasn't sure why she even held back.

"Tea," said the red mother serenely, and led the way to a kitchen roughly the size of the Stellar Concourse.

"You speak," said Aramis deferentially, as the Musketeers trooped in after her. "I wasn't sure that you did."

"There are times for sacred silence," said the Elemental priest, slipping her hood from her shoulders and pushing her mask up to her hairline. She was young, barely forty if she was a day, and wore a streak of dark lipstick across her mouth. "There are times when it is appropriate to speak. Tea is one of those times."

"We should be with him," Dana grumbled. "He's going to get himself killed."

Porthos gave her a reassuring thump of a hip against

hers. "Chin up," she said. "Athos has done a lot of things over the last five years that were practically guaranteed to get himself killed. He hasn't managed it yet."

"Athos the Musketeer," said the priest, trying out the name in her mouth. "Is that what our Olivier calls himself now?"

"He's good at it," said Aramis. "We're not leaving without him," she added.

"Then we had better make sure he does not lose his way while he is here," said the priest with a smile. "House, we will have the chrysanthemum tea. If Mr Auden makes any violent move against his grace the Comte, or if anyone is hurt, please allow Emergency Privilege 3 to apply to all of his guests."

"Certainly, mother," said the House. A fat teapot appeared in a nearby food hatch, steaming.

Dana stared at the priest, who swished her red cloak a little as she crossed the kitchen to collect the teapot. "I feel that his grace the Comte rather underestimated the extent to which his father trusted my predecessor," she explained.

And then she poured the tea into four tiny porcelain cups.

Going home after five years — the place should feel small. But after so many years living in a shoebox apartment in Paris Satellite, it was Athos who felt small amid all this grandeur.

Who needed all these rooms? When it was over, he should give the manor up for good. Donate it to the town:

make them turn it into something practical like a museum or a school.

Or burn it to the ground. Either way.

There were three libraries on the third floor. This, Athos considered for the first time in his life, was excessive. There was the library of the elements, which housed his grandfather's thorough collection of religious and theological texts pertinent not only to the local religion, but also to the history of the Church of All.

He must never let Aramis know that the library of the elements existed, or they would never get her off this fucking planet.

The second library was more of a study, the proper place for the Comte de la Fere to deal with estate matters, paperwork and the like. It had been his father's hideout for most of Athos' childhood, an excuse for the man to smoke cigars away from his wife, and to meet with a parade of serious gentlemen over business decisions and port, not necessarily in that order.

The books that lined those walls were decorative rather than part of a specific collection. Once Athos had taken on the title, he attempted to work in here as his father had done, but found it oppressive and lonely. The library of the elements had a more comfortable couch, and a better view of the mountains.

At the far end of the sprawling central gallery on this floor was the iris library, which had been the domain of Maman. It held very few good memories. His mother was a cool, elegant woman who wore the title of Comtesse better than any other name, but had little time for children.

Athos remembered how the Comtesse would sit him in a corner of that library as a child, correcting his stance and posture and knowledge of the history of Valour with that critical tongue of hers.

When she was not critiquing him, she had very little to say.

Olivier had always hated this room, and Auden knew that.

For the first year of Olivier and Auden's marriage, the Comtesse de La Fere had remained in the house, as she had always done, sleeping in the same suite of rooms, inhabiting this library like a scathing ghost who had opinions about how everything was wrong. She demonstrated neither approval nor disapproval over Auden, though Athos knew he had disappointed her in not choosing a wife (and the preferred option would have been a *wife*) from one of the rare families on Valour she considered equal to the Autevilles or her own bloodline, the Demorrows.

On his first wedding anniversary, Athos awoke to discover that his mother, along with her retinue of three personal assistants and one live-in hairstylist, had moved out of the house and returned to the Demorrow family estate, along with her widowed sister the Marchioness de Lourde.

They did not write, though they exchanged formal cards on the more significant religious holidays for a few years at least.

It had not occurred to him until now that she might be still alive out there.

Auden knew how much Athos – Olivier – hated this library, and so he took it as his own space, once the Comtesse withdrew. He liked to hide here when they had an argument, knowing Athos would never follow him inside.

It was strangely wounding to have the man falling back on those habits now, as if nothing had happened. As if the sword had never fallen on his neck, as if they were not two different people: Athos the Musketeer, and Milord the murderer.

Athos stepped inside. For a moment, he fancied that he could still smell his mother's perfume. Then all thoughts of her fell out of his head, because he was faced with his husband.

Milord sprawled on the antique couch, beneath a wall of watercolour irises and a window that looked out over the violet garden.

He had reverted to the version of himself that lived in Athos' memory – all youth and cheekbones, his silver hair falling long around his shoulders and his feet wriggling bare against the embroidered cushions.

A sword (a genuine sword, not a pilot's slice, Athos recognised it as a family heirloom) lay carelessly across Milord's lap.

"I see you're not a nun anymore," Athos drawled. "I'm surprised you gave up on the new look so quickly. Sister Snow sounds like a peach."

Milord looked at him through his eyelashes. "Sometimes it's best to stick to the classics."

"Yes, and you got murder all over the hands of the last body you wore, so…" Athos gave him a flat smile. "I'm not going to insult you by asking how you survived your execution, this time around."

"Wouldn't tell you if you asked. I have to keep some

secrets. Imagine if you got bored of me." After everything, he was still flirting.

Athos shook his head in disbelief. "What is it you think is going to happen here? Do you imagine I will take pity on you because of what we once shared?"

Milord gave him a frosty look. "I know better than to expect pity of you, Olivier. No, I think you're going to let me go – more than that, you are going to *help* me escape because everyone you love is under this roof."

Athos laughed shortly. "Everyone I love? You mean the Musketeers who all want to shoot you in the head? Yes, I can see where that gives you an advantage."

"We're going to escape," Milord repeated, calmly. "You will call that engie of yours to bring your ship across to the edge of the security field. You are going to walk me out of here, safely, and hand control of your ship over to me."

"You want the *Pistachio*?" Athos said, not sure he had heard correctly.

"I want everything," Milord said sweetly. "I learned a lesson with Sister Snow. Creating a new identity from scratch is too hard, too fraught with extra stress I don't need. But a body I know well – at least as well I knew Auden all those years – that could be useful."

He began to change, silver hair melting into short blond stubble, his body broadening, even his clothes shifting into blue and white. "I'm going to be you, sweet-ness. That should be good enough to get me halfway across the solar system. You are going to let me leave this house as Athos the Musketeer, or I'm going to leave Porthos, Aramis and D'Artagnan in pieces."

Athos could not look at him now – at this strange parody of himself. He turned his back on Milord and went to the window, to the view of the garden that Maman had always been so proud of.

It was beginning to rain, because Valour. Grey streaked across the sky, matching his mood.

"You're not going to get away with this," Athos said, refusing to let anger take over. He pressed his fury into his hands, and pushed his hands against the cold glass.

Real glass, not plexi-glass. The Comtesse de La Fere had prized authenticity over practicality.

"You didn't think I came here only to mock you?" asked Milord.

"I have no idea why you do any of the things you have done," Athos grated, still refusing to look. His hands flexed hard against the window, as if he could claw his own way out through the glass. "But you will not hurt my friends."

"I won't have to," said Milord. "If they think I'm you, they will fall over themselves to help me. And if I can't fool them – well, House always was so compliant when it came to family members."

The panes gave way under Athos' palms, and the glass shattered out across the lawn below. Blood burst from his hands, from a dozen different cuts. He turned to face his opponent, blood smeared across the bright white window ledge.

"No," said the Comte de la Fere. "I think not."

The lights flickered in the kitchen, alerting Dana and the others to the emergency. "Mother," said the House in that creepy formal tone it employed. "I have to inform you that his grace has been injured."

Aramis and Porthos leaped to their feet, teacups flying.

"So we can go upstairs?" Aramis demanded breathlessly.

"Yes – I am so instructed –" but House's voice dissolved into static. "No," it said when it spoke again. "His grace has given the order that no one must interrupt them."

"Them?" inquired the red mother, looking as unflappable as ever. "You mean the Comte de la Fere and Mr Auden."

"No – I – his grace has two voices," House said plaintively. "They have given conflicting orders."

"I'm going up," Porthos said, and made a run for the foyer.

Aramis chased after her. "Be careful! We don't know how many more of those forcefields there are."

"I'm sick of seeing Athos go through hell for that asshole," Porthos growled. "Let me at them both."

"House," the red mother said. "What was the last order that his grace gave you?"

"It concerns the guest D'Artagnan," said the House.

Dana had been about to follow the others out of the kitchen. "What about me?"

"His grace the Comte de La Fere has decreed that D'Artagnan must die," said House.

CHAPTER 29
JUDGES, JURY AND EXECUTIONERS

Athos had taken part in countless duels over the years – against Hammers and Sabres, against New Aristocrats drunk and sober, against his fellow Musketeers. He had never fought a duel against himself.

But Milord was not Athos, despite wearing a semblance of his face and body. Milord's fencing style (which had developed significantly since their days of casual sparring) was formal and vicious, Valour from hilt to tip. He had not conducted a study of drunken Parisian back-alley brawls in between all his marriages, political machinations and espionage.

His loss.

Athos pressed his advantage, taking a fierce joy in being the Comte in this moment, and not the Musketeer. His honour belonged to himself and not to the Crown, and if that meant he was justified in using his free hand to seize anything within reach (a book, a cup, a vase he especially hated) and hurl it at his opponent, then so be it.

"Get out of my house," he growled.

Milord (still wearing Athos' face) raised his eyebrows in a parody of sarcasm. "Get out of *my* house," he replied sweetly.

Athos batted the other man's blade out of his way and stepped in, too close. "This isn't a game."

"On the contrary, sweetness," breathed his husband. "This is the best game we've ever played."

Athos punched him in the face with a bloodstained fist.

Of all the ways that Dana had imagined she might die, it was not at the hands of kitchen implements, ordered to kill her by her best friend.

She didn't know what half these things did, but they were metal and plastic and whirring, and House was about to use them in ways that would make a genuine chef blanch.

Dana backed up into a corner of the kitchen. The red mother's voice was soothing and reassuring as she told the House that the order must have been mistaken, that the real Comte de La Fere would not want his friend dead.

House was audibly struggling against his programming. "The Comte has two voices," he conceded.

"One of those voices is false," the red mother assured him. "Mr Auden is your master's enemy. He has stolen his grace's voice to trick you."

"Does not – that is not logical," House said, sounding genuinely distressed. "Mr Auden is family by marriage. I am to treat him as – I am to protect him as I protect his grace."

A buzzing, rotating knife blade twitched in the direction of Dana's throat. "His grace has a new family now," she blurted out, and looked at the red mother, worried she had said something wrong.

The priest nodded, and smiled. "His grace is now Athos the Musketeer," she said. "He told you that these are his friends: his personal guests. One does not murder personal guests, House."

Dana heard a crash and a yell from upstairs. "He's in trouble, House!" she said desperately. "Please, let me help him. You can kill me later if you're really sure that's what he wants, but let me save him first."

The buzzing kitchen implements hung in the air, considering.

Dana didn't wait. She flew out to the main foyer, where she found Porthos and Aramis battling with the staircase. Porthos was several steps up, and Aramis behind her, but they were both stuck.

"This damned House keeps changing its mind about letting us past the forcefields," Porthos howled.

"He's confused," said Dana. She hesitated, and ran up the stairs and past them both. "He's especially confused about me."

She kept running until she found the third floor, following the sound of a fight. She had no idea which door led to the iris library, but she didn't have to find it, because Athos himself staggered out of a nearby door. He had blood smeared on his white shirt, and across his battered face. No obvious damage.

His grace has been injured.

"Dana," Athos said, his hand tightening on the hilt of

an antique sword, not his usual pilot's slice. "We have to get out of here, now, before he…"

Dana punched him in the face.

He went down with a roar, completely surprised by the force of her fist, and before he could get up again, she shot him with the bright gleam of her pearl stunner.

Porthos and Aramis, who had either won an argument with House or benefited from the red mother's ability to talk sense into AI, came clattering up the last flight of stairs to join them.

"Dana, what did you do?" Porthos yelped.

Aramis gave the fallen Athos a brief once-over and moved past him into the library. "Where's the real one?"

The room, which must have been beautiful once, was a wreck. Silk wall hangings were torn and blood-stained. Pieces of broken vase littered the floor. Books were scattered everywhere. The window was broken.

Athos stood shakily in the middle of it, blood crusting over his hands and a ragged slash in his jacket sleeve showing a nasty cut. He only had eyes for Dana. "How did you know that wasn't me?"

She shrugged. "You were wearing a different shirt, holding a different sword, and you didn't call me D'Artagnan. So."

"He also got your beard slightly wrong," said Aramis, kissing him on the cheek that was not smeared with blood. "It's a very distinctive beard."

Porthos shrugged. "I would have totally fallen for it. Can we get out of here? No offence, Athos, but your House is more unstable than you are."

"Not quite yet," said Athos, his bloody hands still

grasping the hilt of his pilot's slice. Slowly, he walked past them all to the corridor where the stunned Milord still lay.

He looked mostly like Athos, though his skin was a shade or two pinker, now Dana came to compare them. Athos with a mild sunburn.

The real Athos leaned down, allowing the tip of his pilot's slice to scrape against the throat of the unconscious alien.

Dana realised what he meant by 'not quite yet.'

"Athos," she said, barely able to find her words. "We need him alive."

"I have to finish what I started," her friend said, colder than she had ever heard him. He looked broken.

"No, you don't," said Porthos, stepping forward. "You can't go back to that, Athos. You've been blaming yourself for this death for too many years. The guilt was killing you even before he turned up like a bad credit check. You don't have to be judge, jury and executioner this time around."

"She's right," said Aramis, nudging Athos' arm. "We're going to give him back to his own people, let them take some responsibility for his bullshit. And hey, we'll stop a war at the same time. Everybody wins."

Athos pressed the tip of his pilot's slice a little more firmly into Milord's flesh, near the collarbone. "What do you think, sweetness?"

Milord's eyes flickered slightly, and opened. "I'd rather you killed me than sent me home," he said, his words slurred from the stunner.

Athos looked thoughtful. "One of us should get to go home," he said after a long moment, and drew back his blade. "Why not you?"

A sombre party stepped out of the house of the d'Auteville family. Milord, his wrists and ankles hobbled by magnetic cuffs, had reverted to the face Dana knew best, Milord Vaniel de Winter, though his hair was the distinctive silver of the Cardinal's special agent and not the everyday brown of the politician.

Dana noticed that Athos looked at Milord as little as possible, busying himself by soothing House and making some changes to the AI's menu of 'trusted family members.'

Special Agent Rosnay Cho waited for them in the garden, surrounded by engies and darts. Athos had pulled down the security forcefield specifically to let her bring in the ships, and was remarkably unfazed by the resulting destruction of several flowerbeds.

Ro was her usual snarky self. She had changed into a violet flight suit, with matching boots. "They're sending a royal transport to escort us back to the Bastion," she reported. "Finally the powers that be stopped underestimating our prisoner."

Dana nodded. "Are you all right?" Ro hadn't been in good shape last time she saw her.

Ro nodded stiffly. "Your Planchet hacked Winter out of my brain."

Dana blinked at that. "She – I'm sorry, she what?"

Planchet bobbed up out of the *Buttercup*, pleased as punch. "It's not so much a drug as a micro-stud that burrows into the brain stem. Once I figured that, it was easy enough to hack into the right frequency and deactivate the Winter program from having control over or ability to communicate with its victims. I've sent the instructions to the Countess of Clarick, so they can free Marshal Felton. The stud keeps a record of all activity under protected passwords, so it can serve as evidence in court."

Dana stared at Planchet, impressed.

"Yeah, you're really not paying her enough," Ro said in a tone that made it clear she wanted to change the subject. "How are things here?"

"Emotionally devastating."

"Sounds about right."

Dana cleared her throat, feeling awkward. "Look, I'm really sorry that I… that I thought… I mean, that I assumed…"

"What, that I was on Milord's side after the whole murder at the convent thing?" Ro said easily. "Don't sweat it, buttercup. I've been underestimated by better people than you."

"Thanks, I think."

An unreadable expression crossed Ro's face, and she punched Dana's shoulder lightly. "Sorry about your boy."

Dana swallowed, feeling sad all over again. "Yeah. Me too."

The ship that arrived to escort them back to Truth Space – and to the Sun-kissed delegation awaiting delivery of their prisoner – was an eagle-class venturer: *The Stars Divine*, which Aramis knew belonged to the Cardinal herself. It had a gold veneer with starfield tattoos on the fin, and the interior was lushly designed with red and gold in every cabin.

It was beyond extravagant, but no one was complaining.

There was room in the hold for all of the darts, sabres and moths belonging to their group. Once the ships, prisoner and passengers were loaded on board, there was nothing for any of them to do.

Like any decent pilot, Aramis hated being a passenger. It sucked. Normally she might occupy herself with books and poetry, or finding a Fleetnet forum in which to spark off a theological debate or two. She was feeling uninspired right now. They were on limited comms, and besides, she had friends to keep an eye on.

There was a fully stocked bar on board *The Stars Divine*, in which Dana had taken up near-permanent residence, drinking steadily through her heartbreak. It was often Rosnay Cho keeping her company, though Aramis, Porthos and Athos all hovered around Dana as well, making sure there was always at least one of them nearby.

It occurred to Aramis that for all the watching of Dana that they were doing, they should be keeping a close eye on Athos too. He was working hard to act as if nothing of any importance had occurred.

On the third day, not long before they were due to arrive at the Bastion, Aramis cornered Athos in the bar. He sat some distance from the others, who were holding an elaborate cocktail-naming contest.

"You're sober," Aramis noted. "Also you're due for another haircut."

"Maybe I'll let it grow out again."

"Liar."

Athos gave a short huff of a laugh, but his eyes were distant as he glanced at Dana, then back to his own drink, a large mug of black coffee. "If I start drinking now, I won't stop. Maybe when I'm not sharing a ship with *him*."

Milord was locked in a cell in the heart of the ship, guarded by a heavy rotation of Hammers, Sabres and Musketeers. Aramis knew she wasn't the only one who slipped down there occasionally to check he had not escaped.

"What do you think they're going to do to him?" she asked. "His own people, I mean."

"From what Treville told us, they consider him a traitor and a murderer," Athos shrugged. "But they're aliens. For all we know, their highest punishment is a cuddle and a slice of birthday cake."

Aramis slid a look over at Dana, who leaned miserably into Porthos, trying not to make it obvious that she was crying. Rosnay Cho was pretending that she hadn't noticed, ordering more drinks. "I want to tear the bastard limb from limb," Aramis whispered.

Athos saluted her with his coffee cup. "Welcome to the club. But you and Porthos were right. I got to be judge, jury and executioner before, and that was hell. Time to try something new."

Aramis gave him a hug, and slipped behind the bar to pour herself a drink. Champagne, she thought. All the better to toast the downfall of their enemies. "When was the last time you were sober in a bar?"

"Far beyond recorded memory," Athos said solemnly. "Do they usually smell this bad?"

Aramis wrinkled her nose. "That's the carpet. This ship must have been in mothballs for years."

"It's too fancy for every day."

Aramis poured herself a glass of bubbles from a suitably labelled flask, and clinked the glass against Athos' cup. Time to change the subject so hard that there was no going back. "At least we get to skip the drunken confessions part of the evening. That was getting old."

He gave her an odd look. "What exactly do you have to confess?"

"Not me, you." She waited until he had a mouthful of coffee before explaining. "You know, the drunken conversation we keep having, where you beg my forgiveness for sleeping with Chevreuse two days after she and I broke up."

To his credit, Athos did not spit out the coffee, but it took quite the effort for him to swallow. "What the hell, Aramis?"

She laughed at him. "You are cute when you're guilt-ridden."

"I – wasn't aware that was a conversation I had allowed to exist outside my own head."

"Six times, Athos," she told him firmly. "Since Joyeux. For what it's worth, I forgave you five times out of the six."

Athos nodded, looking as if a weight had been taken off his shoulders. It was really quite endearing. "Good to know."

Aramis tapped him on the nose with the cool edge of her champagne glass. "Not everything has to be a melodrama or a tragedy."

Athos had thought he was prepared for this. He had made so many sensible life choices all week. He gave House a more appropriate lockdown procedure when they left Valour, and he fully intended to make proper arrangements for the manor and the estate. He had remained sober, trying to be a good companion for D'Artagnan as she worked through her grief and guilt about the boy that Auden had murdered in order to hurt her.

Athos had even composed a sensible report for Amiral Treville, on the grounds that it was nearly her birthday, and he liked to surprise her now and then.

He trusted his friends to regularly check on the prisoner so that he did not have to, because he was content never speaking another word to that man.

Really, Athos was proud of how well he had handled everything.

They were twelve hours away from Truth Space and the Bastion when the aliens arrived.

Athos was on the flight deck, because his friends were drunk and maudlin and he only got to be one of those things. He hated travelling through space as a passenger (all decent Musketeers felt the same way) but it was easier when standing up here at the business end, watching the stars through the view screen.

The venturer flight crew were Sabres, politely pretending he didn't exist and that none of them had fought duels with him in the last six months; a comfortable falsehood.

"What the hell's that?" uttered Captain Tybalt, a sentence no one ever wants to hear from their pilot.

Athos looked at the blaze of brightness that streaked across their view screen. "That's... not good," he managed, before the blaze became too fierce to look at directly. "Fuck. It's the Sun-kissed."

"They're not shooting!" shouted Magellan, the co-pilot, but that wasn't as comforting as it might have been.

"I don't think they have to shoot at us to destroy this ship," said Athos. He was already running, slapping his comm stud as he went, opening a frequency that alerted everyone on their original extraction team – not just Aramis, Porthos and D'Artagnan, but Cho, L'Etoile and Ducasse too. "Get to the prisoner hold now. Ambush!"

When he reached the corridor outside the hold where Milord was imprisoned, Athos saw the first bodies: two unconscious Hammers, sprawled out by the door.

Aramis and Porthos, their eyes watering from the rapid effect of Sobriety patches, reached him around the same time. Both drew their stunners, allowing Athos to take point.

Inside the hold, four more guards lay unconscious or dead on the ground. At the far end, Milord sat on a bench, electro-cuffed to the wall and surrounded by a forcefield, alert and awake. Looking more like de Winter than like Auden d'Auteville, so Athos could be grateful for small mercies.

The red mother, who had insisted on travelling with them for Milord's trial, stood facing down six figures with bright red skin, light pouring out of their eyes and mouths.

"This is Athos the Musketeer," she said gravely. "He was one of the victims of the prisoner."

The six Sun-kissed delegates turned their bright faces to Athos, and he did his best not to cower under their fierce intensity.

"Friends," he said in the calm, diplomatic tone he had

learned from his father, long before he was old enough to use it. "Do we have a problem here?"

One of the six aliens opened her mouth, and a garble of light and sound poured out. She stopped, tilted her head, and allowed another of her companions to step forward.

"Our lost child is to be collected," that one said in a high-pitched tone. "It was an agreement with your people."

Special Agent Rosnay Cho shoved her way into the cell with L'Etoile and Ducasse. She stood beside Athos with a look of grim determination on her face. "We are charged with delivering the criminal to the Cardinal and the Regence," she said. "They are the ones who made the agreement with you."

All six Sun-kissed tilted their heads back and forth, as if trying to make sense of her words.

"The Cardinal is irrelevant," said one.

"The Regence is irrelevant," said another.

"Our lost child is to be collected," said the original speaker.

"Will there be a trial?" put in a belligerent voice. D'Artagnan, of course. "Will he face judgement for his crimes? Will he be punished?"

Milord began to laugh, a harsh and angry sound. "Oh, sweetness," he said, pretending to wipe tears from his eyes. "You're precious. Don't ever change."

"Our orders are clear," said Special Agent Cho, holding firm.

"*You* are irrelevant," said the main speaker. Light poured into the room, too intense for Athos to do anything but squeeze his eyes shut. When he opened them, Rosnay

Cho, L'Etoile, Ducasse, Aramis and Porthos all lay in a crumpled heap on the floor.

D'Artagnan crouched over Aramis, checking her pulse. She nodded sharply, her eyes wide and startled.

Not dead, then. Athos breathed out.

"What do you want?" he asked, since it was obvious the aliens could do anything they damn well pleased.

"Our lost child is to be collected," the Sun-kissed speaker said, unruffled.

"Take him, then," said Athos. "Be our guest. I can't emphasise enough how little we care about his fate."

D'Artagnan made a small noise of protest in her throat.

Athos rolled his eyes at her. "Do you imagine we have a choice here?"

The red mother addressed the Sun-kissed delegation again. "As the prisoner's religious adviser, I wish to accompany him to your world to ensure he is treated fairly."

As one, the six Sun-kissed turned expressions on her that could only be described as universal sarcasm. "Irrelevant," said one, and the red mother dropped to the ground in a dead faint.

"Marvellous," purred Milord. "My two greatest defenders are all that remain. I feel so blessed."

"Burn in hell," D'Artagnan shot at him.

"Meet me there," Milord snapped back, but it was Athos he looked at, with a sad smile on his face. "No final words, sweetness?"

"Go in peace," Athos breathed, and he meant it. He could not think about vengeance, not now.

A fierce bright light filled the room, dissolving the heavy cuffs on the prisoner's wrists and ankles, de-activating the forcefield. For the first time, Milord looked afraid, pressing himself back against the wall.

"I did my duty!" he protested. "I did exactly what you sent me here to do. I gathered intelligence, I insinuated myself into a position of value in their society. I came *this* close to bringing down their government. I never stopped working for you!"

The main speaker of the Sun-kissed delegates reached out a crimson hand and touched his face.

Light blazed out. There were images and sounds captured in that intense, burning light. Athos saw a ship crash, saw the shapeless creatures that emerged, and saw one die at the hands of another. He saw Auden return to a glowing beacon in the snow year after year, and he saw him broken and angry, destroying that beacon.

Was this a trial? Did this count as evidence? Or was it an interrogation?

Were those crimes enough, to make an entire race turn against Milord, to wage a war in order to take him back? Or had that always been an excuse: an excuse to invade or an excuse to end the war?

The light burned harder, and Milord cried out in pain, in terror.

Athos thought he had been willing to be the executioner again, if there was no other. Now, as he realised what was happening, his whole body reacted against it. Arms wrapped around his shoulders, hands pressed into his mouth, holding him back. In the brightness, he heard a howling cry of protest that, in retrospect, must have come from him.

It must have been D'Artagnan who tackled him to the floor, kept him from hurling himself into the light.

Milord Vaniel de Winter, also known as Sister Snow, and Linton Gray, and Slate, and Auden d'Auteville and a dozen other names, dissolved in a burning ball of light that hurt the eyes. The Sun-kissed delegation bowed their heads, made a chattering sound that Athos did not understand, and vanished one by one, leaving two conscious humans and many unconscious humans alone in the hold.

Athos breathed in the scent of Dana's uniform and skin because any distraction was better than thinking about what had just happened. He coughed, and D'Artagnan released him.

"Fucking aliens," she said with a shaky laugh.

Laughing was as bad as drinking. Once he started, Athos was sure he would never stop. He bit the inside of his mouth, and said: "It's done. How does vengeance taste?"

D'Artagnan gave him a quick, worried look. "Unsatisfying," she ventured.

"Sounds about right." Athos looked around at their many unconscious colleagues. "We're going to get the blame for this, aren't we?"

"Oh, yeah. Big time."

CHAPTER 30
TELL ME ABOUT IT, STUD

The Sun-kissed were gone.

It would take weeks – months, perhaps – to dismantle the war. It would be days before the priests and Sabres and Musketeers and Regence and Cardinal and Amiral accepted the evidence that the Sun-kissed were indeed gone.

Not leaving, not in the process of withdrawing from the battle zone in their many ships, but gone as if they had never been there at all.

It all happened within five minutes of the execution of Milord at the hands of his own people.

The population of the ocean world of Truth had survived the siege well enough, with surprisingly few casualties. All members of the Fleet with Truth listed as their birthplace were given leave to visit the planet and their loved ones.

Porthos, who had left Truth long ago, felt no need to take up the offer. Her family was right here, and they needed her.

There were briefings and meetings and reports to be given. Amiral Treville took it on herself to meet personally with each of her Musketeers. The Cardinal and Regence had better things to do than attend such meetings.

Porthos did not relax. Surely all of them were on the Cardinal's shitlist now. Athos and D'Artagnan, as the two members of the Royal Fleet who had been awake during the execution (and Porthos could kick them both for admitting that on the record) were likely to be blamed for the failure to follow through on the mission as it had been presented.

Sure, the Sun-kissed were gone, but the Cardinal and/or the Regence were supposed to have been the ones who made the grand gesture and ended the war. Not two Musketeers of slightly dubious reputation.

No summons came to explain Athos and Dana's side of the story to the Crown or the Church.

A heavy sense of 'unfinished' hung over them all. There were only so many quiet evenings of wine and subdued conversation that they could survive before one of them (probably Athos, let's face it) cracked and started causing havoc.

Porthos missed Paris Satellite so much that it was a permanent ache in her heart. She wanted her own bed, and her kitchen, and her boyfriends, and the freedom to spend the occasional half day completely apart from her dearest friends without worrying they were about to explode from emotional repression.

Finally, their orders came in to report to Lunar Palais for regular duty. With a few rec hours to fill before their mandatory pre-flight sleeping shift, Porthos invited Athos, Aramis and Dana to join her on the *Hoyden*.

Bonnie provided soup, bread, cake and wine, and left them to it.

After supper, the four of them piled on to Porthos' bunk with the last of the wine. She made sure that Athos and Dana, the two most in need of actual comfort, were properly squished in the middle.

"Let's talk about something else," said Dana, her eyes half closed. "Something a million miles from the war and the rest of it."

So, Porthos told her favourite amusing story about the early days, when she and Aramis were learning to be Musketeers together, and the scrapes they got into. After a while, Athos joined in with descriptions of the most outrageous bar fights they had taken part in across Paris. When he ran out of breath, it was Aramis' turn to entertain.

Finally, Dana was asleep, curled up in a small, tight ball over Porthos' feet. Aramis was nearly there herself, her long hair spilling over Athos' shoulder. "She'll be all right," she murmured. "She'll mend."

Porthos kept her steady gaze on Athos, wondering if the same was true for him.

Athos silently toasted her with one of the wine flasks. "Did you know he had a child?" he said, quite the last thing she had expected to come out of his mouth.

Porthos blinked at him. "Milord – really? Is that even possible with alien biology?"

Athos shrugged. "I looked her up. Morgan de Winter, daughter of Delia and Vaniel. She's three years old, heir to the Countess of Clarick."

Porthos swallowed, not sure what the right thing to say in this instance was. "So Bee – the Countess will look after her?"

"She doesn't seem the maternal type," he said. "Very few New Aristocrats are. That's why we hire nannies."

"There's a special insight into your childhood."

He gave her an ironic smile. "Aramis says I don't share enough."

"S'true," muttered sleepy Aramis.

Porthos thought about it for a minute, and nudged Athos with the foot that wasn't currently being used as Dana's pillow. "Does that mean that in twenty years we're going to have some halfblood alien Countess coming after us for revenge?"

"Wouldn't surprise me. Let's hope someone teaches her to fence properly first." Athos blew out a breath, staring at the ceiling. "She was probably a pawn in his game. Another way for him to bind himself to the de Winter family."

Athos wasn't calling his former husband Milord, Porthos noticed. He never used a name at all. "Were you – if you'd stayed married, if you'd never found out who he was. Would you have had children together?" In his other life, Athos had a New Aristocrat title and an estate to pass down, after all. Just like Bee de Winter.

Athos gave her a thin smile. "We'd talked about it. Just talk, I realise now. We'd have had to use capsules, and if he had donated DNA, it would have revealed he wasn't human. So, no, we would not have had children. At the time, having a family seemed like a genuine future possibility." He made a face. "I would have been terrible at it."

"Hmm," said Porthos, who wasn't so sure after watching him take Dana under his wing over the last several months. She had never thought of Athos as paternal, but the role of mentor suited him, however reluctant he had been at first.

Aramis used one hand to shove her long hair back out of her face. "You should talk to Chevreuse," she muttered into Athos' chest.

Athos patted her vaguely. "Go back to sleep."

Aramis got that pouty look on her face, something Porthos had never seen her do sober, and poked him hard in the ribs. "No, I mean it. You need to talk."

Porthos groaned. "This isn't drunken confession time, is it? I can't cope with drunken confession time. No one cares that you slept with Chev, Athos. We're all over it."

Athos gave her a betrayed look. "You knew about that too?"

"I was there for at least half your drunken confessions. After the fourth time I told Aramis we should write you a note you could read in the morning when you sobered up, but she was still finding it funny."

He glared at her. "I hate you both."

Aramis hauled herself up, trying to look serious. "In my defence," she declared. "It was extremely funny." She tried to poke Athos in the ribs again but he turned her hand aside, slinging an arm around her shoulders instead. Aramis sighed. "I don't like you being the least drunk one in the room. Puts out the balance of the solar system."

"I'm catching up," he told her, tapping her on the nose with his wine flask.

"Not fast enough." Aramis rummaged around in the bed, looking for something. "Where's the clamshell that was here a minute ago? We need to call Chevreuse."

"About what?" Athos asked in alarm. "Please tell me you're not matchmaking me with your ex-girlfriend because we spent one drunken night together nearly a year ago. I cannot emphasise enough how much I don't want you to matchmake me."

Porthos shifted around in the bed and discovered something hard under her elbow. "Found the clamshell," she sang.

"Call her," said Aramis, and this poke turned into more of a punch in Athos' stomach.

"Ugh. Stop it. Why?"

"Because," said Aramis, speaking very carefully and slowly so as not to slur her words. "Chevreuse and Montbazon had a baby after she left Paris."

Athos winced. "What's that got to do with – good for them. All the more reason to leave them alone." He was retreating into his usual polite disinterest, one of the many layers of armour he relied upon.

But oh, Porthos saw where this was going, and it was amazing. She clicked the clamshell open in anticipation. Three seconds after Aramis said the words "I found out very recently that Montbazon isn't the biological father. And you know, Chev didn't do blokes very often. All I'm saying is, you two should definitely have a conversation sometime soon…" Porthos snapped a picture of the startled expression that crossed Athos' face.

"Porthos," he said a moment later, very calmly. "I am going to make you eat that clamshell if you don't delete that image right now."

"Nuh-uh," said Porthos, shoving the unconscious Dana off her foot so she could leap to her feet. "This one's going in the permanent album. Possibly printed on a mug."

She made it as far as the cockpit before Athos brought her to the ground, wrestling the clamshell out of her hands, and she was laughing so hard she didn't even mind.

Also, she had already uploaded the image safely to the Fleetnet servers, so.

"Hey," said Aramis, leaning into the doorway as she watched them tussle. "Got any Sobriety patches?"

"Why?" Porthos howled. Athos held the clamshell triumphantly over his head, and she tickled him just to see him crumple in on himself.

"The Cardinal has summoned Dana to a meeting."

Porthos and Athos both went very still, agreeing to a silent truce.

"Only D'Artagnan?" Athos asked.

"Only D'Artagnan," Aramis said grimly.

"Well, fuck," said Porthos.

The Sobriety patches did their work in making Dana respectable for this appointment, but respectable wasn't the same as prepared.

She was tired, deep in her bones, and no amount of Sobriety could fix that. Being sad was exhausting. Dana's initial shock over Conrad's death had worn off, leaving a heaviness behind. Guilt and dread were packed in around the sadness, and it made for a deeply uncomfortable cocktail of feelings. The death of Milord at the hands of his own people had provided her with no further emotional response.

That probably wasn't a good sign.

Honestly, Dana couldn't care less what the Cardinal had to say.

She cared a little that it was Ro who had turned up, smart in the dress reds of a Sabre, to escort her to this meeting.

"Am I under arrest?" Dana thought to say.

Ro lifted a single shoulder in a gesture that was utterly unhelpful. "Honestly, buttercup, I've no idea. I go where I'm told."

"Yes," Dana said sourly. "That is a thing I know about you."

There was no sign of Athos. Aramis and Porthos had promised to sit on him to prevent him crashing the meeting out of guilt or self-sacrifice or what the hell ever.

Dana fidgeted with the studs on her wrist as she stood waiting outside the Cardinal's office for forty-five minutes after the appointment time. Someone wanted her to know exactly how unimportant was her place in the solar system. Ro stood with her, barely moving or speaking.

"You're still pissed off, aren't you?" Dana blurted finally. "That the Sun-kissed knocked you unconscious, and you missed it all."

Ro gave her a filthy look. "Maybe I'm pissed off because if I had seen and heard what happened, you would have a credible witness to defend you. I don't know if you're going to get out of this one. The Cardinal is furious that the Sun-kissed made her look – well, irrelevant."

Dana lifted her chin. "Like you would have helped me anyway."

Ro rolled her eyes at her. "Yep, keep thinking of me as the villain, buttercup. That's such a constructive attitude." Her comm chirruped. "The Cardinal will see you now."

"Marvellous," Dana growled. "Fun times for all."

The Cardinal's office on Chaillot Station was filled with plants: flowering succulents, which made the air taste spicy on the tongue.

"Ah, D'Artagnan," said her Eminence, setting aside a clamshell to pay attention to the young Musketeer. "So good of you to make time for me."

"I have been expecting you to take an interest in what happened on *The Stars Divine*," Dana said bluntly. Out of the corner of her eye, she saw Ro huff impatiently at her lack of tact.

"Indeed," said her Eminence, steepling her elegant hands. "I read the reports presented to Amiral Treville. You can understand how concerned I am that two pilots under my colleague's command were directly responsible for losing a vital political prisoner during a time of war."

"What war?" Dana said sharply. "The war is over. The Sun-kissed left. You're welcome."

This time, she actually saw Ro slap herself on the forehead. Fine, she wasn't doing herself any favours, but she was sick of pretending that the Cardinal herself hadn't been directly responsible for half of Milord's destructive hijinks.

"Captain-lieutenant Athos has a very troubling record," her Eminence went on. "So many marks against his name for brawling, for behaviour ill-befitting an officer of the Royal Fleet. And of course, there is his known association with the missing prisoner, which makes his culpability in this matter so… disturbing."

"I see," said Dana, leaning back in her chair. "That's smart. You know how much I love my friends, that I would do anything to protect them. But you also know that Athos is Amiral Treville's darling. She would fight tooth and nail to keep him: he's basically untouchable. But you think if you threaten him hard enough, I'll make the grand sacrifice to keep him from being prosecuted."

"Come," said her Eminence. "No one is speaking of prosecution."

"So you don't wish to arrest me for delivering Milord into the hands of his own people? What, then? Are you taking my commission? I thought only Amiral Treville could fire a Musketeer." Of all the things Cardinal Richelieu could do to her, taking away the Musketeers was almost as bad a threat as taking away Athos.

"A resignation letter has to come directly from the Musketeer herself," the Cardinal stated.

Dana actually laughed. "I'm going to resign, am I? You've said nothing to me today to scare me into that kind of desperate response."

Cardinal Richelieu smiled a thin, triumphant smile. "Two Musketeers who share a troubling sexual history with the escaped prisoner turn out to be the only witnesses to that prisoner's escape. The scope of scandal, combined with the success of the Combined Royal Fleet in driving the Sun-kissed invaders back where they came from, *well*, all that suggests there is no need for the Musketeers to exist as a separate fleet any longer. We all serve the Crown. Don't we?"

Dana leaned back in her chair, considering her words very carefully. "What would Amiral Treville's role be in this brave new world of a united fleet?"

"Ah, my dear Jeanne. I'm sure she would enjoy more time to spend with her grandchildren."

Dana stared at the Cardinal. Out of the corner of her eye, she saw Ro standing to attention, her face entirely neutral.

"I am surprised," Dana said finally. "That you think it appropriate to blame the Musketeers for the Sun-kissed taking custody of their prisoner. Considering that we were working under your direct orders."

The Cardinal's face went very still. It was fascinating. Not even a muscle twitched. "The mission parameters were very specific," she said finally.

"Oh yes," said Dana. "The verbal mission parameters that you gave to us via Special Agent Cho – or is it Captain Cho? I lose track. They were almost too specific. That's why it was so thoughtful of you to allow us greater flexibility in our interpretation of those orders, thanks to your written contract."

This time, it was only the Cardinal's eyebrows that moved, but boy did they move. "Say that again," she said coldly.

Dana smiled, and touched one of the studs along her wrist – the one that Athos had pressed upon her for this meeting. It was an expensive piece, a flat bead of platinum with a red fleur-de-lis stamped on it.

At the swipe of Dana's fingertip, the words of the contract sprang up, glowing in the air between them:

> *It is by my orders and for the good of Crown and*
> *Solar System that the bearer of this stud has*
> *done what they have done.*
> **Cardinal Richelieu, timestamp 987398Red,**
> **identity sealed.**

The Cardinal stared at the words, and then at Dana. "Do you want a promotion, Captain-lieutenant D'Artagnan?"

Dana blinked rapidly, taking in the change of tone. "No thank you, your Eminence. I'm still quite new. You know how it is. Learning the ropes. No promotions warranted."

There was a muffled snort from the direction of Ro. Dana kept her gaze fixed firmly forwards.

"As you were then, D'Artagnan," Cardinal Richelieu said, opening her clamshell again, and making it clear that the Musketeer was dismissed. "We'll rattle along as we are for a while longer."

"Sounds like a plan," said Dana. She felt Ro tug at her sleeve, and rose to her feet. "See you back in Paris."

"I'm sure our paths will cross from time to time," said the Cardinal sardonically.

Ro propelled Dana out of the office, and the door spiralled shut behind them.

"Just so you know," said Ro in a steady voice as they walked down the corridor. "That was insanely hot."

"Thanks," said Dana automatically, still more concerned with putting one foot in front of the other without falling over. "Wait, what?"

Ro took hold of Dana's shoulders, crowding her against the nearest wall and kissing her like they were on a burning spaceship about to die.

Dana gasped into the kiss, surprise giving way to *hell yes, want*, and wound one arm around Ro's neck, reeling her in.

"Right," said Ro as they broke apart. "It's not the Sabre uniform, is it? Because I hardly ever wear one of these."

"It's definitely not the uniform," said Dana, grinning at her.

"Okay. Good to know." Ro raked her fingers through her long hair. Dana had never seen her looking nervous before. It was kind of great. "I'll be seeing you, buttercup." She gave Dana a half-mocking salute, and strode away down the corridor.

Dana stayed leaning against the wall a little longer, catching her breath. And yes, sure, she did watch very closely as Ro walked away.

Hell. Yes. Want.

Huh.

CHAPTER 31
WE'LL ALWAYS HAVE PARIS

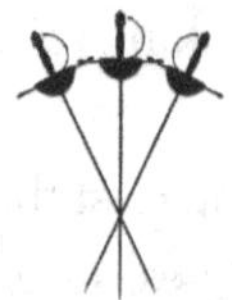

Seven months after the abrupt end of the Second Sun-kissed War, Regence Lalla Louise Renard Royal and her husband, Prince Consort Alek of Auster, became parents to triplets. Royal baby fever had run high for months, and Gossipnode exploded with the anticipation of this happy event.

For Dana and the other Musketeers, life did not change at first, though security details for the royal family immediately became more complex. There were more changes on the horizon to be anticipated.

"Three of them," said Athos dourly, as the Inseparables gathered in the Abbey of St Germain for the age-old tradition of wetting a baby's head. Three babies meant many drinks. "Fifteen years, maybe less, and our jobs will be to keep those three royalings out of every dodgy nightclub, rave, bubble club and whatever the hell teenagers invent to do to themselves between now and then. Never mind Musketeers. We'll be the sex and drugs police."

"Isn't that already your job?" Aramis said archly. "I

wouldn't worry about it, darling. We'll be long gone by then."

Porthos coughed. "Are we going somewhere?"

Aramis pointed a long, elegant finger in her direction. "Don't pretend that fancy Chef Coquenard hasn't asked you to marry him."

Porthos rolled her eyes. "I haven't said yes. Besides, I can be married and still a Musketeer, it's not against the law."

Dana brought a new tray of drinks to the table, and caught the tail end of the conversation. "Is this the part where you convince us you're going to retire to a quiet life as an Abbot somewhere in the outer System, Aramis? Because no one actually believes that."

"I'd be brilliant at it," Aramis protested.

"Surrounded by priests and intellectuals all day, honour-bound not to seduce any married ladies you come across?" Dana actually scoffed. "Yeah, right."

"What about you, Dana?" Porthos asked, to keep the peace.

"Oh, I'm always going to be a Musketeer," Dana said, without hesitation. "Forever."

Athos clinked his glass solemnly against hers. "As is only right and proper."

"There's more to life than being a Musketeer," Aramis insisted. "There's a whole wide universe of possibilities out there."

Dana and Athos gave her identical expressions that clearly told her that she was 100% wrong, and they feared for her sanity.

"For example, Athos," Aramis went on, continuing her thesis. "I can definitely see you in your more mature years, taking up an aristocratic estate somewhere. Not La Fere, of course, something more modest for your noble needs. Only one library. Perhaps you'll find yourself raising a young ward whose chin is suspiciously similar to your own..."

Athos glared at her. "Never going to happen," he growled.

Aramis fluttered her eyelashes at him. "You know Chevreuse and I talk, right? I'm perfectly aware of that trip to Peace you took last time Treville gave you leave for your health."

"Mind your own damn business," Athos said, and knocked back half his drink.

Dana was only half aware that their bickering continued, rising and falling in the background like the energy hum of a musket-class dart in need of recharging. She had stopped paying attention, because Special Agent Rosnay Cho had just walked into the bar.

Her flight suit was pale turquoise, her long black hair spilled down her back, and her manner was all business. She did not acknowledge Dana's presence, but went straight to the bartender.

Dana did not even pretend not to watch the other woman as Ro very deliberately scratched the scar on her face, then lay three fingers alongside her chin.

On high alert, Dana surveyed the bar. "Those three," she whispered. "In the corner. Don't they match the description of the terrorists who tried to disrupt the press conference last week?"

Rosnay Cho knocked back a shot of something highly alcoholic at the bar, and turned around and left with a smirk on her face, still not making eye contact with Dana. She didn't have to.

"That woman," breathed Aramis. "So useful to have around."

"Hands off, I saw her first," said Dana, with pride in her voice.

Porthos glanced casually across at the three men in the far corner. "How are we going to do this? Call for backup? Quietly evacuate the bar? Everything by the books?"

"Sure," said Athos, draining the last of his drink, and wiping his mouth. "Or we can flip the table, draw our blades, see what happens."

Aramis shot him a fond smile. "As always, Athos, I'm in awe of your strategic brain."

"All for one," said Porthos, grinning so fiercely that it was amazing the bar had not already emptied at the disturbing sight.

Athos groaned. "Must we, really?"

"And one for all!" crowed Dana.

"Aren't we beyond team chants and catchphrases?"

"Shut up, Athos. Play nice."

"Flip the table already."

It was, they decided later, somewhere in the top three of best bar fights ever, resulting in six arrests, three dislocated shoulders, and only two major sword wounds. If there was more to life than being a Musketeer, Dana didn't ever care to find out.

ABOUT THE AUTHOR

Tansy Rayner Roberts is an award-winning Australian science fiction and fantasy author who occasionally obsesses about musketeers. She lives with her family in Tasmania.

- Listen to Tansy on Sheep Might Fly, a podcast where she reads aloud her stories as audio serials.
- Read Tansy's stories before anyone else when you pledge to her Patreon: patreon.com/tansyrr
- What tea is Tansy drinking? Find out when you subscribe to her excellent newsletter.

facebook.com/TansyRRoberts

instagram.com/tansyrr

JOYEUX

EXPLORE THE HIDDEN
BACKSTORY OF OUR MUSKETEERS

There's mistletoe growing out of the walls, it's snowing inside the space station, and a scandal is brewing that could bring down the monarchy.

Merry Joyeux, Musketeers! Joyeux on Paris Satellite is a seven day festival of drunken bets, poor decision-making, religious contemplation and tinsel. Mostly, poor decision-making. Aramis is going through a breakup, Athos is haunted by the ghost of his ex-husband, and Porthos is fretting about both of her best friends.

Can they save the space station and the solar system?

A fast-paced, festive space opera novella, Joyeux is a prequel to the Musketeer Space series.

ALSO BY TANSY RAYNER ROBERTS

TIME TRAVEL AND TALKING CATS

If you're looking for more chaotic science fiction with comedy, friendship and yearning, try *Time of the Cat*, a book about time travellers, lost media and talking cats.

Featuring far too many details about Cramberleigh, a TV series that never existed, including a full program guide.

WHEN YOU DON'T HAVE A DRAGON TO PROTECT YOU (AND YOUR ELIGIBLE BROTHER), YOUR ONLY OPTION IS TO BE THE DRAGON.

If you're looking for more classic literature retold with complex SFF worldbuilding, try *The Season of Dragons*, a witty retelling of *Pride and Prejudice* from the point of view of a character very similar to Caroline Bingley, who gets her own happy ending despite all the fortune-hunters and other threats that surround her family.

Yes, Lady Catherine de Bourgh is a literal dragon!